THE BEST OF ENEMIES

Other Titles by
New York Times Bestselling Author

JEN LANCASTER

Bitter Is the New Black

Bright Lights, Big Ass

Such a Pretty Fat

Pretty in Plaid

My Fair Lazy

If You Were Here

Jeneration X

Here I Go Again

The Tao of Martha

Twisted Sister

I Regret Nothing

JEN LANCASTER

The Best of ENEMIES

 New American Library

New American Library
Published by the Penguin Group
Penguin Group (USA) LLC, 375 Hudson Street,
New York, New York 10014

USA | Canada | UK | Ireland | Australia | New Zealand | India | South Africa | China
penguin.com
A Penguin Random House Company

First published by New American Library,
a division of Penguin Group (USA) LLC

First Printing, August 2015

 REGISTERED TRADEMARK—MARCA REGISTRADA

LIBRARY OF CONGRESS CATALOGING-IN-PUBLICATION DATA:
Lancaster, Jen, 1967–
The best of enemies/Jen Lancaster.
p. cm.
ISBN 978-0-451-47109-3 (hardback)
I. Title.
PS3612.A54748B47 2015
813'.6—dc23 2015005844

Printed in the United States of America
10 9 8 7 6 5 4 3 2 1

Set in Bell MT
Designed by Spring Hoteling

For Laurie (and not just because it's your turn)

A man cannot be too careful in the choice of his enemies.

—Oscar Wilde

Love your enemies, for they tell you your faults.

—Benjamin Franklin

A strong foe is better than a weak friend.

—Edward Dahlberg

THE BEST OF ENEMIES

YOU ARE CORDIALLY INVITED
TO HELP US CELEBRATE OUR DAUGHTER

Miss Sarabeth Octavia Martin

ON THE OCCASION OF HER GRADUATION FROM

Whitney University
PFISTER SCHOOL OF MANAGEMENT
CLASS OF 1998

FRIDAY, MAY 29, 1998
Hotel Wintercourt, Carl Sandberg Room
501 N. LAKESHORE DRIVE
CHICAGO, ILLINOIS
8:00 P.M.–11:00 P.M.

REGRETS ONLY
MARTI AND ROGER MARTIN
555-2790

May 30, 1998
Hotel Wintercourt Chicago
501 N. Lake Shore Drive
Chicago, IL 60611

Miss Sarabeth Martin
5746 Garrison Ave
Evanston, IL 60201

Dear Miss Martin,

Enclosed please find the itemized list of your hotel room damages for your records. The charges for each item are as follows:

Steam clean stained sofa: $200

Steam clean stained carpeting: $100

Total: $300

As a recent Whitney grad myself, I understand how youthful festivities can get out of hand. I appreciate your taking responsibility for these charges and wish you the best of luck in your new career. We hope to see you back at Hotel Wintercourt.

Best,
Henry J. Collingsworth
Night Shift Supervisor

YOU ARE CORDIALLY INVITED
TO HELP US CELEBRATE OUR DAUGHTER

Miss Sarabeth Octavia Martin

ON THE RECEIPT OF HER
GRADUATE DEGREE FROM

The University of Chicago
BOOTH SCHOOL OF BUSINESS
CLASS OF 2003

SATURDAY, MAY 31, 2003
Hotel Wintercourt, Studs Terkel Room
501 N. LAKESHORE DRIVE
CHICAGO, ILLINOIS
8:00 P.M.–11:00 P.M.

REGRETS ONLY
MARTI AND ROGER MARTIN 555-2790

June 2, 2003
Hotel Wintercourt Chicago
501 N. Lake Shore Drive
Chicago, IL 60611

Miss Sarabeth Martin
2323 N. Racine, Apt. 2-B
Chicago, IL 60614

Dear Miss Martin,

While I commend you on your recent success, I'd be remiss in my duties if I didn't provide an itemized list of the damages from your celebration/most recent hotel stay. They are as follows:

Steam clean stained sofa: $250

Steam clean stained carpet: $150

Steam clean stained draperies: $200

Replace duvet cover: $100

Replace sofa cushions: $100

Total: $800

Indeed, accidents do happen, sometimes more than once, and I wish you much luck in your future endeavors. As always, we do hope to see you back at Hotel Wintercourt.

Best,
Henry J. Collingsworth
Front Desk Manager

She Said Yes!

and we couldn't be happier!

PLEASE JOIN

Marti and Roger Martin

FOR A NIGHT OF DINNER AND DANCING
TO SHARE OUR JOY BY CELEBRATING THE ENGAGEMENT
OF OUR DAUGHTER

Sarabeth Octavia

TO

James "Trip" Preston
McArthur Chandler III

SATURDAY, JUNE 13, 2005
6:30 P.M.

Hotel Wintercourt Grand Ballroom
501 N. LAKE SHORE DRIVE
CHICAGO, ILLINOIS

KINDLY RETURN ENCLOSED RSVP BY JUNE 1ST

June 15, 2005
Hotel Wintercourt Chicago
501 N. Lake Shore Drive
Chicago, IL 60611

Miss Sarabeth Martin
1600 N. Sedgwick St.
Chicago, IL 60614

Dear Miss Martin,

Enclosed you will find an itemized list of damages from your engagement
party on 6/13.

Steam clean wine-soaked carpet in
Wintercourt Grand Ballroom: $2000

Dry clean wine-soaked draperies in Wintercourt Grand Ballroom: $1000

Replace rack of wineglasses: $400

Replace china for head table: $500

Replace dessert trolley: $600

Reimburse for cost of Young Jeezy ice sculpture: $1500 (to be applied against
the balance for the Goldberg Bar Mitzvah)

Total: $6000

The Ritz Carlton, the Drake, and the Sofitel offer exceptionally lovely and
competitive luxury wedding packages. When it's time to pick a wedding
venue, the prudent would consider all the fine options Chicago has to offer.

Best,
Henry J. Collingsworth
Assistant General Manager

Hey, Party People!

Join us for Sarabeth's final fling before the ring!

Where: Hotel Wintercourt, 901 W. Flamingo Road, Las Vegas, NV

When: May 4–7, 2006

Why: Because it feels GOOD to be BAD!

Who: RSVP to Devon Chandler, Maid of Honor, Sister of the Groom, and All-Around Master of Ceremonies at DChandlerintheHizzouse@aol.com by April 21

Schedule of Events

May 4: Pool Time and Drinks

May 5: More Pool Time and More Drinks, followed by the Thunder from Down Under Show (We don't need no stinking dinner!)

May 6: More Drinks, More Debauchery, and Other Lascivious Acts We Shouldn't Commit to Paper!

Never forget,
what happens in Vegas, stays in Vegas . . .
so you bitches better represent!!

May 10, 2006
Hotel Wintercourt Las Vegas
901 W. Flamingo Rd
Las Vegas, NV 89103

Ms. Sarabeth Martin
1600 N. Sedgwick St.
Chicago, IL 60614

Dear Ms. Martin,

Enclosed is a summary of the damage from your recent stay in the Crystal Palace suite of Hotel Wintercourt Las Vegas. These charges have already been added to your American Express card on file.

Replace plate glass window: $3000

Replace glass coffee table: $400

Repair baby glass top of grand piano: $2000

Water remediation: $5000

Replace panel on custom-built wall aquarium: $7000

Remunerate Marine Biologist for emergency visit and services rendered: $3200

Total: $20,600, billed to AMEX ending in #2606 on 5/7/06

Our motto is what happens in Vegas, stays in Vegas. Coincidentally, this is why we secure your credit card information upon check-in. Much luck with your impending nuptials.

Best,
Bobby Guidice
Hotel Loss Prevention Department

P.S. Per your concern, the shark is fine.

Hotel Wintercourt

LAS VEGAS #1 LUXURY DESTINATION, AS VOTED BY *FORBES* MAGAZINE

MR. AND MRS. ROGER MARTIN

REQUEST THE HONOR OF YOUR PRESENCE

FOR THE MARRIAGE OF THEIR DAUGHTER

Sarabeth Octavia

to

James "Trip" Preston
McArthur Chandler III

SATURDAY, THE TENTH OF JUNE

TWO THOUSAND AND SIX

AT FIVE O'CLOCK IN THE EVENING

AT

The Third Presbyterian Church of Christ

FOUR HUNDRED AND TWO NORTH MICHIGAN AVENUE

IN CHICAGO, ILLINOIS

WITH THE RECEPTION TO IMMEDIATELY FOLLOW AT

Hotel Wintercourt

June 9, 2006
Hotel Wintercourt Chicago
501 N. Lake Shore Drive
Chicago, IL 60611

Mrs. Sarabeth Martin Chandler
7322 Mayfair Road
North Shore, IL 60045

Dear Mrs. Chandler,

This letter is to serve as your official notice that you are hereby banned from
Hotel Wintercourt.

We understand you've already been served on the matter of the injuries our
busboy Javier Domingo sustained when the chocolate fountain was allegedly
up-righted by your wedding party. Despite your bridesmaid's claim the
incident was all just a "delicious misunderstanding," this shall be a matter for
the courts to decide.

Best,
Henry J. Collingsworth
General Manager
cc: Strauss & Malk, Attorneys at Law

CHAPTER ONE

COMMENTS FOR SECRETSQUASH.COM

Posted by AllHailHelenThomas on 9/1/14 at 2:24 a.m.:

What's the purpose of this Web site? Am I witnessing an elaborate piece of performance art, meant to highlight the phenomenon of helicopter parenting? If not, what manner of Kabuki Theater is this? What would prompt you to resort to such chicanery to feed vegetables to your children? Why not simply *model* good eating habits for your children in the expectation they'll follow suit? Certainly that method seems less time prohibitive/exhausting than crafting an entire Red Velvet cake made from pureed beets and broccoli. Consider throwing a little Velveeta on your kids' veggies and calling it a day . . . instead of spending every moment documenting the minutiae of your wasted life.

Katherine "Kitty" Carricoe

North Shore, Illinois
September 2014

"Ashley, I *so* appreciate your volunteering to be Second Grade Snack Mom today. Bless your heart for diving right in!"

I grin broadly, for two reasons—First, to demonstrate how very welcome second wife/stepmother Ashley should feel as the newest member of the Lakeside Elementary School Parent Teacher Organization. Second, when I'm (frequently) complimented on my dazzling smile, I can refer my admirers to my husband, Kenneth "Dr. K" Carricoe, North Shore's premiere cosmetic dentist!

"Um, thanks, Katherine!" Ashley fidgets with the hem of her abbreviated silk shorts, constructed from fabric as thin as tissue paper. How was this garment her home run swing in deciding appropriate garb for Snack Mom duty? Granted, today's unseasonably hot, but most of the other mothers at drop-off this morning were clad in gauzy tunic tops or sundresses, save for new-money Brooke Birchbaum in her obnoxious English riding gear.

(Oh, honey. I let everyone know I had a pony once, too.)

(When I was seven.)

In no way does Ashley fit the mold of the typical Lakesider mother. Around here, we don our Jack Rogers sandals when it's warm and Wellies when the weather turns. While we don't quite "wear pink on Wednesdays," you can certainly see it from here. Expressing one's individuality through fashion is for artists or anyone with the bad fortune of living west of Green Valley Road. No one would dare show up in stiletto ankle booties, particularly paired with itsy bitsy gossamer shorts.

To give Ashley credit, her legs are gorgeous, with long, toned muscles and the kind of smooth, unblemished skin that becomes a distant memory after pregnancy varicose veins take hold. In theory, I understand why she'd opt to highlight this feature. That she's parading said lovely legs around in a pair of hot pants in front of a group of elementary school students is certainly none of my concern.

I mean, my goodness, am I the PTO president or the Taliban?

Still, I'm old-fashioned enough to believe that a mother's shorts should be more "Bermuda" and less "booty." Forgive me if I choose to live in the old-fashioned, bras-are-not-optional world, where wax is meant for *Volvos*, not *vulvas*.

Ooh, I'm *so* bad!

Wax for Volvos—I make a mental note to share this witticism with my best friend, Betsy. She loves it when I spill my PTO war stories. She says hearing about everyone's terrible parenting reinforces her decision not to have children. But I'm confident she'll change her mind about babies eventually. While she and her hubby, Trip, may be on the *Forbes 400 Richest Americans* list, she'll never be *truly* wealthy until she has children.

"Oh, sweetie," I reply, placing a comforting hand on Ashley's bare shoulder (a halter top? really?). "All my friends call me Kitty."

Ashley doesn't have any tan lines on her back, so I assume the rumors of nude sunbathing on a public beach during her French Riviera honeymoon are true. Yikes! Maybe once when I was young, free, and newlywed, I might have been tempted, but breastfeeding three babies has neatly taken *that* option off the table. I refer you again to my bras-are-not-optional statement.

As we size each other up, Ashley toys with her massive diamond ring. My, my, but that's an elaborate set. Her brilliant Asscher-cut center stone—easily three carats—would be magnificent on its own, but hers is surrounded by a dozen round emeralds, set in a wedding band made from three wide strips of braided pavé platinum. I feel like I need my sunglasses to even look at it.

Naturally, diamonds are any girl's best friend, but we Lakeside moms know there's a distinct line between classy and gaudy. Ashley's definitely Krossed into Kardashian Kountry with that sparkly bauble. I much prefer the modest solitaire Dr. K gave me when he was still in dental school at UIC.

I surreptitiously compare our hands. My jewelry—simple wedding set on the left and a family signet ring on the right—is *appropriate*, which is key in a community where fitting in is always the new black. My fingers are topped with short, neat, square nails, finished with Deborah Lippmann's Sandy Camel polish that *Allure* just named a Fall 2014 Must Have.

Hands like mine are made for soothing, for detecting fevers with far more accuracy than any thermometer, for rubbing pajama-clad backs in the middle of the night after a bad dream, for helping sweet little fingers peel a clementine, and for precisely applying sequins on a homemade burlap Father's Day banner. With precariously long, rhinestone-studded French tips, Ashley's are more suited to . . . oh, I don't know, maybe holding dollar bills in a rap video?

Betsy, you're in for a treat when I recount *this* conversation!

Mental note—get ahold of Betsy. We're both so swamped that we don't chat nearly enough these days, even though we live practically within walking distance. But who has time for a walk? I mean, her life is completely insane between running Well Well Well, better known as W3, the nonprofit she founded to bring clean drinking water to developing nations, and keeping up with the demands of being the country's top wealth manager's wife. So many obligations! For me, between manning the PTO, raising my Littles, and updating SecretSquash.com (not to brag, but it's an ultra-popular lifestyle blog), I barely have a minute to run a load of laundry!

Still, I have to *make* time to give her a buzz and chat like we did in the old days. In college, we'd sit down in the basement of our sorority house on Sunday mornings, shaking our heads at all the girls sneaking in the back door after their Walks of Shame. (Some sisters never understood that saving it till pinned is the difference between being a Sigma Chi Sweetheart and a Sigma Chi Slam-piece. Fact.) Bets and I would hang out with a two-liter of Diet Coke and chitchat about everyone's Saturday nights until the bottle was empty. Then we'd trot on over to the White Hen, stock up, and start all over again. We were so close, our Tri Tau sisters gave us the Best Besties Award three years in a row!

I wonder where Ashley went to college?

Skank State University?

Seriously, Bets gets such a kick out of me! She knows I'm never one to judge . . . which is too bad, because I do it *so* well. Now, I have to wonder—how does this Ashley person possibly expect to help her stepchildren with craft projects sporting talons like that? Imagine how much glitter gets stuck underneath them.

Must have been so hard for her when she worked the main stage.

Ha! I'm terrible!

Ashley chirps, "Okay, *Kitty*—what a cute nickname?"

Dear, dear Ashley—nothing says "not yet an adult" more than ending every statement on an up note, as though you're unsure of your own power. A lack of conviction is going to bite her in the booty-shorts real flipping quick. Her stepchildren will eat her for lunch if she doesn't begin to exercise confidence in her authority over them. I mean, Barry Jr. showed up for school today in Pokémon pajama pants and his little sister, Caitlin, wore a tutu. A tutu! Does no one in that home own a pair of *corduroys*? Believe me, this nonsense would have never happened on their mother's watch.

Of course, I overheard Ms. Bevin, the kindergarten teacher with the long, brittle gray hair and tenuous relationship with foundation garments, calling Caitlin's tutu "groovy." No great shock there. I began to question Ms. Bevin's judgment the moment I realized she drove an electric car. Not a hybrid, which makes sense. I firmly believe in going green. That's why I always carry my own shopping bags in the back of my new Escalade. But Ms. Bevin's car? She drives an honest-to-God, plug-your-extension-cord-in-here, hog-up-all-the-best-parking-spots-at-Whole-Foods electric car.

I truly don't get it.

Ashley continues. "Well, Kitty, I was so nervous about bringing the right snack? I mean, I'm really just getting to know Barry's kids and I didn't want to embarrass Barry Jr. by giving the wrong thing to his class?"

Barry Goldman.

Barry, Barry, *Barry.*

Your ex-wife, Lenora, was a saint and the best PTO volunteer imaginable. Her gluten-free, sugar-free, nut-free, dairy-free, wheat-free muffins were the largest revenue-generator in the history of the Lakeside bake sale. (Screw you *and* your store-bought Cronuts, Brooke Birchbaum.) Or what about the time Lenora chaperoned three separate class trips, all in one day? Masterful time management! And, my God, that woman could inflate balloons like a professional birthday party clown. She single-handedly built that bubble arch two years ago at the Children's Carnival of Creativity. When she ran out of helium, she used nothing but the power of her own lungs to soldier through. That's what I call heroic.

But no one remembers Lenora's fine work. Instead, all they can talk about is Lenora's involvement in that sordid *incident* in front of the school, right before she abandoned the family and ran off to Albuquerque to open a hot yoga studio.

On the day in question, I'd already pulled away—exactly as the rules dictate, for it's up to me to set *an example*—when Lenora apparently snapped. Rumor has it she shrieked, "THE DROP ZONE IS FOR LOADING AND UNLOADING ONLY, BITCHES!" before she rammed her Honda Odyssey smack into Merritt Wilhelm and Brooke Birchbaum, who were blocking the exit by having an extended conversation in the middle of the street.

Publicly I condemned Lenora's actions, but privately I admired her dedication to keeping traffic flowing; it was about time that *certain mothers* learned the rules did indeed apply to them, too. (And, please, Brooke barely even needed that neck brace. Hel-*lo*, drama queen alert!)

Ashley continues. "With snacks? I thought back to what I liked as a kid and went with that?"

I nod encouragingly. The good news is we'll save scads of time because she doesn't have to delve too deep into the archives to remember her childhood preferences. I mean, when was she in grade school? Last week?

Ooh, Bets, I am *on fire!*

"I remember one summer vacay, me and my brothers drank nothing but Hawaiian Punch? We had those funny red mustaches for three months!" Ashley tells me. Her eyes are bright and shimmering and there's a light spray of freckles across the bridge of her alabaster nose, making her look even younger than she actually is.

So, pretty much embryonic.

"What a charming story!" I gush. I'm famous within Lakeside for my enthusiasm. Because of me, the school board revoked term limits on the PTO presidency and I've served four consecutive terms thus far. I'm basically their FDR. And if certain board members received free ZOOM! Whitening treatments in exchange for their votes?

Well, it's *for the children.*

"What a treat! Isn't it darling that all the Littles have those same cute mustaches right now?"

I have to stop myself from sighing. Every day, calling my babies "Littles" feels less and less appropriate. I mean, Kord's now a high school freshman and Konnor's started middle school. Sunrise, sunset, eh? Kassie's only in second grade, but I worry that I'll blink and she'll suddenly be slut-shaming sisters in her own sorority house. Tear!

I'd really love to have more kids, particularly since we started so young. Dr. K was in only his second year of dental school when Kord was born. (Related note, the failure rate for birth control pills is six percent. Ask me how I know.) As is, we'll be empty nesters in ten years! I always wonder aloud what we'll do with all that time, while Dr. K replies, "What *won't* we do?"

I've been on a campaign to convince him we should have another child, but he's resolute. On paper, the decision to be finished makes sense, yet I hate the idea I'll never breathe in my own newborn babies' scent again, which smells like the sweetest vanilla powdered sugar doughnuts you could imagine. (My husband insists he prefers a new car smell.) Plus, what happens in a few years when Kassie finishes at Lakeside? Who'll run the PTO then? Merritt Wilhelm, mother to the nose-picking-est brood to ever attend Lakeside?

I don't *think* so.

Ashley beams at me and that's when I notice the gap between her Maxillary Central Incisors. Why would Barry pour all that cash into a skating rink of an engagement ring before fixing Ashley up with a couple of veneers? Everyone knows a bright smile is the best accessory. Priorities, people!

I realize I'm not paying Ashley proper attention, having been distracted by baby fever, so I refocus. After all, being present in the moment is on the Carricoe Family's Always Always list.

"Right?" Ashley says, referring to the little red mustaches. She's clearly delighted that I seem to be taking her side.

Seem to be is the operative term here.

"Hawaiian Punch was a creative and exotic choice for the beverage portion of snack time! The Littles went bananas! Why, do you realize that many of the children in the class have *never even tasted* anything made with high fructose corn syrup or Red Dye number forty?"

Ashley's (imperfect) smile falters. "Did . . . did I make a mistake?"

Hold the phone, what's this?

Do I detect a glimmer of self-awareness beneath all that body shimmer?

I honestly didn't predict that outcome. I'm so used to having to argue with these ninnies, particularly Brooke Birchbaum. Her husband's a senior VP for a certain processed-foods company and she won't shut up about how corn syrup is "just like table sugar!" Oh, honey—is that what you have to tell yourself every time you spend your sweet, sweet blood money on yet another exotic vacation or new Berber carpeting for your McMansion?

I appraise Ashley. Yes, she's in her twenties, but by that same token, she possesses a youthful exuberance sorely lacking in so many of the other mothers in Kassie's class.

Maybe I shouldn't be quite so quick to dismiss her. I could use some youthful exuberance up in here. Why did so many of these women wait until their mid-forties to procreate? Eggs come with an expiration date for a reason! (Trust me, I can *feel* them starting to go rogue down there.) I mean, one of the Midlife Mommies wouldn't even work the bake sale when summoned—said her bunions hurt too much to stand for any period of time. Bunions! Of all things. My ninety-year-old *Gammy Rosemarie* has bunions.

Don't even *start* me on the working mothers. They're an entirely different breed of nightmare. *"Sorry, Kitty, I can't possibly help with the fund-raising calls; I have to depose a witness that day!"* Sure, Ruth Bader Ginsburg, that's fine. But when we can't buy new beakers for the science lab and your daughter's lack of a STEM education leads her to a life as a Hooters waitress, don't cry to me about chicken wings.

Unfortunately, a good portion of the mothers in this school are useless, particularly those with second graders.

I need fresh blood.

I need new recruits to do my bidding.

Between the Oldsters, the Career Barbies, and the Momorexics (those ultra-ripped, exercise-obsessed, untenably selfish women who'd rather spend their entire day at North Shore Spa & Fitness than monitor the playground for bullying, *ahem*, Merritt Wilhelm) there aren't nearly enough proper stay-at-homers for my purposes. What I wouldn't give to have a few polygamous families move to town! *Big Love?* More like big help! Thank God Illinois passed the same-sex marriage act. That should bring me an influx of fabulously involved gay daddies in the next few years, but for now, I've got to work with what I have.

Has Ashley minion potential?

Let's discuss.

On the one hand, Ashley thought it was okay to feed children Hawaiian Punch and Fritos for a snack, because apparently she couldn't get her hands on any Mexican black tar heroin. And yet she *volunteered* for the job of Snack Mom, which is a distinct selling point.

Of course, I wouldn't have to consider converting Ashley if Betsy had been content to get her MRS and not her MBA way back when. Not only would she be the best parent EVAH, but with her business acumen and my ability to organize, our students would have the highest test scores in the state. Mean it.

I guess the investment banking world's gain was Lakeside's loss and I'm forced to manage the dregs.

But *if* I wanted to, how might I bring Ashley around?

Physically, we'd need to dial her whole look back a few (thousand) notches. Her hair's all kinds of wrong. Much too white-blond. Ash-blond, not platinum, sweetie. Never platinum. (Yes, Kassie's hair is that exact color, but she's a natural towhead.) And those extensions? Gots to go, girl. No one could possibly do an entire blowout and still be out of the house early enough to take the kids to Li'l Dippers Summer Sunrise Saturday Swim Club.

Burning all the Forever 21s to the ground should help us with the wardrobe dilemma, but really, everything's going to hinge on how malleable she is.

My brilliant older sister, Kelly, says to never discount anyone because they might be useful later down the line. So I believe a trial balloon is in order.

I wrap an arm around Ashley's narrow shoulders in a conspiratorial manner. "Of course you didn't do anything wrong, Ashley! It's just that some of our Littles' mommies are a tad rigid in terms of their children's diets. Loosen up, be more spontaneous, I always say! These gals should be more 'Carrie' and less 'Charlotte,' am I right?" I don't wait for her answer, because it suddenly occurs to me that *she* was in second grade when *Sex and the City* debuted. "I assume you received the treatise on the evils of nut butter?"

Ashley nods and begins to chew at the cuticle around her thumbnail. Either she doesn't understand the word "treatise," or she's waiting for me to admonish her, but because I'm following Kelly's dictates, I won't take that route.

Too obvious. Too little return on investment.

I continue. "Humorless, right? Peanut butter's not a hate crime!"

Ashley perks up. "Right? When did that happen? We lived on jars of Jif when I was a kid."

This morning, then?

She says, "I tried to give one of Barry Jr.'s friends a PBJ Saturday at soccer practice and his mom literally slapped it out of my hands?"

I nod. "Lacey Churchill."

"Yes!" she exclaims, eyes widening. "How'd you know?"

"Lacey tried to have all of North Shore declared a nut-free zone in 2009." I lean in and whisper, "Her son's not even allergic—she's just afraid of how densely caloric peanut butter is. Doesn't want Jeremiah to chunk out."

Ashley nervously twirls one of her extensions as we speak. "Is it me, or is that, like, cray-cray?"

"Bona fide cray-cray," I agree.

Okay, not afraid to make fun of the parents I dislike.

One point for Ashley.

I explain, "The key with kids is to provide proper nutrition without a lot of conversation. You *ask* them to eat their spinach and you end up arguing until you're prematurely gray. Here's the thing—you don't ne-gotiate. Listen to me—You. Do. Not. Negotiate."

I say all of this while I look directly into Ashley's aquamarine eyes, lined in far too much lavender kohl. I expect to see the telltale sign of colored contact lenses around the periphery of her irises, but as she gazes and blinks, I can't detect anything.

Wait, her stunning tropical-ocean eye color is *real?*

Crap.

Does that mean the gravity-defying, free-range boobs are God-given, too? And what of her small bottom, as flawlessly rounded as a fresh peach? I don't even want to contemplate anyone having come out of the box this perfect. (Save for a small front-tooth gap.)

As I need Ashley to understand how important a healthy, balanced diet is to developing children, I keep my gaze steady, despite noticing she has no dark roots or visible glued-in hair strands.

Damn it. Likely also real.

I continue. "You're the parent, you're in charge. The trick is . . ." I move in for the kill, delighted to be sharing my hard-won knowledge. Yeah, *she* may have the bod of a Victoria's Secret model, but *I* make sure my family takes in plenty of niacin. "If you toss a couple of handfuls of spinach into a smoothie and call it a milk shake, the Littles love it, they drink it, they don't get rickets, and everyone wins."

Ashley gazes up at me with her big doe eyes, framed in heavy, dark (false?) eyelashes. She blinks slowly a couple of times before she finally speaks. "That is the most smart thing I've ever heard."

Two points for Ashley.

She looks over both of her tawny bare shoulders before she says, "Like, Ms. Bevin said that kids are 'sentient beings' and should choose their own path, but I think she's kind of an old hippie with the Ms. business? And maybe she doesn't make the best choices herself?"

Three points for Ashley!!

"Do you have any other hints for me?" she asks. "I'm thinking maybe I should be giving the kids something other than frozen pizza for dinner. Like, nutritious salads? Don't they have vitamins and niacin and things?"

Ah, yes, Kelly was right. Ashley will do. This girl will learn.

Because I'll teach her.

"You mean, do I have an entire lifestyle blog where I post recipes about hiding veggies in deceptively delicious meals called SecretSquash. com?"

Ashley gasps. "Ohmigod! No way! Like Jerry Seinfeld's wife does? I saw her on Oprah a few years ago! Are you going to publish a cookbook? Are you going to be famous?"

I explain, "I'm not in it for the glory. Doing right by children is all that matters to me."

Well, doing right and the occasional page view. How would everyone see how hard I'm killing the mom game without sharing my success on social media?

Although I'm still flashing my show-stopping smile, I notice I'm clenching my fists. Fine, maybe I'd have enjoyed more of my well-earned glory if Mrs. Famous Pants hadn't stolen my idea and beaten me to market.

Damn it, *I* was the one who first hid broccoli inside of chicken nuggets!

Not her, *me*!

I find myself gritting my teeth as I grin, which is problematic. If Dr. K was here, he'd make me put in my mouth guard right now. Clenching is the enemy of healthy molars. True story.

I take a couple of deep yoga breaths to calm myself. *Whoosh* in, *whoosh* out. There, that's better. I can't continue to be frustrated by Jessica Seinfeld, as it's possible she came up with the idea on her own, too. Surely I'm not the first one to figure out how to properly nourish her children.

Granted, some days it feels like that, but it can't actually be true.

I inhale through my nose and exhale from my mouth. There. Getting better. Being able to maintain my cool in a crisis is precisely why I'm such an outstanding PTO president. When everyone else is losing their heads, I'm the one who maintains a laserlike focus. That's why *my* number's at the top of the phone tree.

Betsy believes I'd have been running a Fortune 500 company by now if I hadn't opted for the mommy track. Yet at this point, I can barely even remember what my PR job was like, save for all the cosmos we used to drink after work. And really, it's not as though writing press releases about a new brand of antiperspirant for teens could compare to, you know, *creating baby humans!*

I do recall having fun crafting the client pitches, and the day we landed the fragrance division of Calvin Klein as a client was amazing. They sent over so much free perfume! But about a minute later, I got pregnant with Kord, so now I always associate the smell of my old favorite Obsession with barfing in a metal office trash can.

Definitely no longer obsessed with Obsession.

I breathe in one last time and I am Zen again.

"I don't know how you're so calm," Ashley tells me, wrapping an extension (?) around her French-manicured digit. "If someone famous swooped in on my million-dollar idea, I would be batshit? You are amazeballs for not, like, hating her?"

I'm very strict with the Littles about the "H" word in our home. It's simply not something we say, ergo it's on the Never Never list. Plus, I don't *hate* Jessica Seinfeld. I'm simply disappointed to not have been first to market. If only I'd known about blogging back then I could have staked my claim! Yet what really matters is that my children are thriving because they're properly parented. That I have way more pins than Mrs. Not Shoshanna on Pinterest is an added bonus. (My coco-loco energy balls did make me a household name in the blogosphere. Fact.) Plus, it's against my policy to hate people, even Nana Baba, my overbearing MIL. I don't hate anyone except for those who truly *need* hating.

Like Jack Jordan, for example.

But that's a story for another day.

I appraise Ashley one last time. Time to turn Ashley into an asset. "Sweetie, have you ever heard of a *wonderful* clothing store called Talbots?"

"Um . . . no?"

I hook my arm through hers and guide her down the hall, away from the second grade classroom. "Then do I have a treat for you!"

CHAPTER TWO

GIRL O' WAR: A MEMOIR
CUSTOMER REVIEWS

★ ☆ ☆ ☆ ☆ ARE YOU FLIPPING KIDDING ME?

By: BestSmileEVAH, April 21, 2013

Format: Kindle

Amazon Verified Purchase

I wish I could give this book zero stars. I'm sorry, but how is anyone impressed with this navel-gazing piece of yellow journalism? A "new American classic"? Please. Beth Harbison's Shoe Addicts Anonymous is a million times more classic than this could ever possibly be.

Seriously, are we supposed to buy that Jack Jordan is some kind of saint for donning a flak jacket and traipsing around the Middle East, sharing her Very Important Feelings about the state of the world? Well, I have news for you, Ms. Jordan—some of us do important jobs every single day by raising the kind of children who will eliminate the need for war when they're adults.

So put that in your peace pipe and smoke it!

Jacqueline "Jack" Jordan

Helmand Province, Afghanistan
March 2014

I hate girls.

I do. Can't stand 'em.

I hate how petty girls are. I hate how they'll smile so kindly to your face while they're mentally tearing you to shreds, for committing no transgression other than wearing the wrong shoes.

I hate how girls pass judgment as easily as they'd hand out Halloween candy. I hate how they're more concerned about the content of your closet than the content of your character. Although a few reporters mentioned Margaret Thatcher's power suits when she died last year, Iron Maggie's legacy is that of changing Britain, not changing hemlines.

Margaret Thatcher was young once, but I guarantee she was never a *girl*.

I can't stand the way girls giggle for no good reason. Or all the shrieking, which is as grating as the whispering. Or their inability to use the bathroom alone. What's the story behind that? I've yet to require an escort to the latrine and I live under the near-constant threat of live fire.

Girls are superficial. Artificial. Plastic, not fantastic.

Girls escalate the smallest conflicts until they become epic in scope. Molehills become mountains and tiny skirmishes morph into great wars.

Or, what *they* believe are great wars.

Honestly, it's offensive. I understand the implications of war. I've been a foreign correspondent for twelve years. Trust me, I know what real conflict is. So, raging over who has dibs on wearing fuchsia to the prom or who borrowed your Nine Inch Nails CD without permission or who hid broccoli in a chicken nugget first?

Well, it ain't exactly Kandahar.

There are no girls on the front line. Marines are stationed here as part of the FET (Female Engagement Team) but they're *women.* They're soldiers. Warriors. They do not engage in slap-fights over who looked sideways at someone else's crush. They're tough and competent and I'm not referring to them when I say I hate girls.

That's why I eschew most female friendships, save for Sars. But she's half a world away right now. Wish I were better about keeping in touch when I'm abroad, but between her grueling travel schedule for W3 and the ten-hour time difference, we don't often connect. When I'm not filing a story, I'm in my tiny Kabul apartment, researching my next assignment, so my time's limited and my focus specific.

Sars understands, though. She's always been a good egg. I'm so proud of her work with W3. I hope in some small way I inspired her with my stories of how hard life is for those without access to clean water. After she and Trip made Chandler Financial Group into the premiere wealth management firm, she could have been content to stay home and push out babies, the pampered wife of a wealthy man. Instead, she's been funneling all her time and resources over the past few years to create and manage a nonprofit that builds wells in the third world. I can't imagine a better use of her considerable talent and resources.

Sars and I became friends the day my family bought the house across from hers in grade school. Moving to a new state was overwhelming on top of the other circumstances, but Sars eased the transition.

I remember sitting on the porch swing, watching the movers haul in furniture, when this tiny, birdlike person flew up the stairs to sit next to me, a ball of frenetic energy, eyes enormous behind glasses that even I knew were nerdy. And in one breath, she said, "Hi, you're the new girl! I live across the street. My ma says we're gonna be in the same class. I hear Miss Meyer is pretty nice, even though her spelling tests are supposed to be hard. I don't love spelling. My pa says computers are going to do all the spelling for you in the future, so why bother learning how? Math's my favorite subject. I can divide fractions in my head, no fooling! Someday I wanna be a banker. I already have a savings account where I put all my money from losing my baby teeth. My ma's actually the tooth fairy, but I pretend like she's not. I got two bucks for each front tooth!! We should be friends."

Before I could say a thing, she went on. "There are no girl kids in this neighborhood. Wait, my cousins live down the block. They can drive and they're kinda mean. They made fun of me for liking *Growing Pains* because they say Kirk Cameron's a tool, so I pretend that I don't watch even though I do. He's *not* a tool, but his friend Boner is. Is Boner a dirty word? Everyone laughs at me when I ask. Did I say one of my cousins can drive? Big whoop. Cilla and Gracie think they're so rad because they got to see *Dirty Dancing.* They're in love with Patrick Swayze, but he's, like, seventy years old. Ugh."

She looked at me expectantly. I understood the conversation ball was in my court, yet I had no idea how to respond. I'd already learned more about her in thirty seconds than I did playing Peewee hockey with my old neighbor Jason for two years.

Actually, all of my buddies in Saint Louis were male. Without a female influence for the past few years, I'd become a full-fledged tomboy. I have early recollections of tea parties and lace-trimmed dresses with shiny, buckled church shoes, but at this point, I wonder if I haven't somehow co-opted Sars's memories.

So, I was in the dark about how to address this exotic, bespectacled creature perched next to me, with two elaborate braids hanging halfway down her back, secured with big plaid bows. Noticing her pristine white cotton shirt buttoned halfway down and then tied at the waist like Jennifer Grey in the *Dirty Dancing* movie trailer, I suddenly felt self-conscious in my brother Bobby's old Cardinals tee.

She grinned at me. "You wanna play Barbies?" she asked.

Before I even realized what I was saying, I responded, "Nah, I hate dolls." I instantly regretted my answer, assuming I'd blown my shot at my first real female friendship. Thing was, I didn't *hate* Barbies—I just didn't know what to do with them. When my mom was still with us, I had a few dolls. I don't remember playing with them, though. Mostly I recall my brothers and I just threw them at one another.

Luckily, Sars granted me a reprieve.

"'S okay." She shrugged, adjusting her giant horn-rims. "We can play whatever you want."

Sars was the first female I ever met who could keep up with my brothers and me. Sure, she had that doll collection, and, yes, her mom bought her a lot of frilly stuff, but she never forced any of it on me, and despite her feminine proclivities, she could frontload a jump on a dirt bike better than any of us. (Pro Tip: you compress the suspension in order to keep the throttle steady before hitting the lip of the ramp.) Sars caught air like nobody's business, largely because she understood the geometry behind the sport. She always launched herself at precisely the right second.

She was brilliant and fearless back then. She's still brilliant now, but much more circumspect.

Of course, Sars always said that I was the real adrenaline junkie between the two of us. She claimed I was attracted to anything that made my pulse race.

I'm not sure that's completely true.

The simple explanation is I don't care to sit still. I can't stand to be bored. I'd rather climb Kilimanjaro than laze on the sand with a fruity drink. Give me a campsite over a beach with cabana boys any day of the week. My comfort zone is discomfort. I feel the exact same way about what I do for a living, too. Would I prefer to have kept my first job out of college, covering the Home and Garden beat before going home to my cozy lakefront apartment? Or would I rather report on what it's like to sleep in fighting holes, with nothing but dirt walls as protection from mortars?

Fighting holes. No question about it.

Life's too short to be cautious. That's why I pursued a pilot's license when my peers were working on their learners' permits. Was I the only *girl* in my class who didn't have a date for prom? Yes. But was I also the only *girl* who could execute a perfect aerial barrel roll?

Would I have rather slow danced to Ace of Bass with some high school junior who believed I owed him my innocence because he sprang for a tux? Or felt the rush of soloing over Lake Michigan for the first time?

Honestly?

Maybe I'd have attended prom if any of the boys I liked saw me as a date and not just a pal, but given the benefit of twenty years of hindsight, I believe I did what was best for the long run.

Bobby, one of my brothers, credits Tom Cruise for all my life's choices.

When other kids were watching *Punky Brewster,* we were wearing out the family copy of *Top Gun.* To this day, Bobby, Teddy, John-John, and I can quote every single line from memory. Before you ask, yes, my mother had a Kennedy fixation. Among other things, I've never forgiven her for saddling me with the middle name Bouvier. I'm not often one to express myself in text language, but OMGWTF? *Bouvier?* Want to know who thinks the name Bouvier is absolutely hysterical? Every girl in middle school, save for Sars.

What I'm saying is that after hundreds of viewings of *Top Gun,* I perpetually feel the need for speed. So, when the F-16s fly their sorties overhead, I'm never afraid. I'm jealous. Wish it was me on that hop.

My brother John-John married a *total* girl named Heather. They live in Atlanta where my brother develops software and they have three-point-five children. (She's pregnant. Again.) She spends her days redecorating their museum-quality home. Exactly how many shades of beige are there? Seems as though Heather's found quite a number of them.

I'm forced to exchange pleasantries with Heather when I check in with John. I tell her about the roadside bombs the Ordnance Disposal Team have been defusing along the main drag, and she tries to relate by expressing her frustration over slow-moving SUVs in the carpool lane.

As though her experience was somehow commensurate.

During one assignment, I was embedded with an all-male Airborne infantry unit and had to hike six kilometers through the burning desert to take a shower at the camp where women were stationed. Heather empathized, explaining how John-John wouldn't let her put a jetted tub in the guest room bath.

I just can't with this one. I really can't.

Bears a mention that girls are defined less by age and more by state

of mind. Last winter, Bobby dated Lindy, a woman fifteen years his junior. Even though Lindy wore precariously pointed shoes and had a
whole complicated hair-straightening routine, she also medaled in the
X Games, designed and manufactured her own line of custom snow-
boards, and for fun, she'd scuba dive in dangerous hotspots like the Blue
Hole in Egypt on the Red Sea. Wasn't a trace of *girl* on her.

Sadly, Lindy was too mature for Bobby and they broke up shortly
after I met her.

That reminds me, I owe Bobby a call.

It's two thirty p.m. here, so in Aspen, Bobby should just be rolling
in from après-après-ski about now. After almost ten years of college—
and a dubious claim of having graduated—he moved to Colorado to give
snowboard lessons. He's forty and he still lives with roommates. Yet I
can't disparage his lifestyle because he's the happiest person on earth.

The Internet's cooperating here today—service is sporadic—so I'm
able to connect fairly quickly via Skype.

Bobby's wind-burnt face fills my screen and he smiles with his
whole soul. Bobby's hair is much longer than the last time I saw him,
and the very tips are still blond from his summer spent bartending on
Martha's Vineyard. "'S'up, G. I. Jack?"

"Living the dream," I reply. No sarcasm here—I *am* living my
dream. "How's the powder at Buttermilk?"

"Fresh to death, baby!"

"Nice."

"They keepin' you busy?" he asks.

I could make (and to an extent *have made*) a career of answering that
question alone. There's a saying that war entails long, hot, dusty
stretches of boredom, punctuated by brief bursts of unimaginable terror.
Hate how true this is. A few years ago, an AP reporter was traveling in
the armored Land Rover two cars up from my position in the convoy.
Had the Afghan missile been a single degree off its trajectory, he would
have been the one to cover my passing, instead of the reverse.

No easy day.

Sometimes, the tedium here is palpable, but I know firsthand that
monotony's better than the alternative. I'm always enthralled by the way

the servicemen and -women attempt to fill the void. They're pros at distracting themselves from the sheer loneliness of being so far removed from everyone/everything they love. I keep a professional distance, but the troops here remind me of so many summers ago after my mom was gone, back in the days when my brothers and I were in charge of amusing ourselves while Dad was at work.

Yesterday, I witnessed two warriors battle almost to the death . . . in a potato sack race. This event was immediately followed by a competition to see who could keep a stick upright, using nothing but their foreheads to balance as they spun in circles, growing more and more dizzy with each rotation. As for the Second MEB, Second Battalion, Third Marines' epic remake of Carly Rae Jepsen's "Call Me Maybe"? Catch the YouTube video—my words won't do it justice.

Never an easy day, but sometimes a good one.

There are other days when these same merry jokesters will spend ten hours defusing an insurgent's booby trap. These bombs contain *confetti*, which brings to mind birthday parties and glitter, and not the nails, bolts, and screws that absolutely tear victims to shreds. The dichotomy of any given twenty-four-hour period fascinates me and I'm in awe of our troops' strength and commitment. Whether or not I believe this or any war is justified is irrelevant, because it's my honor to chronicle every aspect of our soldiers' heroic service.

I probably don't need to mention that my love for these servicemen and servicewomen is inversely proportional to my distaste for *girls*.

But I don't say any of this to Bobby. Instead, I respond, "Busy enough." I'll elaborate when I see him in person. Sometimes he needs me in front of him to temper the harsh realities I report. He's truly tenderhearted. A decade ago, he found a litter of kittens dumped by the side of the road. He fed them with an eyedropper every four hours until they were grown enough to feed themselves. Bobby held on to every one of those cats, rejecting each qualified adoption offer. "Where are you and the crew heading after ski season this year?"

My brother stays in Aspen until the snow melts, and then he and the cats head to summer gigs in that year's playground-du-jour for the beautiful people. Given what happened with our mom, her parents set us all up with a small trust fund. Mimi and Poppy pretty much dropped out of our lives afterward, so this gesture was the least they could do. The amount's fairly negligible, but it's enough supplemental cash to keep Bobby from ever having to wear a so-called *monkey suit* and work in an office.

I've never touched my share of the trust. Don't want it.

Bobby's lived all over—Nantucket, the Cape, Southampton, Ibiza, Montenegro, the Cayman Islands, and St. Barts, to name a few. He's always hanging out with celebrities in his line of work. Reese Witherspoon is a pal—apparently she and her husband fell in love with his twist on the Bloody Mary last summer. He says the trick is to add fresh ground wasabi and ginger, which turns a stodgy old brunch standby into something indescribably delicious. He calls his concoction the "Bobby Mary." His inside scoop on the rich and famous is wasted on me, but his lifestyle brings him joy, so I'm glad.

Bobby says, "My summer plan? It's classified. I could tell you, but then I'd have to kill you."

Top Gun quotes will never lose their charm.

Bobby always elevates my mood far more than any prescription SSRI ever could and I find myself grinning back at him. "No, Maverick, really—where are you off to next?"

Bobby suddenly becomes serious. "Gotta level with you, Jack. This life of skiing bumps all day and partying all night is taking a toll on me. I'm finally settling down and going corporate." He holds a straight face long enough for my heart to skip a beat over such a drastic change, and then he can't contain himself.

We both laugh until our stomachs hurt. Bobby seeking salaried employment is as likely as me slapping on a pair of panty hose and hosting high tea.

He's wiping the tears from his eyes when he remembers something. He roots around on a coffee table where Jean-Claude Kitty (brother to Tomba-Cat and Bode Meowler) perches on top of some manner of detritus. Bobby gently moves his cat and digs until he finds what he's seeking. He holds up a newspaper article in front of his webcam. "Check it out."

While I give him points for actually reading a newspaper, it's too blurry for me to see on my end.

"You understand I can't actually read that, right? Summarize, Bob."

"The story's about Trip. Spoiler alert—he just got richer. The article says his returns are topping off in the twenty percent range."

"No surprise there." (Save for that Bobby understands what "topping off in the twenty percent range" means.)

Sars's husband—James Preston McArthur Chandler III, aka "Trip"—is no ordinary businessman. A *Fortune* magazine reporter once said that Trip "possesses the bravado of Donald Trump and the swagger of Jay Z." To me? Swagger's not a selling point. I personally prefer Toby Keith—he's done so much for the troops. But because Trip's such a force of nature, Wall Street absolutely worships him and the media follows suit. Last year, *People* magazine included him on their annual *World's Most Beautiful* roundup.

Trip's a dynamic presence, perpetually swanning about in one of his hundreds of pastel cashmere sweaters. He always looks as though he just stepped off a yacht . . . generally having just stepped off his yacht, *The Lone Shark*. Chandler Financial Group, CFG if you're in the biz, practically has a license to print money, despite the current financial climate. I've always speculated that his success stems from listening to Sars back when she helped him establish the company. But he's far too arrogant to give her the props she deserves and she's too modest to request it.

Honestly?

I'm the only one not riding the Trip Love Train, but I keep that information to myself. Sars radiates contentment whenever I visit her at Steeplechase Manor (yes, her home has a name), so I bite back my scorn and mistrust on the rare occasion we're all together.

But my feelings toward Trip are a *benign* contempt. At least he's always pleasant. My dislike for him doesn't keep me awake at night. Plus, I do my best not to fight with people anymore because I've found it's never worth it.

Working as a war reporter has definitely refined my perspective on conflict. The entire news cycle is dictated by rivalries, whether it's the box scores from the Midtown Classic or the number of gang members shot on the south and west side in my home base of Chicago on any given summer weekend.

My theory is that sometimes enemies are beneficial because that relationship forces each party to improve. Just look at Maverick and Iceman; I maintain they were both better pilots due to said rivalry.

When I was in sixth grade, Miss Meyer assigned us our first real essays. The assignment was to write five pages on anything we wanted. Most of my other classmates penned themes about dogs or their soccer team or what they did over summer vacation. Sars turned in a theme called "The Benifits of a Single World Curency." Funny, but even then she had a head for business, if not for spelling.

Anyway, I explored the War of the Currents in my essay, which refers to the feud between Thomas Edison and Nikola Tesla. I speculated that their mutual hatred drove their success. Personally, I joined Team Tesla the second I read how Edison electrocuted an elephant using high-voltage AC to prove how dangerous it was. (Thanks for the light-bulb, pal, but you're still deplorable.)

There are so many famous rivalries in history, all of them with a story I'd love to have told. Shedding light on the roots of conflict is what drove me to journalism in the first place. What would it have been like to cover the story of Alexander Hamilton versus Aaron Burr? How fascinating to have been a beat reporter when rivals settled tiffs with duels.

Or what if I'd been around when Stalin faced off against Trotsky over control of the USSR? This enmity changed the face of Soviet politics. (Arguably not a net positive.) Better example—how much more skilled of a chess player was Kasparov after playing against Deep Blue? Or Ali and Frazier—their animosity forever upped the standards in boxing.

Or what about Sammy Hagar against David Lee Roth?

Perhaps Van Halen versus Van Hagar isn't quite the same in terms of rivalry and competition, but some fortunate reporter at *Rolling Stone* wrote career-enhancing column inches on that particular battle of the bands.

Documenting the conflict between enemies lights my fire. Gets me out of my sleeping bag in the morning. I wish I had a true and worthy nemesis, an Edison to my Tesla, a Jobs to my Gates, a Nixon to my Frost, driving me ever forward in the pursuit of being the best journalist I can be.

Nope.

Figures that the number one slot on my personal enemy list is Kitty "Flipping" Carricoe, a *girl* to the nth degree.

Had I not hated her so much, I might not have been so eager to take my first overseas assignment. I should give her due credit for being so damned contemptible. If I hadn't left the States, I'd have never embedded, thus I'd never have been nominated for a Pulitzer for international reporting or have written and sold my memoir *Girl O'War.* (Wasn't keen on the title, but my editor insisted. After forty weeks on the *New York Times* bestseller list, I admit he was right.)

I'm about to reply to Bobby when someone leans over his shoulder. The first thing I see is tanned cleavage, encased in a snug T-shirt featuring a beribboned, cartoon cat face. She plops down in Bobby's lap, obscuring most of his face with her ample Hello, Kitty-covered rack.

"Ohmigod, is that your sister?! Hi! Hi, hi, hi! I'm Melody, Bobby's girlfriend!" she says. "I totes can't wait to meet in person! He's told me a scrillion things about you!"

Bobby narrows his eyes. "Nope, not me, never said anything like that. In fact, Jack, I don't like you. I don't like you because you're dangerous."

I reply, "That's right, Iceman. I am dangerous."

Then he chomps at me Val Kilmer–style and we both crack up again.

The best thing about my relationship with my brothers is the shorthand we've established over the decades. We don't need a lot of words to connect with our shared history. One snap of my brother's teeth brings forth the recollection of a hundred games of street hockey, long treks through the Skokie Lagoons, and sitting side by side on the old couch in the dusty family room, surrounded by a never-ending stream of fat Labrador retrievers, watching our favorite movie for the umpteenth time.

And, if I delve deeper, which I'm not often wont to do, the wordless memory of how we were there for one another in the years after we lost our mother. Without her, we were unmoored, rattling around in our Saint Louis home like loose marbles in a box until my dad brought us together with what we considered the greatest movie ever made.

Once we finally accepted she was gone forever, Dad took the job in Illinois, which was for the best. We couldn't move past our loss in the old place. My mother was everywhere—in the bright pink flowers still lining the front walk, in the way her spicy perfume lingered in her closet long after it was emptied, in how every knickknack had been arranged just so. Moving to Evanston was how we excised her ghost.

"I don't get it," Melody says, interrupting my reverie.

"We're quoting lines from *Top Gun*," I explain, attempting to remain patient for Bobby's sake. She seems puzzled, so I elaborate. "The movie? Came out in 1986?"

She giggles. "Well, no wonder I'm confused! I wasn't born until 1993!"

Bobby's expression turns plaintive and even though we're seven thousand miles away, a single glance tells me he's pleading for me to take it easy on this one. He must have a soft spot for her, too.

"Wow," I reply, forcing a smile. "Then . . . you're still just a *girl*!"

CHAPTER THREE

Kitty

North Shore, Illinois
Last Wednesday

"Hi, sweetie! Come in, come in! Oh, my goodness, look at you! *Très* chic! Is that a St. John top I spot?"

As I open the door for Ashley, the warmth of the June day wafts in behind her. The air outside smells like freshly mown grass and the neighborhood's alive with the buzz of dozens of leaf blowers. As of the first sign of spring each year, there's never a moment from dawn until dusk that the air doesn't reverberate with the sounds of all the lawns in North Shore being professionally clipped. Some days it's noisier up here than it ever was when I lived in the city. Thank heavens for triple-paned windows!

I lean in to peck Ashley on both cheeks, my lips never actually grazing her skin. How can Dr. K say that watching the *Real Housewives* is worthless? Those gals taught me air kisses are *so* much more cultured than a hug or handshake.

Ashley's practically unrecognizable from when we met last fall. Her now lowlighted golden-brown hair, lightly flecked with her apparently natural buttery streaks, is pinned up in a side-swept bun, an almost exact replica of Cate Blanchett's style at the premiere of *The Monuments Men*. Gone are the tacky ankle booties, replaced with a simple (but divine) pair of heeled Chanel spectator oxfords. I imagine the numbers on Barry's AMEX have worn clean off at this point.

"Natch!" Ashley squeals and gives me a little spin. "The whole dea-lie's from their new resort collection!"

I could not be more proud of successfully remaking Ashley in my own image. My sister Kelly was right when she told me it's easier to build people up than tear them down.

Well, that's more of the *spirit* of what she said. Kelly's exact quote was "the enemy of my enemy is my friend." Since Ashley was predis-posed to disliking everyone I dislike, particularly after her snafu with Brooke Birchbaum at the fall swim meet, I felt like she should be on my team.

Ergo, makeover.

Ashley seems like an entirely different person from the one I met tottering around on Bambi legs in hooker shoes, delivering highly inap-propriate snacks last September. Now she's tasteful, tailored, and can hide six kinds of veggies in her turkey meatballs. You're welcome, Gold-man family!

And yet . . . at some point over the spring, she managed to somehow *surpass* my image. I mean, St. John? Really? Who can afford St. John in this economy? When did she stop buying Ann Taylor Loft? I find this turn of events distressing. If Ashley were to put her ideas for a trophy-wife-turned-snack-mom lifestyle Web site into action, I might not be able to handle the competition.

So there's no misunderstanding, we don't *need* a Kitty Carricoe, Ver-sion 2.0.

Version 1.0 is doing quite nicely, thank you.

Ashley and I cross through the cathedral-ceilinged, transom-win-dowed, blue slate-floored foyer, past the round maple pedestal table holding an etched crystal pitcher, which brims with my trademark fresh-cut Stargazer lilies and pink and green Pistachio hydrangeas.

"Your arrangement is *to die*!" Ashley exclaims.

"Six hundred and twenty-one Facebook users would agree," I reply. Kelly always says it's not bragging if it's true.

I really did hope to surpass one thousand "Likes," though, and not having reached that number made me anxious. Should I have taken the photo on a sunnier day? Or used a different filter? More "Walden" and less "Amaro"? Do I need to obscure the stems by wrapping a banana leaf around them? Or are my trademark blooms beginning to lose their appeal? Shall I shake things up a bit? Go more kitschy and approachable and display my blossoms in a painted Ball jar instead? Do I mix in some tulips next time?

Or is it just that I'm slipping in popularity?

Please, God, tell me I'm not slipping. That's the last thing I need.

Ashley asks, "Where do you find the little flowers that kind of look like a brain-fist?"

"Here and there," I reply, failing to mention the special order I place through North Shore Petal Pushers every week. Oh, no. *I* made Pistachio hydrangeas happen in North Shore. Not her. Those are *mine*.

The clacking of Ashley's heels echoes throughout the house. We pause for a moment to admire the wall of my black-and-white family pictures, artfully arranged in eclectic frames to form two letter Ks, the first backward and the second forward. (Sort of like Kim Kardashian's logo, except not hideously tacky.)

The K thing has . . . gotten out of hand. We gave Kord my maiden name, as that was always the plan. Then Dr. K was so tickled by all our first names beginning with that letter, he insisted we follow suit with the rest of the Littles, hence altering my preferred spellings of "Cassandra" and "Connor." To me, the alphabetical matching smacked of the Duggars' naming protocol, but Dr. K insisted. For Mother's Day last year, he gave me a monogrammed piece of jewelry to represent all of their names.

The pendant on the necklace reads *KKK*.

Betsy almost burst a blood vessel laughing when I showed her, while her African American driver, Charles, seemed decidedly less amused. I told them both it was the gesture that counted. The lovely, sweet, accidentally racist, completely tone-deaf gesture that now lives at the bottom of my jewelry box.

"You make beautiful babies!" Ashley says and I can't help but feel proud. She points to the photograph I took of Kassie in the North Shore Forest last fall, face radiant with joy as the leaves she's tossing waft down to cling to her fair hair. "My fave."

Although the day in the shot wasn't quite as festive as it appears—while I was trying to capture the perfect photo, Dr. K grew impatient and began to tap away on his iPhone, completely turning his back on the whole scene. I was aggravated he wasn't more supportive, especially since he used this exact picture in an ad for his practice in the *North Shore Shopper.*

Still, no matter what else's happening around me, this photomontage cheers me up. I'm so fulfilled by the family we've created. Once in a great while when I'm frying in the blinding sun at yet another soccer game, or feeling my bum AND brain going numb as I sit on stiff metal bleachers in the natatorium, two laps into the endless fifteen-hundred-meter breaststroke competition, I wonder what my life might be like if I hadn't taken this path.

And then I'm overwhelmed by the guilt over my momentary wistfulness.

But right here in this double-K-shaped display, where all my accomplishments are laid bare in funky metallic frames, I always return to my happy place.

Ashley and I pass the sparsely furnished living room (I prefer to call it "minimalist") and then the dining room, which is so minimal that . . . well, it's actually empty, save for a dreamy handwoven rug in lush shades of crimson and ocher that Betsy found in Indonesia. (Betsy gives THE BEST housewarming gifts. Fact.)

"Your dining table hasn't arrived yet?" Ashley asks. "Ohmigod, how long has it been?"

"Can you believe it?" I fume, hand balled into a fist on my hip in an approximation of outrage. "Who knew it took so long to ship the old-growth beech from Bavaria?"

Truth?

I have no clue how long it takes to ship old-growth beech from Bavaria, having not actually ordered any.

I may not have been *entirely* forthright with Ashley about the status of our nonexistent dining room furniture as we developed a small cash-flow sitch last fall.

See, our financial problems are twofold—first, we bought our place at the top of the market. I was on board with this particular location because no one who's anyone lives west of Green Valley Road in North Shore, at least according to my sister, Kelly. Sure, I grew up in the more rural part of town informally called West North Shore, which was fine as that area was zoned for horses.

Dr. K and I forked over twice what we might have paid a few miles away so our kids could attend the tony Lakeside Elementary instead of Calvin Coolidge, my completely unremarkable grammar school alma mater. Kelly told me that Calvin Coolidge wasn't even offering Mandarin classes at the time! Still, the quaint little Cape Cod we bought was adorable, nestled in the midst of so many old-growth oak trees.

Before we even moved in, we made the business decision to tear down the Cape Cod in order to take advantage of the size of our lot, because that's what everyone does in North Shore. (Hoo-boy, you should have heard what Nana Baba, my ridiculously utilitarian mother-in-law, thought about that!) Now our sparkling new, triple-paned, custom-built, mock Tudor home is deliciously spacious, and the large, oak tree–filled yard has been reduced to a landing strip of grass in the front and the back.

Kelly insisted that only negligent monsters allow children to play outdoors alone, so I'm confident we're better off with the expanded interior space, even if part of it's presently bereft of furniture. But since the housing crash, we've lost a ton of equity and we've maxed out our homeowners' line of credit, just like many North Shore families, so we're a bit stuck. (Not Betsy and Trip, but they don't count.)

Others are floundering, too. I'm sure of it. I saw my next-door neighbor Cecily dropping off items to sell at the North Shore Doubletake consignment store last week. Naturally, I ducked out before *she* could see *me*. Wouldn't want to embarrass her!

The second reason for our cash crunch has been the one-two punch of fluoridated water and sonic toothbrushes. The cavity-filling business is a shadow of what it once was in the candy-coated, sprinkle-topped heyday of the second half of the last century. Back before my father sold Dr. K his North Shore dental practice and retired to South Carolina, he had a staff of four dentists, twelve full-time hygienists, a lake house *and* a ski cabin, and two brand-new Cadillacs delivered to our driveway every fall. Dr. Daddy says cans of full-sugar soda alone paid for my tuition and convertible Cabriolet.

To compensate for the changes in the industry, Dr. K sank a ton of money into building up the cosmetic portion of his biz last fall. Dr. Daddy's old shag carpet and Brady Bunch–style paneled walls are finally gone. The office is so high-tech now! The exam room looks like NASA with all the plasma screens. Unfortunately, air abrasion drills, digital panoramic X-rays, and jaw-tracking technology don't exactly come cheap.

Honestly, the only reason I'm still able to dress Kassie in Hanna Andersson and Billieblush is because of the posts those companies sponsor on my blog.

Ashley interrupts my thoughts. "Hey, is Dr. K around?"

"No, it's his day off, but he was called away for an emergency."

Cookie, his office manager, wasn't specific about what kind of emergency it was, but apparently it was urgent enough that he rushed out of the house like his pants were afire. I'd never complain, but it's funny how he can't quite spring into action to help me, but when work calls? Step aside, everyone!

Speaking of his job, but can we take a moment here to discuss Cookie?

First, what kind of adult calls herself *Cookie*?

Mind you, I'm not jealous. Far from it! I mean, she's a *grandma*. A forty-something grandma, but still. I cannot even imagine how embarrassing that must be. Plus, she tries to be extra chummy with me, as though we're equals, or coconspirators on some great secret. Unacceptable.

I'm miffed by her lack of deference and I don't love how dependent Dr. K has become on her in the past few years. He made a lot of his upgrade decisions based on her recommendations. I miss the early days of helping out at the practice myself. Cookie laughed herself asthmatic when she found my old "Miles of Smiles" promotional flyer, but that "ridiculous ploy" brought in tons of new patients.

At Betsy's last fund-raiser, she asked if I felt threatened by Cookie, which, *impossible*. She's so not in my league. For crying out loud, she rides a motorcycle in the summer, parading around in leather vests without a hint of irony when everyone else is wearing sundresses! And don't start me on the makeup and feathered hair. Feathered! Hey, Cookie, Pat Benatar called and she'd like her eyeliner back.

I do prefer Cookie to the constant stream of nubile young models/ actresses he employs as part-time hygienists. (They generally last until they book their first local cell phone commercial.) Dr. K says the male patients love having hot, young girls in the vicinity of their mouths. (Gross.) He tells me they inspire the men to book their six-month cleaning appointments on the spot. As for his female patients? His cosmetic dentistry practice is up twelve percent with the North Shore mom demographic ever since he hired that glamazon Brandi who goes commando under her scrubs.

I couldn't care less about Cookie, but Brandi is . . . not my favorite.

Last year, Brandi showed up to the practice's Christmas party in a skintight, one-shouldered sheath so low cut that I should have issued a plus-one invitation to her left aureole, as many times as it made an appearance that night. Eventually I stuck a GIVE PLAQUE THE HEAVE-HO pirate sticker over the offending nubbin, which she found hilarious. Apparently she didn't mind as the sticker gave everyone an excuse to gaze at her breasts with impunity.

Thank God Betsy convinced me to borrow one of her Alexander McQueen LBDs that night instead of wearing the twee advent calendar sweater Kassie loves so much. I mean, *maybe* my figure wouldn't sell a cell phone, but between Spanx, a mostly plant-based diet, and a daily combination of Pilates, light reps with kettlebells, and chasing after three children, I can still fit into my old college button-fly jeans. I have no reason to worry.

Although . . . by "fit" I mean "get them almost up my thighs," even though I'm basically the same weight as I was in the nineties, despite the impossible-to-eradicate belly pooch and widened hips. What pregnancy does to the pelvic girdle should be criminal. Kord was in the ninety-ninth percentile for height and weight! He was the size of a watermelon coming out, and not those cute round ones the grocery stores sell now—I'm talking the oblong, submarine-shaped dealies that Baby carried in *Dirty Dancing*.

I'm so lost in thought that I don't even realize that Ashley's been yammering on.

"...so, Barry thinks I should talk to him about veneers or maybe Invisalign to close up the space between my front teeth."

I quickly retrieve the lost thread of our conversation because *this* is not going to happen. "Shame on Barry for trying to change you!" I exclaim. "Your teeth are perfect, honey. Very natural. You don't want to look like a TV anchor, amirite? Bright, generic smiles are *so* last year. The little gap between your front teeth gives you character! You're like a young Lauren Hutton!"

"Who?"

Of course she doesn't know who Lauren Hutton is.

"I mean the model Lara Stone, sweetie."

This seems to satisfy her and she drops the subject.

We need the revenue and I'm sure Dr. K could find a myriad of expensive, dining-room-table-affording solutions for Ashley, but the problem is there's only one person who's allowed to have the perfect smile in the Lakeside PTO.

And that position? Is filled.

"Where are the kids?" Ashley asks. "Seems awfully quiet in here." The house never seems empty or still when they're present. Furniture doesn't make this place a home—my family does. My sweet babies are always racing all over the place, challenging one another to a million different kinds of games, and eating their own weight in chocolate-chip (zucchini) bread!

Of course, the older they get, the less they seem to need their ol' mama. Practically broke my heart a couple of nights ago when Kassie insisted on reading her *Little House on the Prairie* book herself before she went to sleep. There she was, in her massive canopied bed, all alone in a cavernous room, illuminated by the small pool of light from her nightstand, her fine hair spilling around her tiny shoulders, nestled in a bank of fluffy pillows. She looked so small and fragile, I just wanted to scoop her up and hold her forever.

What a bittersweet moment—although I want my children to become autonomous, independent individuals, that doesn't mean it won't hurt when it happens. How did they grow up so fast? Kord has to shave *every day* and Konnor won't let me hug him in public anymore. Some days I just want to scream, *"Where'd my babies go??"*

I tell Ashley, "Kord's at swim camp until Friday, same with Konnor, except it's soccer, and little Kassie's still too young for sleepaway camp, so her Nana Baba is taking her to the Children's Museum and then she's spending the night."

I don't mention that Nana Baba's already called twice—once to complain that Kassie's darling little fringed moccasins didn't offer enough arch support, and then to crow about how much Kassie loved her first Chicago-style hot dog.

Which is so great because I was *hoping* to add hog-lips-and-bunghole to Kassie's diet.

Still, Kassie worships her Nana Baba, so I don't engage.

The upside of the Littles needing me less is that I can finally redirect some attention to my husband. Sometimes I worry I spend so much of my time trying to be the picture-perfect parent and homemaker that I forget to actually be a wife.

Truth?

I can't even remember the last time Dr. K and I ducked into the mudroom for some hanky-panky. The kids always assumed we were folding laundry, which is how that became our code word for sex.

Of course, our mudroom would make any red-blooded American woman weak in the knees, because it's a work of art.

So not kidding. I'm talking Fifty Shades of Mommy-porn.

The walls are white-painted bead board on the bottom. The top part is decoupaged with oversize, vintage nautical maps in the dreamiest patinas of pale turquoise you can imagine. (Best Craigslist find EVAH.) One whole section around the garage door boasts built-in cubbies for each kid, including seats where they can take off their shoes, meaning I never have to see backpacks or sneakers strewn all over the kitchen. There's a massive reclaimed farm sink in the middle of a huge island, designed for folding (or other lay-flat activities), topped with a fat slab of white marble that shimmers in the sun. I especially love the wall of shelves where I display my extensive jadeite glass collection. The floor's the same blue slate of the entry hall and I have a couple of jute rugs strategically placed, which perfectly coordinate with the wicker laundry baskets. In addition, there's another whole wall hosting my built-in home office.

As for the washer and dryer?

Moss green. Custom painted. No lie.

Pretty sure I broke the Internet the day I posted shots of the completed project. Betsy said I was probably going to receive death threats from Martha Stewart. (They met at a charity event, BTW. Betsy's not a fan.)

When I die, I want my ashes scattered in this room.

As for our current marital laundry sitch, um . . . not quite so picture-perfect. My whites haven't been bleached for a while. I'm in desperate need of a spin cycle. The lint trap is *full*. I've been worried that if we don't run a load real soon, Dr. K might send his shirts to Brandi for pressing.

That's why I had a whole date-day planned for us. As soon as Kassie was out the door with her grandmother, I'd hoped to show Dr. K how much more *flexible* I am now that I've upped my Pilates workout. Then I'd make him a luxurious breakfast of cream-topped Belgian waffles containing no pureed pumpkin whatsoever! (I post adult recipes, too. They aren't nearly as pin-able.)

Later, we'd have wine with lunch, followed by a second vigorous wash cycle, and then we'd spend the night chilling in lawn chairs at the outdoor amphitheater a couple of towns to the north, listening to Third Eye Blind perform, our second favorite college band behind Weezer. Jackass Jordan used to claim that Weezer couldn't be anyone's favorite band, because that was tantamount to saying "plain" was the best flavor of yogurt. Wrong! Some of us happen to ADORE all of Fage's fruit-free, sugar-free, lower-fat offerings.

Anyway, LaundryDay2015 was clearly not to be for Dr. K and me, so I figured I may as well start working on the No Screens for Ice Cream program the PTO's implementing this fall. That's why Ashley's here.

I usher Ashley into the breakfast nook, which opens into our professional-grade kitchen and great room. The sixty-inch industrial Wolf Vulcan range with double ovens and built-in griddle/broiler really has allowed me to take SecretSquash.com to the next level. In retrospect, I can't believe I fought Dr. K on the extravagance! In terms of social gathering spots, we also have a media room in the basement, plus a living room and a library on this floor, and four bedrooms and a mother-in-law suite upstairs.

Hopefully someday we'll actually have enough couches and chairs to *fill* all these rooms.

"Why can't we just live here for now and save up for a remodel?" I asked Ken as we walked through our Cape Cod for the first time after closing. I still called him Ken back then. I'm not entirely sure when I started referring to him as Dr. K, although I suspect it was when Cookie started calling him that. "Why take on so much debt when we're still paying off your student loans?"

"It's all about image, babe," he explained. "If we don't *look* successful, then we can't *be* successful. You don't want everyone in town to be all, *'Who lives in that tear-down?' 'The dentist.' 'Then he must not be very good.'* Fake it till you make it. In the dentistry game, image is everything."

Is it? I wondered, although I never said that out loud. Instead, I reasoned, "This house is so cute, even if it is dated." The darling fifties kitchen was right out of my idol Meg Ryan's apartment in *Sleepless in Seattle.* "We're already in the Lakeside school district. Who cares if there's only three bedrooms? We can make the little blue room the nursery for Kassie, while Kord and Konnor can share."

"You're advocating the boys bunk together?" he asked, with what seemed like a smirk crossing his chiseled features.

"Why not?"

He snickered. "I'm worried they inherited their mommy's territorial DNA. You don't have the best track record with roommates, Kit."

Unfair! Granted I'd had only two roommates in my life, but one turned out spectacularly well. I mean, Betsy was my maid of honor! Of course, the *other* roommate situation morphed into a cautionary tale, where the level of aggression escalated from passive to aggressive light-ning-quick. I mean, you speak one simple truth and, bam!

World War Three.

I decided I'd prefer to spend the extra money on a rebuild rather than allow my boys to grow up to be mortal enemies. I feel like that would ruin Christmas. So we tore down, we never looked back, and everyone at my parties circulates really nicely now as there aren't enough places to sit.

Everything worked out as it should . . . even though I wouldn't mind a little more liquidity right about now.

As we sit down at the scrubbed farmhouse table topped by an iron-stone tureen of fresh lemons and a burlap runner, Ashley removes her gum, placing the chewed bit of strawberry-scented neon in her espresso saucer to save for later.

Oh, *honey*.

You can buy all the St. Johns in the world but, as Countess LuAnn says, money can't buy you class.

I open my No Screens for Ice Cream binder and smile to myself, content that in terms of the big picture, the Brandis and Ashleys of the world have nothing on me.

· · · ·

I'm partway through (halfway through) (all the way through) the bottle of wine I'd planned on packing for Ravinia when Dr. K finally arrives home. I've been up here in the den off the master suite watching *Dance Moms*, my guilty pleasure show. I can never quite figure out if I love or hate Abby Lee Miller.

On the one hand, she drives those kids extra-hard, but on the other, they're better dancers for it. Also, I share her opinion that most of the mothers in her orbit are dingbats. I have to wonder if her "bullying" is often just her attempt to herd cats, much like my life in the PTO. Like that time I practically had to frog-march Brooke Birchbaum into the Parental Involvement committee meeting? The irony was not lost on me, so you can see my dilemma in regard to the controversial dance maven.

"That must have been some emergency!" I exclaim from my perch on the Pottery Barn love seat, adorned with the pillows I fashioned from old grain sacks. (My no-sew tutorial has received twelve thousand views on YouTube!)

When I talk, I try to sound flirty, but I wonder if I'm not coming across as slurry.

"What?" He pops his head into the den. His cheeks are flushed and he looks awfully invigorated for having had such an unexpectedly long day. "All I heard was *emergeshesh*."

Darn it! Definitely slurry.

But how was I supposed to spend my suddenly free day? I sure as hell wasn't doing laundry as planned. Except for the three loads I washed, folded, and staged next to detergent-filled Mason jars and sprigs of dried lavender. My Instagram caption? "Laundry today or naked tomorrow!" Which is also kind of ironic, now that I think about it.

If the Littles were here, I'd be ferrying them all over to practices and playdates and lovingly preparing them all manners of meals, but no such luck today. After I met with Ashley, I added graphics to the PTO summer newsletter, wrote a blog post about an exciting new carrot-and-fennel laden pizza (delish!!), photographed the salmon and citrus salad I ate for a late lunch, read the new *Real Simple* cover to cover while I walked on the basement treadmill, rearranged the living room to try to make it seem less desolate (fail), and swapped out the pansies in the window boxes for petunias and verbena after seeing EarthMama's latest Twit pic.

I called Betsy but I never heard back from her. Thought about stopping by with some fresh fudge banana muffins (with bonus kale!), but she may not be in town. She said something about heading to Madagascar last time I saw her. I assume she's taken Trip's corporate jet—must be nice, eh? And even if she was at home, she's been so busy on her newest fund-raising campaign that I figured trying to pop in would be an exercise in futility.

At least, I'm hoping she's just busy. We did have that weird moment when Trip cornered me in their butler's pantry at the end of the last big charity dinner at Steeplechase. I chalked the incident up to our having been overserved. I'm sure Betsy isn't actually mad at *me*. She's not the jealous type. If she was, she'd never have allowed Trip to work so many long hours with his Jessica Rabbit–looking, twenty-five-year-old assistant, Ingrid. Likely her last text was terse because she was swamped. Everything will be fine when we finally see each other.

I mumble, "I opened the goddamned wine because I was out of stuff to do."

"You owe the swear jar a dollar."

Two weeks ago, a cyclist pulled out in front of the Escalade, causing Kassie to exclaim, "What the fuck is his problem?" My first instinct was to laugh hearing that terrible curse coming out of her cherubic lips. But clearly she's heard the word somewhere—*I'm looking at you, Nana Baba*—so I'm actively trying to set the example now.

I take a sip of water and I say, more distinctly, "I said, *'That must have been some emergency!'* You were gone all day. And part of the night."

He enters the den and begins to pull off his shirt while we speak. He's not cut like he was back in his power-lifting fraternity days, but he's in better shape than a lot of men his age, even if he is carrying a couple of extra pounds. (Suspect he doesn't always eat the healthy lunches I pack for him.) Regardless, I'm the appreciative beneficiary of how he takes care of himself. He says keeping fit is an important part of his "professional image." Again, this must be new in the world of dentistry because my father was the most popular practitioner in all of Lake County, complete with a bald spot and a paunch I could barely wrap my arms around as a kid.

"Didn't Cookie tell you I was dragged into a pickup game of hoops with Brad?" Ugh, Brad the Cad, King of the Girlfriend Cheats. Granted, his rep comes from junior year of college, but I'm slow to forgive. I hate anything that smacks of infidelity. Like, I feel physical anger just thinking about any form of unfaithfulness. That's probably why I was so wigged out at Steeplechase for the W3 dinner. Trip's a demonstrative guy and I shouldn't have been so huffy over a meaningless gesture. He's plenty friendly with all the women in his life. He didn't make a pass at me. I'm sure of it now. I just wish I hadn't been so histrionic.

I'm embarrassed about our misunderstanding—I'd definitely hit the vino too hard that night. (Is not a trend, I swear.) Every time I turned around, a waiter was right there to top off my glass. I generally have admirable self-control, but perhaps I was feeling a bit out of place. We were the only couple at Betsy and Trip's event who weren't either high rollers or local celebrities.

"I have a big surprise for you!" Betsy said as we approached the head table in the Steeplechase ballroom. We walked up to a petite, polished brunette in a stunning Carolina Herrera two-tone jacquard sleeveless dress. The top and bottom were the most gorgeous shade of oyster gray with a center panel of midnight blue. The oyster and blue sections were divided by sprays of embroidered daisies in alternating colors. I didn't know love at first sight was possible until I spotted this garment. Suddenly, my darling scalloped, lace-overlay Ann Taylor tank dress felt decidedly pedestrian.

"Do you remember Dylan Blass?" Betsy asked.

Dylan let out the kind of hearty guffaw that seemed at odds with her tiny little body. Her brown eyes sparkled in the glow of the candelabras on the tables. While she seemed familiar, I still couldn't connect the dots. She said, "I doubt it—I was Dyta Blaszczyk back then. *Someone* told me early on that when people can't say or spell your name, you're leaving money on the table. She used the Ralph Lauren né 'Lifshitz' example to sell me. I had it legally changed about fifteen years ago."

Her huge laugh was what sparked my memory. I remembered hearing that sound from a dozen cubicles away. "Oh, my goodness," I exclaimed. "Yes! We were at Eiderhaus PR together right after graduation. I didn't recognize you at first—was your hair different then?"

"Brazilian blowout. Because *someone* used to say that frizz was a *Glamour* Never, not just a *Glamour* Don't."

"Surprise!" Betsy cheered. "I'll leave you two to catch up." Then she excused herself to mingle. I still can't get over how effortlessly Betsy works a room now. She glided away, a vision in a champagne-colored sequin Hervé Léger bandage dress.

Dylan said, "Remember we both worked on the Calvin Klein Obsession launch? Those were the days, huh? All those late nights, using hot water from the coffeemaker to fix our Ramen noodle suppers? That's when you dropped your last-name bomb, which obviously resonated."

Unsure of how to reply, I filled the silence with, "Wow, it's so good to see you." We exchanged air kisses. "What are you up to now? Still at Eiderhaus?"

"Nah. Started my own firm."

"Hold the phone—you're that *Dylan Blass*? Of the Dylan Blass Revolution? With the show on Bravo? You guys brought back the skort! You're seriously amazing!" I said. And I meant it. For the most part. As I was reflecting on our early days, I remembered having to tweak a few of her pitches.

Dylan stretched on her toes to whisper, "Don't worry, I'm better at it all now." She let out another one of those booming laughs. "Thank you again for always guiding me, whether or not I wanted it. Just think, if it weren't for your coaching, I might have never won the Carolina Herrera account. Check out this snappy dress they just sent me! Could you die?"

Yes. Yes, I could.

And just like that, the free twenty-two-dollar striped shirt I'd received that morning from StitchBroker.sg (Singapore's premiere online discount personal shopper's subscription box site) seemed a lot less enviable.

So maybe I was swallowing a little disappointment along with the Kongsgaard chardonnay that night. On top of the whole Ghost of PR Christmas Future, Dr. K saw fit to hand out his business cards to everyone, whether or not they wanted one. I'm usually so proud of his hustle, but I wish he'd shown a touch more discretion with such a sophisticated crowd. Was he offering a luxury cosmetic dental experience or selling a used car?

So I'd say the wine plus envy multiplied by feeling out of place equaled me misinterpreting a completely innocuous gesture. I wince, remembering my reaction.

Dr. K sniffs at himself and grimaces. "I can tell by your expression that I must reek. I went right from the office to the gym and then we had a couple of beers, so I smell like a gym *and* a bar. Lemme hop in the shower and then we can talk." He tosses me his dirty shirt. "Here. For when you do laundry."

"Not exactly the kind of laundry I was hoping for," I grumble. Yet I can't help but admire his lats while he walks away.

He calls, "Babe? All I'm hearing is *nexjussho*."

I hold his shirt to my nose to see if I catch a whiff of Brandi's trademark Harajuku Lovers perfume. Nope. All I smell is my homemade fabric softener (rosemary and lemon oil—seventeen thousand and ninety-six pins within the first week!), cologne, and a slight trace of cigarette smoke, which comes from working in the vicinity of little Miss Two-Packs-a-Day.

Who *smokes* anymore?

Don't answer that, because it's apparently the same people who have *grandchildren* in their *forties*. My God, woman, you are the poster child for bad choices! We should pull Jerry Lewis out of the mothballs and hold a telethon for you!

I ball up his undershirt to use as a pillow while I shut my eyes, waiting for him to exit the shower. I'll steal a quick nap now because when he's done, we're running a load together; I'll be damned if I have to hand wash my delicates myself again.

· · · ·

"Kit, wake up."

I'm shaken into consciousness, muscles aching from not being able to stretch out on the love seat.

"I wasn't asleep," I protest. Technically, I was passed out. There's a difference, although I'm not sure I should argue it.

He sounds anxious as he drops down onto the couch next to me. "Listen, Kitty, you have to get it together, okay? It's important."

I sit up and try to brush away all the cobwebs. I'm all groggy and my light buzz has been replaced with a pounding headache. This? Right here? Is why no one should ever day-drink, regardless of how festive a tight, backlit shot of wineglass condensation looks on Instagram.

I squint at the clock and see that I've been out for a solid three hours. Stupid wine. I scrub at my eyes and chug some water from a Mason jar. I turn to Dr. K and give him a come-hither smile while he takes my hand. Maybe we'll get in a quick cycle after all. "I'm just peachy. What's up?"

He gestures toward the television with the remote. The news is on, but it's paused. "Watch." I lean into him and rest my head on his shoulder, placing my hand on his thigh, but he doesn't pull me toward him. Instead he says, "Brace yourself, babe. It's about Betsy."

And suddenly, I'm wide-awake.

CHAPTER FOUR

WU

October 2, 1993
Whitney University
College of Liberal Arts

Miss Jacqueline Jordan
5745 Garrison Ave
Evanston, IL 60201

Dear Miss Jordan,

Congratulations! We have carefully reviewed your application and all supporting documentation and we are pleased to offer you admission to Whitney University as an undergraduate student in the College of Liberal Arts, with a major in Journalism, for the session beginning August 22, 1994.

Enclosed is a summary of the guidelines you need to review and observe as an entering member of the Freshman class. To enroll, you will need to return the enclosed forms. Housing information will be sent to enrolling students in December.

Congratulations and all hail to the old black and blue!

George Jessup
Dean of Admissions
Enclosures

Jack

. . . .

Evanston, Illinois
December 1993

"We should live in Ellison Hall," I suggest. "Campus is kind of a hike, but the rooms are big. Bonus, right? Plus, it's coed. John-John lived there freshman year and I remember it being nice."

Sars and I are sitting at the breakfast bar, poring over the colorful brochures we just received from the university's housing department. We started off in the family room at her house, but her mom chased us out due to her hosting a Tupperware party later this afternoon. Too bad, because Sars's mom always has fresh-baked cookies in a jar for us and keeps an endless supply of milk on hand. We also never have to drink out of jelly jars over there when all the regular glasses are dirty at the same time, largely because their glasses are never all dirty at the same time. I glance at the sink, brimming with dishes.

Welcome to Jelly-Glass City, Population, Us.

"Ahh! I can't do a coed dorm, Jack!" Sars squeals, eyes huge behind her thick tortoise-shell Lisa Loeb glasses. "No way!"

"Why not?" I ask.

"Um, *boys!*" she replies, like it's the most obvious answer in the world. She seems so keyed up she's practically vibrating in her chair.

My brother Bobby looks up from his spot on the leather couch. He's seated next to Gretzky, one of our enormous black Labs, while inhaling a mixing bowl full of Count Chocula. Until a moment ago, he was intently watching cartoons.

Sometimes I wonder how he's *nineteen* and not nine.

Bobby claims his deep and abiding love for *Scooby-Doo* has only grown more deep and more abiding after taking his first bong hit at college last year. He says he finally understands why Scooby and Shaggy are perpetually so hungry.

"The munchies are *real*," he'd said, like he was sharing a sage truth.

"Why, what'd we do, Sars?" Bobby asks, through a mouthful of cereal. He seems genuinely confused and a bit hurt. Bobby and Sars have been buddies for as long as she and I have. The neighborhood's called us the Three Musketeers for years.

"You didn't do anything, Bobby," Sars explains with a giggle. "I just can't live with boys."

"Is it the smell?" he asks. He sticks his face inside his shirt and takes a whiff, then shrugs. "You get used to it after a while."

It's true.

You do eventually become immune to the masculine stink. Live with it long enough and it's like someone playing a jam box too loud on the el train; you tune it out. For me, three brothers minus one mother plus a host of flatulent dogs and perpetually unwashed bags of athletic gear over many years equals a lifetime of olfactory indifference.

I explain, "Sars, the dorm's segregated by floor—guys on the evens, gals on the odds. Boys won't live next door. You're not going to bump into dudes walking down the hallway wearing nothing but a towel."

"Wanna see a dude in a towel? 'Cause I could make that happen right now if you'd like," Bobby teases, waggling his eyebrows.

Normally, this would prompt Sars to effortlessly lob an insult in return, but today she says, "Um, can I take a rain check?" and shriek-giggles some more as her face turns pink.

Wait, is Sars *blushing*? Over something *Bobby* said? And what's with the affected laugh? I peer at her flushed cheeks. Nah, not blushing. She's probably just coming down with the flu.

"Offer's on the table when you change your mind," he says, returning his focus to the television. He's not sure what to make of her odd reaction, either.

To deflect, I tell him, "Hey, Bobby? I've seen this episode before. Turns out the old man would have gotten away with it, too, if it weren't for those meddling kids."

Bobby slumps down at this news. He seems legitimately disappointed at my having wrecked the ending, and now I feel bad. He's never as good at taking it as he is at dishing it out.

To appease him, I say, "I think Daphne wears a bathing suit in this episode," and he quickly rallies. Bobby's smile returns and he focuses on the screen again. While he watches, he finishes the cereal portion of his breakfast and tips the bowl in order to drink the remaining half-and-half, which he had to use because, guess what? We're out of milk. Dad said for all we drink, he should have been a dairy farmer, not a trial lawyer. In Saint Louis, my mother would make sure we always had at least two gallons in the kitchen and a spare in the garage fridge. Said she hated having to run out in the night to buy more. Yet the one time she did finally run out for more, she didn't come back.

The cream trickles out the sides of Bobby's bowl and travels in twin tributaries down either side of his mouth onto the couch. In Sars's house, this would be tantamount to treason, but no one worries much about sanitation around here. Really, it's not like our house is a showplace, at least not since we moved in. This place reminded me of a small chateau when Dad bought it, what with the stone exterior, pointy roof, and the turrets. But years of indoor touch-football games and ill-groomed Labrador retrievers have turned this castle into more of a dungeon.

Bobby absently dabs at the stray liquid with the bottom of his college logo shirt. Our family consensus is that he applied to USC strictly because he thought it would be funny to wear "Trojans" gear. (Related note? The only other place he applied was the University of South Carolina. Go, 'Cocks!) I guess this is the upside of not having a mom like Sars has. No one's here to cry over the milk spills. Gretzky ambles off his side of the couch to bat cleanup on the spots Bobby missed. See? All fixed.

After Dad became our sole caretaker, he realized our table manners were devolving into that of prison inmates, so he started to take us out to eat more often. He figured we'd learn how to conduct ourselves from watching the other diners. So, thank you, random polite people at Carmen's Pizza, for showing at least *most* of us how to use a napkin.

"Why can't you live around guys?" I ask. I'm genuinely flummoxed. Hell, I'm nervous to live around all the girls. Guys I understand. Girls confuse me with their secret hierarchies and ever-changing alliances.

Sars wrings her hands in a way that looks like she's washing them. "Because it's too much pressure! When you live with boys, you have to be groomed all the time! You can't just go down to breakfast with no makeup on, hair in a ponytail, and sweatpants. Can't be done!"

"Of course it can," I reason. "It's called 'every day of my life.'"

My morning routine entails washing my face and sticking my hair in a scrunchie. That's thirty seconds, tops. Seriously, my makeup bag contains a tube of tinted Chapstick. Once, I tried to use eye shadow and blush, but John-John said I looked like Dee Snider from Twisted Sister. I can't disagree.

"Yeah, you can go without all the trimmings because you're naturally gorgeous," Sars says. "Some of us are going to need Maybelline."

My eldest brother, Teddy, comes shuffling into the kitchen wearing a wrinkled oxford and striped boxer shorts. I notice Sars peeking at his thighs, which are still really buff from years of playing hockey. Who can blame her for looking? I'm jealous of his muscle definition, too.

Teddy's bedhead borders on magnificent and he smells like that time we visited the Anheuser-Busch factory. Since he's over twenty-one, he's done little but hit the bars on Rush Street with his buddies ever since he arrived home for Christmas break earlier this week.

"Who's naturally gorgeous?" he asks. I swear, Ted's always on the prowl. He can run into the Jewel for athlete's foot powder and bulk toilet paper and he'll *still* come out with some girl's digits scribbled on a scrap of grocery bag.

Teddy cracks open the fridge, which contains a stack of near-empty pizza boxes, petrified containers of moo shu pork and Hunan beef, and fifteen crusty mustard jars that will eventually be used as drinking glasses. He has to move a lacrosse ball to get to the orange juice and then chugs straight from the carton.

"Dehydrated much?" Bobby chuckles to himself.

"Munchies much?" Teddy counters.

Sars clears her throat and blinks rapidly. Her throat must be scratchy and her eyes itchy. Makes sense, it *is* cold season. "Um, Jack's naturally gorgeous, of course."

From across the room, Bobby snorts so loudly that our other dog Mikita jumps up from her bed and trots out of the room, her fat rump undulating.

"Whassamatter, spaz? You don't think your sister's good-lookin'?"

Bobby snorts again and Teddy beans him right in the head with the now-empty Tropicana carton. Ted's arm is still a lethal weapon. He was as skilled at football as he was at hockey in high school, which is why so many Big Ten colleges tried to recruit him. However, he had his heart set on Whitney's architecture program, so that's where he went.

I'm so bummed that our time on campus won't overlap, despite his major taking five years. Sure, John's at Whitney, too, but we probably won't hang out much. He's not as close as the rest of us are, likely because he's a narcissistic jerkwad. He's so different from Bobby that everyone forgets they're twins. Fraternal, but still.

Teddy's awesomeness makes up for John's shortcomings. He's very protective of me. (Maybe too protective?) Although Bobby and I are the best of friends, my relationship with Ted is almost more parental. He's always tried to fill in for Dad's logging such long hours to make partner.

Bobby rubs his temple, unwilling to admit defeat. "No, I'm concerned that *you* think she's good-looking."

Teddy pulls up a barstool next to Sars and me, flexing and preening. "'Course I do. We look exactly alike."

Mimi, my mom's mother, was half Japanese, so there's a hint of something exotic in both our faces. Ted and I inherited the high cheekbones and stupid-thick, straight, dark hair from her side and freckles from Dad's Scotch-Irish side. We all have the same small, straight nose and dimpled, determined chin, but John-John and Bobby are more fair, with wavy hair. Ironically, those two actually look like they could be Kennedy offspring, which is one of the many reasons Ted calls them chowderheads.

Teddy, Bobby, and I share a genetic abnormality called heterochromia iridum, meaning our eyes are these weird, multicolored patches of green and yellow with dark blue outlines. I don't like them because the question "What's your eye color?" requires an explanation. We inherited this trait from our mother. Her mutation was much more pronounced, with one eye of golden-green, and the other a smoky blue-gray. When my parents met in law school at Whitney in the early seventies,

Dad would always sing "Lucy in the Sky with Diamonds" because her name was Lucy and she had kaleidoscope eyes.

I hate that song now.

"I always thought you resembled Pierce Brosnan, Teddy," Sars says in a rush, anxiously biting her bottom lip. Again, color flushes across her cheeks. What the hell, Sars? Does she seriously have a fever? She's practically steaming up her glasses.

"Then that means Jack looks like Pierce Brosnan in drag," Bobby crows.

Teddy bristles. "Stop hurting her self-esteem, you douche."

"Make me."

Teddy rises imperiously from his stool. "I will."

Bobby considers his threat and backs down. "Good thing I'm a lover, not a fighter." He clicks the remote. "Hey, be sure to keep it down. *Ninja Turtles* is coming on."

"What are you kids doing?" Teddy asks, returning his attention to us.

"We're trying to figure out where to live on campus. We have to fill out our housing forms and send them in together so we can be roommates," I explain. "And now Sars says she doesn't want to live in a coed dorm, so that seriously narrows our options."

"I thought you got into Stanford, Sars," Teddy says. "Whitney's good, but it's no Stanford."

"I can't go to college without Jack!" she replies.

John-John, self-appointed God's Gift to Evanston, comes sauntering into the kitchen, wearing track pants and Adidas soccer sandals with socks and a perfectly gelled coif. I just want to run my hands through his dumb, stiff, prissy hair and make it messy. I swear he thinks he's Morrissey. I share a bathroom with him and when he's home in the summer, his toiletries fill up the entire counter. "Those two looking for a dorm? They should live in the Virgin Vault."

We consider John-John our most expendable brother, in case anyone asks.

"Wait, where?" Bobby asks, interest momentarily diverted from his beloved break-dancing reptiles. I'm not sure he watches anything that isn't animated.

John replies with his ever-present smugness. "That's what everyone calls Haverford Hall. It's by the Bio building. Killer campus location, but no male visitation, except for fathers on move-in day. That'd probably work best for you, squirt. May as well pack your Melissa Etheridge albums now and greet your lady-lovin' destiny. I see a lot of plaid shirts and big watches in your future."

That's so unfair. Just because I've never had a boyfriend doesn't mean I want to play for the other team. I *like* boys. A lot. I'm just not sure how to let them know I want to do more than arm wrestle with them. (Should I let them win once in a while?)

And if I look just like Teddy, how come guys don't throw themselves at me like the girls have been doing at him since he was twelve?

Ted doesn't mind the attention, though. He's a total playboy. Last summer, he had three dates in one day. He went to lunch with the first girl, hit the beach with another, and took a third to a party. I figured his plan would devolve into a Peter Brady level of sitcom hilarity but he juggled them just fine.

He's probably a better brother than he is a boyfriend.

Bobby takes the juice carton Ted whipped at him a few minutes ago and hurls it at John-John before any of the rest of us can dog-pile on him for being his usual unpleasant self. Pulpy liquid splashes his sweatshirt and he dampens a dish towel to absorb the stain before it sets, grumbling to himself about how he never gets the respect he so richly deserves. I'm not kidding—this kind of stuff happens a hundred times a day here. Dad says this is why we can't have nice things.

Righteously indignant, John tells us, "Whatever, losers, I'm going over to Donnie's house to play Nintendo," instead of good-bye as he heads out the back door. In ten minutes, he'll have forgotten this incident.

Unless he was a girl, in which case I imagine he'd take the slight to the grave.

Ted says, "Live in Wadsworth Hall. Square footage is on the small side but if you're lucky, you'll get a fourth floor assignment. A couple of them have fireplaces, but all the rooms have leaded glass, wide molding, and box beam ceilings."

"They have what?" I ask. Sometimes he forgets he's not speaking to other architecture students.

"That means those rooms retain the original Craftsman style of when first built. Aesthetics aside, Wadsworth's centrally located. You won't care in August, but wait till you pass under the breezeway of the Engineering building in January and the wind hits you. Coldest spot in central Illinois, guaranteed. You'll thank me for shaving any distance off of your walk."

Before we can fill out our forms, the doorbell rings.

"Got it," I say, running down the long hall in my stocking feet. I pull open the huge double doors (large enough to drive a John Deere tractor–lawn mower through, but don't ask us how we learned this) to find Sars's mom.

"Hi, Mrs. Martin! What's up?"

"Hey, sweetie, how are you?" Mrs. Martin places a warm palm on my cheek and it's all I can do not to lean into it like Mikita does when we pet her. She's almost more like a grandma because she's older. The Martins call Sars their miracle baby because they were both well into their forties when she was born.

Mrs. Martin is like one of those sitcom moms we watch on Nick at Nite. Her graying hair's always brushed really nice and she smells like roses. She knows how to make a million different kinds of food and she's always trying new recipes at dinner. She loves to throw dinner parties and on my birthday, she cooks something she calls "Coquilles Saint Jack" in my honor. It's this crunchy, creamy, fishy casserole. Sounds gross, but it's the best stuff I ever tasted. Around here, we know only how to make hot dogs, spaghetti, steak, and reservations. John says he can cook omelets, but won't show us how.

Sometimes when I go to Sars's house for supper, I envy her being an only child and the center of her parents' universe. Then I see all the empty chairs at their dinner table (which is never covered by an ongoing game of Risk) and I remember you can't be lonely in a house like mine.

Mrs. Martin asks, "Can you please send Sars home, sweetie? I could use her help getting the house ready for the party. I wasn't quite as prepared as I hoped!"

"You need an extra hand?" I volunteer.

When she smiles, her eyes get all crinkly and I feel calm and safe whenever she's near. She was once a nurse, so she's really good at making everyone around her feel at ease. "You're such a doll, but, no. The party won't take too long, so don't worry about it. But swing by later—I'm making Peanut Butter Wonder Bars. See you in a bit, sweetie!"

I return to the kitchen where Sars has scooted closer to Teddy. She's pressed against his shoulder, and . . . did she just surreptitiously smell his hair? *Blech.* She jumps when I approach.

"Great news! Your mom's making Peanut Butter Wonder Bars later!"

"She came over to tell you that?" Sars replies, puzzled. "Weird."

"Are those the chewy sort-of-a-cookie, sort-of-a-candy deals?" Bobby asks, suddenly very attentive again.

I nod. "Roger that. Hey, Sars, your mom says you've gotta go home. She needs party help or something."

Sars deflates. "Oh. Okay."

"Doesn't sound like it'll take long. I'm coming over for Wonder Bars later, so no worries. We'll get this figured out before the deadline."

She grabs her stuff from the counter and begins to walk backward toward the door. "Um, yeah, so, like, see you later, alligators! Ha! Maybe we can all go to the movies or something later? As a group? *Mrs. Doubtfire* looks really funny." Except when she extends this invitation, it seems as though it's directed more to Teddy than the rest of us.

When we hear the click of the front door, Bobby turns to Teddy and says, "Someone has a big crush on you, bro."

"Impossible. You guys are her *family.*"

"That's a negative, Ghost Rider. She was practically drooling over your boy here," Bobby replies.

"Wait, *you?*" I say, sitting back down on my barstool, swinging around to Ted. "I mean, no offense, but really? You? Does she like you? I just figured she had a fever or something."

Teddy shrugs. "Used to it. High school chicks dig college guys." To Bobby, he says, "One more semester at USC and even you'll get laid, loser. Then you can finally give Rosie Palm and her five sisters a break."

He turns back toward me. "I don't date high school chicks, but I'm flattered. See, I'm into *women*. Right before break, I hooked up with this Kappa at Henry's Ale House who used her tongue to—"

I tell him, "Please don't finish that sentence. Impressionable youth here. I mean, I'm happy for you, but the whole notion is super-grody."

I'm creeped out to no end imagining my brothers having drunken mash sessions. Although, I bet the idea of *me* kissing a guy likely creeps them out as well, or at least it would until they began to beat the dog shit out of the poor guy. Fortunately, or not, that's yet to happen.

Teddy replies, "None taken."

Hey . . . hold up, here. Let's not be so quick to dismiss this whole notion of Sars dating someone in the family. The idea may hold some merit. What if she did indeed eventually hook up with Ted? Like, when we're all grown-ups?

I begin to consider the possibilities of a Sars/Teddy potential merger. Not the worst idea in the world. The worst idea in the world happened when John bleached his hair and rocked a Caesar cut last summer. Even poker-faced-Dad-the-litigator had to excuse himself from the room when John came in that day.

If Sars and Ted were to couple up, we'd always be invited to her family's Thanksgiving dinners and if you'd ever tasted her mom's apple-cranberry-sausage stuffing, you'd know that's worth the price of admission right there.

"Would you date Sars? Not now, but in the distant, *distant* future?"

"Hypothetically?" Teddy asks. "If we were both single adults, living downtown or something?"

"Yes," I say.

"I dunno. She has potential, but I'll probably always think of her as a little girl in big glasses."

"But you'd be open to the possibility? There's a chance?"

Teddy peers intently at me. "What's with the line of questioning, kid?"

"I'm just saying, if you married her, she'd always be family. Then we could spend every holiday together," I explain.

"I might eventually hit it if you need me to," Bobby offers. I realize he's joking, but he may be a decent alternative if Teddy doesn't pan out. (We can all agree that John-John's not in the running.)

Teddy chucks me on the cheek. "Kiddo, I think it may be time to branch out."

"Meaning?"

Teddy does a weird stretch and his spine crackles like popping Bubble Wrap. I'm glad he's not playing ball competitively anymore. Sports did such a number on his body. You should hear his knees when he walks up the stairs—they're like castanets and he's only twenty-two! "Sars is pretty clingy and I'm afraid she might get too possessive over you. Who turns down Stanford to stay with her friend at Whitney? Stanford calls Whitney 'Shitney.' You need to make some other friends."

Before I can protest that I have other friends, he says, "*Girl* friends. If you don't get some chicks in your life, you're going to become an adult thinking it's okay to live like wolves."

"We don't live like wolves," I argue.

"Um, yeah we do," Bobby counters, gesturing to the disarray all around him. Dad keeps hiring cleaning ladies and they all quit on us without notice. The last housekeeper lasted thirty minutes and stormed out in a huff, muttering something about trying to slap a Band-Aid on a sucking chest wound.

Teddy says, "Do me a proper and don't room with Sars at school. You need a little space away from her. You gotta trust your big bro here. Everyone who lives with their high school best friend in college ends up hating them by the end of first semester. Familiarity breeds contempt. Remember how John-John roomed with Paul diGregorio? We never saw him again after their first semester together. John-John said he didn't meet any cool people until Paul moved out."

"Of course it was hard for him to make new friends," I argue. "He's an asswipe."

Bobby looks away from the television to raise a finger in the air, all parliamentary procedure–style. "Cosigned!"

"No one's arguing he's not a pill," Teddy admits. "But for you, college will be all about spreading your—"

"Legs?" Bobby offers.

In one fluid motion, Teddy nails him with the nearest projectile, which happens to be my American History textbook. It's an advanced placement edition and it's a solid three inches thick. The book impacts with a resounding thud. Ouch. That had to hurt.

"*Wings*, dickweed. I was gonna say wings."

Bobby rubs his shoulder where the book connected. "Oh. Sorry. Hey, the arm's still lightning-fast though, bro."

"Good," Teddy replies. He flexes both biceps and nods to himself. To me, he says, "Point is, it's time to open yourself to new experiences, Jack-o."

I consider what I'm hearing. I love Sars like a sister, but we've been so self-contained as a friend-unit that I wonder if I haven't missed something by not knowing more girls. Maybe it *would* be better for me to branch out? College is the place to experiment, and how great would it be to have *two* best friends? My God, that would be an embarrassment of riches! They could teach me some of the feminine stuff I've never learned, like applying makeup, or putting together cute outfits. A group of girlfriends could help me figure out how to let Derek from my coed soccer league know I want him to consider me as more than just a highly skilled defensive midfielder.

Also?

I really don't want to live like a wolf. With more female influence, it's possible I won't have to.

"You may be onto something," I admit. "I probably shouldn't be, like, so *singular* with the one girl friend, you know? The guys I hang out with are fun, but I can't talk to them like I do with Sars."

Teddy musses my hair. "You don't think you can fly with another partner, but I promise, you can. Remember the end of *Top Gun*?"

"Obviously." Forgetting is a virtual impossibility as many times as we've watched.

"Could Maverick have destroyed those four MiGs if he hadn't allowed himself to trust Merlin?" Teddy answers his own question. "No."

For me, *this* was the most important aspect of the movie, not the superfluous romance with Kelly McGillis. (Yet I did appreciate Meg

Ryan's moxie in telling her man to take her to bed or lose her forever. Could I do the same, substituting "prom" for "bed?" I bet other girls would know this stuff. I'd ask Sars, but she has even less game than me.)

In terms of what Ted's saying, though, Tom Cruise's character had to learn to lean on others to help him get over the loss of Goose. I feel like there's a parallel here and I should finally try the same thing.

"You're absolutely right. I'm . . . going to do it." The minute I say it out loud, I feel it's the truth. "I won't bunk with Sars. But I'll tell her why and she'll be cool with it. I'm sure she doesn't want to lose me, either."

"Smart girl! And don't worry. I'm sure Sars won't let you out of her grip." Teddy claps me on the back. He seems very pleased with himself and then I finally realize exactly who I've been talking to. Teddy's an awesome brother, but he's never one to overlook a prime opportunity.

"Wait, is this because you hope I'm paired with a cute girl and I can introduce you?"

Teddy shrugs. "I said I didn't date high school chicks. I live for hot frosh."

Bobby comes over and sets his mixing bowl and spoon on a plateau of Mt. Filthy in the sink. "You're gonna leave the whole thing to chance? Just gonna live with whoever's assigned to your room?"

"Yeah," I reply. "I will. After all, how bad could it be?"

CHAPTER FIVE

To: Betsy_the_banker@yahoo.com,
DChandlerintheHizzouse@aol.com,
CillaMartinMontgomery@bulldogdesignpros.com,
GracieLouiseMartin@gmail.com,
MelissaAlbertson@RomeVentureCapital.com,
AliciaDaVinci@RomeVentureCapital.com

From: KittyCatKord@hotmail.com

Subject: Pack your mittens, kittens, because
we're going to Las Vegas!

Hi, everyone!

We're SO looking forward to gathering this weekend in Las Vegas to celebrate Betsy's impending nuptials! Devon, sounds like you've put together quite the shindig and we are so flipping excited!!

Please let me know if you might prefer a spa afternoon or cruising the Forum shops instead of three straight days drinking by the pool. This mama ain't in college anymore! Also, if anyone wants to see Cirque du Soleil in lieu of Thunder from Down Under, give me a jingle and I'll purchase the tickets.

This is going to be epic! But tasteful.

Besos!

Kitty

P.S. Apologies to anyone I may have missed with this e-mail.

Kitty

Hotel Wintercourt, Las Vegas, Nevada
May 2006

"You're going to be nice to her, right?" Betsy asks.

I look up from my copy of *OK! Magazine*, where I've been totally absorbed in the cover story about Jennifer Aniston's "baby heartbreak." Jen, sweet girl, I feel for you! But I'm sure Angelina's pregnancy is just a one-off. Like Brad and Angelina could possibly last! I guarantee they won't have any more kids after this one because they are simply not parental. Trust me, no one will ever look to *her* as the paragon of motherhood. You'll come back stronger than ever, Jen, I promise. You're going to find someone better soon, marry him, have tons of beautiful babies, and then win a bunch of Academy Awards if *Along Came Polly* is any indication.

As for those two cheaters? America never forgives adulterers and they're going to fade into the ether, just you wait.

I close my magazine and reply, "Of course I plan to be nice to her. I'm never not nice. What kind of mommy would I be if I didn't set a good example?"

Maybe that's a fib on my part. Sometimes I'm not so nice when it comes to Jack Jordan, but it is truly never me who starts it.

I am an adult.

I don't take potshots at people.

I've never dumped a glass of Bordeaux on another person's head when they disagreed with me at a graduation party; nor have I ever thrown a platter of (the apparently notoriously difficult to clean) room service huevos rancheros in a pique of impotent rage. Never have I body-checked another person—a young mom, no less!—into the ice sculpture of a second-tier rapper. *I* am a paragon of maturity. After all, am I not the one who suggested we forgo the male strip review during this trip?

"Let's have this event *not* be another Rumble in the Jungle," Betsy pleads. She adjusts the brim of her wide straw hat, cautious about too much UVA exposure because she doesn't want to be all sun-spotty at her wedding in a few weeks. That's hard to manage here on the Las Vegas strip. It's already ninety degrees out here and it's barely noon!

We could have avoided the whole three-days-baking-on-an-artificial-beach business if I'd been permitted to organize the bachelor-ette party. My plan would have entailed a long weekend at the Sonoma Mission Inn and Spa. We could have toured the vineyards in the morning and then relaxed in their artisan mineral whirlpools in the afternoon, enjoying world-class cuisine with phenomenal wine pairings in the evenings, but no. Poor Betsy was so torn trying to decide who to make maid of honor—me, her BFF since college or Jack, the egg-plate-tossing psychopath she grew up with—that she asked Trip's tacky sibling to stand up next to her by default.

Congratulations. Everybody loses.

"I'm under so much stress right now with the wedding and with helping Trip launch his company that I literally cannot deal with any more conflict. Please. Work with me here."

"Bets," I assure her, "this is *your* weekend. We're going to make it flipping *perfect.*" This is why you can't blame me for chucking the penis-shaped drinking straws, necklaces, and the Pin the Dong on the Dude game in the lobby trash can when Devon was busy hooking up with the random club promoter she met two nights ago.

I regret nothing.

The cute pool waiter with the muscular calves trots over with a tray of our drinks, and I have to remind myself it's not appropriate to stuff a dollar bill in his waistband.

(Thunder from Down Under, you have ruined me!)

(In retrospect, perhaps I mildly regret tossing out the Pin the Dong on the Dude game.)

He delivers our Virgin Marys without incident, which are the ideal libation at this moment. They're low in carbs, high in vitamin C, and look enough like cocktails that no one will harass us for not boozing it up before lunch. Take note, ladies—you'll enjoy Vegas a lot more if you pace yourself!

"You can't blame me for worrying, Kit," Betsy says. "You two have a history together. A messy, explosive, expensive history. How'd we get here? Can't you just agree to be polite? For my sake? Why does it always have to devolve into the food fight scene from *Animal House?*"

I want to list the reasons we're here, which would read:

Because she's insufferable

Because she's smug

Because she's SO MUCH SMARTER than anyone else

Because she belittles everything about me and my life

Because she can't accessorize

Because she brings it on herself

Because she's not to be trusted

But I don't.

"We'll barely see her. We won't have time to fight," I reason. "Where's she even coming from? Iran . . . istan?"

So I don't quite remember my geography since becoming a mom, but I can recite every line from *Toy Story*, whip up a luscious kale-based lasagna, and get two Littles out the door in less than five minutes. If there was a parenting Olympics, I would medal. Fact.

Betsy stirs her drink thoughtfully, nibbling on a piece of salami from the elaborate garnish setup. Between the meat, cheese, olives, tomatoes, pepperoncini, celery, and tomato, this is our lunch because we're still so stuffed from breakfast. "No, she's been working out of the Baghdad bureau in Iraq, but she's coming by way of Germany, then London, then New York, then Chicago, then here. Poor thing will have been traveling something like three days just to celebrate with me for a few hours. I'm really touched by the effort she's made."

Yeah, Jack's a true saint, because sitting on an airplane is *way* harder than leaving a three-year-old and a six-year-old across the country with an overbearing mother-in-law. Barbara, aka Nana Baba, has been at our town house in Rogers Park for two days and Ken tells me she's already tossed all my celebrity magazines, dug up my pansies because she thinks they're "too pink," taken down our family pictures so the place will "show better" once we put it on the market (not even happening until early spring of 2007) and read every single one of my e-mails. How do I know this last tidbit? Apparently she's been providing a running commentary on them.

Not only does she disapprove of my overuse of the exclamation point, but she, too, finds my relationship with Jack Jordan troublesome.

I wish Ken would put a leash on her, yet when I complain to him about her lack of boundaries, he tells me other people would love to have an MIL who's so committed and helpful. Really? Lemme me know their numbers 'cause I'm happy to give them the Nana Baba hookup.

Betsy unties her bikini straps in order to rub sunscreen on her chest, shoulders, and sculpted upper arms. Sadly, my two-piece days ended after my C-section with Konnor. Sigh. Dr. Patel was supposed to be the best, but I swear it's like he sliced me open with the jagged end of a broken beer bottle. I'm talking full-on Frankenstein. Couple this with those last seven vanity pounds I've been trying to shake and it's skirted-swimsuit-city for me. Betsy's so lucky! She's still as toned and taut as when we discovered the Burdine, Whitney's massive fitness center, second semester of our freshman year. She practically lived there for the next four years!

I dated this guy once who said that Betsy was a "butterface." When I asked him what he meant, he said her body was hot, but-her-face? Not so much. That's when I dumped him. What a flipping butthole that guy was! Such an unfair assessment of a woman I consider gorgeous inside and out. Does Betsy conform to traditional standards of beauty? Depends. She's quite slim and her frame is tiny, even though she's average height. Her nose tilts up and her eyes seem closer together than they actually are because they're such a watercolor shade of blue. She reminds me of that TV actress Christine Baranski. Her features aren't necessarily faultless, but with her fine posture and quiet competence (and with the nerd glasses but a distant memory, you're welcome), the sum of the parts is striking. She's, like, a *handsome* woman. And seriously elegant. Personally, I believe Trip was attracted to Betsy's face as much as he was her figure and her brain.

"Where's she staying again?" I ask, taking the sunscreen from her. I try to avoid saying her actual name whenever possible, as it tastes like poison on my tongue. I worry if I invoke the word Jack too many times, she'll manifest herself Beetlejuice-style and no one wants that.

Betsy reties her top and replies, "She says she found a room at the Super 8 for seventeen dollars."

Of course she did. God forbid G. I. Jane opt to room with the rest of us. Listen, if she's too humble/unfettered/noble to deign to sleep in the ultra-luxurious, super-mod, two-story, four-bedroom Crystal Palace suite with a full glass-countered kitchen, glass bar, glass dining room, and living area with a glass piano, all built around a 10,000-gallon aquarium, then that's just more shark-gazing time for the rest of us.

"Were there no campgrounds or underpasses available?" I can't help but ask.

"You're starting," Betsy singsongs, wagging her garnish stick at me.

"I'm not starting! All I'm saying is her flagrant lack of materialism is simply another affectation." She's no different now than when she began hanging out with the pretentious journalism students at college. While all the fraternity boys and sorority girls were donning matching T-shirts to hit the basketball game at Ryan Stadium, she was skulking around, smoking clove cigarettes, and touting nihilism, whatever that is. (Something to do with Nine Inch Nails, yes?)

"You don't get it, Kit—she says living conditions can be so dismal and depressing overseas that she doesn't like to spoil herself when she's back in the States."

Yeah, that doesn't sound pompous *at all*. Seriously, why does Bets have such a soft spot for this hideous she-male?

"No chance of getting spoiled at the Super 8," I mutter.

"Kitty, please," Betsy implores. "Do this for me. Be cordial. She's as important to me as you are."

Doubt it, I think, but I keep that thought to myself.

After all, it's Betsy's day.

I settle back into my lounger and return to my magazine (and Britney's desperate cry for help!) while Betsy pores over *The Economist*, occasionally tapping away on her BlackBerry. I should simply be in the moment and revel in my time away from the Littles.

I want to revel, yet I'm ashamed about how much I miss their precious faces. I had a panic attack yesterday when I picked up my purse and realized how light it was, unencumbered by spare Pull-Ups (not that Konnor needs them because he's a BIG BOY, but just in case), clean socks, fresh y-fronts, sippy cups, granola bars, washed AND cut grapes in individual Ziploc baggies, antibacterial wipes, Matchbox cars, Kleenex, and my DSLR camera because you never know when the perfect photo op will present itself.

I've called home a few times since I've been here (read = nineteen) and it actually hurts when I hear that they're having a blast with their grandmother. Don't they miss their mama? I'm grateful Nana Baba's such an important part of their lives, and yet I'm bothered that she can swoop in and take over without them ever skipping a beat.

Am I truly so easily replaced?

Especially by a woman who wears socks with Crocs?

I glance over at Betsy, my other soul mate outside of Ken, and decide I need to try harder for her sake. After all, we've been besties for more than ten years and I can't be the sad sack bringing down the party because I'm unable to ignore the tug of my apron strings for three flipping days. Oprah says I need to Be In the Moment, so I decide to reframe all my negative energy by just appreciating my surroundings.

Here we go.

One attitude of gratitude, comin' up!

I begin to take inventory. First, I'm thankful that this is a really beautiful day. Sure, it's hot and a dry heat is still heat, but the water misters are blasting away in the palm tree above us and I'm ten feet away from a cool blue pool. How do they do that? Despite the broiling temps, the water's still brisk enough to totally refresh.

Wait, I just realized that boys are always asking me "why," and now I find myself doing the same thing. Awww! But if I'm concentrating on not missing them, I can't dwell on their delightful inquisitiveness. Instead, I'll ponder this icy body of water.

So . . . is there such a thing as a reverse heater, like a pool cooler? Or do they just toss in giant blocks of ice every day? No, that doesn't sound right because what's coming out of the jets is chilled.

What if—actually, no, it's not important.

Maybe Oprah doesn't want me to dissect *why* the pool is nice to be thankful, just that it exists in the first place.

Plus, the outdoor area is kind of amazing, which is one of the reasons Betsy insisted we stay here rather than the Four Seasons or the Bellagio. With the dense, lush foliage and the tropical birds and the cabanas masquerading as thatched huts, it really feels like we've been plunked down in the middle of an actual coconut grove somewhere, especially with the sound of steel drums playing in the background. And the air smells like mai tais!

Betsy says the Wintercourt Hotel is the most exclusive on the strip since there's no casino attached. And how nice is it to walk in and not be greeted with the chings and chirps of a million one-armed bandits? Fancy pants! That, plus the unbelievably authentic artificial beach (complete with ocean breezes and rum-drink aromatherapy) and I really do feel like I'm somewhere more exotic than Nevada.

Okay, *that* minor sticking point is messing with my gratitude attitude, too.

Ken keeps promising me that he's going to whisk me away to the Caribbean, but he's been so busy it's yet to happen.

I've been obsessively Googling this little beach I heard about from this really smug mother at Kord's kindergarten. Brooke Birchbaum says there's a place at the tip of Little Cayman that has luminescent pink sand! And it's so secluded that she and her husband even had it all to themselves last year. The hotel staff packed them a picnic lunch and they spent the day snorkeling in the azure sea, eating the freshest fruit they ever tasted, and just reconnecting as a couple.

By reconnecting, I'm fairly sure she meant doing it.

Can you *have sex* in the sand? Or does that leave grit, like, everywhere? Is it good friction or bad friction? I don't like Brooke enough to have this conversation. I should ask Kelly—she always knows this stuff. Regardless, I'd sure like to find out for myself because the Caymans sound like heaven. After she told me about her trip, I applied for a passport that I keep in my purse because the minute Ken decides we're going, I will be *ready.*

I decide to nap and dream of pink sand beaches because it's going to be another late night, but I've barely closed my eyes when Alicia flops into the lounger next to me. "Jesus! Why's the water so cold?" she exclaims, wrapping herself in one of the plush teal-and-white-striped towels strategically placed on every chair.

Alicia's another one of the bridesmaids. She and Betsy met in grad school and, up until she took a job in San Francisco and Betsy started working with Trip, they were employed by the same firm. As she's pro–*The Bachelor* and anti–throwing food or drink at me, she's good people. "I'm, like, all nipped out," she says, pointing to her bikini top. "What's up with that?"

"Right?" I say. "It's bizarre. How do they keep the water so cold?"

Alicia notices our drinks and raises the flag on the back of her chair. "You're drinking bloodies? Perfect! I could use a little hair of the dog right now. Ugh, why do I feel so shitty? I never got hangovers in college. I'd wake up in some frat rat's bed and be naturally adorable, hair tousled just right, all smoky-eyed from mascara. Walk of Shame? More like Walk of *You Wish*. But now? I drink three glasses of wine at a client dinner and I spend the next day trying to keep my office from spinning. Shit, wait, I totally forgot about the body shots! Tequila! *That's* why I feel like ass. Did you tequila-up, Kitty? You seem awfully bushy-tailed."

"No, the liquor pools in my C-section scar and not my belly button so it's too weird now," I truthfully reply.

Alicia peers at me over her sunglasses, saying, "Kit, I will give you a thousand dollars if you never mention your C-section scar again. No joke. I have cash."

This is the downside of being with women who've never had kids. They don't understand that we moms aren't *complaining* when we mention our sacrifices. I reply, "What? It's part of the miracle of life. My scar's a badge of honor."

"As is telling me stories about how you ripped *down there*?" She winces and shakes like a Golden Retriever after a dip in the lake.

"The tearing's not really a badge of honor. That just sucked and now every time I sneeze, I'm rolling the dice."

Alicia holds up a hand. "Nope. No. Don't say another goddamned word. I was so skeeved out that I didn't fuck anyone for a month after you told me that story the first time. You think you've got scars? Well, I got news for ya, sister. I'm scarred, too. Mentally."

"We're all too old for body shots," Betsy adds, yawning and stretching, each lean muscle rippling as she moves. "Still, last night was epic."

Last night was, indeed, epic. We chartered a limo to take us to the theater where the Thunder from Down Under was performing (didn't hate the show) (at all) and at one point, we were all hanging out of the sunroof, hooting and waving champagne bottles like a bunch of kids in an eighties movie montage and not the adults we actually are.

"Pfft, speak for yourself. I plan to never be too old for body shots," Alicia says, rubbing Banana Boat oil on her flat brown stomach.

"Welcome to Cougartown, population you," Betsy says.

"Gimme a few years, but then, yes. Absolutely. I plan on going full Jackie Collins," Alicia replies, likely contemplating all the leopard print she's going to buy once she hits forty. "Hey, where's everyone else?"

I tell her, "Gracie and Cilla went to float in the lazy river over by the children's pool, I believe Devon's sleeping—"

"With a bartender," Alicia helpfully suggests.

"Seems likely," I admit.

"So, who's left?" she asks.

"Um . . . Melissa!" I say, snapping my fingers. I'd say I have mommy-brain today, but it's really more like Veuve Clicquot–brain. "Melissa said she was going to hit the buffet. Wait, how did she not eat this morning? The spread was legendary!"

When we woke up, our personal butler (!) had arranged a ridiculous in-room breakfast for us to help soak up some of last night's booze. We came downstairs to a mighty spread and were greeted by servers foisting goblets of fresh-squeezed juices and champagne on us. Personally, I avoided the cocktails, instead diving into the raw bar, laden with briny oysters and shrimp the size of clenched fists, bracketed by piles of cracked crab claws and lobster tails, surrounded by dozens of pots of different varieties of cocktail sauces and citrus mayonnaise.

At first, I felt a little guilty indulging in a seafood feast in front of the massive aquarium spanning the suite from the first floor to the second. I could have sworn the tiger shark was glaring at me with his unblinking black eyes, as he circled around in the tank, but then I realized he was probably just lusting after my caviar-topped blini. Who wouldn't?

(Also, I'm pretty sure there's no such thing as shark sashimi, so it was fine.)

If the seafood bonanza wasn't enough of a treat, what of all the perfect little petit fours from Vanille Patisserie, Betsy's favorite bakery in Chicago? Or how about having our own personal chef in a giant white toque, crafting truffle-laden omelets on demand, and the mile of steam trays on the glass counter, brimming with favorites such as eggs Benedict and mini-quiches and prosciutto-wrapped asparagus?

For Betsy, none of the gourmet offerings could hold a candle to the simplicity of the authentic biscuits and sausage gravy flown in directly from The Ol' Breakfast Joynt, our favorite late-night haunt at Whitney. She was teary when she realized what Trip had done.

Note to self: In my next lifetime, I need to marry a millionaire.

Betsy breaks out the biggest smile I've seen from her all weekend. Her teeth are ultra white and beautifully capped. (Well done, Ken!) "You know that means Melissa's playing blackjack, right?"

"Really? Kinda early for gambling," I note.

"Not at all. In fact, I'm shocked it took her so long to hit the tables. Must have been biding her time." Betsy looks over both shoulders and then leans in conspiratorially to whisper, "Missy can count cards. She majored in math at MIT. Over the years, she's paid for her house, her car, her tits, and her Stanford MBA with winnings."

"Huh. Isn't card-counting a form of cheating? Seems like . . . not the most ethical behavior for someone in the financial service industry," I whisper back.

Betsy and Alicia exchange a look I can't quite read—it's not pity, right? Do they feel like I won't understand? Oh, *whatever.* I think sometimes they hold back on business-y talk because they doubt I can keep up with them, being just a stay-at-home mom and all.

Please.

If they witnessed how I single-handedly saved the Chicago Park District's Toddlers and Tambourines music program with my keen managerial skills and ability to delegate, they'd be hitting *me* up for advice.

"Wait, what about Jack? I almost forgot she was coming!" Alicia says. "Oh, my God, did you ever read the exposé she wrote about the conflict in Darfur? The way she risked her life to interview those rebels? Whoa. I literally cannot wait to sit down with her and hear all about it."

I roll my eyes so hard I can see the inside of my skull.

"Are you two still having your little tiff from college? What was that, like, nineteen-ninety-who-cares? You guys aren't over it yet?" she asks.

"If by 'having a little tiff,' you mean total and utter thermonuclear destruction, then, yes, yes, we are." I glance over at Betsy, who seems pained. "However, despite my wishing she'd die in a fire, I'm planning to smile and nod, so if there's an issue, it won't be me who started it."

Betsy's spine stiffens and she very deliberately says, "Because it won't start, of course."

"Because it won't start," I agree.

I wish I felt as confident as I sound.

· · · ·

The Intrepid Girl Reporter is perched on the edge of the one uncomfortable chair in the whole place, a piano bench that appears to be crafted out of steel beams and icicles, because God forbid she allow herself to nestle into the squashy, U-shaped ten-seater couch where everyone else is. Her arm rests on the glass top of the piano to her side, next to her tumbler of plain water. Not even Evian! Just regular tap. Naturally, she droned on about how water is more precious than oil in the desert. Betsy nodded and asked a bunch of questions about access to wells and stuff, but she was just being polite. Personally, I had to excuse myself to go pummel a pillow in the room I'm sharing with Alicia.

And the hair! Holy crap! Her head's practically shaved. Like, the full Sinéad O'Connor. She said she buzzed it off herself *to get rid of the lice*, as though that wasn't the most shameful statement ever uttered in recorded history. Instead of being all "Cooties!" the rest of the girls kept telling her how brave she was.

Ugh.

Look at her, leaning on that piano like she owns the place.

". . . then I'm on this deserted beach in K.L., watching the sun rise, and it's as though the Lord himself were wielding an enormous paintbrush and—"

I interrupt, "I'm sorry, *where?*"

She narrows her eyes at me, as though I'm challenging her.

I'm not.

Well, not really. Much.

I'm just saying Miss World Traveler might want to ratchet the level of self-satisfaction down a thousand notches or so for those of us too busy raising fine young Americans to faff about on other continents.

I reach for the margarita on the table next to me, which the butler's been serving in ginormous crystal tumblers. This thing must weigh five pounds. It's like a fucking carton of milk!

Whoopsie! I just dropped an F-bomb! Bad mommy! I have to remember it's *flipping*, not *fucking.* Little pitchers, big ears.

I actually have to use both hands to lift my glass to my lips. Like, my arms are tired from drinking these all night. (Or maybe the butler wanted to help me tone up, in which case, thanks, Jeeves!) Betsy catches my eye and I sip and smile beatifically, before innocently sucking the grains of salt off my upper lip. Nope. No problems here! Me and my other best friend Jose Cuervo are doing just fine.

"K.L. is Kuala Lumpur—it's in Malaysia?" Is it just me, or did she say that extra slow, dragging out "Mah*laaaay*sha*aaaa*" as though I'm developmentally delayed (we do NOT use the r-word; it's on the Never Never list) and won't understand her otherwise? "I assume you're familiar? It's the home of the Petronas Twin Towers. Anyway, I'm with a documentary crew and we've been—"

Blah, blah, blah.

Braggity-brag-brag.

Look at me! I'm Jack Jordan! I travel around the whole world with nothing but a notebook and my own moxie! I shave myself bald! I'm wearing nasty jungle boots, a ratty scarf, and a tactical shirt with lots of buttons, because I would rather die than dress appropriately for a bachelorette party!

She drones on. ". . . the chiaroscuro of the sunrise, which is the inter-play between dark and light . . ."

How is everyone not barfing into their own handbags right now over the sheer pretentiousness of what's coming out of her mouth? And the nerve of assuming I don't know where Malaysia is!

". . . it was as though a box of crayons had been left melting on the sidewalk. The burnt sienna oozed into . . ."

I know where Malaysia is. I am quite familiar, as a matter of fact. The night nurse my parents hired for us after I had Kord was from Malaysia.

I think.

No, I'm sure of it. Malaysia. Wait, excuse me, Jack, Mah*laaaay*shaaaaa. That makes her Mah*laaaay*shiaaaaan. I take a swig of my megaton of margarita to congratulate myself on remembering that particular fac-toid. Ekaterina didn't last long, though. Did not care for how she'd bounce around the house in flimsy baby-doll jammies without benefit of brassiere. I mean, it's not like Ken would even look sideways at another woman, but still. Best not tempt fate. Plus, I realized I could do it all on my own because I am SUPERMOM!

Woo!

Am I drunk?

Mayhaps I should slow down.

Cripes, I forgot how chatty this blabbermouth can be. Must have blocked it from my memory as, like, a protective mechanism. Forgot about how she used to grill me all the time. Do you know what it's like to have someone question your every move? To comment on your every action? She was so weird—she acted like she'd never spoken to another girl before.

For more than a decade, she's been saying that I'm the problem and that I don't like women, but what's so funny is that I had zero issue liv-ing in a sorority house full of them. Not a single issue. Maybe I didn't have an actual best friend until college, but that's only because I was always so close with my sister. I play well with others. I do. So, clearly it wasn't me because *I* was part of a sisterhood. An integral part. *She* didn't even get a bid!

Wanna know why she failed so spectacularly? She brought up Mah-*laaaay*shaaaaa.

So smug. So self-righteous. Like earlier, when I accidentally mentioned my jagged C-section scar again? (Sorry, Alicia.) She was all, "The women of Iraq would kill to have your first world problems. Let's talk about the state of maternal fetal medicine in a war zone. Did you know that the average adult Iraqi mother is subject to—"

I immediately tuned her out, and not just because of the smug. I kind of can't bear to hear her terrible stories about what it's like for moms in other countries. If I were to actually listen to her, I would literally run to the airport, hop on the next plane headed east, and go home to hug my sweet baby boys until the end of time.

In fact, if I had to get to my kids, I would run all the way to Mah*laaaay*shaaaaa.

I watch Betsy's whole face glow as she listens to Lois Lane prattle on about her experience running with the bulls in Pamplona. Oh, please, Miss Ernest Hemingway, tell us more!

"Sars, there I was, in my white shirt and red bandanna . . ."

Argh! Stop calling her Sars! That's not a name; that's a coronavirus! Her name is Betsy, you asshole!

Darn it! That's another dollar in the swear jar.

I can't understand how Betsy can like us both. They have nothing in common anymore, save for a shared childhood. Pretty sure Bets hasn't been on a dirt bike since the first Bush administration.

I need to take the spotlight off of this blowhard.

"P.S., FYI, I am familiar with Mah*laaaay*shaaaaa. Betsy." I cut my eyes over to Jack to see if she corrects me. She doesn't but I can tell she's dying to. "Remember our night nurse? She was from there. You know, Mah*laaaay*shaaaaa," I say, delighted for the chance to prove Jackass wrong. I raise my marg in victory.

"Ekaterina?" Betsy says.

"Yes."

"Ekaterina who worked for you? Back in 2000? With Kord?"

"*Yes.*"

"Oh, Kit, no," Betsy says gently. "She was from Macedonia."

"But they're close to each other, right?" I ask, trying to shrug it off. "Common mistake."

Betsy pats my knee. "It's actually an entirely different continent."

Jack's snort is so abrupt and profound that I flinch, which causes me to accidentally lose control of the hand holding my margarita glass, thus setting off a chain of events I'd . . . rather not discuss.

For the record?

I didn't start it.

Mah*laaaay*shaaaaa did.

I hope the shark is okay.

CHAPTER SIX

Jack

....

Seven Miles over Ohio
Last Saturday

I dropped everything the minute I heard.

I hate that Bobby had to give me the news. He's not equipped. His insular, good-time, party-boy lifestyle is the defense mechanism he's created specifically to avoid dealing with the grim reality of the real world. That's why he was the one who cried, not me. All I could do was spring into action. Guess that's how I'm wired.

Maybe I've seen too much in the field, too much sadness, too much destruction, too much suffering. I've witnessed and documented the nadir of human behavior. I wonder if I'm not somehow inoculated against having more profound feelings when others leave this mortal coil? The Operators I've met in the field always speak of creating a Chinese wall between feelings and duties. Said it's the only way to survive after the war's over. Perhaps I've taken their words to heart.

I suspect I started to shut down long before I worked in the trenches. Teddy said we all changed after Mom. I hardened my heart, whereas Bobby started to wear his on his sleeve. Ted overcompensated and John-John, well, I guess he's remained his consistently unpleasant self.

Some things never change.

I glance down at my wrist and I have to smile. John was right about one thing—I do love a big watch. I'm not one to splurge, but when I saw the MTM Special Ops Black Military model that day Sars dragged me through Neiman's, I had to have it. With its titanium bracelet, carbon-coated case, and antireflective sapphire crystal, I figured it would last forever. After more than ten years in dozens of war zones, I can confirm it's stood the test of time. (Pun intended.)

Wouldn't let Sars buy the watch for me, though. She perpetually believes I'm broke. Couldn't be further from the truth. I've socked away almost every cent I've earned. And the trust's still untouched. I could live off of what I made from *Girl O' War*'s movie rights alone, had I not donated such a large portion to Sudanese relief efforts. Before you ask, no, I had nothing to do with stunt-casting Jennifer Aniston as the lead. Don't start me on the fiction that was the shower seduction scene. I never even *met* General Petraeus, but truth takes a backseat to Ms. Aniston's backseat in a lace thong.

Anyway, the plan's to put in another ten to fifteen years of doing what I'm doing and I should be set to retire. To settle down, if it's not already far too late.

To be clear, not with General Petraeus.

According to my fancy watch, I'm due to land in forty-five minutes. I don't want to start a new documentary on my laptop and I just finished reading the latest book on Vladimir Putin. As I transition out of the Middle East, I'm brushing up on Russia. Putin has designs on restoring the USSR to its former glory. Chances are, I'm headed there for the long haul. I plan to be ready.

Flipping through the pages of the *American Way* magazine stuffed in the seat pocket in front of me, I pause to examine the spread on the Crystal Palace suite at the Vegas Wintercourt. Glad to see Tigger the tiger shark is still alive and swimming. We did give him a scare, though.

Scanning the article, I realize that night may not have been my finest hour. When I arrived in Vegas, I was filthy and exhausted, yet I'm often filthy and exhausted in the call of duty, so that wasn't the issue. I guess I wasn't comfortable with the whole situation. For once, it wasn't Kitty's fault. That night, Kitty was but a gnat buzzing around my head. A minor annoyance, at best.

Sure, she irritated me with all her silly chatter about Australian strippers and *Us Weekly* and injecting broccoli puree into chicken nuggets (?), so I admit to baiting her about Malaysia. Her expression was priceless. As always in the case with Kitty, the bitch had it coming.

But for once, Kitty wasn't the main problem.

What had me riled was that I didn't want Sars to marry Trip.

There. Said it.

I realize what poor taste it is to bring it up at a moment like this, but maybe if Sars had listened to me back then, everything would be different now.

My concern stemmed from what I saw earlier that day in the international terminal at the airport. I'd just disembarked from my British Airways flight, cleared customs, and was headed toward the connecting departure gate in another terminal. I was beat and a little disoriented, but I was instantly wide-awake the moment I spotted Trip—pastel sweater and all—in the priority boarding line for an Air France flight. And then I noticed he wasn't alone. I assumed the attractive young Latina wasn't a business associate by the proprietary way he was grasping her shapely behind.

I called over to him and I'm sure I saw a flash of panic cross his face, before he pretended to gaze right through me. With that one look, he confirmed my every suspicion.

I was not about to let this go. As a reporter, my job is to delve into the heart of the story, regardless of the outcome. An ocean of people separated us, but I pushed through them. Narrowing the gap between us, I vaulted over a group of French students who were sitting on the floor of the gate playing a card game and I plowed past a passel of disgruntled fanny-pack-clad tourists, but I was too late. He'd already boarded the plane and the snooty gate agent refused to confirm or deny that Trip's name was on the manifest. "Ess not your biiiisness," he'd sniffed.

The damn French'll disappoint you every time.

(I hang out with a lot of marines; I may be biased.)

Already agitated when I arrived in Vegas, I broached the subject with Sars immediately. She wouldn't even entertain the thought of impropriety as Trip had just dropped a load of cash flying in all of her favorite treats. To me, his extravagance smacked of overcompensation. A guilty conscience.

I distrusted Trip from the moment we met. He was one of those guys who'd simultaneously charm you while glancing over your shoulder in case someone more important was to walk by. Or maybe he was mentally undressing them? He was always so cagey, it was hard to tell.

He and Sars met at some U of C mixer for MBA students and she was instantly smitten. I knew she really loved him; Sars was never so superficial that she'd date someone for his money. Growing up an only child on the lake in the upper-middle-class area of Evanston, she was familiar with living well. That Trip's family lived so much better than her version of well was an added bonus.

But I always had the feeling that beneath his Ivy League veneer and perma-tan beat the heart of an operator. An opportunist. A snake-oil salesman. Unfortunately, despite my investigations after I "allegedly" saw him in the airport, I couldn't unearth the full evidence needed to prove my theory. So all I could ever do was smile and wish Sars well. Whenever I visited Steeplechase, their sprawling North Shore estate complete with guardhouse, she seemed extremely happy. So even though it went against my every instinct, I eventually stopped probing.

Sars and Trip had lived nine years without incident, even though I could never shake the feeling that there was always some sort of darkness under the surface, lying dormant . . . until the time was right.

· · · ·

"There she is! There's our girl!"

Teddy runs over and sweeps me up in a massive bear hug, spinning me around so hard that I get dizzy. "Quit it!" I demand as he whirls me around faster and faster. "I think I'm going to throw up!" When he doesn't stop, I add, "I think I'm going to throw up on *you*, Joel."

Terry, Ted's spouse, clucks, "You're kidding! *Top Gun* lines? Already? You've been together *thirty seconds*! That's a new record. I told you I should have made up a sibling BINGO card. Y'all are *too* predictable."

"Technically, that line was from *Risky Business* in reference to Guido-the-killer-pimp from the car chase scene," Teddy replies.

"'Porsche, there is no substitute,'" I add.

Terry shrugs. "Sorry, not familiar."

Teddy rolls his eyes. "You're killing me, Ter, I mean it. Last week I said I wanted to receive total consciousness on my deathbed and *this one*"—he pokes Terry, who giggles in response—"was all, '*Should we write that into your living will, honey?*' Pretty sure your never having seen *Caddyshack* is grounds for divorce in this state."

"Do what you need to do, babe," Terry replies. "That means more cake for us." Terry owns an incredible little shop in the Andersonville neighborhood of Chicago called The Confectionery, which specializes in homemade candies, like toffees and caramels, and baked goods, such as exotically flavored cupcakes, including my favorites, the blood orange Dreamsicle and the Maharani, which is a curry lemon curd with sweet basil cream.

I'm not the only one who swears Terry's treats are the best in all of Chicago. The place opens at ten a.m., which means the line forms at the door every day by eight thirty a.m. On the days they sell mini-pies, it's more like seven thirty.

I hug them both to me again. Feels so good to be here, back beside my family. Teddy loops his arm around my left shoulder and Terry grabs me on my right side as we head toward the baggage carousel in one cohesive unit. At times like these, I wonder why I work so far from everyone I love.

"Not for nothing, Tedster, but you are better-looking every time I see you." Not flattery, but hard fact. Teddy was striking in his teens and twenties, but now that he's older, he's practically breathtaking. Pretty boys always go in one of two directions—they turn into James Spader with the wrinkles and paunch and male-pattern baldness or, if they're very lucky, they head down the less trodden path, the Rob Lowe/Daniel Craig/Sean Connery route, improving with age like bottles of Château Margaux. "What's your secret?" I ask. "Do you have a portrait of Dorian Gray in your attic? If you still look so good, who looks bad in your place?"

At the same time, we all say, "John-John." Not sure if it's time or the demands of four kids and a vapid wife or just plain old karma, but the last time we saw him at the new baby's christening, he was almost indistinguishable from our father. John and Dad looked more like twins than he and Bobby do anymore, much to John's chagrin and Dad's delight.

"Girl, *I'm* his secret," Terry insists. "We juice now. We're juicers. Had to do something to counterbalance all the carbs. I'll make you some in the morning. I do a blend with kale, apples, and celery that'll knock your socks off."

"It's really delicious," Teddy says, while vehemently shaking his head and choking his own neck, eyes bulging comically behind Terry's back. "Definitely better than the mini-pies."

"Trust me, anything will be gourmet after all the MREs I've eaten," I say to appease them both, referring to the bland, cold, prepackaged field rations I normally call dinner.

We circle around the baggage claim to wait for my luggage. A seemingly endless supply of identical black roller bags whiz past us. How often does someone take the wrong suitcase when they all look so much alike? I don't even have to tell Teddy when mine chugs past—he can automatically deduce that the dusty old green duffel belongs to me.

We load up Terry's Outback and I feel like a child again in the backseat, with my doting parents up front. "Tell me everything, hon," Terry says, navigating out of the four-tier parking garage at O'Hare. "How long do we have you?"

"I won't know more about that for a few days," I reply. "The wakes begin tomorrow and then the funeral's on Wednesday. But I can take as long as I need."

Terry's face softens. "I'm so sorry, hon. This is devastating."

"Thanks, Ter, I appreciate it," I reply. I swallow hard, trying to hide my emotions, but almost too overcome not to. Terry really feels like a second mom to me, significantly different from the original (obviously), but better in so many ways.

Teddy asks, "You mind bunking with Bobby and the boys? They should arrive later tonight." A few years ago after I was transferred from Baghdad to Kabul, I shipped my few things home to Terry and Teddy. They wanted me to have a place I truly could call home, so they set up a little apartment for me in their basement. However, ninety-nine percent of the time, it's Bobby who uses it as a crash pad between his winter and summer gigs. I'm not sure he *has* to so much as he *wants* to be there with all Terry's mini-pies. (I suspect if Terry were to make a full-sized version, Bobby would move in forever.)

"I packed Benadryl and an inhaler, so I should be set." I've developed an allergy to cats as an adult, which I guess is a benefit even though I love them. Pets can inadvertently tether you to one place, so never being able to have one made it easier for me to move about at will. I'll be glad to see Bobby's crew, though, as they're particularly sweet. He has the kind of cats who head-butt you to demand kisses. I always oblige, and then spend the next two days sneezing and scrubbing at my watery eyes.

Terry glances at me in the rearview mirror. "Whenever you do leave, which will be too soon, bee-tee-dubs, what's next? Any chance we can convince you to take a stateside assignment in the near future?"

"Not unless Putin relocates. Believe I'm off to Russia next. If ol' Vladimir keeps up with his current level of nonsense, I could be there for a while," I reply, mentally ticking off his ever-growing list of transgressions.

"Ooh, Putin!" Terry replies. "I *hate* him! But . . . I kind of love him a little bit, too. I know all the shirtless bear-wrestling and posing on horseback is propaganda, but I don't care. He's just the most perfect Bond villain ever."

Teddy gives Terry's shoulder a good-natured rub. "Only you, Ter. Only you."

We're almost to their home before Teddy remembers something important. "You got a call today, Jack-o," he says.

"From?" Given the news, it stands to reason people would know I'm back.

"Kitty Carricoe."

I slump down in my seat. "Damn. I forgot I'd have to deal with her. Was it awkward?" I ask.

"Why would it be awkward?" Terry demands. Terry can sniff out the faintest trace of gossip like a truffle pig in a forest.

"No, it wasn't awkward," Teddy replies. "That was a million years ago. It's you who has the issue with her, kid, not me. *I* always liked her. Plus, with all her big blond hair, red lips, and trapeze dresses? She was the shit back then."

"They dated briefly when I was a freshman," I explain.

"Jealous?" Teddy asks, arching an eyebrow.

Terry gives Teddy the side-eye and replies, "Survey says . . . no. But it sounds like there's a story. Dish, please."

I lean into the front seat to explain. "Their brief relationship and subsequent breakup caused this whole chain of events that took us from being the best of friends to the best of enemies."

"This is already my favorite story ever," Terry says, eagerly glancing back at me in the rearview mirror. "What happened?"

"What happened is, we started to act like eighteen-year-old girls. She said something that pissed me off, so I stormed out, then she made a big stink out of an innocent mistake I made, then John convinced me to seek revenge. The whole thing went back and forth, escalating in severity and, bottom line, we almost got kicked out of the dorms because of it. Clearly we've never gotten over it because each time we're together, we're at it like two wet cats in a burlap sack."

"How have I not heard any of this?" Terry asks.

"Because it's mortifying and I'm desperately ashamed of my behavior," I reply.

"That's how you know it's a good story. Do continue!" Terry signals and expertly navigates the Outback down the off-ramp. We've reached the Andersonville area and should be home soon.

I explain, "Our whole feud took on a life of its own. Normally, when something like this happens, both parties agree to hate each other and go live entirely separate lives. But because of Sars, we keep getting thrown back together and each time it's been a disaster."

"Wait, this is the girl who almost killed the shark?"

"Yes."

"And she dumped the chocolate fountain on you at Sars's wedding?"

I clear my throat. "*Allegedly.* Trip's lawyers eventually made the whole incident go away. But if that had happened—and the attorneys are vehement that *it did not*—I'd have had so much chocolate on me, it would have been as if I'd leapt into a pool of it. It was—allegedly—everywhere. In my ears, up my nose, in my underwear. I mean, *everywhere.* I went through a bottle of shampoo trying to wash it all out of my hair."

Terry nudges Ted. "Take note, please. I want this to happen to me before I die."

I interject, "I promise you death by chocolate isn't as great as you'd imagine."

"I prefer to be the judge of that."

Personally, I *wish* that I could be covered in scalding hot chocolate every single day of the rest of my life if it would erase the memory of the look Sars and her parents had on their faces when they saw the end result of our shared grudge. I'd do anything to take back that moment.

I can handle having an enemy, especially as I believe that good can come of conflictual relationships. But poor Sars has always been the innocent in all of this. The bystander. The sweet kid in a bad neighborhood, just trying to ride her bike to Grandma's when she gets caught in gang cross fire. I'd always secretly hoped that somehow Kitty and I could find a place of understanding and give back to Sars what we inadvertently took away by ruining the end of her wedding. And bachelorette party. And engagement party.

But now? Now it's far too late.

I say, "I'm dreading seeing Kitty tomorrow because she'll make an impossible situation exponentially more difficult. I'm warning you, the coming days are not going to be a treat. I apologize in advance if I turn into a bitchy *girl.*" The more I contemplate what's ahead of me, the more I twist the hair in my stubby ponytail. My brothers could always tell when I was stressed in school, because I'd end up with these long, panic-based banana curls—until I finally chopped it all off second semester of my freshman year.

Terry is a paragon of compassion. "Oh, honey, that's terrible! But you have to tell me—what could that awful wench have done to cause such a ruckus?"

I love how Terry's on my side, ready to defend me, whereas Teddy's already sputtering with laughter as I explain.

In retrospect, the story *is* hilarious, and maybe if I hadn't reacted so badly due to my immaturity, shock, and surprise, she'd have never pulled that business during rush and I'd have left her hair alone, so she wouldn't have destroyed my stuff and the Sean situation wouldn't have come to pass . . . Long story short, we'd never have reached this point.

I take a deep breath, give my locks a few extra twists, and finally say, "The fight started when Kitty claimed Ted dumped her because he was gay."

Teddy's laughing so hard he's gasping for air, while Terry scratches his five o' clock shadow, as he always does when deep in thought, trying to piece this all together.

"Um . . ." His voice is as rich, deep, and melodic as James Earl Jones. If he weren't committed to being a pastry chef, he'd make a killing doing voice-overs.

Terry looks like what Val Kilmer should have grown into, had he fulfilled the promise of his golden youth back in the *Top Gun* days. His hair is still fair and full, and jawline square as ever. He's lean in all the spots where Val became puffy and he's so strong from hoisting fifty-pound bags of flour all day. He certainly wouldn't need a tub of Vaseline to try to squeeze into a fitted Batman costume. (No offense, Val.) And a steady regime of injectables and microdermabrasion has kept his skin as fresh and unfurrowed as the day I met him back in 1996. Is he forty-two? Is he twenty-four? No one can tell.

I explain. "*That's* why it's funny now. At the time I thought she was just being a megabitch."

Teddy finally manages to compose himself. "I wasn't mad. I was relieved. We parted as friends because she was the catalyst to my being honest with myself, even if it took me a while to come out to all of you. I remember thinking, *'If this smokin' hot chick isn't doing it for me, no woman ever will. I can finally stop overcompensating.'* And P.S. she was a freak in the sheets. Big-time."

I grit my teeth. "What a poseur. She'd always tell me she was saving it until someone gave her his fraternity pin."

Ted hoots with mirth. "I pinned her all right."

I shriek, "Augh! No! Again, I'm going to throw up on *you*, Joel."

Teddy snaps his fingers. "Actually, no—wait. My bad. I'm remembering wrong. The first night, she went on and on about the whole boyfriend/committed relationship thing, too, so I figured we weren't going to happen because I wasn't in the market for anything serious. Her tune sure changed after a couple of drinks. Two grenadine-spiked Zimas later, I literally couldn't peel her off of my jock. One time, she—"

I throw up my hands. "Stop. I mean it. Kabul didn't give me PTSD, but your story might."

"When did all this happen?" Terry asks.

"Between Thanksgiving and New Year's Eve in 1994," I reply.

"And when did we meet?" He steals a glance away from the road to look to Teddy.

Ted replies, "October of 1995. I saw you for the first time on Halloween at Sidetrack in Boystown. I got your number that night. Remember? You were done up like Tori Spelling in *90210*?"

"Aha! All the pieces finally fit together. Blond hair, red lips, trapeze dress," Terry replies as the streetlight illuminates his wide grin. "Donna Martin really did graduate."

We pull into the garage behind Terry and Teddy's amazing Arts and Crafts home with the original millwork and stained glass. As we exit the garage, stretching and breathing in the warm night air of the backyard, Terry says, "I can't speak for you, Jack, but I want to bake this Kitty lady something extra nice. I feel like I owe her a debt of gratitude. Can I send her a treat? What kind of pie says 'thanks for being too much woman for my man?' Key lime? Rhubarb?"

"Cherry?" Ted suggests, snickering.

"Stop it, you. Really, I'd like to make her something," Terry insists. "Would that be okay?"

"Only if you add broccoli," I reply, only half kidding.

"Consider it done."

The guys are all smiles and jocularity as we bring my gear into the house, but I'm more solemn, worrying about what comes next. I offer up a short prayer that, no matter how tomorrow shakes out, I won't throw the broccoli pie at Kitty.

Because Sars always deserved better.

CHAPTER SEVEN

♥ From the Beautiful Mind ♥ of Miss Katherine Kord

July 23, 1994

Hello, future roomie!

I'm psyched you live so close to North Shore! We can ride home together and hang out during vacations! Sorry we can't meet in person before we leave for school—this'll be my last year working as a camp counselor here in Wisconsin. Am seriously SICK of dealing with all these brats. It's going to be a looooong time before I wipe someone else's nose again, I promise you that. Hoping to snag a job at Express in Old Orchard Mall next year—employee discount, baby!!

You're bringing a futon, yes? I'll have my sister Kelly's mini-fridge and portable TV—she just graduated and moved to the city, so she doesn't need them. Dr. Daddy (I know, I know, but the name makes him happy) is buying me a computer, too. You're welcome to use it! So awesome that your brothers are building us a loft for our beds—how many and how cute? Inquiring minds want to know! (I have a serious boyfriend, but that doesn't mean I can't look!) I'm also sneaking my Cabriolet onto campus. Frosh aren't supposed to have cars, but without wheels, how would we shop?!

Go to Crate and Barrel for your comforter—buy the twin in the Marimekko Unikko Bright print. (Orange and fuchsia flower print on a white background.) Get their mother-of-pearl desk lamp with the beige shade, too. I already bought some fun pillows for the futon. We can decorate more once we're moved in.

Can't wait to meet your friend Sarabeth! She sounds awesome and I'm so excited she'll be in Wadsworth Hall with us!

Quick reminder—have everyone send in your sorority recommendation letters if you haven't yet. Greek life is key at Whitney, so you'll want a running start. Are you a legacy anywhere? My mom was a Tri Tau, as was my grandma and Kelly. Triple legacy, baby! I tell everyone that I plan to consider ALL the houses, but we all know where I belong.

Aw, crap, I think I heard the little lunatics coming back from arts and crafts. UGH. Gotta scoot! See you soon!

Besos!
Kitty (that's what my friends call me and we're going to be best friends forEVAH!!)

Kitty

....

Whitney University, Central Illinois
October 1994

"How hot are *you*? You're totally smoking. For real."

As of this moment, Jackie's a serious ten. Not kidding. Who saw this coming? Definitely not Jackie, as she's still gawping at herself in the mirror, completely gob smacked. Like, her mouth's literally been hanging open ever since I did the big reveal five minutes ago. Granted, I have mad makeover skills, but wasn't aware she had that kind of raw material under all those ill-fitting hockey shirts and sweatpants.

I arranged a signature daytime look that makes the most of Jackie's natural attributes. After applying black liquid liner cat-eye style with a neutral matte powder shadow, I brushed on layer after layer of Great Lash to make the crazy-kaleidoscope iris colors pop. (I skipped the base because her skin is, as we say in French, *da bomb*.) I finished her off with the same awesome brownish-bronze shade on her lips that Shannen Doherty's been sporting lately.

I back-combed Jackie's long hair for volume and to show off how piece-y her cut is. Stefan says these layers are the new take on the seventies shag and this style's about to become The Next Big Thing. I also lent her a fab knee-length plaid swing dress (picture a modern Mary Quant), fat-heeled Mary Janes, and my favorite velvet choker.

"You look just like Phoebe Cates," I say.

She knits her brows. "Have I met her? You've introduced me to so many girls already that I can't remember who's who."

What Jackie doesn't know about pop culture could fill a book. Mean it. Last week, she asked me if *Courteney Cox* lived in our dorm, because she kept hearing that name. "Phoebe Cates is the actress who took off her bikini top in *Fast Times at Ridgemont High.*"

Jackie seems puzzled. "That's good?"

"Very good," I confirm.

She returns her attention to her reflection. "You're a miracle worker," she says, practically pressing her face into the mirror for a closer look.

I wave her off. "Please. I'm not Jesus making loaves out of fishes. I'm more like . . . Mary Kay," I reply. "Fact is it's a lot easier to sculpt marble than, say, oatmeal. Your skin, for example? Your pores literally make me rage-y."

Jackie flushes and touches her cheek. Her modesty is super-refreshing. Whenever anyone tells my sister Kelly she's pretty, she's all, *"Yeah, and?"* because she's heard it a million times.

Jackie stammers, "My—my skin's nothing special."

I sit down to refresh my own makeup because I need considerably more foundation work than she does. I'm so fair that if I skip mascara or eye/brow liner, I look like a newborn baby rat.

I rest my elbows on my desk where the lighted makeup mirror's arranged on my textbooks. As I paint my inner lids with blue kohl, I ask, "Are you kidding? I've never seen you with a single blackhead, let alone a full-on, stressed-out, pre-period Vesuvius, despite washing your face with hand soap. *Hand soap.* I don't even want to mention your visible abs. I didn't know *girls* could have those. Fortunately, I'm not a jealous person, because I'd probably be consumed by the little green monster right now. No lie. Do me a proper and don't let my boyfriend see you all dolled up. I couldn't compete!"

Seriously, Sean's super chummy with Jackie. He thinks she's hilarious.

Jackie does this all over body-roll, like she's trying to shimmy away from the compliment. Instead of just accepting her accolades, she goes, "What's wrong with hand soap? Skin is skin." Then she flops down on the futon next to the mirror, legs akimbo, as though she's sitting in the dugout, waiting for her turn at bat.

"Knees, please." I have to keep reminding Jackie she's wearing a dress. I swear sometimes that wolves raised her, but at least she's open to learning. She quickly crosses her legs in a decidedly more ladylike manner, just like we've practiced. " *'Skin is skin'?* You're messing with me, right?" I peer back at her from the reflection in my mirror.

"Maybe not wearing makeup has been good for my face." She pokes at her eyelid with a newly manicured finger. "Hey, this stuff will come off later, right? It's not permanent?"

This girl is just too precious for words sometimes. We've started reading *Brave New World* in my Freshman Lit class and I feel like I'm Bernard Marx (the hero, obviously) bringing John the Savage into Utopia. She doesn't understand our modern ways either, but she will and everything will work out great eventually. (Haven't finished the book yet, but I'm sure there's a happy ending.) So I tell her, "Honey, it's *eyeliner*, not a tattoo. You can wash it all off in about fifteen seconds. Later, though. Not now. And not with hand soap."

Jackie's makeover is like those infomercials where they find some ratty old hunk of metal in a scrap yard. Looks all beat up and worthless, right? But then they dip the piece in a special chemical bath and presto-change-o, all the scum dissolves and a valuable object's revealed!

Jackie's totally a shiny silver doubloon now, which is amazing because when we moved into our room together two months ago, she was a bit of a sartorial train wreck. When I saw that her makeup bag was basically a tube of lip balm, I was nervous. When she put up the *Top Gun* poster, I was all, *"What's up with that?"* And when she pulled out of her bag *seven different kinds of sneakers?* Yikes. But I gave her a chance and I'm so glad I did. She's now my best, best friend and I would, like, take a bullet for her. Mean it.

I always had close girlfriends, but I was never as tight with them as I am with Jackie. For example, I appreciate how smart Jackie is, despite buying the wrong comforter because she couldn't tell the difference between the poppy and the tulip-printed Marimekko bedding. (Actually, no biggie—the mixed florals look faboo together.) Plus, she's a great listener and seems so open to new experiences. Her default answer is, "Sure! Let's do it!" I can't believe she can fly a plane by herself—how, like, *brave* is that? I'm still so nervous about driving that I have to take the back roads all the way home to North Shore, instead of using the expressway. We're totally the Odd Couple, but in a way where our respective strengths, like, *compensate* for each other.

Sean's right, Jackie is really funny, even though her quips go over my head sometimes. She kept giggling over how I was "farding" when putting on her makeup. (I still don't get it and I *did not* eat beans.)

The biggest bonus of being roomies and best friends is that her brothers are TCFW—Too Cute For Words. (Not the crabby one, though.) The guys took off their shirts while they were building our loft and . . . rowr! They kept saying, *"It's so hot in here."* Later, my sister, Kelly, and I were all, *"I'll say it was hot!"*

Teddy's especially nice-looking. If I wasn't dating Sean, I'd have been ignoring Teddy extrahard, alongside of Kelly. (Kelly says the fastest way into a guy's heart is to be dismissive of him.) Jackie believes I'd get along better with Bobby, who's supernice, albeit kind of a stoner. I dug his laid-back vibe, but he's all the way in California for school, while Teddy could drive down here from the city in less than two hours.

Again, doesn't matter because I do not cheat on boyfriends. Ever. Sean and I have been together since the first week of summer camp this year. He was a counselor on the boys' side up in 'Sconsin. I thought he looked way cute in his puka shell necklace and tank top, so I tacitly ignored him, per Kelly's instructions. Works every time! He finally sidled up to me at the campfire and we started talking. I was psyched to hear he was starting his junior year at Whitney, and when he mentioned he was not only in the best fraternity but also premed with hopes of becoming a plastic surgeon, I knew he was the one for me. All summer long we'd sneak away from our cabins to make out in the boathouse. (We never went below the belt. Kelly says pretty girls don't need to put out, although a little bit of me might wish she was wrong.)

Anyway, I've been excited to go Greek ever since I started hearing my mom's stories about dances and hayrides and all-night gossip fests. Once Kelly pledged and lent me her awesome letter sweatshirts, I was even more sure I wanted to belong. Plus, a lot of her friends are still here on campus, so I have a built-in social circle already. Unless I rob a bank or wear sweatpants to class or something, I'm guaranteed a Tri Tau bid. I'm still planning to attend parties at each campus sorority, though. Let them fight over me, right?

I'm superexcited to go through rush, which starts today. That's why I insisted Jackie finally let me style her. Thing is, rush is a delicate dance of looking your best while saying the right thing without bragging, of highlighting academic success without sounding like a mega-dork (*ahem*, Sars), and of showing them you're entertaining and freewheeling, but not so entertaining or freewheeling that you're going to flash your ta-tas at the SAE house and ruin your chapter's rep.

"Are the rush parties fun?" I asked my mum and Kelly back in August when they were helping move me into my fab new dorm room. I still can't get over our great fortune—Jackie and I randomly were assigned one of the gorgeous fourth floor rooms with the beams on the ceiling and the stained glass windows. We totally scored on the half bath, too. How nice is it to share a sink with one person, as opposed to fifty?

Best part of our little piece of Wadsworth Hall is we have a *fireplace*! The University would have kittens if we tried to burn anything in the hearth, so on Parents' Weekend, Mum bought us a big ol' fern to fill that space instead. With our color—if not pattern—coordinated comforters, lofted beds, *and* a futon, we totally have the best room on campus.

I'm so stoked about our space because we could have ended up like Jackie's weird little friend Sars—she and her roomie basically live in a closet behind the elevator on the second floor. I don't know why, but their room smells exactly like spray cheese. Super-disturbing.

"Of course the parties are fun, honey," my mom replied. "You'll—"

My sister started speaking over our mom. "Rush parties are bullshit."

"Language, Kelly!" Mum admonished.

Kelly paid her no attention. "Please. The *'parties'*?" she said, making air quotes with her long, elegant fingers. "Yeah, parties in name only. I'm talking no fun, no boys, no booze." She stopped herself. "Not that you'd drink until you're legal, I mean." Then she winked at me. According to the ID she gave me, I'm *totally* legal.

Mum pressed her lips together and shook her head. We discovered long ago that when Kelly begins her conversational-bulldozer thing, it's best just to step out of her way. She said, "These stupid rush events are more like when we have high tea with Great-Aunt Eleanor. Stiff, awkward, hot, overly formal, and you have to smile until your face cracks off.

But we do it because when the old broad finally kicks it, we'll be rolling in dough. The payoff's what's important, so you've gotta put your game face on."

"Kelly! We see Aunt Eleanor because we love her!" Mum cried.

Kelly completely ignored our mother. "I'm not wrong. Also, and this is key, everyone's perfectly groomed . . . or at least the girls who hope to have a social life over the next four years are."

"Freaking out now, thanks," I said, suddenly anxious. "I assumed I was just going to talk about fun stuff with a bunch of cool girls."

Mum stopped folding a sweater to place her hand on my shoulder. "Sweetie, rush is more like a job interview."

"Then I'm hosed!" I exclaimed. I'd never actually interviewed before—my only jobs thus far had been helping in my dad's office and working as a counselor at the tennis camp I attended for eight consecutive summers. Somewhere around my sixth year, everyone just assumed I'd eventually join the staff once I was old enough and it never occurred to me to say no, despite the fact that I'm not a fan of kids. At all. In fact, I wouldn't be surprised if I ended up one of those child-free career women who's far too busy and important to even consider marriage until she's really, really old. (At least thirty.) I'd take an engagement ring earlier, though. Big fan of jewelry.

Mum smoothed my hair over my shoulders in an attempt to calm me. "Kitty-cat, these parties are where you demonstrate how you'd fit within the group. You're not having conversations to make friends so much as you are trying to make a positive impression. No one wants to live with someone they don't like. Be chipper and bright—pretend you're talking to Regis and Kathie Lee."

"P.S.," Kelly added, "rush is not therapy; no one wants to hear your probs."

"Be chatty, not catty?" I asked.

Mum smiled. "That's a nice way to look at it. Because everyone'll have a different point of view, avoid bringing up anything controversial, such as politics or religion. Talk less about Nelson Mandela and more about . . . Michael Jackson."

"Who's Nelson Mandela?"

"That's the spirit!" Mum said, chucking me on the shoulder.

(I actually wasn't kidding, but I guessed not knowing important stuff was why I headed to college in the first place.)

I replied, "You're saying I should be myself, only a better version of it? Won't that be hard to keep up after a while?"

"Get through rush. Pledging is entirely different. Everything's more casual and you'll gravitate toward girls who share your interests. But during recruitment, members have their guards up. Rush is hard on them, too. It's not actually fun for them to cut rushees," Mum explained.

"Disagree. It's *plenty* fun," Kelly countered, with a wicked chuckle. "Someone wrongs you? Boom. Cut. Done, bitch." Noticing that we were both frowning at her, she added, "What?"

Mum blinked hard and then cleared her throat. "The members are as anxious to find new sisters as you are to pledge. If every day were rush, no one would join. Sorority rush is a necessary evil—imagine a dozen of the worst parties you'll ever attend, followed by four years of tradition and fun and female bonding. You'll form the friendships that'll last the rest of your life, so it'll be worth it. All of my best girlfriends were once my Tri Tau sisters. We wouldn't all be friends now if we didn't endure the nonsense in the beginning."

On learning that some of the sisters could be as cutthroat as Kelly, I was suddenly scared. Did I even *want* to be a part of something that sounded so exclusionary and conformist?

Mum unpacked my trunk as we talked, pulling out the kind of dresses and heels I didn't know I needed for rush parties. She even made me bring the navy suit I wore to my great-grandpa's funeral for Bid Night. She removed the tissue paper she'd packed between each layer of clothes in my trunk, placing it all neatly in the little garbage can by my desk. When we'd assembled my stuff at home, Mum had said the right outfit was a must. I finally understood why.

"Plus, you don't have to be, like, *beautiful* to pledge," Kelly said, flipping her trademark long blond French braid over her shoulder. Sometimes when she flings her braid, it smacks people in the face, which brings her great joy. (Is best to stay on Kelly's good side. Trust me here.) "But you have to try. Make an effort with your appearance. If the sisters see you can't even bother to iron or put on lipstick, then that tells them something about the kind of lazy active you'd be. If you don't get a bid, you may as well transfer to University of Illinois, because you'll have zero social life here. Fact."

That sealed it—I was rushing whether or not I wanted to.

I figured I'd be more comfortable at the parties if I had someone courageous with me, so I sought out the bravest person I know. With Jackie rushing, too, I've regained my initial enthusiasm.

I feel Jackie would benefit from hanging out with more girls and I'm fired up for rush to go well for her. My ulterior motive is she meet other people so she can lose that Sars person like a bad habit. Sometimes I suspect that Sars wants to make a suit out of Jackie's skin, all *Silence of the Lambs.*

What a flipping geek Sars is! Her book smarts are inversely proportional to her social IQ. No exaggeration. Earlier this fall, I brought both of them to a party at Sean's frat. Never again. Sars spent the whole night giggling and leering at the Beta brothers instead of actually *talking* to them, like she was at a fourth grade cotillion or something. Awkward. (Mind you, that's *after* Sars let me fix her unibrow!) She comes from a totally nice, normal family, so I don't know what her damage is.

The frat brothers thought Jackie was a ton of fun that night, but after she crushed them so soundly in table hockey, they all assumed she was, *ahem*, Playing for the Pink Team. From then on, I had her start calling herself Jackie because it's way less butch.

Also, the *arm wrestling*? No.

I'm lucky to have learned the ropes from Kelly, even though sometimes she terrifies me. I'd be royally screwed if the only female role model I had was *Sars*. Granted, I'm still a virgin (by choice, thank you very much) but even I know that talking about differential equations in a frat house is a total boner killer.

I know all about Jackie's brothers (believe me, I've asked) but I wonder what the story is with her mom? That's the one area where she's ultraprivate, so I have no idea how she may have died. She's said a few things about how when she was little, her mom was a great cook and the house was always really immaculate, but that's about it. She must miss that so much—I know I would. I figure she'll eventually open up and when she does, I'll be there for her. Because that's what best friends do.

Without having any chicks in her life, save for Nerdzilla, Jackie never learned the basics, like how to put on perfume (spritz away from the body and walk into the mist) or that it's just as important to shave your toes, too, lest you look like a hobbit in flip-flops. In fact, Jackie was cutting her own hair when we met. No lie. She'd literally gather her locks in a ponytail and hack off the bottom. I was horrified when I saw this. I said, *"Why not perform your own lobotomy while you're at it?"*

When we were home over October break last week, I brought Jackie to my salon in North Shore and my stylist Stefan gave her a proper trim. Even though she seemed anxious for the first time since we've met, she allowed us free rein.

When Stefan turned her around in her swivel chair to reveal her fab, piece-y bob, she said, "It's uneven!"

Stefan rolled his eyes. "No, girl—this is *choppy*. Your old cut was *chopped*. Did you cut it yourself?"

"I did," she admitted.

He ran his fingers through her long layers. "Miss Kitty, you slap those scissors outta her paws if she ever tries that again. Don't *make* me come down to that fancy college."

Jackie agreed to maintain the look, although today's the first day she's actually blown it dry, and that's only because I forced a vent brush and a hair dryer into her hands, coaching her through the entire process. (She said it was harder than the first time she landed a plane on instruments.) I had to promise her we'd go hiking in Hawthorn Woods later as a compromise.

Worth it.

"Are you ready to rock rush?" I ask, giving her a final once-over.

"Sure!" she replies, executing the slow twirl I taught her. Fabulous! But then I notice something.

"Hold up, are you not wearing the panty hose I laid out?" I ask. I glance at the futon and see the package exactly where I left it.

"Because it's warm out, I won't need 'em," she says.

I snort. "Um, yeah you do. I don't care if it's a nice day, you *will* wear hose. Nonnegotiable. At Ol' Miss, girls rush in hundred-degree temps and ninety percent humidity. Yet you won't see a single one of them without their nylons." I toss her the egg-shaped container.

Jackie catches the package like she plays third base professionally and then sets it down on her desk. The mood in the room completely changes for some reason. She toys with the hem of her dress and becomes very quiet. Then she hangs her head to the point I can't look her in the eye, with all her heavy hair around her face.

"Hey, are you okay?" I ask, bending over to see her face. "Is all this too much? We can take off the mascara."

She says nothing in reply.

Shoot, what's happening here? I press on. "Or we can put your hair back in a ponytail if you're uncomfortable. Do . . . do you not want to go through rush? I thought you were on board. I'm so sorry if I badgered you, if this isn't what you want."

Seriously, it's important not to be peer pressured into something you're not ready to do, at least according to the Tori Spelling movie we just watched. I note how tense Jackie is and I want to do anything I can to make her feel better, so I try smoothing her hair just like my mom does for me when I'm anxious. That seems to help.

"It's silly," she finally replies. "It's just . . . Ugh, you're going to laugh at me, Kit." She chews on her bottom lip, all pensive and intense. I don't let out a peep about how she's eating all her lipstick. We can fix that later.

"You can tell me anything," I say. "Whatever it is, I'll keep it in the vault. No judgment here." I place one hand on her shoulders and pretend I'm locking my lips with the other one before tossing the key.

She takes a couple of measured breaths and then exhales loudly. "Um, in fourth grade, after my mother . . ." She trails off.

Oh, crap, I didn't mean to make her upset! Not today! But she is, and I can't blame her. How would I handle it if Mum died? I'd likely be devastated, always and forever, but at least I'd still have Kelly. To exist without any strong female influence to teach me to never mix plaids and stripes? Unimaginable. Jackie's struggling for words, so I suggest a more delicate term than *died*.

"After your mother *was gone?*"

She meets my gaze, and seems to appreciate my trying to help.

"Yeah. *Was gone.*" Her tone turns acidic for a moment, which I totally get. Loss sucks. But, why *specifically* is she bitter about losing her mom? Was it a car accident? Terminal disease? Plane crash? Random act of violence? All I know is that it had something to do with milk. I wish she'd tell me so I could help.

Jackie says, "After my dad was left in charge. He's a great father, but he wasn't so skilled at domestic stuff. Yet what choice did we have? So on Halloween, he was the one who had to help me with my costume for the school parade."

"Were you still in Saint Louis then?" I ask, still trying to figure out the whole mom mystery. They'd moved when she was a kid, but I'm not sure exactly when. Should I try to look up Saint Louis newspapers on the microfiche in the library? Maybe there's a story because her mom must have been pretty young. Or is that a massive violation of privacy?

"Uh-huh, we were. I wanted to be Batman, but Dad suggested I try something more girly because he worried I was being unduly influenced by my brothers. Anyway, I listened to his advice and decided to be Smurfette. We found a white dress and a blond wig and a bunch of blue makeup to cover my skin. I planned to paint my legs with the makeup, too, but Dad figured the blue would get all over his car's cream-colored seats, so he found some tights at the drugstore. They were sized for toddlers, but I managed to squeeze into them somehow. Willpower, I guess. Long story short, the tights began to suppress my circulation, I passed out, and the school nurse had to cut me out of them . . . in front of my whole fourth grade class."

"Oh, honey. I'm so sorry. That's horrible," I say, giving her a squeeze. First her mother, and then she had to deal with that kind of humiliation? So not fair.

"Not my finest moment," she replies. "After that, my dad promised me he'd never make me try to be all femmy again, so that's the last time I ever wore panty hose."

Who knew so much baggage could be attached to a simple scrap of fabric? After hearing her story, I'm astounded that she let me take ahold of her like this. I can't believe we've built this kind of trust already and I'm not about to blow it by snooping into her past. She'll share when she's ready.

But, desperate to make her feel better now, I grab the panty hose and say, "Then you don't wear these things. I insist. If any sorority girl looks at you sideways, she'll have to deal with me. I won't put on mine, either." Then I hug Jackie again, wishing I'd have been there all those years ago to make her feel better.

She rewards me with a small, tight smile. "I'm being ridiculous, aren't I?" Jackie asks, taking the plain plastic egg back from me. Earlier, I removed the outer packaging because I didn't want her to see I'd bought queen-size and feel like I was insulting her. She's trim as can be, but her legs are so long, the bigger size is the only way to keep her crotch from riding around down by her knees.

"You're not ridiculous in the least. Here," I say, moving the big fern out of the way of the hearth. "Let's have a ritual burning, like the hippies used to do with their bras."

She laughs, breaking the suddenly somber mood. "I'm *for sure* being ridiculous now." She cracks open the egg and pulls out the offending garment. Then she kicks off the Mary Janes. "You can be my wingman anytime. Cover me, Goose, I'm going in."

"*Top Gun* quote?" I ask. When we hung out with her brothers at home last week, it was all movie dialogue, all the time. I didn't get it but I didn't hate it.

She shoots me a thumbs-up. "Roger that, Ghost Rider."

"Then you *must* be rallying," I say. Jackie gingerly steps into one leg before yanking them up her thigh. Noting how her blood's still circulating just fine, she pulls on the other side and then steps back to assess the damages. "How do they feel?"

She runs her palms up and down the length of her calf. "Um, silky?"

"Any discomfort?"

She lowers herself into a series of squats, lunges, and impressive karate kicks. "None."

I smile because my work here is done. "As long as you don't snag them on any sharp objects, you'll be fine."

I can't put my finger on how or why, but I feel like this exchange has somehow brought us to a new level in our relationship, and that makes me so happy. Despite how we differ, Jackie's awesome and I want us to be friends forever. And very soon, sorority sisters.

Jackie's not terribly comfortable with big displays of emotion, so instead of saying anything mushy, I change the subject. "You want to grab some lunch before we do this whole party thing? They'll serve food at each party, but we're not actually supposed to eat it for some reason."

Jackie raises an eyebrow. "That's bizarre, right?"

"So bizarre," I confirm.

We're just closing our door before heading to the cafeteria when we notice some kind of . . . *creature* skulking along in the shadows down the hall. As the thing draws closer, I realize that it's Sars, Her Royal Dorkness, the Weenie Queenie, lurching all club-footed toward us in a pair of sky-high heels she's clearly never even tried on before.

I admit Sars's A-line dress is cute, but the rest of her look is right out of *The Rocky Horror Picture Show*. Wish I were kidding. Thick red gloss bleeds far outside of her natural lip line and her lids have been swept with deep navy shadow from the lash line all the way up to her eyebrow. She appears to have been punched in the face a whole lot of times. In lieu of applying the mascara, Sars seems to have simply poked herself in the eyes with the wand multiple times, which looks even worse behind the travesty otherwise known as her Coke-bottle-bottom glasses. Two blazing orange streaks adorn the apples of her cheeks back to her ears, completing her "look."

"Whoa," Jackie says, not realizing she's speaking aloud. She immediately smacks a hand over her mouth. "Shit, Sars, I'm sorry."

"Too much?" Sars asks, pointing to the face Picasso himself must have painted. (Am also taking Art History this semester.) "It's too much. Sorry, I'm still pretty new to makeup."

"It's a lot of look," I confirm with as much diplomacy as I can muster as I lock our door. Yet in my head, I'm all, *"Holy crap, the Tri Taus are going to laugh you clear to Champaign-Urbana."*

"Can you fix her up, too?" Jackie asks, eyes searching my face. She's well aware that I'm not a huge fan of her dweeby, clingy little buddy. "For me?"

The last thing I want to do is spend more time with this hideous troll, but I feel like helping Sars may be yet another tipping point for Jackie and me. Jackie's never asked me for anything. For her to reach out is a huge step forward.

So I sigh and accept my fate, covertly squeezing Jackie's hand as I do because, whether or not I like it, these two are a package deal. "Okay. For you."

To Sars, I say, "I'm going to need a clean slate. Go scrub. And when you think you're done, scrub again." We shuffle back into the room where I make Sars wash her face in our half bath.

Of course I have to tell her not to use the hand soap.

I send her downstairs to put in her contact lenses (why would she not wear them in the first place if she has them?) and when she returns, I sit her in a chair, draping a towel over her dress.

Sars beams up at me with her mousy little grin and buggy eyes and I can't help but soften. I haven't been her biggest fan, but I'm not Kelly and I don't get off on being deliberately cruel to people. Plus, she's important to Jackie, which means she's going to have to be important to me. If it's on me to transform her look and stick close to her at the parties to help if (let's be honest, *when*) conversation gets awkward, then so be it. Every sorority needs a true bookworm to help raise the collective GPA, so I'll make it my job to pitch Sars as Tri Tau's resident nerd.

For Jackie.

"Do you have any rush advice for me?" she asks, shifting anxiously in her chair. Jackie's back on the futon, legs neatly crossed, grinning at the both of us. This must be how a little kid feels when his divorcing parents decide to give their marriage one more shot.

I decide to fix that which I find the most immediately grating.

I say, "Sars really isn't the best name to use during rush. It's memorable, but not in a good way. Kind of makes me think of a disease or something."

"Okay," she agrees. "Should I go by Sarabeth?"

"Eh," I reply. "That's kind of a mouthful and expensive to put on a pledge paddle. No one wants to buy that many wooden letters for her li'l sis. They're like three dollars each! Anyone ever given you a different, shorter, cuter nickname?"

"Nope," she replies.

Of course no one has. I try not to sigh out loud. This one's not going to make my job easy, is she? Still, if she has any shot at pledging, I have to boost her confidence in any and all ways, starting at the very beginning.

I say, "Then, let's find a super-fun abbreviation. Why don't we call you, oh, I don't know, maybe . . . *Betsy?*"

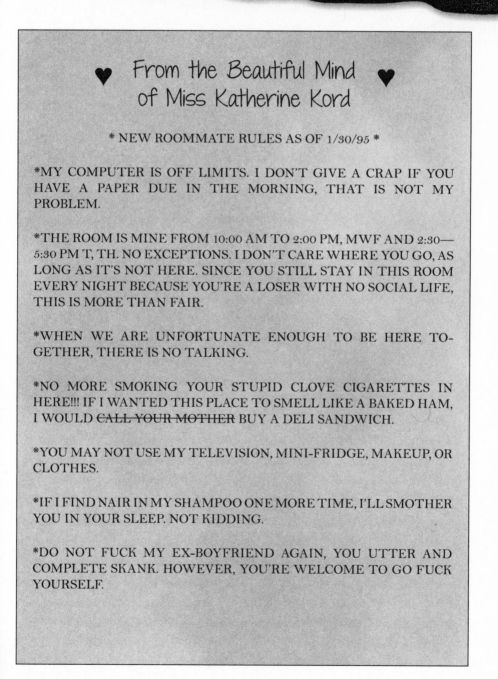

CHAPTER EIGHT

♥ From the Beautiful Mind ♥
of Miss Katherine Kord

* NEW ROOMMATE RULES AS OF 1/30/95 *

*MY COMPUTER IS OFF LIMITS. I DON'T GIVE A CRAP IF YOU HAVE A PAPER DUE IN THE MORNING, THAT IS NOT MY PROBLEM.

*THE ROOM IS MINE FROM 10:00 AM TO 2:00 PM, MWF AND 2:30—5:30 PM T, TH. NO EXCEPTIONS. I DON'T CARE WHERE YOU GO, AS LONG AS IT'S NOT HERE. SINCE YOU STILL STAY IN THIS ROOM EVERY NIGHT BECAUSE YOU'RE A LOSER WITH NO SOCIAL LIFE, THIS IS MORE THAN FAIR.

*WHEN WE ARE UNFORTUNATE ENOUGH TO BE HERE TO-GETHER, THERE IS NO TALKING.

*NO MORE SMOKING YOUR STUPID CLOVE CIGARETTES IN HERE!!! IF I WANTED THIS PLACE TO SMELL LIKE A BAKED HAM, I WOULD ~~CALL YOUR MOTHER~~ BUY A DELI SANDWICH.

*YOU MAY NOT USE MY TELEVISION, MINI-FRIDGE, MAKEUP, OR CLOTHES.

*IF I FIND NAIR IN MY SHAMPOO ONE MORE TIME, I'LL SMOTHER YOU IN YOUR SLEEP. NOT KIDDING.

*DO NOT FUCK MY EX-BOYFRIEND AGAIN, YOU UTTER AND COMPLETE SKANK. HOWEVER, YOU'RE WELCOME TO GO FUCK YOURSELF.

Jack

....

Whitney University, Central Illinois
January 1995

Who knew how dirty girls could fight?

I assumed words would be Kitty's eventual weapon of choice, so I was unprepared for exactly how devastating her silence could be.

Growing up, my brothers and I settled our arguments with a well-timed uppercut or a roundhouse kick and then it was over. Maybe a game of HORSE if the problem was of a more philosophical nature. Then our beef was settled. Forgotten. Forgiven. I almost wish Kitty had punched me—I'd probably feel better right about now.

If Kitty wasn't happy with me last semester, why didn't she say so? I'm like a computer—I can operate only given the proper input. Can't fix what I don't know.

My plan from the beginning was to be the ideal roommate, making the effort to be as neat, quiet, and pleasant as possible. Whenever Kitty suggested anything, I always responded with enthusiasm, even when her ideas took me outside of my comfort zone. (Panty hose, anyone?) Like a butler, I tried to anticipate what she needed before she ever had to say so. For example, as soon as I deduced she didn't care for the guys in my journalism class, I stopped bringing them to our room for group project work. Out of courtesy. Because I *cared* about *my* roommate.

Truth is, I believe the boys in my class made her feel dumb, especially because they weren't charmed by all that big, fluffy hair that she's always tossing around. To these guys, brains trump beauty all day long, which is why they busted a gut when she said, "Wait, aren't you supposed to swim parallel to the shoreline when there's an Apartheid?"

That's when my friend Simon held up his copy of *Time* and said, "It's called *the news*, Kitty. Perhaps you should read it."

Granted, Simon was snotty and officious. I apologized on his behalf later, yet I was taken aback by her glaring lack of social conscience. Who could be so blissfully unaware of an entire government built on racial segregation? If college has taught me anything thus far, it's that I've had it very easy growing up in well-off, suburban America, regardless of any past family drama.

(As for Kitty? She was born on third base and assumes she hit a triple.)

I can't figure out where she and I went wrong. Was she somehow jealous of me? Highly illogical. She's the one who flitted from sorority house to house during informal fall rush. All the girls loved her and each chapter's after her to pledge. I suspect I was only asked back to a handful of places for their formal January party because I am—no, *was*—her friend and they assumed they had to take me if they wanted her. What's to envy about being an also-ran?

Clearly I must have committed some transgression; otherwise why spread rumors about the person who means the most to me in the world?

The way she couched the whole conversation, all that faux concern? The quivering lip? The watery eyes? What an actress. She must have been taking tips from her unholy sister. I bet Kelly's fat braid conceals the "666" birthmark on the back of her neck.

Kitty sat me down over lunch at the mall on New Year's Day, pretending to be oh-so-troubled. She grabbed my hand, all serious, and she said, "I'm not sure how to tell you this, so I'm just going to come right out with it." Like she was going to say she had two weeks left to live or something. Then she spewed her ridiculous lie and I was blindsided.

So how was I not supposed to respond, "Don't say Teddy's gay just because he doesn't like *you*."

Honestly, I'd wanted to spare her the pain of the inevitable breakup. I knew she wasn't going to hold Teddy's interest when they first hung out together over Thanksgiving and I tried to warn her. The whole virgin thing might initially have seemed like a challenge to him, but when he realized she was serious about keeping her V-card out of his wallet?

Check, please.

I probably shouldn't have accused her of not being smart enough to read the situation, which I'm sure entailed Teddy trying to let her down gently. I possibly shouldn't have solidified my case by bringing up other instances where she's said dumb things, like when she asked if the Electoral College had a football team. And maybe after I called her an airhead, I shouldn't have stormed out of the food court, taking the bus home instead of waiting for her to drive me, but I didn't want to hear anything else she had to say. When you tell lies about my brother to protect your own precious ego, you're telling lies about me.

Sars (whom I will *not* call Betsy) says she doesn't want to be in the middle of this because she's friends with both of us. She says we should consider her to be Switzerland. Once I cooled off, I realized I'd been hurtful, so I asked Sars to please broker peace. I thought she could bring us together to talk it all out. I figured that as close as we'd become, we could find some common ground, but Sars said Kitty was resolute.

Kitty hasn't uttered a word to me since that day at the mall. To think I almost told her about my mom!

So it's been quiet around here. Very quiet. The tension's so thick you could slice it up and serve it on a platter. That's why when our phone rings, I practically jump out of my skin, even though I'm in here alone. I believe Kitty's at the gym with Sars for step aerobics before this evening's Bid Night rush parties, but can't be sure. I asked where she was headed but she chose not to respond.

I pick up the receiver. "Hello?"

"Jackie!" says a friendly male voice on the other end of the line. "What's shakin', babe?"

"Not much," I reply automatically. "Wait, who's this?"

"It's Sean. How was your break?"

Ugh, how do I even answer him?

"Fine. How was yours?"

"Too short, as always. You back early for rush? Are you excited? It's Bid Night! You're at the finish line now! Tomorrow, you'll officially be a sorority girl."

Wait, why's Sean on the phone *now*? I know he kept calling Kitty after she got together with Teddy over Thanksgiving. I assumed he was trying to woo her back, so I always went to Sars's room so they could speak in private. I've never had a boyfriend, so the whole uncoupling process is a complete mystery to me. I recall when Teddy dumped girls in the past, they were always finding reasons to drop by the house or phone, sometimes for months afterward, so I figure no breaks are ever completely clean or immediately accepted.

Still, it's been almost six weeks.

That's a little stalkerlike, right?

Can this guy not take a hint?

Kitty told me she and Sean were over as soon as she started seeing Teddy. At the time, I thought that was a shame because he was really nice. He seemed kind and thoughtful, always asking after me and re-membering random facts, like the soccer position I played in high school. He was one of those guys who'd smile often, and laugh easy, re-ally listening to what others had to say. But Kitty said Sean was pres-suring her to take their relationship further, so maybe the good guy act was just that—an act.

He must be obsessed with her to be sniffing around here *again*.

Or, wait, what if this is a different Sean and Kitty was actually cheating on Teddy with a third guy?

"Are you Beta Theta Pi Sean?"

"Jack, it's me. 'S'up with the confusion? You got more than one Sean calling or something?" he asks in an amused tone. "A plethora of Seans. No, a gaggle of Seans. Perhaps a herd? A pride?"

I reply, "No, I just assumed this was a new Sean since Kitty broke up with the old one after she started dating my brother at Thanksgiv-ing. Dude, I don't want to tell you how to conduct yourself, but it's a new semester. Maybe it's time to move on."

If he's still trying to win her back after pressuring her so much she broke it off, I'm going to protect her, even if she no longer has my back.

There's a long pause on the other end of the line.

"Jack, please do me a favor and tell her I'm gonna call her back later."

"Okay, I'll leave her a message."

See? I'm still helping, even if she won't talk to me.

As I'm due to get ready for tonight anyway, I'm happy to have ended the call. I figured I may as well go through the last round of rush if there's a chance I could fit in somewhere. But this time I plan to be there on my own terms, in my own clothes, discussing my own interests. At the Theta house, I spent twenty minutes listening to a debate over whether the sorority sisters were Team Kelly Kapowski or Team Lisa Turtle—I didn't even know who those people were. Still don't, so I wasn't unhappy not to be asked back.

My only nod to Kitty tonight will be donning panty hose, not because I want so badly to conform, but because I'm wearing my cotton graduation dress (a gift from Sars's mom) and it's flipping cold outside.

No.

Not flipping. Fucking. It's *fucking* cold outside.

As we aren't so lucky as to have a full bath, I grab my soap caddy and take my stuff down the hall to the shower after I lay out my outfit, complete with plastic egg canister.

When I finish, Kitty's back in the room.

"Hi?" I say tentatively.

No response. Naturally, she's still not speaking to me. But she's not here for long. Her Caboodles case is already gone, so I assume she's been getting ready in Sars's room and forgot something.

Since I'm a *decent* person, I won't interfere with their friendship, especially as Kitty seems to be coaxing Sars out of her shell socially. I don't have to like it, though.

I try to dry my hair as Kitty had previously shown me, but can't quite manage working the brush in conjunction with the stream of air. I keep blasting myself in the ear. How can I land a Cessna, yet working a vent brush entirely eludes me?

In the end, I scrape everything back into a ponytail, with a few jagged layers escaping here and there. With the chunks flat around my ears, I resemble George Washington. Hopefully sorority girls dig historical figures.

Because of the hair snafu, I'm running way behind. So, when I realize I have the wrong-sized panty hose—wasn't I supposed to buy Queen?—I'm forced to wear the pair I have.

I struggle to squeeze into them, visions of fourth grade careening through my mind. Even the bed wetters and paste eaters were laughing at me that day. I'm still mortified. Desperately pushing the imagery out of my head, I try the trick of dampening my hands and coaxing the fabric up my legs, which is the only reason the crotch isn't hanging to my knees. As is, we're at half-mast on my thighs and now I have to walk like I'm part of a chain gang, taking tiny, mincing steps.

So here goes nothing.

· · · ·

I thought I could rally, play through the pain at these rush events, but the stupid hose have thrown me due to poor circulation. The blood's no longer getting to my brain, which is why I forget all about proper party protocol, such as "sit like a lady" and "don't eat." But the Kappas are serving Peanut Butter Wonder Bars! And if I cross my legs, there's an excellent chance I'll faint.

Such is my level of distraction, I don't remember to ask any of the sisters about themselves, nor do I seek out common interests. I did okay in rush before because I basically went through the journalist's way of writing a story. Everyone thought I was engaging because of my *who, what, when, where,* and *why* questions, but this time, I'm too rattled to remember. I'm palmed off from girl to girl, rather quickly. I'm blowing it. I discern this from the tight smiles that don't reach their eyes, but I don't know how to right my trajectory. I'm sinking fast.

I can't seem to stop myself from complaining about Kitty, either, sharing thoughts such as, "She thought no one wanted to play Sun City because it was a shitty venue!" and "Every time I mention Nelson Mandela, she brings up the *Thriller* album!"

Tonight is not my finest moment.

Still, I hope there's one sorority girl who'll fight for me, who'll see past what's awkward and unpolished. Who'll understand that I have talent and drive and that I'll be a great friend and a fine sister. That I'll work tirelessly for their philanthropies. At the very least, that I'll win their intramural softball and soccer games for them.

Funny, but I always assumed Kitty would be that girl.

I receive no bids.

As I stand here in the hallway of the administration building where all the rushees have gathered for results, I'm envious watching everyone else open their envelopes, scream, and hug the girls all around them. I never felt so different until this very moment. What's wrong with *me*? What don't I have that those girls want?

I wish I wasn't so disappointed. Simon says the whole Greek system is silly and trite and archaic, but I figured that was just his defense mechanism. I suspected he secretly wanted to be a part of it all, too, just like I do.

Or maybe I did a terrible job during rush because subconsciously I wanted to reject them before they could reject me, like girls have been doing my whole life?

If so, then why does my heart feel so heavy?

I trudge home to my dorm, passing the well-lit sororities where members yelp with joy as new pledges drop by for more hugs and their first letter sweatshirts.

I'm on the futon in my room, all alone, so angry with myself for having failed. My gaze lingers on various portions of the room and each area makes me feel melancholy for the bond Kitty and I briefly shared. There's the chair where *my friend* performed my first makeover. And how about the sink where *my pal* and I accidentally spit toothpaste on each other when we were brushing our teeth after we drank all that pear schnapps she bought with her sister's ID? *My companion* and I laughed so hard we collapsed on the floor together. Or how about after midterms when me and *my good buddy* stayed up all night watching Meg Ryan movies and then, sometime around four in the morning, punch-drunk and full of chocolate-covered pretzels, re-created Tom Cruise's "Old Time Rock and Roll" dance?

While I'm looking around, I spot some garbage sticking out from behind Kitty's desk. *And she calls me messy*, I think, bending over to re-trieve the cardboard cup that goes around the L'eggs egg. That's when I notice the size—extra small. Extra small? Odd, because neither one of us wears extra small.

I don't dwell on my find, as I'm busy wallowing in self-pity.

Welcome to Sucktown. Population, Me.

• • • •

Later this week, when Sars comes back from her first official sorority event, cheeks pink with excitement and the glow of belonging, I learn the full story.

Kitty had returned Sean's call in Sars's room after bringing all her gear down there. Sars told me that Sean had no idea his girlfriend wasn't actually still his girlfriend. According to Beelzebub, I mean *Kelly*, I guess she always advised Kitty to firmly establish herself with her next beau before officially ending it with the current flame, so that's what Kitty had done. With finals and the holidays, she was able to string him along without their hanging out together. Since Kitty's relationship hadn't panned out with Teddy, she'd planned to fall back into step with Sean. But I blew it for her.

Perhaps someone should have *talked to me* and *told me the plan.* I'd have been on board.

Looks like that's when Kitty snapped, going from never having been dumped to twice in one week. Sars said Kitty rushed out, but then returned so quickly that Sars assumed she'd simply hit the bathroom. But apparently she used that time to swap out my proper-fitting queen-size nylons for the tiny pair belonging to pint-sized Lisa Wu who lives across the hall.

Kitty's the one who sentenced me to hobbling around for the entire night of rush, which led to my demise.

Even though I was the injured party, I still wanted to talk to Kitty because I never intended to screw anything up for her. I wasn't being malicious, but maybe after my harsh words in the mall, she didn't believe me. When I told her she reinforced every dumb blonde stereotype, she reacted as though I'd slapped her. Later, I tried to apologize but she just looked right through me, like I didn't exist.

Seriously, I would rather take a punch. At least then the hurt would come with an expiration date.

I've been hiding out in the Student Union lately because my room is too tense with Kitty coming in and out. Sars said I could hang in her room because her roommate isn't coming back this semester. (Supposedly, it's mono, but what kind of mono takes six more months to cure? The kind that requires diapers, I suspect.) Sars and Kitty both pledged Tri Tau, so it doesn't make sense for her to take sides. Am I a terrible person for wishing she would anyway?

I'm sitting down here in the oak-paneled Rathskeller with a coffee and a tin of Djarum clove cigarettes. I'm surrounded by girls proudly displaying shiny new badges shaped like arrows and kites. I blow smoke in their direction when they get too loud.

I'm lost in thought when someone yanks my ponytail. I turn around to find John-John. He lives on the other side of campus and the computer science classes are far from liberal arts, so we rarely run into each other. Which is fine. However, I must be in a state because I'm actually glad to see him.

(When I tell Bobby about our encounter later, he says, "John-John, the last refuge of a scoundrel.")

"Whazzup, spaz?" He folds himself into the café chair across from me. Without an invitation, he grabs my paper cup of coffee and takes a deep swig. "Blech. Not enough sugar, too much cream."

"I'm sorry." Great, now I've even gotten coffee wrong.

He leans over the table to poke me. "Sorry? *Sorry?* Who shit in your cornflakes, kid? 'S'matter with you? Why so emo?"

I sink into my seat. "I don't even know where to start, John. Maybe I'm down because in wanting everything, I've inadvertently wound up with nothing."

He smirks and pats his intricately gelled coif. "Um, okay, *Sylvia Plath.* Make sure you get the oven real hot before you stick your head in."

"Will do."

"Shall I fetch you a bell jar, milady?"

"I'm good, thanks."

"You're no fun. Why aren't you fun? Have the pseudo-intellectual j-school drama queens done a number on you? Shall we discuss Important Things? Wait, what the fuck are these, Jack?" He picks up the red tin and opens it to find the cigarettes. "Whoa, are you *smoking*? No way! Ooh, I'm gonna tell Dad!"

I look him squarely in the eye. "Do that."

He cocks his head and peers at me like an entomologist examining a never-before-seen species of beetle. "Why aren't you fighting back? You're like a pod person all of a sudden. And where's your pledge pin?"

In sotto voce, I share my shame. "I didn't get in."

"But I just saw Sars upstairs wearing her pin. Wait, hold on—you mean the human calculator scored a bid and you didn't? The *hell*? Thought you were Tri Tau all the way. Do they not want to win the soccer intramurals?"

He was home during Christmas break, too, so he already heard Teddy's side of the story—that he wasn't into Kitty, and broke it off. I brief him on everything that's gone on since then.

"Duuuuuuude," he says, drawing out the word. "Your roommate is a *thundercunt*. No joke. What kind of person takes a painful childhood incident and then uses it against you? That's fucked-up. Who does that?"

I glance up at him. "Aside from you? You've been doing just that for years."

He shrugs. "I'm allowed to; I'm family."

John assumes a more aggressive posture as he begins to formulate a plan. He looks as though he's Patton about to deliver that famous speech to the Third Army. "Are you gonna take it from this bitch? No. Nuh-uh. Jordans don't go down that way. Jordans don't quit. Remember when Teddy played an entire quarter against New Trier *after* he broke his collarbone? Why'd he do it? *Because Jordans don't lose.* You need revenge. You require justice. Remember how it went down with my roommate Paul? I have experience with this. She took something from you, so now you're gonna take something from her. Time to buzz a tower."

I'm more of a turn-the-other cheek kind of person, but where has that gotten me? To an uncomfortable living situation and shared custody of my best friend. Perhaps John's words have merit. He can't always be wrong, if for no reason other than the law of averages.

". . . kill or be killed, that's the way of the jungle."

I glance over both of my shoulders. "Not going to kill her. I want to be real clear about that."

"*Metaphorically* kill her. You've got to strike first or she's going to beat you with a sock full of shit while you're asleep."

"Metaphorically again?"

"Yeah, you hope. So kick her where she hurts."

"Which is where?" I ask, genuinely puzzled. "Actual kick or metaphorical kick?"

He pats his fancy do. "Kick her in her crowning glory."

. . . .

When John drove me to the Kmart off campus for supplies, this seemed like a capital idea, but now that I'm in the middle of executing his plan, I'm less sure.

I watch as the glistening trail of shampoo circles the drain; then I rinse away the evidence, squirting some pinecone air freshener to mask the telltale smell of Paul Mitchell's awapuhi fragrance.

Will her hair come out all at once, or will she shed small chunks over a period of time? I wonder. And should I even be attempting this, or am I blowing any chance to reconcile? I vacillate as I stand here clutching both bottles.

I catch a glimpse of myself in the medicine cabinet and realize I look absolutely unhinged. There's some crazy in my eyes.

No. *No.*

A rational person doesn't behave like this. I should stop.

I'm stopping.

I've stopped.

Not happening. Teddy always says I should pay attention to John's advice in order to do the opposite. So I shove the bottle of Nair behind a box of maxi-pads in the cabinet under the sink and I place the depleted shampoo bottle back into Kitty's shower caddy.

Resolved to be the bigger person, I'm exiting the bathroom when Kitty and Sars come bursting into the room.

"Hey, Jack! A bunch of us are going sledding on Squires Hill! Come with! It's gonna be awesome!" Sars calls. She's bundled up in a down jacket and a scarf knit in sorority colors, which is wrapped around her neck about fifteen times. Between the big coat and all the layers, she looks exactly like she did when we'd toboggan back in sixth grade. She's the same degree of excited, too. She hasn't forgotten her need for speed.

I've been dying to sled on Squires Hill ever since Teddy went for the first time five years ago. Given the angle of the hill and the span of the run, it's supposed to be the most incredible rush. I even stole a tray from the cafeteria last fall in anticipation of the first snowfall. Unfortunately, Simon and the rest of my j-school buddies think all the Whitney traditions are super-lame, on par with dressing in matching outfits to watch the Cotton Ginners play football or swimming in the fountain during the annual Mini Daytona go-kart race weekend, so I had no takers when I suggested sledding earlier. I could go alone—or call John—but both options seem equally sad.

Kitty, who's still yet to acknowledge me two weeks after the fact, tells her, "Sars, this event is for *sorority sisters only*. GDIs and losers not allowed." She reaches into her closet for a pair of gloves. "Kitten's got her mittens, so away we go!" And like that, they're out the door.

I can actually feel my blood pressure rise. Before I can talk myself out of it again, I dump the hair remover into her shampoo bottle and mix vigorously.

Revenge is indeed mine.

But . . . shouldn't it feel more sweet?

· · · ·

After NairGate, I could have lived with her "spilling" that India ink all over my prissy comforter. Never cared for all the flowers in the first place. I'm happy to use Simon's extra Mexican blanket. More my style.

When she whacked three inches off the end of my ponytail in the dead of night after I had all those pizzas delivered to her sorority house? No problem. I simply chopped off the rest to just below my ears. No fuss, no muss. "The Rachel" cut is already played out anyway.

I could even live with her swiping and selling back my Biology book, using the proceeds to stock her fridge with pink liquor. Kind of wish I'd thought of that first. I could use a couple of extra bucks—smoking imported cigarettes is expensive.

But coming home from class to find she's shredded my *Top Gun* poster into a million pieces? My prized possession? My favorite item in the world? The one thing that I could look at to feel better all those years ago?

You do not mess with Maverick.

If studying Pearl Harbor in my History of Conflict Reporting class is teaching me anything, it's that aggression will not stand. Force will be met by force. Channeling FDR, I revise his famous speech and pledge to myself the following:

No matter how long it may take me to overcome this premeditated invasion, I will win through to absolute victory. I will defend myself to the utmost and I'll make it damn certain that this form of treachery will never again endanger me or Tom Cruise. Hostiles exist within this room and there's no blinking at the fact that my territory and my interests are in grave danger. With confidence in myself and an unbounding determination, I will gain inevitable triumph, so help me God.

Kitty shouldn't fear *fear itself*; she should fear *me*.

I grab the address book from Kitty's tidy desk, pens neatly gathered in a pink Tri Tau mug, pencils in a green one, paper clips lined up one by one, equidistant apart. I open to the S page. I find exactly what I'm looking for, because I'd have laid money on this stupid cow alphabetizing by first name.

I channel my fury into confidence. I pick up the phone and dial, doing my best to imitate Kitty's flirty sorority-girl tone. "Hey, is Sean in? Um, Sean, hi, it's *Jackie* . . . Yeah, Kitty's roommate . . . Ohmigod, right? Listen, are you busy? See, I have, like, a whole fridge full of liquor and no one to drink it with . . . I know, that *is* a dilemma . . . Nope, she's gone for the weekend . . . I agree, that really would chap her bony white behind . . . Okay, Sean. See you in ten."

I hang up the phone with a trembling hand and open a wine cooler to steel my nerves. I tilt the bottle back and chug until there's nothing left but a fine scrim of pink bubbles. I taste Skittles when the carbonation causes me to burp. Then I grab a second bottle and repeat the process. I have ten minutes to down enough liquid courage for what's about to happen next.

Not my ideal first-time scenario, but one does what one must.

War is hell.

CHAPTER NINE

Kitty
....
North Shore, Illinois
Tuesday

"You're still going? You're actually *leaving*?"

I wince at how shrill my voice sounds. I'm already devastated and now I'm stunned to find out my husband won't be by my side when I need him most. How am I supposed to get through tomorrow without him?

"Babe, the weatherman says if I don't leave before the torrential rains coming down from the west hit, I won't get out at all. Haven't you seen the flooding on the news? In Minneapolis, people lost their *homes*," Dr. K replies, managing to somehow make me feel guilty for being too distracted to pay attention to precipitation in cities where I don't live.

Dr. K opens a couple of dresser drawers, scouting for anything he might have missed. Pulling out the pair of lace-up board shorts that effectively conceal his love handles, he tosses the brightly patterned swimsuit into his overflowing Tumi suitcase. He gives the bag's contents a final once-over before mashing it down and zipping it shut, satisfied to have not forgotten anything. Yanking the heavy bag off the bed, he drops it onto the floor. The thump reverberates throughout the long, empty upstairs hallway.

Calm as can be, Dr. K reasons, "Let's be logical here. I miss the conference, I'm behind the curve on advancements in crown lengthening and provisional bridges. I'm behind on advancements, I'm doing the practice a disservice. I'm doing the practice a disservice, then everyone who counts on me for the most up-to-date dentistry techniques will take their business elsewhere. Bottom line? My patients *need* me in South Beach."

I guess I understand the learning component, but do those patients *really* need him lounging poolside in flattering board shorts? I say, "From a business perspective, okay, but right now I need—"

He cuts me right off. "Plus, I already paid for everything. I stay home, we're out the four grand anyway. You have four grand to throw away like it's nothing? I sure don't."

After writing checks for all three of our mortgages on top of all of (most of) (okay, some of) our regular recurring monthly nut, I'm not sure we have *forty* dollars left in the joint account. Too bad North Shore Savings and Trust doesn't accept Keurig K-Cups as currency. I'm K-Cup-rich after featuring their 2.0 brewer on SecretSquash. I'd assumed the marketing firm I partnered with would send a check, not four gratis cases of Jamaican Me Crazy pods. Seems like all my sponsors are starting to pay in goods and services, not money.

My stomach churns at our current skate on the financial edge. How'd we cut it so close again? I've been economizing all over the place, even making my own cleaning rags out of the kids' outgrown pajamas instead of purchasing paper towels. While everyone on Facebook praises my green initiatives, they have no clue it's not by choice.

We're not facing a massive, "come up with twenty thousand now or the nuns will lose the school" kind of monetary imperative. (And I'm so fortunate that if the unthinkable did happen, my family would help.) Instead, the issue is that our expenses are unrelenting. There's no single, devastating tidal wave of debt; rather our financial boat is perpetually adrift on choppy water. I can juggle. I can negotiate. I can keep us afloat from month to month, but the idea of living this way indefinitely makes me seasick.

Dr. K believes I should go back to work, but who'd hire me with two years of professional experience followed by a fifteen-year gap? What are the marketable skills I've honed since then, mastering clothdiapering? Throwing elegant but affordable parties? Do I go back to public relations? Would I have to start out as an intern again? And if I were to take a job, who'd run my families' lives? Who'd be there to bring the Littles home from school? Who'd make sure everyone ate well and did their homework? Dr. K says we can hire a nanny to handle day-to-day duties like ferrying the kids to practice, but the commute is our best time together. The boys have come to view the car as a safe place, where they can confide in me about topics they're not comfortable discussing around the dinner table. I want to hear that Kord had the fortitude to say no when offered alcohol for the first time and that Konnor was worried about being perceived as a bully. I can't help my kids with their issues if I'm not there.

For a long while, SecretSquash neatly filled the financial gaps. Even though I generate a ton of clicks, pins, likes, favorites, and retweets, the way in which and how much I'm being paid has changed diametrically since last year. Something will have to give soon, but what?

I wish Dr. K had consulted with me before committing to the Miami conference. When he makes decisions alone that impact all of us, I feel as though I'm not part of his team. Couldn't he have earned those continuing medical credits online, no swimsuit required? That four grand would cover what we still owe the landscapers. Thank goodness I was able to maintain our lawn service by bartering a free root canal for Hector or else I'd be out there with the hedge clippers myself. Oh, the field day the HOA would have if our grass grew higher than the maximum three-point-five inches! (I know exactly what they'd say, having once been the one wielding a pitchfork and lighted torch in better days.) (P.S. I may owe Cecily next door an apology.)

I realize I'm obsessing over our finances and I feel like the worst person in the universe for losing sight of the big picture. How petty I am to worry about a few measly bills, a time like this. The accident proves that the rich are just as fallible, just as mortal as every other poor schmuck.

Regardless of our now nonexistent savings account, it's imperative for me to put on a brave face. I must be that paragon of strength, even if it means I show up for the funeral tomorrow alone.

Still, I can't fathom standing there in a black dress without my support system, my rock, the light of—

"See ya in a week, babe!" he says, pecking me on the cheek before trotting down the back stairs, suitcase in tow.

"Whoa, wait, am I not even taking you to O'Hare?" I say, shutting the drawers behind him before following him to the kitchen. I assumed we'd at least spend some time together on the way to the airport. I need to process my heartache and he's barely been around for the past few days.

"Cookie figured your hands would be full with everything, so she's driving me. Plus I arranged for my mom to come help with the kids for the week. *You're welcome.* Hey, we got any Smartwater for the road?" He opens the Sub-Zero PRO 48 with the glass-fronted door and begins to root around. This peek-a-boo refrigerator was once my dream, but *that* dream is over. I had no idea how taxing it would be to keep my chilled items on display every single day. As pin-worthy as my veggie cornucopia may be, sometimes I just want to fling a pizza box in there and not have to worry about anyone judging me for how neatly I merchandise my kale, carrots, and banana peppers.

Before I can plead my case again, I hear the enthusiastic toot of a car horn coming from the driveway. I peek out the side window to see Cookie in the front seat, taking a drag on her cigarette, not a care in the world. She exhales plumes of smoke at the tangle of Mardi Gras beads hanging from the rearview mirror of her Scion. I bet her car smells like Keith Richards and estrogen pills.

"Ride's here!" he says. He leans in for what I assume is a proper kiss, but instead he bends down over the burner I'm standing next to. He uses a wooden spoon to taste the white bean ragout I'm simmering to pair with pan-seared sea bass to feed everyone staying at Steeplechase. "Not your best. Bland. Add some of that pink Himalayan salt. Love to the kids, see you next week."

Then just like that, he's out the door. Faintly, I hear him say, "Hey, Cookie Monster!" before they pull back down the drive.

Much as I'd like to, I can't indulge my disappointment because his learning new techniques will make the practice more profitable. I have to believe his effort will pay off soon.

Hopefully in cash money, and not just dental floss.

After reaching for the salt, I sample the ragout first to determine exactly how much to add. I take another bite for good measure, letting the portion linger on my tongue and penetrate my soft palate to really get a sense of how it tastes. That's when *I* slowly start to simmer.

How can he say the ragout is bland? I'm sorry, but this dish is *flipping perfect*. The chopped aromatics give the stew depth and complexity. Adding more sodium would overpower the delicate interplay between the tomato, garlic, and pancetta. The flavor isn't meant to shout in your face; rather, it should whisper sweetly in your ear.

I notice I'm clutching the Himalayan saltcellar like a baseball I'm about to whip to center field. For a brief moment, I contemplate how satisfying it would feel to throw this container at the fridge's loathsome glass door.

Before I can wind up for the pitch, I'm startled by the sound of my cell phone.

If you want it/Come and get it . . .

I've been crazy in love with David Gray's music for years, hence the ringtone. But now? Now I'm starting to despise him because I've come to associate this song with Dr. K's aggressive student loan collection calls. How's this debt not yet settled? I could have sworn we'd paid them all off last year.

Crying out loud . . .

Plus, while I did the right thing by leaving a message at Jack Jordan's brother's house (WHERE HE RESIDES WITH HIS PARTNER BECAUSE I TOLD YOU TEDDY WAS GAY), I've been dreading her return call. That's why I'm especially jumpy about the phone. Jack and I don't play well together under the best of circumstances, so this? This is an apocalypse waiting to happen. We've thus far avoided each other because the wake has been stretched over the past few days to accommodate everyone. Tomorrow we won't be so lucky at the funeral or the private gathering afterward.

Once upon a time, a ringing cell phone was full of promise, the prelude to a date or an awesome party. Now either it's a demand for money or Lacey Churchill needing to complain some more about Jeremiah's teacher reading aloud from *The Perils of Paul, the Peanut Butter Beagle*.

"Lacey, sweetie, please," I said when I made the mistake of answering earlier. "I promise you this is simply a cute children's book, totally age-appropriate. There's no agenda and the sales go to support animal shelters. Homeless dogs and cats are helped and no actual peanut butter's involved. Everyone wins."

"The book's an attractive nuisance," Lacey replied, absolutely discounting reason. "These kids are being systematically conditioned to crave pulverized nut spreads. Like brainwashing. Extra-crunchy brainwashing. The school is colluding with Big Peanut Butter, I just know it. I sense Jif's sticky fingerprints all over this story."

Fortunately, my phone's caller ID says it's Kelly. I don't see her much since she relocated to West Palm Beach with her pro-golfing husband and two daughters a few years ago.

"Yo, Kitty-cat! You rich yet?"

Is this sarcasm or a subtle barb? I've kept our financial issues on the down-low because I'm mortified, so I'm shocked Kelly's picked up on my deception. But I decide to follow her advice to ABD—Always Be Denying, so I don't offer any info that might confirm her suspicions. "I have no idea what you mean," I reply, trying to sound breezy.

"I mean, you've got a dead Chandler on your hands. I bet the life insurance policy alone is eight figures. Possibly nine. They didn't have heirs, so you've got to be a benefactor. The estate needs to throw a few bucks your way, amirite?"

Jack used to insist that Kelly was the anti-Christ. Oh, please. While Kelly can be—

Kelly tells me, "Listen, this is important."

Thank goodness, I think, hoping she might offer some advice or solace, given—

"When you get your share of the inheritance, be a pal and pick up a new Range Rover for me. I *hate* mine. Mean it. I can't believe Brett cheaped out on the Evoque instead of buying the full-sized. I'm embarrassed to drive this subpar model to the club. You realize I won't even valet park at Mirasol? Too shameful."

Perhaps Kelly's not Mother Teresa, but she's always looked out for me. And regardless of how much we might need a temporary cash infusion, I'd live outdoors before taking a cent from the Chandler estate.

"Make a note, I want the Four Zone Climate Comfort pack. Got that? Obvi, cold weather's not a problem in West Palm, but that's the only model with the shiatsu seats. My Evoque doesn't even have adjustable lumbar support! It's like Russia or something! I asked Brett, *'What am I supposed to do? Drive around in an SUV that can't offer a post-tennis ass massage, like a* poor?'"

Sure, Kel's not for everyone and can come on a bit strong, but her heart's in the right place. Once when we were kids, she—

"Supercharged. God help you if it's not supercharged. Are you writing this down? Write it down, your memory's for shit. I want the LCD displays on the first *and* second row seats. I need separate surround sound for the stereo. I have to be able to play my music outside of the wireless headphones for the DVD player because if I have to listen to those little fucks blather on about 5SOS any more on the way to ballet class, I *will* pull a Susan Smith. Not kidding."

Fine. She's Satan.

Before I can say a word, the back door flies open and Nana Baba enters in a tornado of vaguely blue-tinged white hair, paper bags from the Jewel, and cat-themed, elastic-waist clothing.

"Why aren't you keeping this locked?" she demands, pointing at the door Dr. K exited moments earlier. "Any lunatic could let themselves in, and then where would you be?"

I think, *Likely exactly where I am right now, seeing how one just did.* But I say nothing, pointing to the phone at my ear by way of excuse.

She makes tsk-tsk sounds as she unpacks grocery sacks full of Pop-Tarts, mini chimichangas, and a frozen patty-based product called "Chykyn Wingzz," which I suspect contains neither chicken nor wings.

"Kel, I'm sorry I have to go—Nana Baba's here."

"Ahh! Kill it with fire!" she exclaims before hanging up on me.

Kelly is Satan, but at least she's *my* Satan.

I paint a polite smile on my face and say, "Nana Baba, thanks so much for coming up to stay with us because I'll be in and out over the next few days. The boys are both on day trips with friends and won't be home until late tonight, but Kassie will be thrilled to spend the evening with you." I'll give her that: the Littles adore her. I suspect it's because she swears and watches soap operas with them.

"Where's my girl? Kassie! Kassie, baby! Your Nana Baba's here!" she calls and her words echo.

"Sorry, Baba, she's down the street at a birthday party. We'll pick her up at five o'clock."

The last thing I needed was Brooke Birchbaum's spoiled daughter Avery's party. I had to shell out more than a hundred bucks to buy one of the lower-priced items on her registry. A *gift registry*! For a child who isn't even a decade old! Because Avery's bash is award-ceremony-themed, Kassie needed a noteworthy new outfit for posing in the step and repeat area of the red carpet, too. Paparazzi. *For eight-year-olds.*

How ridiculous has this whole competitive-birthday-party enterprise become with the swag bags and professional DJs? There's such pressure to outdo the previous fete that the costs have skyrocketed. Fortunately, this is one instance where I'm glad to have access to sponsored merch, or else we'd never be able to keep up. For example, last month, Merritt Wilhelm served fresh sushi brought up from Katsu in the city for over two hundred guests! Have you priced hamachi lately? Unreal! (P.S., I'd have been impressed if her son Winston had eaten more maki rolls and less of his own boogers.)

Ashley's been planning a bash for Barry Jr., and her flower budget's twice as much as what my folks spent for our peony-and-gardenia-based wedding centerpieces and rose wall. I wish someone would say, "Enough already!"

However, that person won't be me. I'm not about to be the one parent who doesn't go along and causes my children to be singled out, especially when there's no reasonable alternative.

Nana Baba screws her face up and I can tell I'm about to be hit with a tsunami of judgment, which is ironic considering she's standing there in a cats-wearing-tiaras printed sweatshirt with the caption *Pussies Rule, Dogs Drool!* cross-stitched across the bottom. "How far away is she?"

"The party's a couple of blocks east of here." Lake-adjacent, Brooke Birchbaum always claims, even though she'd have to scale the neighbor's eight-foot privacy fence to catch a glimpse of water.

"Two blocks? And you're driving her?"

Wait for it, wait for it . . .

"What, are her legs broken? She can't walk home? When I was eight, I was riding the bus by myself all the way from Belmont Ave up to the Superdawg. Their malteds were the boss."

Two points to make here: first, leaving my door unlocked for thirty seconds is bad, yet allowing a child to roam free-range just north of the third largest city in the country is good? Second, each time Baba tells this story, she's a little younger in it. When I heard the tale initially, she was thirteen. At some point, she'll be navigating Chicago's public transportation system on her own as an embryo floating in a cup of amniotic fluid. Ha! A cup of Nana Baba. I'll be sure to share this little nugget with Bets—

Damn it. For a blessed second, I forgot.

I begin to tidy up the already immaculate kitchen as an outlet for my nervous energy. I spray a homemade vinegar solution on the counters and wipe with a cloth printed in the yellow racecars Konnor absolutely could not sleep without for a six-month period. "I wish I had your confidence, Baba, but I'm not comfortable with an eight-year-old managing herself. We'll pick her up."

"That kid needs more fresh air."

"We'll roll down the windows."

"She needs exercise."

"Outside of tap, ballet, field hockey, tennis, and tae kwon do, what do you suggest?"

"Mmmph." She stows all her groceries, completely obscuring my fridge staging, and begins to poke through my cabinets. "Where do you hide your coffeemaker?"

I gesture toward the Keurig. "Right there."

"That's not a fancy can opener?"

"Nope." She sidles over to the Keurig, dubious it's not meant to pry lids off of creamed corn cans, eager to correct me.

I inquire, "What flavor pod would you like? Hazelnut? Mountain Blueberry? Ethiopian Yirgacheffe, perhaps?"

She's still manhandling the appliance, unconvinced it makes coffee. "What the shit are you trying to say? And where do the grounds go in? Why isn't there a burner on this thing?"

The path of least resistance will be to make the cup for her, so I invite her to get comfortable while I brew.

I present the steamy Fiesta-ware mug on an old oak barrel tray made of wine staves (complete with cooper's mark) along with a small, coordinating Fiesta-ware bowl of raw sugar cubes, a pair of tiny silver tongs shaped like birds' feet, an adorable vintage cow's head creamer filled with half-and-half, a couple of linen beverage napkins, and a plate of orange zest shortbread cookies and darling little pecan tartlets. When I serve her, Baba holds up one of the tartlets. "What's in here?"

"Pecans, sugar, eggs, flour, vanilla, cinnamon, and some heavy cream."

She casts a gimlet eye. "You know what I mean."

I'm so not in the mood to argue. "Sweet potatoes."

She sets the tartlet down on the other side of the tray so fast you'd imagine it was radioactive. "Did you get my e-mail?"

Did you get my e-mail? I'll take "What Are the Five Most Terrifying Words the Elderly Can Ever Utter?" for two hundred, Alex.

Wait, those are the second most terrifying. The first are, "I'm moving in with you."

Fortunately, I was savvy enough to provide my old Hotmail address years ago, or else my SecretSquash in-box would currently be brimming with urban legends, virus-laden gifs of dogs playing the piano, and chain letters written in multicolored Comic Sans font. I haven't purged anything in that account for a while, so I take an educated guess as to the content.

"What a patriotic story!" I say. Easily, fifty percent of all her forwards include American flags and bald eagles.

"No, not that one. The other one."

There's zero benefit to telling her most of her mail goes unopened, so I guess again. "The monkey who uses sign language to communicate with her fluffy kitten? So cute!"

"I sent that three weeks ago."

I nod noncommittally. "Are you talking about the list of all the uses for apple cider vinegar, or why I should never again park in the garage at Old Orchard Mall?"

She dunks some shortbread into her coffee, then takes a bite. Through a mouthful of crumbs, she says, "Are you daft, girlie? I mean the one about Trip. Did ya read it or not? Whole lot of rumors flying around right about now. Figured you'd have the inside track on the truth."

"Baba, now is not the time for *unfounded rumors*," I reply, with more acid in my voice than intended.

Nana Baba's fairly unflappable, so she doesn't match my tone. "Suit yourself. Hey, that clock right? It's four p.m.?" She points to the display over the stove.

"Yes, of course."

"Then I got a hot date with Dr. Phil. Lemme know when we're picking up Kassie." With that, she takes her coffee and ambles up to her mother-in-law suite over the garage because she prefers to recline on the Tempur-Pedic while watching her "stories."

She shan't be missed.

To keep the peace, I'll pretend I didn't see her snatch up the rejected tartlets first.

Of course, I'm curious as to what kind of ridiculous conspiracy she's touting now, so I open my MacBook and log in to my old Hotmail account. My password's still "Macaroni," named for my childhood pony. Ugh, there's so much crap in here. Nana Baba's e-mails take up most of the entire first page and I sort of want to kill Dr. K for setting her up with an iPad because now she can forward me nonsense from anywhere.

I click on the note she mentioned and skim the contents. Hoo-boy, here we go again, New World Order . . . Trilateral Commission . . . the Masons . . . secret meetings in a bunker under a mountain in Colorado. Come on, Nana Baba—you're better than this. One would imagine a woman who single-handedly raised, nurtured, and provided an under-grad education for four young children in the city after her husband passed away would have more sense. *Delete.*

I read the subject line of every e-mail before sending them to the Big Trash Can in the Sky. That way I'll be prepared if—no, *when*—Baba quizzes me during her week here.

You've Gotta Read This! No, I actually don't. *Delete.*

You won't believe what happens next! I bet I would. *Delete.*

The REAL story behind Hussein Obama's Birth Certificate! Maybe it's time to switch over to CNN, Baba. *Delete.*

AmAzinG DOg VidEo Will HaVE U Cryin! Probably. *Delete.*

If I had a dollar for every fw: fw: fw: that I run across here, I could actually pay the landscapers.

I Can't Stop Thinking About You. Sure, you can't stop thinking about me. Specifically, you can't stop thinking about how I buy my kids' shoes with inadequate arch support, about how I spend too much time building an online presence, about how I don't put enough starch in Dr. K's shirts. *De—*

Hold on.

This e-mail isn't from Baba at all.

This e-mail is from Trip. I feel my heart begin to pound inside my chest and a sour taste in the back of my throat.

Kitty,

I wasn't joking when I propositioned you in the pantry. My feelings for you are real. You pulled away and pretended you weren't interested, but I understand your game all too well. Players recognize players.

Remember—I always get what I want. You and I are going to happen and the sooner you recognize that, the better. Things are changing around here and I'm in a position to make your life very easy. Call me on my private line at (312) 555-1820.

XO,
Trip

According to the time stamp, he sent this e-mail approximately seventy-two hours before his Gulfstream jet depressurized and crashed into the shark-infested waters around Belize.

All those on board perished.

I barely make it to the sink before I vomit.

CHAPTER TEN

CHANDLER FINANCIAL GROUP MEMO

TO: All Employees

FROM: Henry Allen Black, Interim President

SUBJECT: Funeral Services

The office will close today at 1:30 p.m. so that employees may attend the funeral for our beloved founder and friend, James "Trip" Chandler III, who tragically passed away last Wednesday when his plane crashed into the Caribbean Sea off the coast of Belize.

Services will be held at 3:00 p.m. at Harris Brothers Funeral Home, located at 155 Western Ave, North Shore, IL. For those who require transportation, a charter bus will depart at 1:45 p.m., parked at the Randolph Street exit, returning to Chicago after the service.

We ask that you don't speak to the press out of respect for the family in this trying time. Please direct any inquiries to Leigh Ann Kingsley, corporate counsel, ext. 3606.

In lieu of flowers, Mrs. Sarabeth Chandler has asked that donations be made to the W3 Clean Water Initiative.

Jack

....

Chicago, Illinois
Tuesday

"You okay, Jack? You're a little green around the gills."

I don't know how long I've been sitting at this antique leather-topped desk, staring at the phone in my hand. Perhaps if I stare long enough, what I heard won't be true and the roiling nausea I feel will cease.

"Jack, seriously—you need some ginger ale or something? Plastic trash can? Looks like you're about to hurl. Why's that? You didn't have any of my Bobby-ritas last night. Thought it was just Terry and me working the tequila like a boss. Or, like bosses."

Bobby comes over to the banker's desk, where I'm still motionless. How long have I been here? Five minutes? Five hours?

Terry and Ted created this work space for me, located in a little nook off the main living area in the basement. The fine, old desk is nestled between two bookcases full of all the volumes I didn't care to lug all over the world. There's a small but elegant and efficient galley kitchen down here, too, where all the stainless steel appliances are top-of-the-line, yet apartment-sized. As always, the fridge was stocked with every manner of treats for my arrival.

I have one of the two small bedrooms in the back of the apartment and Bobby has the other. My room includes a regal, four-poster mahogany bed that's so tall I have to climb a step stool to get in. Once mounted, I sink down into a billowy cloud because Terry's layered three feather-beds on top of the mattress. (He calls it my Princess and the Pea bed—says this makes up for all the times I sleep in a tent.) The sitting area's up front and it boasts a beautifully aged, button-tufted, leather Chester-field couch, which is flanked by a couple of wingback chairs. The whole scene is reminiscent of a gentlemen's club or an old English manor.

Funny, I haven't covered the Home and Garden section for more than a decade, but still retain the lingo. This place is a far cry from my usual digs.

Normally I'm so grateful for how my family insists on spoiling me when I'm in the States, despite my protests. Visits here entail fluffed pillows and a never-ending stream of gourmet meals, but right now the luxury is cumbersome. Discordant. I feel like I should be sitting on a metal folding chair in a cold room with damp, bare cement walls. I don't deserve any creature comforts for having been so derelict in my duties as a friend.

Trip triggered my internal alarm bells from the first day. Because I didn't want to lose Sars, I kept my concerns to myself after she so thoroughly rejected what I thought I saw at the Air France counter. Thought my interference would be the Kitty situation all over again. Yet with this new information, I'm certain my initial assessment was on point. He was not to be trusted and I fear the repercussions may be far-reaching.

Bobby passes me a steaming mug. He lowers himself into the club chair across from me, after nudging a snoozing Bode Meowler out of the patch of waning sun. Feels like a storm's gathering out there, both literally and figuratively. "You're making me nervous with that scowl, Jack," he says. "So drink this, you'll feel better."

I take a whiff of the smoky, lemony concoction. "What is it?"

"An experiment. Terry might expand into the space next door and open a café. I said he'd bring in more business if he served cocktails that went with cake. Teddy says booze doesn't go with cake, so I'm proving him wrong." He points at the mug. "It's my take on the traditional Hot Toddy. There's Irish whiskey, Earl Grey tea, and a citrus simple syrup I make with sugar, a bunch of lemons, a couple of blood oranges, and a secret ingredient."

I take a sip and can feel the soothing vapors rush down my throat, warming me from the inside out. When I exhale, I feel like I'm walking through a lemon grove in Tuscany. "Amazing. I'd order this in a heartbeat. Imagine a cup served with a plate of scones."

"I know, right?"

"What's the secret ingredient?"

Bobby makes the shape of a heart with his thumbs and fingers. "Love. Splash of single-malt scotch for earthiness. But mostly love."

"What does Terry think?"

He flashes me the heart-hand again. "Only problem is he wants to call it a Hot Teddy."

"Gross."

"Cosigned." He hooks one leg over the arm of the chair in order to get more comfortable. "Anyway, nice job of dodging my question. You're upset, so spill. Who were you talking to? What's going down? More bad news? Hope not."

"You remember my friend Simon?" I ask. I begin to worry at a ragged cuticle around my thumb.

Bobby scrunches his eyes shut, trying to remember. "The rugby player?"

"Definitely not." There was no mistaking Simon for an athlete back then. I used to have better-developed quads than he had. Surely still do.

"He came home with you for Thanksgiving a few times? Pasty kid, real pretentious? The one who couldn't decide if he was Sid Vicious or an English professor? Kept saying 'Anaïs Nin this' and 'Anaïs Nin that.' Spoiler alert, I still don't know who Anaïs Nin is."

I fondly remember a young Simon, so intense with his pipe tobacco and his elbow-patched cardigan, worn over a red capital-A anarchy symbol T-shirt. He'd accessorized his dissonant look with black eyeliner and white-boy dreadlocks. His persona was all over the map, back in the days when we'd try on new identities like a stack of Gap blue jeans, desperate to figure out which one fit best.

God, we were so young then.

"That's him. He's a deputy managing editor for the *Times* now. Lost the dreads, kept the sweater."

"Good call. He keep the pretention, too?"

"Little bit," I admit. "Anyway, he phoned because he remembered my connection with Sars. Says they're breaking a huge story on Sunday regarding the Chandler Financial Group. He has confirmation from three independent sources, at least one within the SEC, so I don't doubt he's onto the truth. The short of it is, CFG clients were anxious about Trip's passing."

"He was kinda their poster boy, yeah?"

I nod. "Trip was definitely the face of the group. So, investors started pulling their accounts at the news. A few were able to cash out, but now Simon hears that the money isn't there to handle the onslaught of requests and everyone's beginning to panic."

"Like that scene in *It's a Wonderful Life*?"

"Yes, but on a global level."

"Where's the money?"

"Therein lies the problem."

Bobby's eyes grow wide. "Holy shit. Did Trip pull a Bernie Madoff or something?"

"For Sars's sake, I hope not, even though evidence points in that direction."

"Aw, Sars. She doesn't need this, too," he says, empathy causing his voice to crack. He's been profoundly impacted by Trip's passing, crying more than anyone else at the first calling hour. Sars ended up having to comfort *him*. Ted and I worry that Bobby's too delicate for his own good.

Wracked with emotion, he says, "Poor kid, especially after losing both her folks in the last two years. Fuck cancer. Fuck cancer *hard*. I'm glad we're all here for her now."

I nod, aching with the guilt of not being around when either of her parents passed away. Bobby said Sars was inconsolable. I was out of range in Sar-e Pol, not hearing the news about either Martin parent until far too late. Sars said she understood why I wasn't there and that she forgave me, but I've yet to forgive myself. Her folks were such kind, loving people, always finding reasons to create a celebration for anyone they knew. Teddy getting a learner's permit? Better bake him a cake shaped like a car! Bobby's braces coming off? Let's take the whole neighborhood to the candy store for caramels! Jack's first byline? Champagne by the case. They could not have been more proud of Sars, particularly after she founded W3. If there's any blessing in this instance, it's that they aren't here to see her so crushed.

Bobby clears his throat and tries to get a handle on himself. "If Simon's right, Sars is in for a shit show. I used to work for a real fun guy in Southampton five years ago. Name was Gidon, came from Israel. Cool accent. Made all his dough in the family diamond business and retired real young. Lived in a huge mansion on Meadow Lane, right on the beach. I'd run the bar at his parties, which were historic events. He'd hire actresses and models to dress up like Greek goddesses and they'd feed guests grapes and give 'em shoulder massages."

"You and I orbit entirely different planetary systems," I blurt, marveling at how far removed our worlds are from each other. "Sorry, Bob. Didn't mean to interrupt your story."

"Nah, it's okay. Club Gidon was pretty surreal for me, too. For example, we'd go through a hundred bottles of Cristal in a night, easy. Guests all went nuts for this raspberry-vanilla puree I'd add because Gidon loved anything raspberry. I'd try to tell him, 'Cristal doesn't need accessories,' but he didn't care. Said the raspberries reminded him of growing up in the Golan Heights. Anyhoo, the Madoff thing happened and the guy was wiped out. Boom, everything he'd invested was gone. The next summer, I stop by his place the first weekend and it's all shuttered. Foreclosed. The bank took his cars, too. I heard he's working as a club promoter in New Jersey. Sad, sad story and now I'm bummed any time I see a pint of raspberries. Jesus God, please don't let this happen to Sars."

I slam my fists down on my thighs, hard. "Damn it, I should have protected her! I should have convinced her that Trip was no good!"

Bobby grabs my hands and holds them steady. "Whoa, take it easy, slugger. Number one, there's no proof yet, right? So far it's all hearsay. And number two, how could you have known anything? What, are you a psychic now? If so, we need to have a very important conversation about Powerball numbers."

I can't accept his solace. Because I stood by and did nothing about Trip, I'm essentially complicit. "I wish I'd trusted my gut. Why wasn't I more insistent when I went to Vegas for her bachelorette party? I knew that was him at the airport in New York all over some other woman. He was so smarmy, so slick, but covered it up with that veneer of old money and Ivy League respectability. I should have made Sars listen. Better for her to have had a small hurt than this heartbreak."

Satisfied that I'm not going to punch anything else, Bobby lets go of my hands, picking up the antique brass pheasant-shaped object on the corner of the desk, turning it this way and that for inspection. I always wondered if he wasn't a little ADD with his inability to sit without fidgeting.

"But that's not your job," he says, finding the hinge on the back of the pheasant's neck that opens to reveal a hidden reservoir. He opens and closes the pheasant's head, like Pac-Man gobbling pellets. "You aren't responsible for protecting everyone. People have to make their own decisions and live with their own consequences. Remember how Mom was always saying that?"

"How'd that work out for her?"

He snaps shut the head, which makes a clacking noise. "Don't go there."

"I'm not wrong."

"I'm not saying you're wrong. I'm just saying you should be logical, Jack. What were you gonna do? You aren't Sars's keeper. Never were. She's a grown-ass adult. Think about what Dad was always saying to us as kids. 'Not your circus, not your monkeys.'" He begins to toss the item back and forth; each time it lands with a satisfying smack on his palms. "Hey, what is this thing, anyway?"

"That's one of the vintage inkwells Teddy started collecting in college," I reply. "Remember? He kept this one on his desk. The best ones are the lion and the jackal—they're here somewhere, too—shelf in the living room, I think?"

Bobby halts his game of catch to look at me, brows knit, genuinely confused. "Inkwell collection. In college. When I was busy collecting tequila bottles. How did we not know he was gay?"

I begin to pick at my nails again, finally tearing off the offending bit of skin on my thumb. The area begins to bleed and I blot at the tiny bead of red with the bottom of my shirt. "Probably because I'm a lousy reporter."

Before Bobby can disagree, Teddy materializes behind us, scooping up the inkwell and placing it back on the desk. "Are you making her feel bad again, cock-muppet?" He cuffs Bobby lightly on the back of the head.

"I wasn't! I swear!" he protests, holding up his arms to protect himself.

"I thought you'd be with Sars," Teddy says.

"I took the morning shift. *She's* going to be there this evening," I say, not wanting to use her actual name. Even now, Sars is helping to manage Kitty and me, advising each of us where to be when so that we may avoid each other. This isn't fair. Our stupid feud should be the last thing on her mind.

Teddy perches on the edge of the desk, clean-shaven with closely cropped hair, clad in a sharply creased pair of khakis, a crisp, pale yellow oxford, a summer-weight blue blazer, and loafers so shiny they glow. He's quite the contrast to shaggy Bobby in his faded cargo shorts, Tevas, and Día de las Muertos T-shirt. "So, why are you a lousy reporter, Pulitzer Prize–nominated Jack Jordan?"

While I explain what's transpired, we gravitate out of the crowded office nook, resituating ourselves in the seating area of the little apartment. Teddy and I sit at opposite ends of the gracious old Chesterfield, while Bobby opts for a wingback out of striking distance. All the cats immediately swarm me, settling in my lap and around my shoulders. Tomba-Cat purrs against my ear so loudly that I have to strain to hear conversation.

"Not to be morbid, but it sounds like Trip died at just the right time," Teddy says. "And there's poor Sars, holding the bag. Does Simon believe investors will go after her? Even though she's not part of the company? Didn't Madoff's wife lose everything?"

My heart begins to pound in my chest. "Say that again."

"Madoff's wife lost everything?"

I stand and the cats go spilling off my lap. The boys dart away in all directions as I begin to pace. "No. You said Trip died at just the right time. *He died at just the right time.* How can I be so blind?"

"Hereditary astigmatism?" Bobby volunteers.

"That's a rhetorical statement, you ass-jacket," Teddy says.

"You're a rhetorical statement," Bobby replies, picking up a pillow and hugging it into his chest.

I walk back and forth behind the sofa as I work everything through. "Why didn't this occur to me sooner? Rescuers didn't find the whole jet, just an easily identifiable tail piece, complete with registration numbers, part of a wing, a couple of seats, and a few other floating artifacts. Where's the oil slick? Where are the bodies? Why wasn't his usual pilot flying the plane? How does no one else have questions? This strikes me as, *'Here's a simple answer for a complex question, move along, nothing else to see.'*"

Teddy narrows his gaze. "Are you saying . . . ?"

"Exactly," I reply. "That's exactly what I'm saying."

"Could he be that insidious?" Teddy asks, more to himself than to anyone else. "Would he go that far?"

I reply, "People aren't always rational when it comes to money. Remember that story I wrote about the Taliban commander who turned himself in for the hundred-dollar reward?"

Teddy muses, "You almost had to feel sorry for the guy, right? There he was, pointing at his WANTED poster, saying, *'I am him! Please to give me my reward now!'* and then didn't understand why he was being dragged off in cuffs."

Bobby's eyes dart back and forth as we talk, tennis match–style.

"Do *not* feel pity. That guy plotted two separate attacks against Afghan security forces. Spend five minutes with the wounded in the med center at the Ramstein Air Base and any compassion you feel for that piece of garbage will disappear right quick," I snap.

Teddy quickly backtracks. "Whoa, of course, Jack. I'm sorry. Didn't mean to sound insensitive. But I follow your point—people will always surprise you in what they're willing to do with enough cash on the line."

"You also believe it's possible?" I confirm.

Bobby throws his arms wide, which causes his pillow to fall and almost knock over a vase on the coffee table, which Teddy quickly rights. "What the hell are you guys saying? Like the crash didn't really happen? Like Trip somehow faked it all? Come on! This is real life, not the movies!"

"Bob, you never believe that anyone could have a darker side or base motives. I wish I had your optimism about human nature, but I've seen people at their worst," I say. "He had the means and the motive."

Bobby's cheeks begin to redden. "Uh-uh. No. That's the kind of crazy conspiracy talk you hear on late-night AM radio. Not finding a whole plane doesn't mean shit. Water recovery can take a lot of time depending on tide and wind. Lindy and I went diving in Belize once and the barrier reef really messes with how everything flows. We were swept so far off course that we almost didn't get back to the boat and she was an expert. No. I don't buy it. They found the black box—the plane clearly crashed. Don't make it all worse by disrespecting the dude's memory. Uncool." He eases forward to retrieve his pillow. "Major league uncool."

Dad always said Bobby's patented refusal to see the worst in anyone is both his greatest blessing as well as his biggest liability. "Still," I insist. "Consider the ramifications if the plane *didn't really crash*? What if Trip knew he was under SEC investigation and he somehow made it *seem* like there was an accident?"

Teddy's wheels are turning, too. "Like John Burney writ large?"

"Bingo," I say.

"Writ *what*?" Bobby says, clearly frustrated with both of us. "Explain, 'cause you sound nuts."

"John Burney was a prominent businessman who'd fallen on hard times back in the seventies," I tell him. "Somewhere in Alabama, I believe. No, Arkansas. Not important. Anyway, his company had gone under and he was facing lawsuits, financial ruin imminent. One night, he was involved in a car accident on a bridge. Instead of waiting for help to arrive, he climbed over the railing, dropped into the water, and swam away. The police, and everyone else, assumed he was dead, his body having floated down the river."

Bobby flashes a victorious grin. "Tides, man, I'm telling ya."

"Bobby, she just said he swam away and he was fine," Teddy said.

I don't want to upset Bobby any more than he already is, but I need Ted's help to piece this puzzle together. "Burney basically bolted and created a whole new life for himself in Florida. Even remarried and had kids under an assumed name. Neither his first wife nor business partners had any knowledge of this, so they filed for and collected his insurance. Seemed like the perfect crime."

Teddy jumps in to add, "Except it wasn't. That dumb bastard ended up coming back to Arkansas to visit his father and he was found out. A judge allowed his beneficiaries to keep the money on a technicality—something about the settlement being fairly disbursed. Of course, Burney's insurance company turned around and sued him."

While Bobby remains upset and unconvinced, Teddy and I gather steam. We were an unbeatable team when we'd play two on two against John and Bobby as kids. While the twins were more proficient in hoops than Teddy or me, he and I always won because we mastered the art of unspoken communication. With one look, we could anticipate any move the other would make.

I say, "Wait, there was a man in Indiana who did the same thing not too long ago." I quickly Google the information to confirm. "Yes! Marcus Schrenker! I knew this scenario seemed familiar. Same situation as what could have happened with Trip, right down to this guy being an investment advisor. He was in financial trouble, so he crashed his single-engine Piper Meridian and made it look like an accident. He even sent distress calls to air traffic control about a broken windshield and bleeding face."

Bobby clutches his pillow ever tighter.

"Terry and I saw that story on *20/20*," Teddy says. "The difference between Schrenker and Burney is that Schrenker's crime was premeditated, whereas Burney capitalized on a happy accident. Schrenker was quickly found out and caught because he did a shit job of covering his tracks. Like, there was no blood in the plane or around in the field where it went down. The windshield was intact, too, suspicious given the distress call. However, if he had more means, more time to plan, and an aquatic crash instead of terrestrial? Wouldn't have been so easy to spot the fraud."

Bobby's shaking his head no with great vehemence. "Sorry, Cagney and Lacey, not buying what you're selling. If cops thought there was any possibility of Trip being missing and not dead, then how'd Sars get a death certificate so fast? Remember? Dad was going to have to do that with Mom, until . . ."

Teddy squares his jaw. "Until we had confirmation."

We're all quiet for a second, remembering.

Bobby's the first to break the silence. "So we know for a fact that there's a seven-year waiting period when there's no body."

Gently, I say, "Normally, yes, and you make a valid point." Bobby unclenches at the compliment, while Ted's expression is that of having just bitten into a lemon. "You're missing the two mitigating factors. First, in situations of imminent peril, like a plane crash, the presumptive death period doesn't have to elapse for a death certificate to be issued."

"Say what?" Bobby asks. "English, motherfucker, do you speak it?"

"Remember me covering a lot of the aftermath of 9/11 before I went overseas? That's when the rules changed. Expedited procedures were established for the beneficiaries of those who perished in the Towers. In some cases, decedent DNA wasn't identified for years, but because of the imminent peril factor, death certificates were issued immediately and insurance companies paid families very quickly."

"What's the second part?" Ted prompts.

I shrug. "That Trip's a Chandler and the rules are different for them."

Trip's family helped settle this country and they've been building their fortune ever since, first in shipping, and then in timber, railroad, copper, and eventually, electronics. If history is any indication, this family has been virtually untouchable for almost two centuries. Regardless of the crime's nature, from his cousin's recent alleged drunk driving escapades to his uncle's alleged insider trading to his great-great-grandfather's alleged mistress's alleged strangulation, no Chandler has ever had a charge stick.

I can tell Bobby's wavering, but he's not yet fully persuaded. "Still, this is some tin-foil-hat level of speculation, especially because I don't believe Trip was smart enough to pull off something like this. When *I* think you're dumb? Bro, you're dumb."

"You used to be smart, thousands of bong hits ago," Teddy says.

"And you used to bang chicks."

Teddy doffs an imaginary bowler hat. "Touché. You may continue."

Bobby nods curtly. "Thank you. Anyway, last night, when Sars was reminiscing about how Trip put his dirty wool suits in the washing machine when they first started living together? Not smart."

"That's a function of coming from privilege, not of a lack of intelligence," I argue. "I'm sure that was his first time ever touching his own dirty laundry. Plus he can't be dumb—he went to Yale for undergrad."

Teddy snorts to himself. "So did W."

"You're not helping," I say to Teddy. "Bobby, if Trip somehow had diminished capacity, how'd he get through U of C business school?"

Bobby replies, "You mean, outside of his family donating half of the campus's buildings? Easy. He had Sars. Remember how she said they met the first week of classes at that mixer? He knew she was smart and he made her help. And he probably copied off of her."

"Huh," I say, temporarily stymied. "I can't argue that theory. Anyone who'd run around on his spouse would absolutely cheat on assignments."

Bobby continues. "Plus, you guys can't be right because the numbers don't add up. I'm telling you, faking a plane crash with a single turboprop Piper like the Indiana Shanky guy? Yeah, that makes sense because older planes only run about six hundred thou. Pricey, for sure, but it's still doable, you know?"

Teddy looks astounded. "Six hundred thousand dollars is 'doable' to you? Since when? Yesterday you said your current net worth was thirty-two bucks until you get your payment from the trust."

"I bought a burrito, so it's more like twenty-four now. Wait, I had an horchata, too. Make it twenty-two. My point is, Trip's model of Gulfstream? That'd be hella expensive. Those things run, like, sixty mil. Nobody's gonna shell out those duckies to perpetrate a fraud. So, *post hoc ergo propter hoc*—"

"Have you been watching *The Good Wife* again, Bob?" Ted asks.

"Is it a crime to appreciate how Kalinda works a skirt? So, yes, but that's not my point." Bobby crosses his arms over his chest in triumph. "My point is, *Counselor*, no one would spend sixty damn million dollars to fake his own death, so I rest my case."

My phone buzzes and I glance down at the text Simon's just sent.

I sit back down, pointing at my phone's display. "You're right, Bob. No one could or would sacrifice sixty million bucks . . . unless they were sitting on the *seventeen billion* that's currently MIA from investors' accounts."

We each stare in silence at the message.

Oh, Sars, I think, *what has Trip done?*

CHAPTER ELEVEN

Kitty
....

North Shore, Illinois
Tuesday

"How's your summer going?"

Keep it together, Kitty-cat, I tell myself. *You can do this. Do not freak out. You are their PTO president. The second these moms sense weakness, bam! That's it. Junta. Or hostile takeover. Or whatever it's called when there's a vote of no confidence and the democratic, fair, pretty leader's ousted. You want to end up on the bottom of the phone tree list like your neighbor Cecily, not even deemed responsible to call one person, let alone ten? No. No flipping way. Not happening.*

I smile broadly and say, "Oh, it's been *to die.* Just the best, Merritt! And thank you for asking! You must tell me all about yours! Don't you dare skimp on a single detail, either."

Naturally, Merritt Wilhelm is still done up in high-speed moisture-wicking workout clothes, gun show on full display, lest anyone doubt for a second she spends all day at the gym. She launches into an exhaustive description of some house on some body of water somewhere. Don't know. Can't care. Not listening. I'm not here to make small talk. All I want to do is find my kid and mother-in-law, exit this damn party, and have a few minutes to sort out my racing thoughts.

"*. . . water as clear as can be!*"

I cannot piece this together. What am I missing? What did Trip mean when he wrote that things were changing? Was he leaving Betsy? How could that be? I never heard of a moment's discord between them! And how could he believe that I'd be the kind of woman who hooks up with her best friend's husband? Ugh, I feel sick again. I can still taste the bile, even though I shoved three pieces of gum in my mouth after I brushed my teeth.

"... *jet skis, a pontoon boat* ..."

Was I somehow accidentally untoward with Trip? He always flirted with me, but I thought he was being friendly. Because I'd occasionally banter back, did he take my naturally sunny nature as an invitation? Yes, I can be flirty—flirting is an effective, everyone-wins tool for getting others to do your bidding. But my flirting isn't of a sexual nature and I'd never flirt with anyone I actually crushed on—that would violate everything Kelly ever taught me! And, hello? Happily married! Smiling with my eyes and giggling on cue do not an adulteress make!

I'm worried, though—did Trip have a notion I wasn't happily married? Why would he? Did he know something I didn't? Do Dr. K and I not present a united front? No, that's crazy. We're fine. Fine! We're great! Every married couple has ebbs and flows. This isn't about my husband. This is about a man who was so used to getting his way that it never occurred to him someone would say no. But that raises the question, was Trip a cheater?

"... *the* most *adorable fudge shop* ..."

Sure, as much as Trip traveled, he'd have the opportunity to step out on Betsy. In theory, he could have a gal in every port. And plenty of women would throw themselves at a rich man. His assistant Ingrid was always making sausage-eyes at him. Did he not have the kind of integrity it took to say no to the gold diggers? What if there really was something going on between him and his assistant? Had Betsy an inkling?

Oh, *Betsy*.

How am I going to face Betsy this evening? I'm embarrassed to have this insight into her marriage. And I can't say anything about this e-mail because she'd be devastated. I will *not* make her feel worse just to ease my own burden. I can't reveal he was anything short of wonderful.

I'll take it to my grave before saying a single negative thing about that low-down, dirty, son of a biscuit.

"... I said, 'Who cares about market price? Just bring me the damn lobster salad!'"

I'm fixated on his "things are about to change" line, though. Almost seems ... prophetic. I wish I had a sounding board, someone who might talk me through this. But I can't trust anyone around here. Who'd keep the whole thing quiet? My neighbor Cecily? Please. Brooke Birchbaum? Ugh. Ashley? What kind of insight could that ding-a-ling provide? I imagine the inner workings of her brain look a lot like those old commercials where monkeys try to open suitcases. Bash, bash, where's my banana?

What about Kelly? She gives great advice. Then again, she's so calculating that she'd try to find an angle to exploit the situation to her own advantage and that's not okay.

I can't gauge how Dr. K might react if I shared the e-mail with him. Truth? I'm afraid to find out. What if I told him and he *didn't* somehow explode in a pique of jealousy, ripping his shirt and beating his bare chest in rage? Not overreacting would feel worse than overreacting. Was Trip actually onto something between my husband and me? Ironic that Betsy's the one person I can bare my soul to, only to be the same person who'd be devastated by the info.

"... manicure, pedicure, seaweed wrap, hot stone massage ..."

I *cried* for that despicable philanderer. Sobbed. Bawled until my eyes were tiny slits and I had to ice them and breathe into a paper bag to stop hyperventilating. Mourned over how this loss would impact my best friend. Yet now I wish he was alive so I could slap his weasely face. The nerve thinking he could just dangle the promise of financial security and I'd run to him, screwing over Betsy in the process. Disgusting. Contemptible. *Grody.*

"... 'tap water? Did we lose a war or something?'"

Too bad Jack Jordan's a lunatic because she's the one person who looks out for Betsy as much as I do.

Would she ...

No.

Could I . . .

No.

I feel dirty for even considering seeking her input, and yet, it's not the worst idea in the world. She *is* smart. Some might say too smart for her own good. (Usually me.) But she may have the kind of perspective I so desperately need right now.

"*. . . what would I do with a butler? What wouldn't I do is more like it!*"

How do I approach her after all this time? How?? Do I . . . compliment her? Discuss a shared interest? Save for Betsy, there's no common ground between us. Is it possible being reasonable and honest would be enough? Feel like I have no choice but to find out.

"*. . . digest carbs? Oh, honey, no.*"

Okay, new plan. I'll get her alone tomorrow. I'll kill her with kindness. She'll be surprised at first, and likely distrustful—no, *profoundly* distrustful—but I'm really good at this sort of thing. I worked in PR. I know how to spin. I can win over people. I mean, did I not convince that famous old astronaut to spend the day with Konnor's fifth grade class? At my behest, they even were permitted to try on his helmet! And if it wasn't for my influence, hundreds of children across the country would be eating brownies without a shred of kale in them. And my crusade for mandatory skirt and short length enforcement at North Shore Senior High? You're welcome, every testosterone-fueled teenage boy who can finally pay attention in class because he's not too distracted by young, bare thighs.

So that's it. I'll be nice.

I can do it.

"*. . . and I'll be devastated if you don't think so, too.*"

Feeling vaguely less queasy, I smile at Merritt and pretend to agree with whatever it is she's just said. "Of course I do, Merritt! Of course I do."

* * * *

"What in the actual shit was that all about?" Nana Baba asks from her spot in the backseat next to Kassie's car seat.

I glance at her in the rearview mirror. "What do you mean?"

"That party. Never seen anything like it."

Brooke Birchbaum spent a mint on this event, starting with the celebrity look-alikes. I've been in such a state that at first I thought Brooke
had finagled the *actual* Adele and Leo DiCaprio to serve mocktails to
the children.

I'm sure she'll save that until Avery's *ninth* birthday.

The Cirque du Soleil–type performances, the screening room at the
end of the red carpet, and the salon area with the mani/pedi and blowout stations were all completely over the top, no expenses spared.

Nana Baba is shell-shocked. "And the statues. I can't get over the
candy statues."

Brooke commissioned a European sculptor to create The Avery, a
life-sized take on the traditional Oscar statue, only shaped like her
daughter and crafted from marble. A Swiss chocolatier created gold-leaf
covered, caramel-filled, miniature Averys, which are just one of the
items in the Hollywood-themed swag bag. Other goodies include a yet-
to-be-released DVD of the new Pixar film and related plush toy and a
photo frame with AVERYWOOD affixed on the bottom right hand corner,
fashioned like the HOLLYWOOD sign. There're professionally decorated
sugar cookies shaped like film reels, movie cameras, and popcorn boxes,
with mini-cupcakes embossed with Avery's monogram, as well as a
sparkly Swarovski headband and a child-sized Return to Tiffany heart
bracelet. The kit wouldn't be complete without a glittery eye shadow
and lip gloss gift set, as well as a digital camera.

Astounding.

Kassie had handed off the bag to her Baba as soon as she stepped
into the car, completely blasé over the contents, having received such
largesse more than four times already since the summer began. (Would
it be wrong to list one of the spare iPad minis on eBay? Asking for a
friend.)

"The gift bag!" Nana exclaims, holding up each item for inspection.
"Must be fifty dollars' worth of stuff in there!"

"Probably a lot more than that," I say, doing the math in my head.
"The Tiffany bracelet alone is in the one-fifty range."

Nana is fuming. "Christ on a cracker, one hundred and fifty god-damned dollars? For kids?"

Kassie slaps a hand over her mouth to keep from giggling.

Baba's on a tear, cat sweatshirt heaving as she draws a breath. "You spoil them like this now, and what happens later in life? Are they ever going to be satisfied? No! What do they do up here when kids turn six-teen? Give 'em their own condo? These kids are going to make shit adults! Give 'em everything now and it sets an unrealistic expectation for the future. How do you justify that kind of excess with children?"

"I don't and I can't," I reply, already dreading what I'm going to have to miracle up for Kassie's next party. Do I even *have* any more fa-vors to call in? I bet half the reason everyone's paying me in swag now is because I opened that door myself. I took nice things in trade because I didn't want to tell my kids we couldn't afford the newest/latest/greatest.

Maybe Kassie would like some kind of Keurig-themed event?

"This bag is why the whole country's going to hell on a Handi Wipe," she says, causing Kassie to burst out with fresh peals of laughter. "Everybody's greedy and they gotta make a splash, so they cut corners to make more money and they don't follow the rules. Saw it with the Savings and Loan crisis back in the eighties and nineties and the aughts are still reeling from the subprime mortgage market. What kinda mo-ron takes out a million-dollar mortgage when they know they can't af-ford it?"

I glance back at her. "You'd be surprised."

"Insanity, that's what it is. Plain old insanity. Personally, I never worried about keeping up with the Joneses. Don't give a flying f—"

I cut her off. "*Fig.* A flying *fig* about the Joneses."

She nods, pleased that I seem to agree with her. "Goddamned right."

While Nana Baba's lack of pretension is refreshing, I wonder if ap-pearances are now so important to Dr. K having grown up without them. He was Captain Credit Card in college, dressing in as much Polo and Hilfiger as the rest of his fraternity brothers, so I never even real-ized he came from a more working class beginning until well into our relationship.

Kassie lays a small hand on Baba's arm. "Nana Baba, will you take me to Superdawg tonight? I didn't eat anything at the party and I'm hungry." Brooke had the event catered by a two Michelin-starred molecular gastronomy chef best known for his ability to turn any flavor pairing into a gelatinous, foam-covered cube. "All the food looked like Jell-O. Yuck."

Baba pokes me in the shoulder. "There may be hope for this one."

I sigh and think, *Well, at least there's that.*

CHAPTER TWELVE

Jack

....

North Shore, Illinois
Wednesday

"Nice panty hose," Kitty whispers under her breath to me. "You hoping to fail at sorority rush again?"

Why am I stunned that she's starting with me?

"You're un-be-*fucking*-lievable," I hiss back. "Show some decorum! God! What is wrong with you?"

We're halfway between the funeral home and Steeplechase, protected from the light drizzle by the broad canopy of the old-growth oak trees in Sars's neighborhood. Those of us at the house beforehand opted to walk to and from services earlier when it was still sunny. Harris Brothers is only about half a mile away from Sars's home. With so many expected mourners, we didn't want to take up additional parking spaces.

I was secretly relieved to see the discreet presence of well-dressed security guards at the funeral home, looking like every other attendee, only bigger, beefier, and wearing sidearms. The only thing that could have made today worse for Sars would have been confrontations with angry investors or any member of the media who didn't fiercely love Sars.

Even now as we walk back to Steeplechase, the guards flank us to the front and rear, which is why I won't call attention to whatever asshattery Kitty has in mind. She'd be on the ground with an ex-SEAL's knee on her spine before she could say "flipping."

When we left Harris Brothers, Kitty and I had been walking on either side of Sars. Somehow along the way, we were elbowed away by her low-rent cousins Cilla and Gracie and now the three of them are a few paces back. I'm grateful Sars's parents aren't seeing this; they'd be so hurt and disappointed to witness her greedy relatives circling, assuming there will be some potential opportunity for financial gain. I'm sure these vultures haven't the first clue as to how trusts and estates law work. There's no way the whole shooting match isn't earmarked for Sars. However, as the SEC scandal won't break until Sunday, everyone believes there's cash in play.

I hope these bottom-feeders are still there for her after.

But I doubt it.

"I was *paying* you a *compliment*," Kitty says, thrusting out her lower lip, pretending to seem hurt. "I assumed you'd show up here in jungle boots. But look at you, all tailored and chic. I'm touched you made the effort; I know it's super-hard for you, being a she-male and all."

The only reason I don't scream, "She has a gun!" is because I don't want to make a scene with Sars so close behind us.

She is right that I made an effort. Terry insisted on buying an appropriate funeral outfit for me, so I'm wearing a dress that's black and fitted, with some kind of gauzy floof around the waist. But it has pockets, so I like it, even though the pantsuit I keep at the house would have been perfectly serviceable. Terry claimed he had to take over dressing me because I looked like "a state senator from Asswater, Iowa, ready to crown the winning hog at the county fair."

Fine. It's not a great suit.

Terry found me a pair of pumps with heels I could manage and *appropriately* sized nylons, so I'm fixed up like everyone else at the funeral. I appreciate Terry mothering me, even if he did mention something about ritually burning my suit to excise the ghost of 1992's Hillary Clinton.

With as much calm as I can muster, I whisper, "Go fuck yourself, Carricoe." I try to calm my nerves, so on edge from a night spent compulsively trying to verify my hunch about Trip. Simon's confirmed the SEC has a real case and they're in the final stages before indictments are passed down.

The more I dig, the more "convenient" Trip's death seems. I'd wager he took the money and ran to some country without US extradition. With that kind of cake, he could buy his own island and private military force.

Even Bobby believes me now.

Of particular concern is Ingrid, Trip's personal assistant for the past three years. She came to him fresh out of college, so I wonder exactly what duties she was qualified to fulfill in his employ. As I scanned the Internet for photos of Trip, I noticed she was perpetually in the background, so it's clear she rarely strayed from his side. Then . . . where is she today? Why wouldn't she attend the service? No one's seen her and I find her absence highly suspect.

"Go flip *myself*? Why don't *you* go flip *Sean*?" Kitty replies, every word full of venom.

I stop in the middle of the sidewalk. "For Christ's sake, are you still beating the *flipping* drum? You're almost forty, Kitty. Say fuck if you'd like. No one cares. Truly."

She stops next to me. As we stare each other down, a couple of the mourners have to step around us and I notice one of the guards giving us the eye. I return his look with a discreet shake of my head and he moves on.

"I am not in the mood for your crap today, Sasquatch. We're here for Betsy."

"Yes," I agree. "We are here for *Sars*."

She grits her teeth. "Today is about supporting *Betsy*, you complete and total waste of newspaper ink."

I take a slow, even breath. "I will not stoop to your level. And I know *Sars* appreciates our efforts."

Kitty grabs my wrist with her bony hand, so I spin around and take ahold of her other wrist. We look like we're about to square dance. Then she pulls in very close to me and says, "You are on thin flipping ice, *Bouvier*," taunting me with my hated middle name. "I will cut you. For real." Her words are slow and deliberate, and so close I can smell her breath. Honestly, I was expecting notes of creosote, not Wrigley's Doublemint Gum.

The wind begins to pick up because foul weather's blowing in from the north. If I didn't know better, I'd guess the gathering clouds and graying skies were Kitty working her crazy witch magic.

But I'm not afraid.

I stand up to my full height, push my shoulders back, and reply, "Yeah? Then you should throw another margarita glass at me. Crystal, if you have one."

Thunder rumbles in the distance. I'm sure if I were a witch, I'd be more powerful than she is, because good always conquers evil in fairy tales. As if on my cue, I see a lightning bolt slash the darkening sky over the lake. The thunder grows more persistent.

Her eyes are blazing and she's as stiff as a cobra about to strike. *"Are you implying that I can't afford crystal? Ooh, don't you know everything, Jackass Bouvier Jordan, girl reporter. Being temporarily overextended is not the same as broke!"*

"Yes, I—wait. What'd you say?"

Before she can respond, Sars comes upon the two of us, throwing her arms wide and bringing us into a three-way hug. "The only thing that's keeping me from shattering into a million tiny pieces right now is seeing the two of you get along. Thank you. I understand the depth and breadth of this sacrifice. I love you both so much. Now let's hurry home before the rain hits."

• • • •

After the most awkward three-way hug in recorded history, Kitty and I both exercise heroic self-control, largely by staying as far away from each other as possible at Steeplechase. Avoidance is made easier given the buffers of Teddy, Bobby, Dad, and all the available square footage. Bobby even goes so far as to engage Kitty in conversation. (What did they discuss? How to hide zucchini in an edible?) I wonder why Kitty's husband didn't come with her. Surely he could have closed his office early—tooth bleaching isn't exactly a life or death matter. Plus, I thought both couples were close. Even if Trip and Ken weren't friendly, he should be here for his wife. Personally, I had to insist Terry not join us because

I hated for him to lose an entire baking day at the height of Wedding Cake Season. (John made noise about coming, but no one wanted that.)

I'm proud that for the first time in the twenty years since our initial falling-out, nothing goes awry between the two of us. This feels somehow historic. We don't snipe or glower at each other. We neither posture nor pose. No one is slapped with a slab of smoked salmon and all the canapés remain gravity-bound on their silver serving platters. I can actually leave a party without a ruined outfit or an earful of chocolate. What a shame that Mr. and Mrs. Martin's final memories of the two of us are our being separated by busboys.

As I wander through the somber crowd (who aren't so despondent they can't gobble up the caviar blini or Kobe tenderloin), I view Steeplechase in a different light. Financial success has never been important to me, so I'm often oblivious to the trappings of wealth. In a world where running water feels decadent, a Japanese toilet seat that warms, washes, and dries is practically beyond my comprehension. Teddy, who's never seen Steeplechase in person, was agog at some of Sars's and Trip's possessions, such as the Matisse in the library or the Georgian Chippendale sofa in the solarium. From my days on the Home beat, I recognized the curves and the carving, but had no clue this item could cost anywhere from fifty thousand to one million dollars.

One million dollars.

For a couch slowly fading in the sun.

Viewing this home through Teddy's eyes, I finally recognize the extent of the opulence. I never discussed dollars and cents with Sars, but it's well-publicized that Trip's father follows Warren Buffett's inheritance philosophy: "I want to give my kids just enough so that they would feel that they could do anything, but not so much that they would feel like doing nothing." About ten years ago, Trip's parents set up a foundation similar to that of Bill and Melinda Gates, tirelessly giving away the family fortune to worthy causes.

Could Trip have perpetrated such a fraud because he felt he was denied his birthright? Was he furious that the Chandler riches flowed like water through so many generations, only to go dry when it was his turn at the tap?

Finally confident that I won't act out, Dad and my brothers leave together before the worst of the rain begins to fall. They're heading south for dinner in the city with Terry and with Dad's lovely long-term girlfriend, Gloria. He sold the old place in Evanston after we all finished college (or claimed to have finished) and bought a modern, open-concept loft on the Gold Coast. Said condo contains no flatulent dogs nor guest rooms. This omission is not by accident. He's the happiest I've ever seen him, probably because Gloria dotes on him and he's no longer forced to drink his Dewar's out of old mustard jars.

Cilla and Gracie are staying here with Sars, so I'm comfortable leaving her and heading back to Andersonville. I was invited to dinner, but I visited Dad and Gloria two days ago and I'm anxious to continue my sleuthing, starting with Ingrid's whereabouts. Maybe I didn't protect Sars before, but if that man is still somehow walking the earth, I'll find him. And I won't tell Sars anything until I have hard, fast proof. Trip was a scoundrel, but he was her scoundrel and I want her to hold on to the good memories for as long as possible, even if that peace lasts only until the Sunday news cycle.

I will not let my best friend down again.

Sars and I are saying our good-byes under the grand portico, waiting for a valet to bring my car from the parking area by the helicopter pad. We're midembrace when there's a mighty flash and a huge crack.

For a second, everything goes white.

When the smoke clears, we see that one of the massive old oaks on the periphery of the property has been struck by lightning and a limb the size of a Subaru is strewn across the driveway, blocking the gate. No one's hurt, but someone will have to be called to clear the area, so we return indoors.

Ever the compassionate soul, Sars says, "You want to get out of that 'monkey suit,' don't you, Jack? Go up to Great Meadow and look in the closet. Trip's sister keeps some things here and she's about your size. Please help yourself."

Even at her nadir, Sars is sterling. "Aw, Sars, you will always be my Goose."

I kick off my shoes before sprinting up one of the two grand staircases that lead to a bridge that connects one side of the second floor to the other. Because Steeplechase is so large, Sars gave each guest room equine-related names, to honor the home's past as the Sausage King of Chicago's weekend horse farm.

I turn down the hall to the right, having to stop and read each placard, passing Breeder's Cup and Saratoga. I find Great Meadow across from an open gallery between wings where oil paintings of each generation of Chandler are displayed.

After I change into sneakers, yoga pants, and a snug yet stretchy black hoodie, I exit the guest room, dress in hand, when I notice Kitty stepping into the gallery. I lunge back into the room, hiding behind the door so she doesn't see me. I'm determined to leave here before we have an incident, so I'll simply wait her out.

She inspects Trip's portrait with great reverence. He's standing on the prow of *The Lone Shark*, peach sweater casually draped around his shoulders, face raised to the light, as though the sun shines only on him. Never have I seen smug so perfectly captured in oil.

She runs a neatly manicured finger along the scalloped gold frame, likely paying homage. Of course this ninny would consider Trip's death a telling blow, a tragic loss for society, a dreadful—

"Rest in peace, motherfucker," she snarls. "Rest in peace."

So . . .

Kitty and I may share a sliver of common ground after all.

CHAPTER THIRTEEN

NEW POST ON SECRETSQUASH.COM

Who Wants Lemonade? Kassie Does, Kassie Does!

Is there anything more adorable than a Little running a lemonade stand at the end of the driveway? Survey says . . . no! And how proud does sweet Kassie look here in her pinafore-apron? One, please!

There's sooooo much to love about setting up a lemonade stand with your kids this summer! A few of the many benefits include:

*Developing a work ethic

*Gaining an understanding of planning and budgeting

*Exercising creativity and fine motor skills in building and decorating a booth

*Appreciating the value of earning a dollar

*Learning to give charitably by donating a portion of the sales

*Crafting a quality product full of fresh, wholesome ingredients

Basically? A lemonade stand's a win/win for everyone!

To begin our project, Kassie and I sketched out what her dream stand might look like and—MORE AFTER THE PAGE JUMP

Kitty

....

North Shore, Illinois
Wednesday

Okay, here's my chance. I've been psyching myself up for this since last night. Operation Be Nice to Jack starts now.

With my gold-medal, ten-out-of-ten-dentists-approve grin, I lean in and say, "Your dress is to die! Mean it. That peplum? Love. And I so admire how polished and pulled together you are, right down to the stockings." I speak to her using my most loving, mommy's-tucking-you-in-now whisper. "You'd kill at rush right now. You should be really proud of yourself. What a lovely woman you've become."

"Fuck you in the fucking eye, you fucking fuck," Jack retorts, practically shoving me in her haste to distance herself. We're on our way down Betsy's street, coming back to her house after the funeral for the WASP version of sitting Shiva. Betsy's about fifty paces behind us, what with her cousins swooping in to surround her, then clinging like a couple of barnacles or kids who refuse to get into the bath. Cilla and Gracie's profound displays of grief feel self-serving to me. I'm not sure I trust their intentions.

To Jack, I say, "I wish you'd take the compliment. I'm absolutely sincere. You really are radiant. Your hair! Your skin! You're still such a Phoebe Cates!"

"Eat a dick, thundercunt. Or don't. Nah, you wouldn't. I bet that's why Sean slept with me." She whirls around and plants herself on the sidewalk, taking a highly aggressive posture. She's acting just like that angry silverback gorilla the kids and I saw the last time we went to the zoo, thumping her chest and stomping the ground. Please, someone shoot this ape with a tranquilizing dart!

I gasp, "My goodness, such language! I'm glad there are no children around to hear your potty mouth!" A couple of Betsy's neighbors have to walk on the median to pass by us.

Jack rolls her eyes. "No one cares what you have to say, Soccer Mom. Hey, don't you have any balls to inflate? No? That must be why Sean picked me." Then she grabs my wrist, squeezing the dickens out of it, and tells me, "Listen, I don't want any of your shit because I'm here for Sars."

I gently take her other wrist, as though to calm her. We appear ready to do the fox-trot. Fortunately, I understand how to de-escalate a situation, having learned from raising boys. This conversation is getting out of hand and I want to make sure we're both mellow, so I come in close to speak slowly and clearly. "Please, Jack, Betsy doesn't need you starting yet another scene."

"And Sars doesn't need some broke housewife sniffing around after her money," she says. "That's right, I learned all about your finances. I'm a famous reporter, you know."

Before I can defend myself, Betsy reaches us on the sidewalk. She throws herself between the middle of us, hugging and saying, "The only thing that's keeping me from shattering into a million tiny pieces right now is seeing the two of you get along. Thank you. I understand the depth and breadth of this sacrifice. I love you both so much. Now let's hurry home before the rain hits."

• • • •

Despite Jack's terrible attitude on our walk over here, I pledge to not let her suck me into anything. I will be the adult here, even if she won't.

Betsy's being so stoic, so strong. She barely shed a tear during the service. I admire her so. I thought I'd have to be her pillar, but she's the one maintaining a brave facade for us. Right now, surrounded by so many people who love and support her, she has to feel buoyed, but I imagine once the last car pulls away, the impact will hit her. And I'll be there for her, as long as it takes.

I decide that I'm simply not going to think about Trip's e-mail again. That's the only way I can deal. Somehow it was a prank or a joke gone wrong. Perhaps a glitch in the system. Didn't happen. Even if there were bad intentions on his part, nothing came of it. When Trip knew he was at the end, in those few precious remaining moments on the plane,

I bet his thoughts were of his one great love, and not some unrequited crush.

I'm done obsessing.

It's over. Moving on.

"That you, Kitty?" Jack's brother Bobby sits down next to me in the solarium. Rain falls in earnest now, running down the glass roof in rivulets, coming so thick and fast that the view of the lake is obscured. Earlier, the wind whipped so hard that the normally gentle waves of Lake Michigan bashed against the seawall, sending sprays upward of six feet.

Bobby looks desperately uncomfortable in what are surely someone else's clothes. The neck on his white dress shirt is too tight, so he's left it unbuttoned behind his sloppily knotted tie, while his pant cuffs hang onto his shoes. Likely he's not the only Jordan to have had assistance dressing today. "Been a while, huh? How ya doing?"

One might imagine I despise the entire Jordan clan, but I don't. Mr. Jordan is a jovial old soul. I'm embarrassed on the rare occasion I bump into Teddy (things went a bit too far too fast during our brief courtship) (before completely going sideways, I mean), but I don't hold any animosity and he's always pleasant. Bobby's my favorite—he's a genuinely nice person, and I wish I could have spent more time with him way back when. He's always been kind. After the carnage known as the Fourth of July at Steeplechase, Bobby was the first to find a steak for my eye before he whisked Jack away. He's good people. (John-John, I can take or leave.)

I tell Bobby, "I'd be better if we weren't here for my best friend's husband's funeral."

He clinks his beer against the glass of chardonnay I've been carrying but haven't touched. "Word." He takes a sip and the dense foam gets caught on his upper lip.

"You've got a little . . ." I point to my lip.

Bobby swipes at his mouth with the back of his wrist and I laugh because it's the same unaffected gesture he'd have made twenty years ago. "Wait, that called for a napkin, didn't it?" He begins to look around at the crowd in the other room. "Shit, did my dad see me do that?"

"No one's paying attention to us in here." I lean in to stage-whisper, "Don't worry, I won't tell on you."

"Kool and the Gang." He takes another pull on his beer. "Hey, how come you're not drinking your wine? It's bad luck not to take a sip after you toast."

"Not into wine today, I guess. Tastes bitter."

"Wait here."

He sets down his glass and trots off to the bar. A minute or so later, he returns with a highball filled with a creamy, iced concoction. "This is what I serve when people seem sad. I call it a Jordan Almond. Didn't have crushed nuts for the rim, so you'll have to pretend they're there. Now we'll toast again and then you won't have bad luck."

I taste the blended drink, which is really more of an alcoholic Frappuccino. There are coffee undertones from the Kahlua and the rich, nuttiness of actual almonds from the Amaretto. Between the sugar and the alcohol, it feels like a hug in a glass.

"This is delectable," I tell him.

"I normally hide some lychee nuts in there, too. Good source of vitamin C and they add a real nice perfume to the whole thing," he says. "I don't tell anyone I put 'em in because they'd just argue. They don't know what's good."

He and I chat about his adventures over the past few years. Seems like he's been everywhere, even the beach I'm dying to see in Little Cayman. Said it's one of his favorite places in the world.

Sigh.

Anxious for more travel-by-proxy, I ask, "Where are you off to next?" envisioning some new, exotic locale.

He sets down his beer and begins to unbutton his shirtsleeves, rolling back the cuffs, as though he's ready to really dig into our conversation. He was the best listener years ago, which worked well when I was such a talker. I notice he already ditched the sport coat after the service and figure it's only a matter of time before the tie comes off, too. I always did appreciate his sincerity.

He tells me, "I was in Nantucket when I heard about Trip. Gotta be honest, his death hit me pretty hard. We hadn't met more than a dozen times and we weren't best buds or anything. But something about him going out like that really made me reassess."

I wrap a napkin around my glass to catch the condensation. "How so?"

"Well, there I was, doing my regular summer share house, working my bartending job, having a good time, like ya do."

I smile. "Like ya do," I repeat.

"Then here's this guy on the screen and I'm all, '*I know him.*' See, the networks are covering the story all over the place about his plane going down. Like, he *mattered.* His death was important enough to break into the baseball game. The Red Sox. On a Boston station. Trust me, that's a big deal. So Trip dies, and he leaves so much behind—a wife and an industry and a home like this. He created this whole legacy, you know? Even though the both of us were close to the same age, he had, like, a *permanence* about his life."

Now that the napkin's damp, I begin to roll little bits between my thumb and forefinger. "There isn't a permanence about yours?"

Bobby sighs and begins to pick at a loose thread on his pants. I see that it's hard for him to sit still. Know the feeling. "Nah, not in any kind of way. I thought, '*I'm not tethered to anything.*' Being unattached always made me so happy, up until Trip's passing. Didn't know what else to do, so I packed up all my shit and came back here. Not planning to return to Nantucket this summer, and I'm not sure what's next. Staying with Teddy and Terry until I figure it out. Being footloose has been the plan ever since I got done with college."

I touch his knee briefly. "Not to interrupt, but did you ever actually graduate?"

"Yeah. With a 3.85, not that anyone believes me. The family was going through some stuff back then, so I didn't want 'em all having to come out to Cali just to see me in a cap and gown. Should have, though, 'cause I've never heard the end of it."

"What was your major?"

"Chemical engineering. That's why I'm a great mixologist."

I'm surprised to hear this. Last I knew he was majoring in General Studies. "I had no idea! Quite impressive."

He waves me off. "Eh, it's not. Originally I wanted to be a chemical engineer so I could make my own drugs. Didn't. But could have."

We both laugh. "I miss being twenty-two," I admit.

Bobby sighs. "Yeah, but I'm perpetually twenty-two and that's no great shakes, either. That's why Trip dying hit me so hard. Makes me wonder if I didn't miss something in my life of no house, no kids, no big job, no obligations."

I take another sip of my Jordan Almond. "Houses and obligations and jobs are overrated."

Bobby tilts his head and looks at me. I'd forgotten he has the same multicolor-eye thing as Jack. The gold and green and blue all swirl together in a crazy tapestry of color. "How so?"

Bobby was always good people, and this conversation reconfirms it. He's so guileless and without judgment or agenda that I find myself opening up to him, letting the real Kitty shine through all the exaggerated PTO President, SecretSquash, Super Mom veneers.

"Consider yourself lucky that you didn't get sucked into the matrix, Bob. Growing up on these towns along the lake, well, you know. You get what it was like here. We had expectations of what our lives should be like as adults. We're the first generation who hasn't actually done better than their parents and that's . . . hard to swallow." I wad up more napkin bits as I make this admission.

He looks at me intently. "Hard to swallow how?"

"For example, my husband and I didn't want the crummy little bungalow in our price range. We wanted the nice five-bedroom place like our folks had. Actually, better than our folks had. Felt like we deserved it because it's what everyone else has. So we overextended ourselves in order to keep up with our peer group and now I live in constant fear that it's all going to come crashing down."

I glance down at the growing pile of shards on the floor.

"Whoa," I say lightly, trying to lessen the impact of the truth I've just spoken. "Not sure I've ever said any of that out loud. This drink must contain truth serum or something."

What's going on with me? I haven't even shared these thoughts with Betsy. Why am I comfortable enough to say this now? Is it that Bobby's basically a big kid, so he feels nonthreatening?

Bobby's still intent on speaking seriously. "So you don't own your stuff. Your stuff owns you?"

"Exactly." As we talk, I can feel my chest start to loosen, like my lungs aren't being pinched in a vise quite so firmly. "You have to keep up around here or you'll be a social pariah. God forbid you don't have the best car or house or washer and dryer."

His eyes grow wide and I notice that tiny splotch of gray on the lowest part of his right iris. He used to call it his "paint spill." "You don't really compete over washing machines, right? That's nuts."

I nod, remembering how much traction I gained when everyone saw my laundry room for the first time. "Believe it. Everything's so competitive, even parenting. No, *especially* parenting. I mean, we go into debt to make sure our Littles have the right backpack, the right shoes, the right jeans, because if they don't, they'll be bullied."

Bobby finally removes his tie and shoves it in his pocket, the end flap still sticking out. The effect is that of his shirt blowing a raspberry. Did I not totally call it? "That sucks. I think we had it easier growing up."

"My God, yes, because we didn't have the online component. Our bad behavior never ended up on Reddit or BuzzFeed or YouTube. Thing is, the nature of bullying has changed, too. Your kid isn't safe anywhere. Used to be if someone didn't like you at school, you go home, they can't reach you. With social media, your kid can be harassed twenty-four-seven, across a dozen different platforms. The flip side is your child might *be* the bully, and a whole lot of parents are too involved trying to make enough money to buy the right backpack, shoes, and jeans to be around to keep that behavior in check."

I think about Brooke's daughter, Avery, who's already showing signs of turning Mean Girl. I worry for Kassie.

Listening intently, Bobby nods. "And then there's the whole privacy thing, right?"

I drain my drink and fight the urge to lick the froth off the sides of the glass. "What do you mean?"

"I meet people all the time when I'm tending bar. People talk to me like I'm a priest or hairdresser or something. Having a whole bar between us makes them feel safe. So they tell me about their lives. Most folks out there are well meaning, but they're not content with just making sure their kids have needs met. They gotta put it all online. I know, because they show me their Facebook pages."

I swallow, my throat suddenly very dry.

He goes on. "Like, it's not enough to bring their kids to meet Mickey Mouse at Disneyland. They have to take a billion pictures, put 'em all over the Internet, and rub the vacation in everyone's faces. I gotta wonder, at what point does the trip stop being about you and your family and start being about showing off to the rest of your timeline? It's weird. That's why I don't do social media. Not my thing. Mostly I use the Internet for Skype and checking snow reports. I do like where they put captions on pictures of cats, too. My favorite is the one where the cat's in a suit, all, *'I should buy a boat.'* He's holding a newspaper. Cracks me up."

I clear my throat. "Bobby, you know I have an online presence."

"Yeah, but you post about vegetables and stuff, right? You're not making documentaries of yourself, selling your life off to the highest bidder, one picture at a time. You wouldn't plaster your veggie site with shots of your kids because there are too many pervs out there living in their mom's basement." He stops himself. "Wait . . . shit. I currently live in a basement. You know what I mean."

I'm afraid I do know what he means.

Bobby's addressed a topic that I've preferred not to examine too closely. I was vehement about never publishing photos of the Littles online. But then I made this amazing fondant-covered Cowboy and Indian carrot cake for Kord's tenth birthday and he was so cute in his fringed leather vest and ten-gallon hat that I broke my own rule and posted the shot. My page views jumped exponentially, so once in a while after that, I'd let through the occasional snapshot until it became a regular thing.

I'll be honest—I didn't hate the positive feedback. I liked having people recognize my labors and tell me I was good at something. Parenting is so hard sometimes, so thankless, that it's nice to have the effort appreciated.

While I'd never, ever embarrass the Littles by sharing their potty training stories or showing them, say, having a bath, I wonder if I haven't done them a disservice by allowing my pride to overrule my better judgment and letting their images be seen at all?

Or is just being referred to as a "Little" in and of itself fodder for bullies?

By turning SecretSquash into more of a lifestyle blog, I've definitely improved our day-to-day existence. Yet in so doing, I wonder if I've sold out somehow. Is it possible that Dr. K has grown distant because I've been too busy trying to document a perfect life, rather than actually live it?

Considering this possibility gives me a shooting pain in my temples. I press down on the area with my fingertips to see if that relieves some of the pressure.

"You okay?" Bobby asks.

I'm done spilling my guts for now, so instead of explaining, I say, "Changes in the weather can make my head ache."

He stands, ready to spring into action, as always the gentleman. "Want me to find an aspirin for you?"

I grab my abandoned wineglass, gesturing for him to sit. "I'll try this medicine first." This time, the wine doesn't taste so bitter.

"Good call."

We sit quietly, each of us working on our respective drinks.

Bobby breaks the silence that has yet to grow awkward. "I'm proud of you and Jack. If there ever was a time to put your differences behind you, today's that day."

I nod, saying nothing about our horrible scene on the sidewalk. But we got past it, and that's what's important. Bobby lowers his voice and moves in closer as though he's about to confide in me, but I don't feel tense like I did that time Trip hit on me. Instead, I feel comforted and familiar, pleased that he wants to reveal some small, private truth.

Bobby says, "I gotta be honest—you and Jack are a lot alike."

I snort into the chardonnay. "We couldn't be more different," I argue.

"I've always said it and you never agree, but that doesn't mean I'm wrong. You have problems because you're both really strong willed, you know? You're both so sure you're in the right that you likely come away from situations with wildly different perspectives. You say black, she says white, and then you fight to the death over something that's actually gray. You ought to compare notes someday. I bet what you think you hear is way different from what's actually said, and vice versa. Come to terms with that and you two might be friends yet." He drains his beer and sets the glass on the coffee table. A waiter immediately squires away the empty.

"I need one of those guys at my house," I quip in lieu of telling him why he's deluded. He's too nice for me to argue with now. Before I can say anything else, Bobby glances down at my watch.

"Whoa, is that the time? We've gotta get going soon. Dinner in the city with the fam! Gotta motor. Good seeing you again, Kitty. Take care of yourself."

"And I should take care of Betsy, too," I say.

"And of yourself," he repeats. "Catch you on the flippity-flop."

He leaves and I'm left alone with the sound of the rain, which isn't loud enough to drown out my thoughts. I feel like I've just been on a therapist's couch for an hour, full of new information and insights demanding my attention, whether or not I want to deal with them.

Jack was very close with her brother Bobby when we lived together, but she never gave him enough credit. She didn't value his kind of intelligence. She never grasped that there's more to being smart than using SAT words. I remember once when we were with him over October break, she was telling him about something in the news and it was clear he needed a second to process. He asked her a question to clarify and she got frustrated and snapped, "I can explain it to you, but I can't understand it for you." The look on his face—so hurt. He laughed and shook it off, but I could tell he was bothered.

Whether it was his intention or not, Bobby brought up an awful lot of what's not quite right in my life. I realize I have some areas to address once Dr. K comes home. We can't continue on our current course and we need to figure out how to navigate.

Maybe Trip wasn't the only one on the cusp of making changes.

Crap.

While sitting here with Bobby, I forgot about the whole *thing* for a second.

There are so many people in this house right now, celebrating Trip's life. I was on board yesterday, but now I'm simply angry. He wasn't what he seemed. Period. I can deny all I want, but if I'm really honest with myself, I know he was hitting on me, because he did it so many times before. I can whitewash the behavior by claiming he was flirty, but he wasn't. A part of me was always flattered to hold that kind of power, that he'd absolutely be willing if I ever complied.

How do you do that to your wife? The person who stood beside you as you built your empire?

I wonder, did Betsy even really *want* to leave CFG? Or was she forced out by those who negated her contributions because she was considered "the wife"?

Maybe Betsy founded W3 for the same reasons I created Secret-Squash, only on a much grander level. Personally, I was content where I was. I'd have happily stayed to manage the dental practice forever—I mean, I practically grew up in that building. Mum was always running over there to help Dr. Daddy. Kelly and I would often do our homework in the lobby, just to spend time with our parents between patients. I hung out enough that I eventually learned how to do everything—file charts, generate bills, answer the phone. If I could be a fine helper at fourteen, I definitely could have continued to manage everything long-term as an adult.

I still could, actually.

Perhaps that's the answer to a lot of our problems.

If I were to take over Cookie's job, we wouldn't have to pay her salary anymore. That'd be a relief, considering what she makes an hour. If I managed the office, I could still be a mom and run the kids to practice and take care of the house. I'd probably have to lose the blog, but that might be a good idea as the Littles get older. Maybe I can reclaim our privacy while forging newer and stronger bonds with Dr. K.

No, wait, *Ken*. Form new bonds with Ken.

This is a capital idea. I'm calling him right now.

I reach in my bag for my phone, but before I can dial, lightning strikes out front and the party is thrown into chaos. A massive tree comes down outside and blocks off the whole driveway.

I immediately offer my assistance in organizing the cleanup, but Betsy manages the whole show, delegating like a boss. So I decide to slip upstairs to the end of the hall by the portrait gallery to make my call. This is where it's the most quiet, so I'll actually be able to hear my husband when we talk.

I wonder if I haven't *really heard him* for a while now.

I dial but he doesn't answer, so I leave a message outlining my thoughts. Ken will love this idea, especially as strapped as we are. Losing that salary would be such a boot off of our necks. Cookie will have to understand that this is a business decision.

And if she doesn't?

Well, I can't worry about her.

I gaze up at all the portraits on the wall. I try to imagine coming from the kind of family where everyone's commemorated in oil paint. Sure, Dr. Daddy did well, but he didn't come from a dynasty like the Chandlers. Grand-pappy was a farmer, which is likely why my dad developed such a solid work ethic. None of Trip's forefathers look like they ever lifted anything heavier than a gin martini their whole lives. Yet they are stern and formidable in their own ways, each one perched behind a massive desk, or seated in a stiff chair.

But not Trip. Nope.

He's standing there on a yacht, breeze ruffling his hair, gazing out at the water like he owns the whole damn world and everything in it. I feel guilty having such murderous thoughts over a man who's already dead. Yet I can't go back downstairs right now because the only thing anyone's talking about is what a swell guy he was. Such lies.

Maybe it's the wine and the boozy Frappuccino talking, because I can't help but look at his portrait and say, "Rest in peace, mother-flipper. Rest in peace."

Jack emerges from the shadows behind me, and I almost jump out of my skin, both shocked and humiliated.

Oh, yeah, I need *this*. Now I'm going to get a lecture from the Great Jack Jordan over how I shouldn't be so disrespectful and how I'm a terrible person and—

"I think the bastard's still alive. You and I need to talk."

CHAPTER FOURTEEN

Jack

North Shore, Illinois
Wednesday

"This is your daily driver? This colossus? Are you transporting troops to the front line? Bringing relief supplies to South Sudan?"

Kitty tightens her jaw in response, glaring straight ahead. I'm not harassing her; I'm genuinely curious. The Escalade is the largest nonarmored personnel carrier I've seen.

I try to better explain myself. "I've been in smaller Humvees. What's the MPG? Six on the highway, five in the city?"

Her knuckles whiten as she clutches the steering wheel of the enormous land beast. In a clipped tone, she replies, "Thirty minutes ago when you yanked me into that bedroom at Steeplechase, you swore we could put aside our differences to figure out what happened to Trip. *We must pool our resources, Carricoe,*' you said. *'It's imperative we share what we each know. We have to team up to track him down,*' you said. *'For Sars,*' you said. You promised on our best friend's life to behave. You can't keep a promise for half a flipping hour? For Betsy? I knew I shouldn't have agreed to this because you're never going to change."

Oh, the Martyred Saint Kitty Carricoe. Such a victim. Do her shoulders ache from lugging that heavy wooden cross around all day? I wonder. I keep my eyes fixed on the horizon in order to not roll them.

Keeping Sars top of mind, I offer a mild response instead. "That's where you're wrong. I absolutely did not break my promise. I've neither assaulted your character nor belittled your life. *That* was our deal; I'm sticking to it. Did I say, *'You are anally raping the environment and perpetrating the spilling of blood for oil in this vehicle?'* No, regardless of how true that might be. Or did I say, *'How important must you feel driving around in a car that costs a hundred times the GNI of Micronesia?'* While a valid point, again, I did not verbalize it."

Crickets.

I continue. "I was simply stating the fact that this is a very large car. The square footage is greater than the bedsit I rented in Baghdad. That's all. Big car. Small apartment. I was making pleasant small talk."

Kitty dodges the storm-fallen limbs on the streets of North Shore with a fair amount of aplomb, considering the girth on this whale of an automobile. The Escalade is surprisingly sprightly. Nimble. This vehicle is Hyacinth Hippo, the ballerina en pointe from *Fantasia*, the convergence of grace and bulk and style.

She says, "No, you were posing a story problem. *'How many cubic inches of smug can Jack Jordan pack into one conversation—GNI? Bedsit? Micronesia?* Really?—*before Kitty Kord Carricoe presses the ejector button on the passenger seat? Solve for x.'"*

I crane my neck for a better look at the dashboard, which has more lights and indicators than that of an old WWII Tiger Moth cockpit. I'm suddenly, irrefutably impressed with the advances in the American automotive industry. Way to go, USA! When did all this technology come onto the marketplace? I've been away from the States for too long; I feel I've missed everything. "This behemoth has ejection seats like the F-14?"

Kitty shoves a hank of her damp blond hair behind her ears. We were both drenched while running from the house to her Space Shuttle, which she'd left on the street because it won't fit under the archway to Steeplechase's parking pad. Our respective exits were staggered to escape detection. I purposely lingered to make arrangements with one of Sars's staffers regarding a drop-off for my rental car once the main gate's unblocked. Kitty and I agreed to spare Sars any hint of us colluding. Until we have concrete proof Trip is alive, our operation is covert. Clandestine. We're headed to Command Central, also known as Kitty's house.

Kitty says, "Soooo sorry now that I didn't spring for the Sarcasm Detector along with the Surround Vision, Power-Folding Third Row, and In-Dash DVD System. BTW, only you would reference some stupid plane, when everyone else would talk about that awesome part in the James Bond movie." More to herself than to me, she mutters, "FYI? This is why people thought you were weird in college."

I'd defend myself, but she might not be wrong here.

Still, a lack of ejection device is disappointing. And yet the vehicle started without benefit of key and the heated seat is neatly warming my rain-soaked clothing, so I'm pleasantly surprised with Detroit's finest. I mean backup cameras and—

"Did you say there's an In-Dash DVD player? Meaning one could watch a movie in here? Like on a 747?" I ask.

What a boon that would have been back in Saint Louis when we used to take road trips in my mother's Country Squire station wagon, eighteen feet long and sided in more fake wood paneling than your average rumpus room. Our only entertainment was listening to John Denver on the cassette player and making up games that somehow all culminated in punching John-John. At the beginning of our ten-hour pilgrimage to see Mimi and Poppy, my mother would be uncharacteristically cheerful and enthusiastic, but by the time we passed the first HoJo, the temperature in the car would drop, while her shoulders would ride up by her ears from tension, and she'd clutch the wheel like . . . well, a lot like Kitty right now.

Good times.

Kitty takes a right turn with enthusiasm, causing the tires to make noise in protest. "Relentless. You are flipping relentless. You have no clue what it's like to drive downstate for meets and matches and scrimmages and games because procreation is far too pedestrian for the Girl O' War. Well, here's a newsflash for you—children eventually get bored in the car, no matter how much you engage them. Their attention spans are only so long. To keep them from going rogue or pounding on one another like caged beasts, sometimes I let them watch a movie. For safety. And sanity. So, please enough with the sanctimony."

"Stop the car," I say. "Now."

In response, she brings the car to a halt, at no point hydroplaning on the rain-slicked streets. Again, I'm captivated. The only auto I ever owned was Teddy's beige 1989 Honda Prelude. We called it the Honda Quaalude, as there was nothing exciting about it.

"New deal," I say, making a concerted effort to not escalate. "You are going to cease the display of raging narcissism, assuming that everything I say is somehow meant to disparage. Let me be clear. I. Am. Not. Slamming. You. Not today, anyway. You can't take everything so personally. We have to put our petty bullshit aside, at least for now. When we're done and when we have resolution, we can hate each other again and you can resume writing your fake book reviews."

Although the rain's pelting the car with drops the size of silver dollars, we're so well soundproofed that I can hear her catch her breath. "How did you—"

"Water under the bridge. Today is our tabula rasa. As part of this fresh start, I pledge to better explain myself so there's no opportunity for misinterpretation."

Kitty loosens her death grip on the wheel ever so slightly. I continue. "For example, when I asked you about the DVD player, I wasn't condemning your parenting skills, despite previous interactions where this may well have been the case. I've baited you in the past. I own that. However, today I was contemplating how much better family vacations would have been had we access to entertainment. The caged beasts? Were us. My comments weren't about you, Kitty. Because it's not always all about you. So, let's start over. Please. For Sars."

"Sure thing," she says, now-loosened fingers tapping out a beat on the steering wheel. Is that real wood I spy? Polished cherry? Elm, perhaps? Wait, is the leather portion *heated*, too? My God, is this car real life?

Kitty nods, more to herself than to me. "We'll begin again, turn over a new leaf. Start all flipping over. We'll be two caterpillars busting out of our cocoons, morphing into Monarch butterflies."

"Exactly! I'm glad you've decided to be reasonable."

"Of course. I'm well-known for being a reasonable person. People see me and say, *'That Kitty Carricoe is one reasonable gal.'* And I'll begin to be reasonable right here, right now, as soon as you apologize for calling me a raging narcissist. Because couching an insult in a pledge to move forward? That is HORSE PUCKEY."

"You're misunderstanding me yet again. I didn't say *you* were a raging narcissist. I said you were *displaying* raging narcissism. Two entirely divergent meanings."

"There is no difference," she says, through clenched teeth.

"Of course there's a difference. There's a marked difference," I reply. "The difference is subtle, but crucial. Nuanced. Let's deconstruct the semiotics of my statement—"

Kitty begins to violently poke at the wood-grained panel between us.

"What are you doing?"

She stabs some more. "I'm looking for a hidden ejector button because, *semiotics.*"

"Wait," I say, piecing together the possible reasons behind her reaction. "Is this an instance where I should simply apologize rather than detail why the evidence will eventually reveal the validity of my position?"

Kitty turns to fully face me, hugging her arms across her damp chest, the cords in her neck taut as guitar strings. "Ding, ding, ding."

"Oh. Then . . ."

Ugh, I'm going to have to prostrate myself in order to convince her. Take one for the team, no matter how unjustified, so I cross my fingers behind my back. I don't have to mean these words; she just has to believe I mean them if we're to help Sars.

Oh, *Sars.*

The image of meeting her for the first time is still crystal clear. There she is, all skinny limbs and owlish glasses, leading me across the street, intent on being my friend no matter what. I've never felt maternal stirrings, but something about those narrow shoulders and beribboned braids touches me and I feel doubly protective of her. I said I'd do whatever it took to help her, and apparently that pledge includes swallowing my considerable distaste now.

So I say, "I'm sorry, Kitty. I was wrong and I apologize."

Which doesn't feel as soul-crushing as I might have imagined.

Kitty must buy my apology, because she flips her blinker and pulls back out onto the road. What smooth yet responsive acceleration!

In the spirit of détente, I suggest, "We should create a code word. Something that will let the other know when we're tripping her trigger. We could, um, we could say . . ." I scan my mental Rolodex for the best word choice. Mayday? No, too obvious. Geronimo? Too campy, and possibly offensive to Native Americans. "Ah, I have it! We could say *pan-pan*, which is a maritime and aviation signal for urgency when repeated three—"

"*Semiotics*," Kitty interrupts. "We'll say *semiotics* when the other person is making us feel stabby. Once is plenty. That work for you?"

Semiotics is simple, elegant, and concise. I concur. "Semiotics it is."

"Aces."

In silence, we pull down what I presume is Kitty's block. The homes are huge, but seem comically incongruous to the size and shape of the respective lots. This street reminds me of when our first in a series of obese Labs used to curl up on Tom Kitten's cat bed. Sarge would cram every ounce of his bulk into that tiny square of cushion, rendering himself into a canine muffin top. Same effect is happening in this neighborhood— there's not a square inch of real estate not spilling over with over- blown new construction. When I lived in the city after college, I had a larger front yard at my apartment building and more space between my complex and the property next door. Why surround such stately homes with so little land? If Teddy was with us, he'd be in a pique of aesthetic displeasure.

Probably not an opinion I should share with Kitty.

Instead, I offer a positive affirmation. "These beautiful houses have such tidy yards. Landscaping can't cost much with so little grass to mow."

Kitty scowls. "Semiotics."

Wait a damn minute, how did that statement merit a *semiotics*? I attempt to clarify. "I was merely stating that in terms of square footage to hourly rate—"

"Semi. Otics."

I hold up my hands in surrender. "I give up. We'll just ride in awkward silence." And undeniable comfort.

We pull up to a sprawling home with a steep roof, highlighted with peaks and arches and gray timber over white stucco, so expanded and overblown that there's room for only a couple of flowering bushes before the whole thing bleeds onto the sidewalk. As we pull down the drive back to the garage, I note that the house spans the depth of the property. At Steeplechase, one doesn't get a sense for the magnitude of the home because the dwelling is proportional to the amount of land and trees around it. Here, the house is a sore thumb hulking over a tiny parcel, meant for something cozy, like the original bungalows and small ranches.

Kitty expertly navigates into the garage while I hold my breath, sure she's going to clip a side-view mirror. Oh, my God—the mirrors fold!

"We're here," she announces. "Brace yourself for my mother-in-law, Nana Baba. She's *the worst.*"

"In what respect?"

Kitty exhales with such vigor she fogs a portion of the windshield. I bet this car neatly handles interior condensation. "Long story."

I follow Kitty through a garage like I've never seen before. Even Teddy would be impressed. Never has it occurred to me that a garage could be more than just a place to disassemble a dirt bike, or house hundreds of old newspapers, oily rags, and paint cans.

Instead of poured concrete, rife with oil stains, these floors are finished with a gleaming, glinting material that resembles a granite countertop. There's a massive wall of shelves, each containing an identically sized Rubbermaid tote, all with detailed labels such as GREAT ROOM CHRISTMAS VILLAGE DECOR, PART I OF III. Another wall is covered entirely by pegboard. Rakes, hoes, shovels, and clippers are all impeccably hung Tetris-style. Other than the five bikes neatly tucked into a rack in the corner next to a pristine lawn mower, there's not a single item that isn't hung or boxed. The garage windows are not only spotless, with nary a spider carcass in sight, but adorned with curtains in a lightweight fabric. And, instead of reeking of gasoline, the space is lightly fragranced by . . . the holidays?

"Am I having a stroke, or do I smell Christmas in here?" I ask.

Kitty digs for her keys and says, "Peppermint's a natural rodent repellent. Every couple of weeks, I soak cotton balls in peppermint oil and then strategically stash them throughout the garage."

I announce, "Kitty, I'm about to say something flattering, so please accept the compliment at face value. We clear?"

Not meeting my eye, she nods curtly.

"Okay. The peppermint trick is really clever. Also, I could live in your garage."

Kitty stops in her tracks and scans my face for mockery. Sensing none, she says, "Thank you. I don't like chaos, so I work hard to keep my home clean and organized." She unlocks the door and we step out of the garage and into a stunning space with lots of white wood and map-covered walls. "Attractive kitchen, too," I say.

"This is the mudroom."

"I don't know what that means."

Before she can reply, Kitty is broadsided by a small pink and yellow plaid cannonball that's come flying around the corner. "Mommy!! You're home! Yay! Nana Baba said to be nice to you because you're sad."

Kitty picks up her daughter with one deft motion and hugs her close, burying her face in her daughter's hair. "I am sad, sweetie, so thank you. Compassion is one of the Always Always values we talked about, remember?"

Kassie nods.

"So you are a kind little girl to worry about someone else's feelings and I'm proud of you. Very good listening! Now, Kassie, I want to introduce you to an old . . ."

Kitty pauses, clearly struggling for the right word to define our relationship.

"Nemesis? Foe? Antagonist?" I offer.

"Friend," Kitty says with some decisiveness. Behind Kassie, she mouths, "She's eight," and vehemently shakes her head.

"Semiotic?" I confirm.

"You think?" she replies. Gently, she places her little girl back on the ground. "Kassie, please say hello to my old friend. Please call her Miss Jack. We went to college together. She's also very sad today so can you help me give her an extra special welcome to our home?"

Kassie throws a small but surprisingly clean hand up at me. "Pleased to meetcha, Miss Jack! How come you have a boy's name?"

"Because my mother had an unhealthy obsession with a dead president," I reply.

"Did I mention my daughter is *eight*?" Kitty asks pointedly.

I haven't had much interaction with children since I was one myself, but I see that speaking to them as though they're adults is not the right call. I quickly adjust. "My full name is Jacqueline." I kneel down. Over many years of speaking to sources, I've learned that interactions are always more positive when the other person's eyes are parallel with my own, rising or lowering myself depending on their level. "You know what's hard to spell? *Jacqueline*. It's J-A-C-Q- Wait a minute, Q? Who puts a Q in a name? So I shortened it to Jack."

"Ha! That's why I'm called Kassie. There's a lotta letters in Kassandra. Too many, if you ask me. Same with my mom. She's K-A-T-H-E-R-I-N-E, but that's sooooo long, so she's Kitty. I have a friend named Bo. Two letters! He's very lucky."

"Sounds like it," I agree.

She looks at me long and hard, taking in every bit of my face, coming in so close her forehead touches mine. Finally, she says, "Your eyes are funny colored," and touches my orbital bone.

"Funny ha-ha or funny weird?" I ask.

"You're funny," Kassie giggles. She scrunches her shoulders and covers her mouth with her hand as she laughs. Then she throws one hand on her hip and declares, "I am going to be your friend, Miss J-A-C-K."

I stand back up. "Hear that, Kitty? Kassie is going to be my friend."

Kitty pets her daughter's long corn-silk locks before planting a kiss on her temple. "Can you do me a big, big favor and go tell your Baba and your brothers that I'm home?"

Kassie is doing a little jig around the room, finding it impossible to stay in one spot. I remember how I could never hold still at her age, either. (When do I grow out of that stage? I wonder.) She exclaims, "Yes! Are we all going to play a board game? I'm thinking . . . Trouble or Sorry."

I tell Kassie, "Your mom and I are trying to avoid anything to do with Trouble or Sorry. Do you have Candyland?"

Kassie shakes her head, hair flying out in all directions. "We don't have Candyland. Ask me why. Please, please! Ask me why."

"Okay, why?"

Kassie's already cracking herself up before she can say, "Because my mom can't hide broccoli in candy!"

"She's said this before?" I ask.

"Once or twice," Kitty replies. But instead of growing taciturn like my mother would when the boys and I would tell our Little Johnny jokes over and over, Kitty gives her daughter a big squeeze and says, "And it's hilarious every time! My turn. Knock, knock, Kassie."

"Who's there?"

"Olive."

"Olive who?"

Kitty yells, "Olive you and I don't care who knows it!"

Kassie squeals with fresh delight and there's more hugging and tickling. As I observe their unabashed mutual affection, I'm hard-pressed to recall a single time when my own mother responded similarly. When we'd get too riled up for her liking, she'd lock herself away in my parents' bedroom, Tom Kitten in tow.

Collecting herself, Kassie asks, "You got any jokes, Miss Jack?"

"Sure. How about this? There are two muffins in an oven." I glance at Kitty and say, "No, wait, there are two *zucchini* muffins in the oven. One zucchini muffin turns to the other zucchini muffin and says, 'Whew, it's hot in here.' And the other zucchini muffin says, 'Oh my God, a talking zucchini muffin!'"

Kassie reacts as though I'm the unholy love child of Jerry Seinfeld, George Carlin, and Lisa Lampanelli, rolling with laughter as she dances around the room. She's still sputtering when Kitty says, "Eight-year-olds are the most appreciative audience on the planet. Fact. Anyway, sweetie, I'm so sorry but Miss Jack and I have some work to do. We'd love to have you join us, but we're going to talk about really boring topics so I bet you'd hate it."

"Like grown-up lady stuff when you talk to Miss Ashley?"

"Yes, just like that."

"Blech. No, thank you, please." Kassie scratches her head as though in thought. "I'm going to find Nana Baba and tell her that funny joke."

"Good idea," Kitty replies. "I'm sure she'll love it."

"Will Miss Jack tell me another joke before bed?"

I glance over at Kitty, but I can't read her expression.

"Depends," I reply. "Do you like elephant jokes?"

With deadpan delivery, she replies, "I don't like them . . . *I live for them!*"

"Then it's a date," I reply.

"Okay, then. 'Bye, new friend Miss Jack!" She scampers off into the recesses of the home. As she propels herself up the stairs, I can hear her exclaim, "Zucchini muffins!" and I can't hide my grin.

"Stop smirking, *Bouvier*. She's eight. She's still at the age where she likes everyone." But she says this without rancor. "Anyway, let's talk in here."

I follow her out of the mudroom and to the kitchen proper. I sit at an old wooden table, heaped with bowls full of lemons. Why so many lemons? Is Kitty starting a lemonade stand? And what is it about women and kitchens? Mrs. Martin used to have a sign that read No Matter Where I Serve My Guests, It Seems They Like My Kitchen Best. Is kitchen-gathering a portion of the girl code I never learned? My brothers and I always headed as far away from the kitchen as possible because the chairs weren't as comfortable as the couch, and also because no one wanted to accidentally be crushed in a landslide of dirty dishes.

"Let me change out of these wet clothes and check in with my husband. Hopefully I'll catch him before he goes out to dinner," Kitty says as she trots down the hall. "Back in two shakes. Stay right there. Mean it. Don't go anywhere."

By the time I reply, "Where would I go?" she's already upstairs.

．．．．

"Where the hell are you, Bouvier?"

Kord, Konnor, and I are all gathered in rocking gaming seats in front of the gigantic television in the basement. After ten minutes of waiting, I couldn't resist the siren song of what sounded like action.

"Mom, Miss Jack's down here with us!" Kord, the elder son, calls. Kitty hustles down the basement stairs. "She's KILLING IT on *Madden NFL*! How come you never brought her over before?"

"Hey, Mom!" Konnor says, brightening when he sees his mother. "You want a turn?"

Kitty bends down to fix Konnor's wrinkled collar. "Love to, but not now, kiddo. Miss Jack and I have some business to discuss upstairs. But don't forget, you still owe me a rematch."

"Mom's almost as good as you are," Kord tells me.

"You play *Madden 15*, Kitty?" I ask. I'm surprised to hear she joins in her children's games. My mother would always retreat when we broke out the Atari. She said the electronic beeps gave her a migraine.

"I have many talents," Kitty replies lightly. "Boys, did Baba give you dinner yet?"

"Yeah, we ate around five o'clock," Kord replies, gaze fixed on the game.

Kitty places a finger to her ear. "Beg pardon?"

Kord shoots her an apologetic grin. "*Yes*. Sorry, Mom, *yes*. We had the spinach lasagna."

As they all interact with one another, with their blond hair, toothy grins, and patrician features, the three of them look like a page ripped out of the JCPenney catalog.

"That's great, sweetie!" She places a conspiratorial hand on his shoulder and leans in close. "So, what'd you really eat?"

"Busted!" Konnor said in the same kind of smug, you're-gonna-get-it tone I thought emanated exclusively from John-John.

"Frozen pizza. But I split a bag of spring mix salad with Kassie and Konnor," he says.

"How many colors?" Kitty asks.

Kord raises four fingers, eyes back on the game. "I added those sliced mushrooms, plus red peppers, black olives, and pepperoncini."

Wow. Only under threat of martial law would my brothers or I consume anything healthy at that age.

Kitty holds out her palm. "Up top, my man." Kord rewards her with a high five. She returns her attention to Konnor. "As for you, don't pretend you weren't playing *Medal of Honor: Airborne* while I was out. Rated T for Teen means *not you*, my twelve-year-old friend."

Konnor's mouth hangs open. "How did you . . ."

"I'm on top of everything that happens under this roof. Okay, guys, you have fun! We'll be upstairs if you need anything. Jack, shall we?" She so handily makes this order sound so much like a request that I find myself complying without argument. Who'd have guessed *Kitty* could be a commanding presence?

As we climb the basement stairs, I'm curious as to her methods. "How'd you know about the pizza and the video game? Nanny cams?"

Kitty's now dressed in an outfit similar to mine, hair pulled back in a loose bun. We look like those women in the tampon commercials, drinking wine with lunch. "Nothing that high-tech, I'm afraid. Just finely tuned MSP—Mom Sensory Perception. You see, Kord had an oil stain on his shirt from drippy pizza cheese and I saw crumbs on the counter. My spinach lasagna isn't greasy and doesn't contain cornmeal."

Wow. My mother would never have picked up on those clues. "Okay, then how'd you know about the younger one?" As a reporter, I'm trained to observe my surroundings, especially when embedded. With so much danger in the field, one uncalculated move could mean the difference between life and death. "I didn't notice a *Medal of Honor* game box sitting out anywhere."

Kitty tells me, "Motherhood is the ultimate game of high-stakes poker. You want to win, you have to know how to read your kids. You learn their tells and anticipate their next moves. For example, Konnor's cheeks were flushed. When I touched his collar, it felt damp, as though he'd recently been worked up about something. *Madden 15*'s a fine E for Everyone game, but doesn't provide that level of adrenaline rush, so I speculated he'd been playing *Medal of Honor.* That's our only Rated T for Teen game. On that hunch, I glanced at the shelf where we house the boxes and spotted open space between alphabetically arranged *Mario Kart* and *Minecraft.* Case closed."

· · · ·

Our tentative truce holds while we compare notes and form our plan of attack. Finding Ingrid is our first priority. "Here's how we play this— I'll ping my NSA contact who owes me an off-the-books favor. He can very quietly run the gamut from recording cell phone calls to tracing credit card activity on Ingrid and anyone in her family."

Kitty furrows her brow. "On a scale from one to ten, how legal is that?"

"A ten."

Kitty begins to chew on her lower lip, as though in thought. "Really? Because that sounds like something a super-villain would do."

"Oh. I reversed the numbers. One, definitely. Probably more like zero."

Without hesitation, Kitty says, "Big no. Big, fat, huge, screaming no."

"Kitty, do you want to help Sars or not? This would all be through unofficial channels, not part of the public record."

"Help Betsy, yes. End up in *Orange Is the New Black*, no. Look at this face. I would be the Piper character and I wouldn't have an ex-girlfriend there to protect me."

"Kitty, I see no other alternative."

Kitty's voice ratchets up a note. "Yeah, because you only see what you want to see. Tell me again why we can't go through official channels." Kitty begins to police up our dirty dinner plates. To give due credit, her spinach lasagna was superb. The roasted eggplant was an unexpected addition and the ricotta had a touch of something sweet— cinnamon, nutmeg? Her meal made me want to learn to cook. But just because she knows her way around a kitchen doesn't mean she understands the complexities of conducting an investigation.

"Kitty, a Fort Knox's worth of money is missing. A crime on this level had to involve more than a single person. We have no idea who else may have helped perpetrate the fraud. Dozens could have been on the take, paid to look the other way. Starting an official investigation could tip off Trip. I'm sure he's fled to a country without an extradition treaty. My suspicion is he's fled to someplace cushy and relatively easy for us to look for him, like Monaco, but if he finds out someone's on his trail, he could go deep undercover somewhere impossible to travel to, like Equatorial Guinea."

"*Where?*"

"It's a small country in Western Africa, south of Cameroon."

"Never heard of it."

"Exactly." While Kitty rinses our plates, I add, "I suppose you're also opposed to monitoring Ingrid's banking activity or hacking security cameras in her neighborhood?"

She bangs flatware into the dishwasher in response.

"Fine," I reply, growing frustrated at her rejection of each viable solution. "If you're not comfortable using modern, covert technology, we can go old school by interviewing associates and potential witnesses. We can stake out her domicile. But I'm afraid we'll inadvertently tip off Trip. Or, God forbid, Sars."

"A stakeout, Jordan? With cold cups of carry-out coffee, sub sandwiches, and us hiding behind an open newspaper in the front seat? That would be a fab way to approach the situation, if we lived in, say, 1976. Shall I start calling you KoJack now?"

My bonhomie dissipates with every obstacle Kitty throws in our path, but at least she's stopped calling me Bouvier. "Listen, I can always do this without you."

"Like I'm going to let you hog all the credit and be the big hero to Betsy? No. No way."

"Then what's *your* plan, Kitty? Forgive me if I sound dubious. I wasn't aware that you learned a lot about in-depth reporting on your, um . . . *squash Web site.*"

That was probably uncalled for.

Kitty bristles in response. "I guess if you had any friends, you'd be aware of the concept of"—she makes air quotes—"'social media.' It's 'media' for people who aren't 'socially retarded.'"

We hear a gasp from the doorway to the dining room, where Kassie stands in a long cotton nightgown, trembling with fury. "MOMMY, YOU SAID THE R-WORD! Not funny! Avery called Winston the r-word last week and I told her she was being hurtful. She didn't care, but *I do*. No one's supposed to use words on the Never Never list!!"

Kitty hustles over to Kassie and scoops her up, bringing her back to the table to sit in her lap. "Oh, honey, no. I'm so sorry, but you misunderstood me. Mommy didn't say the r-word in a way meant to be cruel. She was using the literal definition of retarded, which means slow or stunted."

Kassie thrusts out her chin, unconvinced. "You sounded hurtful."

"Sweetie, even though you heard what sounds like the exact same word, the intent is entirely—"

"You realize this discussion is the very essence of semiotics," I observe.

She barks, "Not helpful!" at me as she whisks Kassie upstairs to explain without benefit of my assistance.

While I wait for her return, I poke around the first floor. Doesn't seem to be enough furniture for all the square footage, but what do I know about decorating? I don't even have a bed in my Kabul apartment, just a thick mat for sleeping, a small desk, and a few changes of clothing. I no longer keep anything there that I'd miss if I couldn't get it back. I used to have more personal items, but the previously safe Kabul, aka the Kabubble, grows more dangerous by the day. Makes sense to travel light. As our troops withdraw, the Taliban's turned its focus on attacking Afghan citizens. Last year, a suicide bomber blew up a nice Lebanese restaurant near the news bureau, my usual haunt whenever I was in town.

As for ISIS kidnapping and executing journalists?

I can't. I simply can't.

For the first time, I'm not so anxious to return to Afghanistan. I used to believe that living like Kitty would be death by a slow, quiet form of asphyxiation, gasping for air until an eventual fade to black, but nothing I've witnessed here seems unpalatable.

In the hallway I stop to inspect her happy family photos. If this afternoon, and this wall, is a slice of her reality, I realize I don't hate Kitty's life.

I might, in fact, envy a few aspects.

After I finish my house tour, I help myself to a glass of water. I open a cabinet to find dozens of matching glasses, all lined up in equidistant rows. Our Saint Louis house was once similarly organized, but I don't recall my mother garnering any pride or joy from keeping the chaos at bay. Mostly I remember her executing her motherly duties with equal parts anger and detachment, until—

"Would ya look at that—no fancy bottled water for you. I also believe Chicago tap water tastes best."

I regard the blue-haired woman who's sidled up next to me. "Nana Baba, I presume?"

"And you're The Jackass?"

I take an overly enthusiastic gulp and then have to wipe off my top lip. "That what she calls me?"

Nana Baba offers a cagey half shrug. "May have let it slip once. Assume you have similar names for her, though. You can make a lotta plays on the word Kitty."

I can't keep from smirking. "I may or may not have explored those possibilities."

She gives me a brisk pat on the forearm. "Aha! Then you're guilty of name-calling, too. Sounds like you've both cast stones. My advice? Gotta let it go."

"Why do you say that?" I ask.

"What does a grudge get you at the end of the day? Nothing but indigestion. You carry anger around and it just gets bigger. What was a handful eventually grows into something that'll break your back. Years ago, I was best friends with a neighbor on the other half of our duplex, but we had a falling-out over who was supposed to shovel our shared walkway. Our stupid little fight turns us into enemies and then no one shovels the walk. We're waiting to see if the other'll cave. My husband gets tired of wading through the snow to get the mail, so he goes out to shovel after a real bad storm and the walk was covered in the wet, heavy stuff. We didn't know he had a weak heart until it was too late."

"I'm so sorry to hear that."

"Was a long time ago, but thanks. All's I'm saying is sometimes you have to forgive your enemies."

We move back to the table and she sits down across from me, removing her glasses. I worry that she's about to cry, but instead she huffs hard on each lens, and then rubs a cloth napkin across the lenses.

"So . . . Mr. Rich Guy's not dead?"

What? "How do you . . ."

She puts her glasses on again. "Thin walls. Why would anyone build themselves one-a-these McMansions but cheap out on the insulation? Don't make any sense to me. I could hear everything she told my son on the phone earlier."

With tact, I reply, "Sometimes just because you can eavesdrop doesn't mean you should eavesdrop."

"Eavesdropping, overhearing. Potato, poh-tah-to." Dropping her voice to a whisper, she says, "You really gonna call the NSA?"

"Shall I assume you 'overheard' what we talked about at the table, too?"

Her gaze is keen behind her bifocals. "Lemme just say this, don't install a fancy intercom system if you don't want nobody hearing what you have to say."

Is Kitty hip to the intercom scheme? Wait, what am I saying? Of course she is. How else would she have a bead on everything that happens under this roof? Well played, Kitty.

"You're a piece of work, aren't you, Nana Baba?" I ask this without malice, as my impression is that life's made her tough and full of moxie, the antidote to all things "girl." Yet I can see why this behavior might frustrate Kitty.

Nana Baba puts on an innocent face. "Me? Never. Anyways, nice meeting you. I gotta get back to the *Wheel* before the commercials end. Do me a favor, though. Be nice to Kitty. Yeah, she's high-strung, kind of like a poodle, but she's decent people once you get past the annoying yipping. She's a lot easier to work with than against." With that, Nana Baba grabs a couple of little tarts out of the cookie jar and is on her way.

Moments later, Kitty appears, an odd expression on her face. Had she been on the intercom?

"I have good news and bad news."

"What's the good news?"

Kitty begins to rake her fingers across her scalp as though she's about to stick her hair in a ponytail. "I've found Ingrid's roommates and know where they'll be tonight."

"What? You were gone ten minutes! Impossible."

She slides into the seat across from me. "No, totally possible, and exactly as I explained. And P.S., I didn't commit treason."

"Then I'm all ears. Do tell."

"I checked out Ingrid's LinkedIn profile but that didn't tell me anything I didn't already know. So, I went to her Facebook page and tabbed through her timeline. Still not a ton of info, because she uses privacy settings. But I was able to see her Group Memberships and Likes and some of them were kind of specific, such as the six thirty a.m. spin class she attends. So I started tabbing on the others in that group and cross-referenced the overlaps with Instagram, Tumblr, and Vine, to see who was a friend and who was just a follower. I figured out who she @-replied most often on Twitter and followed that rabbit down the hole until I stumbled across a tweeted exchange about erasing a DVR'd episode of *Basketball Wives*, and, voilà, roommates."

I admit, "I guess if someone was able to live-blog the Bin Laden raid, it's possible . . ."

"I'm sure that's as close to, 'Wow, Kitty, you're amazing,' as I'm going to get, so I'll take it. Anyway, you and I are off to the Monaco tonight."

"What's the Monaco?"

"It's a nightclub in the city. You and I are going clubbing. Tonight."

"And that's the bad news."

"No," she replies, clawing at her head. "The bad news is we might have lice."

CHAPTER FIFTEEN

Kitty

....

Chicago, Illinois
September 1999

"Kitty, can you *please* look this over for me? If I send out another press release about our client being in the 'mist' of prepping for next year's Fashion Week, I *will* get fired."

I take the page from Dyta, the high-energy, yet completely hapless new account manager in my department. "Don't you worry. I'm an expert proofreader. My roommate's a terrible speller so I had to double-check all her papers in college. Good thing, too, because I once saved her from turning in a paper describing the steps she'd implement for an effective initial pubic offering. Definitely not what she meant to write."

Dyta sits on the corner of my desk. "I don't get it." She's wearing Obsession, my favorite perfume, but for some reason it's bothering me today. Like the musky notes are too musky. Weird.

"A public offering is an initial stock sale. A pubic offering is a successful Saturday night."

Dyta looks at me from behind her veil of wiry bangs. I'm dying to get ahold of her with some control serum and a round brush. Frizz isn't, and will never be, the new black. "I don't get it."

Oh, honey, I think. *You are not cute enough to be this dim.*

"Work it out, every word. You can do it."

Dyta's eyes widen. "Oh!" Then she lets out an enormous bark-laugh that's disproportionate to her tiny body.

I scan the document and make the needed corrections, then offer a few suggestions for improvement.

"You rock, Kitty Kord."

"Happy to help," I reply. "And if you need advice on anything, doesn't have to be work related"— *such as your hair, sweet Jesus, please let me help you tame that bush*—"you just ask, okay?"

Dyta crosses her legs and swings her foot. At least her shoes are cute, so there's hope. "So what's the word for the weekend? Doing anything fun? If you don't already have plans, some of the Calvin Klein account team are going to Barleycorn after work. Will you come? And let me buy your first round?"

I rub my midsection. "I will take you up on this, and soon. Today's bad, though. The Pad Thai I ate is *not* settling well."

Imagining the thick, pink shrimp I was so excited about an hour ago now makes my stomach cramp. Then again, the six Diet Cokes I've chugged so far today can't be helping either.

I tell her, "I kind of feel like vegging on the couch with my roomie. It's so sad. We live together, but I never see her—she's a junior analyst at Goldman and her schedule's just nuts. We're SO due up for some girl time. Pop some corn, put in a Meg Ryan movie, you know? Ooh, or maybe Winona!"

More than anything, I need a good old-fashioned chitchat because I have to figure out what to do about Ken. I love him. I do. But I'm not up for the long-distance thing and I need an exit plan before we get too serious. I haven't told him Betsy and I plan to move east in the spring when our lease ends. Chicago's great for a lot of reasons, but if either of us really want to make names for ourselves in our respective fields, we need to be in New York City. Betsy's dying to work on Wall Street proper and Eiderhaus's biggest clients are serviced out of Manhattan. I want in on that. Thankfully, HR has already approved my transfer. We just have to find a place (I loooooove the *Friends* apartment even though I know it's fiction) and figure out the subway, then, boom! New Yorkers!

Despite all evidence to the contrary, Chicago's actually a small town. Between everyone I know who grew up in and around my suburb, my friends from tennis camp and my parents' country club, plus all the Greeks at Whitney who also moved to Lincoln Park after graduation, I feel like I'm still in high school. I can't go anywhere without bumping into someone familiar. I'm always, "Kitty, the dentist's daughter," or "Kitty with the wicked backhand," or "Kitty, the North Shore cheerleader," or "Kitty from Tri Tau." (Or, "Kitty, Kelly's sister," which, frankly, terrifies everyone even though she's seriously mellowed.) For once, I'd like to know what it's like to be *Katherine*, with no preconceived notions.

I feel like I could find that in New York.

Ken and I met at a Tri Tau/Sigma Chi mixer as sophomores and I let him pursue me until first semester of our junior year. Is it sad that the chase was the most exciting part of our relationship? We've been together ever since. Thing is, we've always enjoyed each other's company and I'm content. I never mind when anyone calls us Barbie and Ken. It's just that I'm not . . . challenged. He's sweet as can be and anxious to provide us with a nice lifestyle, hence dental school, but there's nothing about him that drives *me* to be better. He doesn't discourage my dreams, but he's not exactly cheering them on, either.

Mind you, I don't want a Betsy-style boyfriend with all the intense highs and lows. For such a composed woman, her breakups are surprisingly theatrical, perpetually ending with massive fights, followed by lots of crying and a week where I nurse her back to sanity with *Buffy* marathons and pints of ice cream until she's ready to slap on a pair of stilettos and try it all again. I tell her she's got to start dating smarter guys, knowing some intellectual equality would lessen the fireworks, but she never listens. Nope, it's always either bartenders or liberal arts grads, which are basically the same thing.

I suspect that after staring at numbers all day, Betsy enjoys the interpersonal drama. She'd never even kissed a guy before she pledged and didn't have a serious boyfriend until senior year, so she was definitely behind the curve with guys. She's having fun figuring out the dating nuances most of us first encountered in high school, so if dramatic is how she wants to play it, I'm down.

Naturally, Jackass Jordan disagrees, telling Betsy her romantic tempests are "unhealthy" and "problematic." Whatevs. Who cares what she thinks?

My stomach churns audibly.

"Hey, you all right?" Dyta asks, raising her pencil-thin brows. Look at them—they're like two tiny commas on her face. Ironic that she doesn't have enough hair there, yet far too much elsewhere. She is crying out for a spa day with me. She just doesn't know it yet. "Where'd you have lunch?"

"I ate the rest of yesterday's takeout from the new place on Delaware—Phuket, Let's Get Thai."

Dyta hops off my desk. "Ooh, bad news! I saw Lissy Ryder puking her guts out earlier this week after eating there. You should probably go home. Like, *now*. Typhoon a-coming, if you know what I mean."

A tsunami of nausea hits me and I break into a cold sweat. "You may be right."

"Feel better," Dyta says, taking four giant steps back from me.

"Food poisoning isn't contagious," I tell her.

"Yeah, it's just that these shoes are suede. Later! And thanks for proofing my copy!"

I e-mail my boss to let her know I'm sick and pack up my laptop to work from home. I make haste leaving the office, anxious for some fresh air.

I call Kelly to commiserate while I walk down Michigan Ave to the bus stop. I wish Kelly lived in the city now. She spent six months working in marketing after graduation when she met her now-husband, Brett, at my parents' club. He was Green Valley Club's golf pro, but he's recently been accepted onto the PGA tour. They married ten months into dating. They now live in North Shore with their adorable toddler, Sophia, and another baby on the way. When Kelly wants something, she doesn't mess around.

"So you're nauseated?" she asks.

I clutch my roiling stomach. "Yes."

"I see. Let me ask you—does the idea of a dirty ashtray make you want to barf?"

I feel the bile rise in my throat. "Yes, every day of my life, largely because I hate smoking."

"Okay, what about biting into a raw onion? One of those big red Bermudas Dr. Daddy puts on his burgers."

"Sure, but I have food poisoning. The idea of any foodstuff makes me want to hurl."

"Are you peeing a lot?"

"I had six Diet Cokes today, so, clearly."

"Do you have any cramping?"

"Only because I'm due for a period."

Kelly clucks her tongue on the other end of the line. "Interesting. And how do your tits feel?"

"What kind of question is that?" She loves trying to trip me up by saying whatever's the most shocking and outrageous. As always, I take her bait, stopping short in the middle of the sidewalk in front of the Hancock Center. "I don't know; how do *your* tits feel, Kelly?"

I'm mortified when I realize I've caught the attention of a mustached police officer on horseback. I lower my head and keep walking.

Undaunted, she replies, "Tender as fuck, thanks. Brett accidentally grazed one with his elbow last night and I almost sent him flying through the sliding glass door. Tell me something, Kitty. Where are you?"

"Almost at Watertower Place."

"Cool. Do me a proper and cart your happy ass to the Walgreens on the corner."

"That's where my bus stops."

"Perfect. When you get there, go inside and buy yourself a pregnancy test. What the hell, why not buy two?"

I feel a sudden stab of dread. "I don't need a pregnancy test, Kelly. I'm on the pill."

She snorts. "Oh, sweetie. Go piss on a stick and then tell me how that whole birth control pill thing worked out for you."

• • • •

Why are there so many choices here? Yes or no? Red light, green light? Which one do I buy? There should be a single, uniform test so I don't have to stand here and debate whether a plus sign or a double line is going to dictate my whole future.

How do I do this? I've never purchased a pregnancy test before. Do I shop based on price? Do I buy in bulk in case I get a false positive? What's the best brand? First Response? ClearBlue Easy? EPT?

I don't know.

The irony that the wall of condoms are housed right next to the pregnancy tests is not lost on me. Way to rub salt in the wound, Walgreens.

Okay, here's what I'm going to do. I'll grab the cheapest *and* the most expensive tests, I'll toss them in my basket, and then I'll get the heck out of here. I will go home, try one now, one in the morning like the directions instruct, and then I will call Kelly and tell her she doesn't know what she's talking about and everything will be fine.

Yes.

This is a solid plan. I will approach this problem with my usual systematic organization and all will be well.

I sweep a couple of boxes into my basket and then I cover them up with a box of panty liners. If I see an enema between here and the register, I'll add that, too, for camouflage purposes. I quickly walk away from the tests.

No enemas between there and here.

Which is fine.

Now I'm going to get in line, give my purchases to LaShonda, the sweet cashier (with the cute rhinestone-studded manicure) who can never remember my name, despite my daily Diet Coke purchases. Then I'll shove everything into my bag and go home.

I can do this.

I'm five deep in line, waiting my turn when I hear, "Kitty Kord, is that you?"

Don't turn around, don't turn around, don't turn around.

Now's an excellent time to pretend I'm not Kitty Kord. I am a random and anonymous young professional girl named Katherine. In New

York. Here, I can buy as many pregnancy tests as I'd like without worrying the news will travel back to my family, my friends, my old teachers, my ex–tennis coaches, my sorority sisters, or any one of a thousand other people who might judge me.

LaShonda brightens when she hears my name and she waves. "Hey, Miss Kitty! How you doing this afternoon?"

I smile and offer a weak fingertip-wave in return before plastering a smile on and turning around to face whichever nonstranger is behind me. For a blessed second, I don't recognize the deep tan and the eyes like stained glass because they don't belong here. Yet once I do, then I truly want the floor to open up and swallow me whole.

My anxiety-tinged mortification takes the form of nervous chatter. "Bobby! BoJo! Bob-bay! Vinnie Bob-a-rino!"

Oh, my God, stop talking. You are not a *Saturday Night Live* skit.

"Bob-o-link."

Mean it. Shut it down, self.

"Robert Bobby Robby Rob Jordan!"

But I am apparently unstoppable.

Bobby's bemused by my greeting. As am I.

"So . . . what's shakin', Bob-bacon?" I pour on the false brightness, attempting to block the contents of my basket with my computer bag. "What are you doing in town? Thought you lived in California full-time now."

No, I'm *sure* you live in California because you never came back the summer after your first junior year. And sometimes Betsy sticks your postcards on our fridge. Why are you here? Here today, right now, witnessing my abject humiliation, and not back in LA writing postcards?

AND CAN YOU SEE WHAT'S IN MY BASKET, DAMN IT?

I don't say any of that, though.

He still exudes that laid-back beach vibe I used to so appreciate. "Yeah, man, still doing the LA *thang*, still taking classes. Should be done in December, though. Got some gnarly family stuff going on, so I came home for a visit. Y'know, running interference. Met my dad for lunch and now I'm doing errands because I have time. And what time is it? It's time for Fritos." He shakes the bag at me.

I practically dislocate my shoulder trying to hide my basket behind me. *Please don't glance down. Please don't glance down. Please don't glance down.*

"Super. Sounds so great!"

He gives me a slow, appraising grin. "Nice to see you again. You look happy, Kit. Pink cheeks and all, kinda like a glow. Grown-up life agrees with you." He notices LaShonda motioning toward her open register, sun glinting off her rhinestone-studded nails. "Hey, it's your turn at bat. When you talk to Sars, tell her I'll catch her on the flippity-flop. And you take it easy, Kitty."

Take it easy why? Because you think I'm pregnant because you can see what I'm buying?

"You betcha. See you later!"

I maintain eye contact while he pays the other cashier for his gum and Fritos in the hopes he won't spot my purchases. "LaShonda, do you mind double-bagging everything?"

Did he notice the tests?

Can he see them now?

His expression tells me nothing.

She replies, "I surely will, Miss Kitty," with a kind nod. "I threw in a Twix bar, no charge. You have yourself a blessed day." She counts back my change, gives me my still-ill-concealed merch, and I practically sprint away after saying thank you. My bus is waiting at the stop, so I'm able to board before Bobby can catch up to me. I pay my fare and find a seat in the front.

As the bus chugs up the Outer Drive, I try to decide what's worse—possibly being pregnant or the way Jackass Jordan will gloat when she finds out.

From where I'm sitting?

Both options make me feel sick.

· · · ·

This test must be defective.

Stupid cheap test.

I try again.

This test must be defective, too.

Stupid expensive test.

Yet I can't escape the obvious truth, which is that I need to buy more tests.

• • • •

"Yes, I actually do enjoy always being right," Kelly says. She brings me a bone china cup on a silver tray with sugar cubes and slivers of lemon, the very portrait of domesticity. She makes it look so easy. I watch as she expertly navigates her sunny kitchen, pouring hot water from the kettle into a teapot. "Give this five minutes to steep. It's ginger tea and it'll save your life."

I inhale the vapors. "Mmm, nice. I appreciate that the scent of it doesn't make me want to immediately puke on your parquet."

"Ginger's your best defense against nausea. Ginger ale, ginger tea, ginger root, what have you. Works in any form. Also, carry a bag of oyster crackers at all times."

"What's wrong with regular saltines?"

"They're bigger, denser, and higher in calories. You'll eat more than you mean to and being pregnant doesn't give you license to become a fatty."

"You are the very model of compassion."

Kelly tosses her braid over her shoulder. "You want a hug? Go to Mum. You want the truth? Come to me. What's the plan?"

I've peed on so many sticks this past week, I could build a log cabin out of them. Every single test I took came back positive, so I scheduled an appointment with my doctor, who confirmed the results. Congratulations! I'm screwed.

"I'm still weighing my options. I'm only six weeks along, so I have time to decide whether I should . . ." Ugh. I can't even finish the sentence. "I mean, you know I'm steadfast in a woman's right to choose; I'm just not sure if that's a choice I can make for myself."

And that's why I'm stuck in limbo.

Betsy was stunned that I was even considering other options.

"What's to think about?" she asked, a couple of days after my confirming doctor's appointment. "You said you want to dump Ken and you're looking to get out of this town. A baby makes both those choices impossible. Why abandon your goals for what amounts to a pharmaceutical mistake? You've never even wanted children!"

I replied, "It's not that simple, Betsy. I was all Team No Way until Kelly had her baby. Little Sophia gives me . . . pause." The first time I held that precious child, I felt like I'd been pulled into another dimension, as the weight of her in my arms felt so *right*. But I wasn't sure how to explain that to Betsy.

"It absolutely is that simple," she argued. "You like Sophia? Great. Babysit for her. Buy her outfits from Baby Gap. Put her school picture on your desk. Just don't let your feelings as an aunt cloud your better judgment."

"I know, in theory, termination is the clear choice. Thing is, this isn't about me only—Ken has a say, too." When I told him I was pregnant, he immediately dropped to one knee and proposed, saying, "We get to jump-start our future together!" Then he maxed out his credit card to buy me the best ring he could afford.

Although his reaction made me fall in love with him all over again, I haven't yet said yes.

When I mentioned Ken, Betsy practically exploded, leaping up from her spot on the couch. "No, he has zero say! What kind of fucked-up patriarchy are you subscribing to where he has dominion over *your* body and *your* choice? My God, somewhere in North America, a chill just went down Betty Friedan's spine."

"Was she a Kappa at Whitney?"

"Oh, my God, Kitty, please do not reproduce!"

I was shocked by her reaction. Where was the rancor coming from? I walked over to Betsy and held her shoulders. "Bets, you've never spoken to me like this. Ever. This is so out of character. What's going on with you? Are you okay? Is your job putting too much pressure on you? I feel like I don't know who you *are* right now." I searched her wild eyes. "Is my reasonable, rational, supportive friend in there? If so, can you maybe send her out?"

Betsy was shaking beneath my grip. "Don't you understand? I'm not upset about *me*, Kit. I'm upset about *you*. I don't want to stand here while you throw away what could be a brilliant career to step right into our mothers' sensible heels. Is that really the life you want? Getting roasts into the oven and planting flower boxes and volunteering for the PTA? Look at Kelly—she was the most badass chick to exist and now she knits. *Kelly knits!* And not with the bones of some virgin she sacrificed, just regular old needles. You can't go Stepford. You can't turn into one of those women who are all smug when I tell them I don't want kids, all 'You'll change your mind!' with a wink and a nod, like they know my heart and mind better than I do. That's so obnoxious. That's so not you. You're meant for more than pushing a stroller to Mommy and Me classes."

And yet, a part of me didn't think that sounded like the worst thing in the world, especially as Kelly's borderline blissful. (In as much as she can be while still being Kelly, that is.)

"What if I'm not meant for more, Bets? What if I'm meant for exactly this?"

"You *are* meant for more! Of course you are! You're Kitty Kord—you can do anything once you set your mind to it. You took me from the nerdiest freshman at Whitney and made me into a Tri Tau. I'd be such a loser without your intervention. You have the rare ability to step in, orchestrate change, and make everyone thank you afterward. Look at all your success at Eiderhaus so far! Don't waste that gift on carpools and playdates. Please."

While I let what she said sink in, she ran into her room and came back with her Day Planner. "Look, we can schedule the appointment right now, you go in, it's done, you take a day to recover, we eat ice cream, I hold your hand while you cry, but then you move on with the life we've been talking about ever since graduation. No harm, no foul, no one needs to know."

I said, "I would know."

And that's the hurdle I can't clear.

. . . .

Little Sophia toddles over from her play mat and pulls on Kelly's blouse to be picked up. Kelly scoops her up and sets the baby on her lap. I have to stop myself from reaching out for her.

"Would you look at this kid?" Kelly says. "She's perfect, right? She walks around in a state of constant wonder and every time the dog barks or the bell rings or she takes a shit, her little mind is blown. There's no job I could hold that could ever compare to being here, witnessing her figuring out her life one handful of Cheerios at a time. She's the greatest gift I can imagine. She taught me what real love is. Will she be an estrogen-addled teenager someday? Yes. Will I hate her then as much as she hates me? Yes. I accept that, which is what makes now all the more precious."

"What are you saying? You won't hate Sophia," I argue. "Mum and Dr. Daddy didn't hate us when we were in our teens."

She pours the tea, careful to keep small fingers away from the steamy teapot. "Of course they did. Why do you think we were shipped to tennis camp in Wisconsin all summer, every summer?"

Huh.

"*You* were a terror, maybe, but I was nice."

"Ha! So you don't recall your shrine to Marky Mark and your subsequent Vegas-style freak-out when Mum took down your clippings to hang the new wallpaper? I thought we were going to have to shoot you with a tranquilizing dart. How about when you forced us all to that Vanilla Ice concert for your birthday? Mum. Me. Dr. Daddy. At *Vanilla Ice*. What about when you decided you were English and would only speak in that horrific British accent? But you didn't know the difference between Brits and Aussies and you were always wishing us a 'g'day'? Do you have any idea what a self-involved pain in the ass you were? You were the worst. We *all* hated you."

"We're all tight as can be now. Whatever I was like as a teen, I grew out of it," I say.

"Yes, we do grow out of our difficult phases because it's the cycle of life. Understanding what to expect is half the battle. So if you decide to say yes to Ken and to get married, and really to go through with everything, then I'll be here to guide you and show you what to look out for, like I always have."

"Kelly, I'm so confused. I don't know what to do."

"Just keep thinking about it, weighing your options. Figure out what's most important to you. The right decision will hit you out of the blue and your path will become clear. You have some time; take it."

I wrap my hands around the cup, trying to absorb some of the warmth. "My mind is spinning off in a million different scenarios and each one makes a degree of sense."

"You'll figure it out. But, P.S., in the spirit of full disclosure, having a kid *will* ruin your vagina. For the rest of your life, it's going to feel like a map you can't quite refold. Thought you should know. Other than that? Two thumbs-up for babies! Right, Soph?" Sophia reaches around and grabs ahold of Kelly's braid. Sophia sucks on the end of it while dandling on Kelly's knee to the chant of, "Two thumbs-up! Two thumbs-up!"

If motherhood could tame the savage beast that is Kelly, what might it mean for those of us who *aren't* borderline sociopaths?

• • • •

I leave Kelly's when Sophia goes down for her nap, largely because Kelly threatened both my and my unborn child's life if we dare disturb her sleeping daughter. She sends me off with a couple of cans of ginger ale and a bag of oyster crackers.

I sip and nibble on my drive back to the city from the burbs, and my stomach settles. My route south takes me past all the pretty homes and the huge trees with leaves just beginning to turn. I loved living up here as a kid. I wonder, would I want all of this again with Ken at my side? Or is the lure of life in New York and becoming Katherine too strong to ignore?

And even if Ken and I were to get married, we surely couldn't afford a North Shore life for years. At best, we'd be able to swing a condo somewhere off-trend, like Rogers Park, and that's with my parents' help.

I just wish I knew what to do. Regardless of what decision I make, I'm sure I'll spend the rest of my life second-guessing myself.

I have to park four blocks away from the apartment because there's a Cubs game today. I make my way past drunken fans, and each time someone comes too close, I find myself automatically protecting my still-flat stomach.

Maybe I subconsciously know what to do after all.

I unlock the three dead bolts on the three-flat's main front door and climb the stairs to our place, where I work three more locks. If this is the kind of security the Big Ten, Yuppie enclave of Wrigleyville requires, how much scarier would Manhattan be? I find myself cradling my stomach again.

"Bets? You here?" There's no answer, but I'm not surprised. She spends a lot of Saturdays at the office. The message light on the answering machine is blinking with two new messages. We'd planned to upgrade to voice mail, but decided the expense wasn't worth it since we were moving anyway. I click PLAY.

"Hey, babe—it's Ken. There's something small, gold, and shiny here, and it's waiting for you. Gimme a buzz when you're home. Love you."

I feel myself smiling. The second message begins.

"Sars, it's Jack." She sounds upset. Well, too bad because (a) a lot of people have problems and (b) I'm sure she deserves whatever it is that's bringing her down. "I'm . . . livid. I need to talk. I can't believe her nerve. I really can't. If she thinks she can just waltz in and be a mother now after—"

I erase the message before I have to listen to another vile word. The mystery of whether or not Bobby saw the contents of my basket is solved. Funny, but I thought I could trust him.

Oh, well.

Still, I cannot fathom the kind of nerve it takes that woman to call *my* home and comment on *my* life and *my* decisions. On the rare occasion we're forced together, I've actually felt sorry for her. Once in a while I think, *How did we go so far off track that we can't even be civil?* And then something like this happens and I remember all over again.

Jack Jordan thinks *I* can't be a mother?

She's so wrong. So flipping wrong.

I'm Kitty Kord, and I can be anything I want. And now, my choice is crystal clear. Without another second's hesitation, I pick up the landline.

"Hey, Ken, it's Kitty. I'm about to make you the happiest man in the world."

CHAPTER SIXTEEN

Jack

....

Whitney University, Central Illinois
January 1995

This was a mistake.

My mettle lasted thirty seconds, the exact amount of time it took me to place the call to Sean. My ego has written a check my body can't—or, rather, is terrified to—cash.

I open another wine cooler. Liquid courage shouldn't taste like Froot Loops. I ought to imbibe something bracing—a shot of scotch, a jigger of rye, a belt of whiskey. This is the beverage equivalent of Hello, Kitty. (The Sanrio cat, not the evil roommate.)

Is sex going to hurt? And where do we *do it* in the room? I'm concerned the lofts won't be safe to hold the weight of two people in one bed. (Suspect my brothers built it that way on purpose.) Last semester, Kitty and I watched *9 1/2 Weeks*—I'm not going to have to do *all of that*, am I? How does the standing-up part work? Will I need Jell-O? Should I have painted my toenails?

I'm proactively embarrassed. As in I'm already embarrassed and nothing's even happened yet.

What if he was just humoring me about coming over?

Yes, that's it. He's not coming. Why would he come? It's bone-chilling outside and snowing like mad. No one's going to walk all the way from the Beta house to Wadsworth Hall in this weather. I'm clear on the other side of campus.

There. Off the hook.

Simon invited me to a performance at the experimental theater tonight. They're doing an all-male version of *Little Women* in an earnest, nonhilarious way. I assume the show will be truly terrible, but at the moment, it sounds better than *Cats.*

Yes. That's what I'll do. I'll join Simon. I will grab my coat and my scarf and—

Knock, knock.

Crap. He's here.

Crap, crap, crap.

No. I sound like Kitty. Shit, shit, shit.

"Hi, Jackie, it's Sean."

If I were to throw myself out the fourth floor window, what are the odds I could land on my feet? Yes, I'd likely shatter a few bones, but there's a decent amount of snow accumulation. Injuries suffered from defenestration may be worth it. Or I could—

Knock, knock.

"You there? Did you leave the door unlocked? Here, I'm going to try. Coming in." Sean opens the door (DAMN IT) and I have nowhere to hide. "Yo, Jackie, what's up?"

"Hi. Is it freezing out?"

This?

This is my opening line?

Well, aren't I the femme fatale? I don't necessarily want to seduce him, but I also don't want to *not* have the option to seduce him if I suddenly find my nerve again. Weather talk. Super sexy. Perhaps I can bring up NPR next, with a side of Nelson Mandela. Bet he'd love to hear how I use baking soda and newspaper to draw the stink out of my soccer cleats.

"Probably, but my buddy gave me a ride." Sean shakes the snow out of his light brown hair with the swoopy bangs and shrugs off his jacket. Instead of tossing it on the floor, he hangs it neatly on the back of my desk chair. "Lemme see what we've got." He takes my bottle from me to inspect the label, which includes an anthropomorphic kiwi with a straw-berry in a headlock. The liquor company isn't marketing this product to adults, are they? "What flavor?" He takes a sip and then puckers his lips. "Jolly Rancher?"

I nod. "Basically." I'm so nervous that I reach to twist strands in my ponytail, forgetting that I cut off my hair.

He takes a seat on the futon, just like he's done the dozens of other times he's been to our room, acting utterly at home. Why is he not un-comfortable when I literally want to shimmy up the chimney Santa-style to get away? I realize we were friends before, but everything's about to change. (Possibly.) (If I don't throw up/pass out/run screaming from the room, I mean.)

"Hey, you cut your hair. I like it. Very French."

Should he be all over me already? Or not? Is this considered a booty call? Do we make casual conversation first? How does this work? Do I put on an Al Green CD? Would Nitzer Ebb be okay instead, since I don't have any Al Green? (Simon's been schooling me on industrial music.)

He's looking at me as though he expects an answer. I have to say something here. Um, okay, how about . . . "Have you been to France?"

Not bad. Not great, but not bad.

"Yeah, a few times with the family. We travel a lot. Instead of big Christmas presents or extravagant birthdays, we go on trips a couple of times a year. That's why I don't have a car. My mom and sister love France—it's where we'd go every time if they had their way. I like Paris, but I'd rather hit London. Great pubs. Favorite is the Dog & Duck. They're all named like that over there, too. The Elephant & Castle, the Bull & Bush. The English are big on ampersands, no idea why. I've been all about the ales on tap *and* the drinking age for a while. France is more for wine guys, which is not really my groove."

"Does that mean you're not a wine cooler guy, either?" Ahh! He's not going to drink? Does that mean we just get to it, then? No alcoholic Starbursts to loosen us up? What irony that the only person in my orbit who could advise me here is Kitty.

He shrugs. "Don't get me wrong. I'm definitely a free drinks guy.

Didn't realize anyone drank wine coolers anymore. Who came up with these anyway? Like someone was sitting around eating melted Fla-Vor-Ice and they were all, 'You know what would be a fantastic addition? Cheap, carbonated wine.'"

"I burped a couple of minutes ago and I swear I could taste the rainbow." Oh, my God, what am I saying? Shut up. SHUT UP.

"Nice. Up here." He holds up his palm for me to slap. Is this how the American Mating Ritual begins? Exchanging high fives? Is that the protocol? High fives, then chest-bumps, then bro-hugs, then naked?

"Before I forget, I brought you something." Condoms? Is it condoms? Should I hope for yes or no? I don't have any. Should I have any? I'm sure Kitty doesn't have any, either. I feel like I ought to have my first kiss before I buy my first prophylactic. "Here."

I examine the round object he's given me, desperately relieved to see it's not manufactured by Trojan. I look, then do a double take, utterly surprised and delighted by his gift, which is embroidered with a fighter jet. "Is this what I think it is? A pilot patch from Top Gun training?"

I'm sewing this onto my jacket the minute I find some thread. And learn to sew. Teddy can teach me—he's able to cuff his own pants. But that doesn't mean he's gay, *Kitty*.

"Yep. Miramar, baby. My cousin graduated from the Navy Fighter Weapons School a few years ago and he gave me this patch. Thought about you when I ran across it over break and figured you'd appreciate it. But then Kitty and I ended so I didn't have a chance. But here we are, so there you go."

"I love it, thank you. My brothers are going to be seriously jealous." I'm really touched that he remembered something so important to me. "Do . . . you want a wine cooler?"

He pretends to look pensive. "Hmm. Sometimes you've just got to say, 'What the fuck.'"

I feel the grin spreading across my face as slow and sure as the sunrise. "You're quoting from the wrong Tom Cruise movie."

"Close enough. And at least we're not going to U of I."

"Pfft. U of I wishes they were Whitney."

I grab a cooler for him and sit on the other side of the futon, tucked far into the corner, to the point I feel the arm digging into my back. I do appreciate how he's making this easier on me. He leans over and I brace myself (IS IT TIME FOR LOVE, DR. JONES?) but he just clinks his bottle on mine. "Proost."

"What language is that?"

"That's 'cheers' in Dutch. We went to Holland for spring break a few years ago. No one else says it. Kinda my thing."

I curl my legs underneath me and angle myself toward him a bit more. "Where else have you been? My family does a lot of hiking in national parks and we snowboard all the time, but we've never traveled internationally."

"You've got to get on that. Travel's the best, man. You hang out in a different country? You're a different person there," he says. "Like, it changes you for the better. So far, we've been to England, Holland, France, as I mentioned, and also Italy, Germany, Switzerland, Australia, New Zealand, Brazil, Mexico, Belize, Panama, and Dominican Republic. South America was my favorite by far. The trip we took to the DR is why I want to be a plastic surgeon. Yeah, I'll make bank—not gonna lie, that's a draw—but I also want to do volunteer missions someday to help kids with cleft palates."

"How did I not know this?" I ask.

"Kitty never talked about me?"

"Not about anything important. I mean, I know how many Polo shirts you own and that you're Beta's pledge educator. Also, you drag your right toe on your tennis serve and it wrecks your sneakers. Might want to work on that."

I had to talk about athletic shoes somewhere, didn't I? I should watch *9 1/2 Weeks* again because I'm pretty sure Kim Basinger never blathers about going to Lady Foot Locker. Argh.

Yet Sean doesn't seem put off. Rather, he's all smiley and affable, as though he's somehow enjoying chillin' here on the futon with me. I never really had an appreciation for Sean before, despite his Ping-Pong prowess, but I'm starting to discover his appeal. There's something vaguely Bruce Willis about him, with the quiet confidence, piercing eyes, and strong chin. He's kind of rugged and seems like he'll be even more handsome as his mileage increases, like how a bomber jacket improves with age and distress.

(Am I shallow for noticing he has a better hairline than Bruce Willis? Has Kitty rubbed off on me?)

He knocks back a long sip, and then takes a perplexed look at the bottle. "Interesting. I detect notes of . . . cotton candy? As for Kitty? I'm better off without her. You want to know the most fucked-up part?"

I move closer. "Um, obviously."

"She kept trying to negotiate with me about sex. Said she'd only do it if I gave her my fraternity pin. Listen, I'm graduating next year and I have to keep my grades up if I want to get into UCLA med school. I've got to buckle down so hard I'm living off campus in an apartment next year. Plus, I'm in charge of pledge education. I have a shit-ton on my plate. There's ten solid years of school and residencies and fellowships in front of me. The last thing I'm going to do right now is get preengaged, you know? I told her, if that's what you need, then I can wait. I'm cool. Why am I telling you this? I can't believe I'm telling you this. Anyway, so instead of taking it slow with me, the last actual gentleman on earth, she hooks up with your brother and then lies about it? I don't get it."

"Yet she wanted to give it to you; I can see your dilemma."

He grins and I notice he has a dimple on the right side. "Forgot you were funny, Jackie. Always liked hanging out with you. You owe me a rematch. You cannot consistently be that good at foosball. You can't."

Ugh, stupid Jackie. That name has never fit. "Do me a favor and call me Jack."

He nods, seeming to digest my request while scanning my face. "You seem more like a Jack. Jacks are badass, you know? All of 'em. Jack Nicholson. Jack Nicklaus. Jack LaLanne."

"Please. Jack LaLanne is, like, a hundred years old." At this moment, I've almost forgotten about being nervous. Sean is smart and, by virtue of my pants still being on, chivalrous. Why would Kitty throw all this away for Teddy and his microscopic attention span?

"He's still doing one-armed push-ups! LaLanne could kick my ass *today*, so my point's valid. Who else? There's Jack Ruby."

"Interesting you bring him up, considering all my siblings and I were named after Kennedys."

"See? I pay attention. And how about Jack Kennedy? All those guys he saved on his PT boat? *Badass.* Then you've got the one-two punch of Jack Johnson and Jack Dempsey, pun intended. Thesis statement? Jacks London *and* Kerouac."

"I may fall spontaneously in love at your knowing how to pluralize Jacks." Then I blush furiously, not having realized what I was saying until it was too late.

UGH, THIS IS WHY BOYS DON'T WANT TO DATE ME.

Somehow determined to save me from my awkward self, Sean says, "Eh, not the worst reason. Better than being into someone for their Ralph Lauren shirts, right? Speaking of worse, do you really want to drink these wine coolers? I'm worried they'll give us diabetes."

"They're horrible, right? Like cough syrup, sans the whimsy."

He stands, holding out a hand to help me up. His grip is warm and firm. "Let's go do something fun. We're young, we're free, and it's Saturday night. Let's burn shit. Figuratively. Or we can go back to the Beta house, where they probably will burn something literally. Last week the pledges torched a couch. Now we have to sit on the floor in the TV room."

I tell him, "The only event I heard about tonight is an all-male version of *Little Women* at the experimental theater."

He looks at me long and hard. His gaze is . . . smoldering. Is that a thing, smoldering? Now I kind of wish he would make a move on me. Yes. I would indeed be fine with that. "I'm going to pretend I didn't hear that. I may have to drink this bottle of glucose to erase the image from my mind. Okay, you and me? We're making a plan. You have boots?"

"I live in Illinois and it's January; of course I have boots."

"Then I presume you have a warm coat, mittens, and a hat. Possibly some long underwear."

"Affirmative, Ghost Rider."

"Then suit up, Maverick; I feel the need for speed."

• • • •

"You're a lunatic. Take that as a compliment."

"You're a complete wuss. Not a compliment."

"I don't want to fall and break my hands, wreck my career before it even starts."

"That's a fancy way to say, 'I'm chicken.'"

We're at the bottom of the highest run on Squires Hill, where the sledding is every bit as good as I imagined. I just won a bet by taking the hill standing astride dining hall trays, riding them like two small, square skis. The whole crowd burst into applause when I finished upright.

"Bawk, bawk," he replies.

The flurries are still coming down and the moon's out, making the hill almost bright as day. I feel like I'm in the middle of a snow globe. There are dozens of other students out here with us and for once, no one cares who's Greek and who's not or who's drinking hot chocolate instead of swigging schnapps. We're just a bunch of big kids enjoying the rush. Tonight is absolutely the most fun I've had since starting college.

I stopped feeling nervous around Sean about three hours ago, right after I made my first trip down the hill at the front of a two-person toboggan. Told Sean I was likely the better pilot, so he acquiesced and I was the one to steer. We wiped out in a spectacular fashion because we were going way too fast, our tilted sled sending a spray of icy snow out twenty feet. I've crushed him so handily every time we've raced back up the hill that I assume I've inadvertently entered the Friend Zone again.

Can't believe I've not suggested we arm wrestle. But I'm sure I will.

So, when Sean eventually suggests we get out of our wet, freezing cold clothes back in my dorm room, I take the statement at face value.

Um . . . way off on that.

Did falling asleep half dressed in his arms start World War III when Kitty arrives home twelve hours early, jumping to a conclusion that wouldn't technically be true for another three months of our covert dating?

Abso-flipping-lutely.

And worth it.

CHAPTER SEVENTEEN

To: Undisclosed Recipients
From: North_Shore_Brooke_Birchbaum@gmail.com
Subject: Good and bad news

Hi, all!

Thanks a million for coming to Avery's party. Good news? She's still over the moon about the fun and friends. You are all simply THE BEST. She'll be sending her own thank you notes out shortly.

The bad news? Well, there's been the teensiest wrinkle to what otherwise was the MOST PERFECT DAY! Your child may or may not have been exposed to lice. But fear not, fellow moms! I've already arranged to take care of any child who may have been impacted. Please call Denise at Hair I Go Again (contact info on attached VBC) for your confidential, prepaid, in-home delousing.

Have a wonderful summer!

Brooke B.

Attachment: VBC, Click to Download

Kitty

The Monaco, Chicago
Wednesday

"I vote we deal with the lice in the morning and we leave for the Monaco now," Jack says.

"Right now?"

"Yes."

"Like this?" I point to my yoga pants, bare face, and damp bun.

"*Yes.*"

I remark, "You've never been to a nightclub, have you?"

"I have been to clubs all around the world," Jack replies.

"I don't doubt that, Miss Global Entry. But how many of these clubs were in the *first* world? Any place the women wear those burlap sacks over their heads? Doesn't count," I say.

"Number one, offensive, number two, they're called burkas, and number three, you don't see devout Muslim women in Western clubs *at all* in the Middle East."

"Let me explain something to you, Jordan—we're not in Kabul. You might be the hottest chick to ever don a flak jacket in Over-there-istan, but here in Chicago? You wouldn't make it past the door like that. Nor would I. Granted, I haven't been to a club since before Kord was born, but I'm sure nothing's changed. We show up at eight p.m. in exercise togs and the doorman will laugh us down the street. We need to work on our look before we venture anywhere."

Jack stamps her foot. "Wrong. I am not your Barbie styling head and this is not Queen for a Day at the Omega Moo house. Makeovers? Not happening. We need to interrogate the roommates, for *Sars*, so let's hustle."

"Jack, I'm not fighting you. Let me explain in terms you understand," I tell her, with as much patience as possible. If I can't convince her why I'm right, we're destined to fail. "Would you, say, minesweep in board shorts and a tank top? Of course not!"

"Are you referring to minesweeping, which is the act of mine detection, or mine-clearing, which is an entirely separate entity and entails the physical removal process?"

"Either-flipping-or," I reply tersely and then I stop myself.

Calm blue ocean. Calm blue ocean.

Okay. Better.

I say, "My point is, the minesweepers and the mine-clearers wouldn't dare head into danger without their gloves and helmets, right? Running pell-mell into a field of potential landmines could be a death sentence, yes? I'm trying to prevent our accidentally getting exploded. Metaphorically."

Grudgingly, Jack admits, "Well, protective equipment *is* a key component to survival, should the process go awry. I've written about soldiers experiencing great success using the Guartel Inflatable Mine Shoes, which allow them to—"

"Super!" I crow. "You grasp the concept. Perfect. Then consider this—you and I are heading into a different *kind* of battle tonight. If we show up to the Monaco in yoga pants or mom jeans or a Junior Leaguer shift, we're done before we begin. We can't get in without having properly groomed, having dressed for success. We want to blend and we need the right kind of camouflage."

"So you're saying we participate in a makeover, which, I've already established, is a no."

"How do you not get this? I am *not* advocating for a makeover. Makeovers, wonderful though they may be, are not appropriate here. Makeovers are for nineties movie montages. Makeovers turn you into someone more elegant, *beaucoup* sophisticated, *trés* refined. To go 'clubbing,' we're striving for less elegant, less sophisticated, and less refined. Even if our mission is to go in all CIA, we need to *look* DTF."

"DTF?"

"Down to—never mind. We need a *skank-over*. Remember at the end of the movie *Grease* where Sandy got all tarted up in the shiny cigarette pants and poufy hair? That's the game plan. We need to be made *under*. And I have just the person to call for help."

. . . .

"Awesomesauce!" Ashley coos, sweeping the final coat of body glitter across my collarbone. "Ohmigod, if the PTO could see you now! You should put your new look on your blog. Everyone would pin the crap out of this!"

"For sure!" I reply, knowing my posting this outfit is as likely as me sharing my secret Snickerdoodle ingredient with Brooke Birchbaum. (Homemade pumpkin pie spice with grated, crystallized ginger.) "But in case I forget, you're still a total lifesaver, thank you so much! I owe you a massive favor. And a favor from Kitty Carricoe? Is money in the bank. Fact."

Upon the news of our last-minute club-themed costume party (the easiest explanation), Ashley came rushing over with cases of cosmetics, scores of fake hairpieces, and stacks of dresses. I chose the only garment that would accommodate both a strapless bra and a pair of Spanx. The downside is the halter holding up my bodice is made of chain link, which is freezing cold against my skin. But at least I'm not Jack, stuck in a hot pink pleather one-shoulder sheath with a gigantic, daisy-shaped cutout up the side and *Pretty Woman*–style, thigh-high platform boots.

"Where'd you learn to do all of this? Are you a makeup artist or film costumer? If not, you should be," Jack says. I can see why she'd be incredulous, with Ashley all radiant and summer-chic in a blousy Tory Burch tunic, Jack Rogers wedges, and skinny white Bermudas, hair simply secured in a low, messy bun.

"Eh, I helped on some music videos, nothing real serious, though. This was my daily style before Kitty taught me to be all classy," Ashley replies. "I'm taken way more serious now, totes legitamittens!"

"Then well-done. I'm a completely different person in this outfit. I feel like Mata Hari," Jack says, turning back and forth in front of the mirror, far less distressed than I'd expect. Ashley's given Jack straight-up Kardashian-inspired hair, slicked back from her face and pulled high and tight, with a fake ponytail that hangs all the way to her waist. To make the extension seamless, Ashley's braided the ends of Jack's real hair and wrapped the piece around the clip of the fall, in a woven crown. Her makeup is fairly minimal, save for the J.Lo–style false mink lashes, so long and full they graze her cheekbones when she blinks. "The shoes will probably end me, but otherwise, I'm all ready for *the costume party.*"

"How do you like your look, Kitty? Bet you wish Dr. K were here to see you!"

Actually, that's not untrue. I'm a sleazy kind of hot, too. Whereas Jack's all smooth and sleek, I'm leonine with my flowing, clip-in golden mane and air-brushed bronzer. I'm less Snack Mom and more MILF right now.

"It's fab! I should borrow all this hair again so Kassie can trick-or-treat as Rapunzel. Where did you get all the clip-ins? I thought you never wore extensions," I say.

"Barry and I are into cosplay."

So I probably won't borrow the hair again.

Ashley circles around me, not completely satisfied. "Something's missing . . . oh, I know." She reaches into one of her tubs and pulls out what looks like a set of chicken cutlets. Without a second's hesitation, she's suddenly rooting around inside my bodice.

"Buy a girl a drink first!" I cry. Yet when she's done, I do appear . . . perkier. Like those three full years of breastfeeding never actually happened.

"Better, right?"

I have to agree. Can I purchase these from her?

Jack says, "Ashley, you are a girl to the nth degree . . . much to our collective advantage. Thank you."

"No probs! So, who's having the party tonight?" Ashley asks, packing up all her lotions and unguents.

"Some of the hygienists from the office," I reply.

"Cool! Gotta run. You both look *to die*, so have fun! Kisses!"

We depart soon afterward, but not before Nana Baba nearly wets herself laughing at us. Even though she understands what we're doing and why the costuming is necessary, we can hear her choke and snort all the way down the drive.

We climb into the back of the cab and give the driver our destination in the Gold Coast downtown. "You ladies workin' tonight?" he asks with a leer.

"That depends. Are you planning on collecting a tip tonight?" Jack replies. After that, he stays quiet.

"So we're ready," she says to me. "Ashley's makeunder is kind of genius."

"Right," I reply, "but we still need some help. Do you know anyone who has recent experience attracting women in their twenties?"

Jack places a quick call to Bobby and relays his advice. "He says we need to get a table with bottle service and offer the girls free drinks."

I feel an irrational twinge of something—jealousy?—but I can't even imagine why. I'm a married mom of three and he's a man-child.

Even if he is a decent listener.

"Bobby says that's the second fastest way to win them over."

I shake thoughts of him out of my head and refocus on what's important. "What's the first fastest way?" I ask.

"Free drugs."

"Bottle service it is."

· · · ·

Without Ashley's careful ministrations and her "chicken cutlets," we'd have never been granted entry to the Monaco. We'd have never mixed so seamlessly with the rest of the clubgoers. Ashley's makeunder has delivered us halfway to the finish line, but we still have to find answers.

We reel in Ingrid's roommates, all of whom I recognize from their Instagram accounts, with a story of a breakup and "grrrrl power" and a boyfriend's stolen credit card. Tonight we're calling ourselves Patsy and Edina in honor of *Absolutely Fabulous*, a show Jack and I used to watch together. To "prove" our story, Jack even flashes her platinum AMEX (really?) with her shortened first name on the front.

Now that we've convinced the girls to join us at our table, I assume Jack will take over from here. After all, she's the trained journalist.

Ha!

Five minutes into her White House Press Corps, impeachment-grade, rapid-fire questioning, I have to drag her into the black-walled, smoked-glass, unisex restroom by her ponytail.

"You are blowing it!" I hiss.

"I'm not blowing it!" she hisses back.

I cross my arms over my chicken cutlets. So buoyant! "You're blowing it and you know it. I thought you were a journalist! I thought you knew how to finagle information out of people! I thought you understood how to infiltrate a community by posing as a member of the community."

She begins to twist a strand on the long tail. "I'm used to straightforward fact-gathering. Pitching hardballs. I'm less comfortable with the clandestine, undercover business of investigative reporting. Despite my respect for writers like Barbara Ehrenreich and Pam Zekman, I guess I'm no Nelly Bly."

"No kidding."

As we glower at each other, men and women filter into the dark restroom, a few to use the facilities for their intended purpose, but most to either couple in the stalls or sniff cocaine off of house keys they're dipping into small vials. Every time the door opens, we're hit with a blast of electronic dance music.

"This is fascinating!" Jack says in a low voice, attention diverted by a mesh-shirted, muscled man partaking of the booger sugar. "I always assumed one needed a white suit and a mirrored table to snort lines Scarface-style, but that's not true. While I've toured the poppy fields where Afghans harvest the raw opium from inside the seedpods, which is the first step in making heroin, I've never seen—"

I clap my palm over her mouth, which she instinctively bites.

After the screaming and subsequent wrestling, I rinse the now tender flesh under the faucet. I tell her, "Stop. Talking. You're killing our game here with the earnest Lois Lane thing. Fact. If we didn't spring for three flavors of Cîroc—you're paying for those, by the way—they'd have already bolted because you're coming on like Demented Diane Sawyer. Or Crazy Katie Couric."

She protests, "But—"

I dry my hands on a paper towel before generously slathering the bite with sanitizing gel. "Nope. No. Don't want to hear it, Batcrap Barbara Walters. The new plan is, I'm in charge. You will sit there quietly and drink premium flavored vodka when you're not busy dancing. No, do not give me that face. Yes, you *will* dance—this is a nightclub. People dance. You are people. But mostly, you will drink and be quiet. If you are addressed, you may offer one of the following responses: 'OMG,' 'WTF,' or 'STBY.' Do not share opinions. Do not mention semiotics. And for crying out loud, say *nothing* about Malaysia. I am not negotiating; this is how we're rolling. You had your chance to lead and you failed. Kitty's in charge now. Not Jack. Get it? Got it? Good. Let's head back now before they realize something's up."

She follows me out the bathroom door into the pulsing music of the club, where the bass is so profound I can feel it vibrate clean through me.

She asks, "What's STBY?"

"Sucks to Be You, which is what the code means, not a personal opinion. You, zip it. Not kidding." When we approach our table, I grin at Hallee, Shay, and Blake, Ingrid's roommates. I have to raise my voice for them to hear me. "'S'up, bitches! Edina needed a little breakfast cereal to turn it up. Don't worry, she's legitamittens now. Totes sorry we didn't bring enough to share with the rest of the class! Tear!"

Blake, Shay, and Hallee nod while Jack gawps at me openmouthed, which earns her a solid stomp on her instep under the table. She kicks me back. I pinch her and she elbows me in the chicken cutlet. I grab ahold of her ponytail and that immobilizes her. By way of explanation, I say, "She always gets a little violent before she starts to roll. Ignore her. If she convulses, we'll shove a spoon in her mouth so she doesn't choke on her tongue."

Jack removes my hand from her hair, offering us a terse, "OMG," in response.

What's interesting to note is that *I'm* the Mata Hari here, not Jack, because it's me who turns the conversation to the information we solicit.

"Have you guys ever had, like, a bad roomie? I had one in college a couple of years ago. She was the wooooooooorst. Mean it," I say during a quieter part of the music, while avoiding Jack's poisonous glare. "Total she-male, but that didn't stop her from banging my boyfriend."

"Like, I don't even have time for more bad roommates," Hallee says. "So we share a place with this basic bitch named Ingrid, right?"

Jack relaxes a little bit when she sees that my line of questioning is headed somewhere.

Hallee continues. "So last week, she's all boohoo, but then on Tuesday morning? Hashtag gone girl while we were all at work."

"You have *jobs*?" Jack asks and I pinch her. "OMG!"

"Um, yeah? I'm a receptionist, Shay does graphic design, and Blake teaches spin classes, hashtag SoulCycle. Anyway, Ingrid took none of her good shit, either. Left her jewelry, her major electronics, and her shearling coat, hashtag mine now."

"Are you worried?" I ask, ignoring how Jack's pinching me back.

"Hells, naw! Bitch Bogarted all my sluttiest La Perla thongs," Hallee huffs, one eye on us, one scanning the crowd for attractive potential bathroom partners. "She'd best stay gone girl, far as I'm concerned."

"Right?" Shay added, giving her leopard-print tube top a judicious yank. "I don't like to throw shade, but I haven't even *worn* the new gingham Juicy Couture bikini she took. And she, like, tore off the tags and left them on my bed for me to clean up. I can't even. I've been texting and texting, but all afternoon, it's been all Message Error, Message Error. She's oh-tee-gee."

"Is it your opinion that she seemed to have left in a hurry, and if so, what precipitated this act?" Jack asks. I deliver another ninja table kick and she clears her throat and says, "I mean, WTF, STBY!"

"For reals," Blake agrees, sweeping a curtain of straight, tawny hair over one shoulder. "What I don't get is why go off the grid with my duffel bags? I'm not here for it, you know? I have a bunch of them for the gym and for dance practice and work and stuff and she snatched 'em all. I mean, yassss for her not stealing my Kate Spade suitcases, but they were right next to each other in my closet. Why grab the ones with stank on them? Like, I get she was upset over her boss buying the farm and all, but to take off two days later, with our premium shit? I'm all, 'Cuntasaurus Rex much?'"

When the girls go dance, Jack pounces on me. "So Ingrid went from mourning Trip to stealing new bikinis and skimpy underwear in a matter of less than a week? Why? And where did she travel that's out of text range? Cell phones work all over the world, but outside of the US only with an international plan, which tells me (a) she's likely away from the continental United States as of this afternoon and (b) her trip wasn't premeditated."

"What does it all mean?" I ask.

Jack's words come out in a rush, as she tries to finish her thought before the Beyoncé remix ends. "I'm trying to connect the dots. Why would Ingrid leave valuable possessions, but take multiple heavy canvas bags? Did she grab said bags on Trip's instructions, perhaps to ferry large amounts of cash? That's my best guess. But where might he have stashed the cash? Through the Foreign Accounts Compliance Act, the IRS has cracked down on US citizens hiding money in offshore accounts over the past few years. Even places like the Caymans and Switzerland are beginning to comply, so money deposited in a bank seems somewhat unlikely—"

"We need more information. We have to get into the apartment. We've got to see what's on her computer," I say.

"Affirmative," Jack says. "Breaking and entering? On it. But I'll probably need to change shoes first and put on underwear."

"You're not wearing underwear?"

"I'm exposed from hip to thigh. Where would I put them?"

I shudder. "Thank goodness my lessons about sitting like a lady finally sank in. Also? Eww."

She twists a bit of her fake hair. "Yeah, tell me about it. Once on assignment I went a month without a shower. This feels worse. Far worse."

"Well, sorry to hear it. Mean it. Anyway, I have an idea. How much cash do you have, Jack?" A cocktail waitress comes by to police up our empties. She points at the empty Cîroc Coconut bottle and I gesture for one more. On Jack's tab, naturally.

"About three hundred bucks? Plus a debit card and other assorted plastic. Why?"

I look over both my shoulders to make sure the waitress is gone. "Go buy us some drugs. We need bait."

"*What?* Are you *crazy?* How about (a) no, and (b) how would I even go about purchasing illegal substances?"

I grab the back of her ponytail so she has no choice but to look at me. "Let me get this straight—breaking and entering is fine, but buying three grams of ecstasy from a guy in the bathroom is out of the question? Do you want to help Betsy or not? I got us this far, Jordan. Do your part. Bring this home."

Jack stomps off to the bathroom, ponytail swinging, and returns five minutes later.

"I'm both pleased and disheartened at how easy it is to buy drugs here," she says, gesturing toward what looks like a bag full of Skittles in the top part of her thigh-high boot.

"What the actual hell, Jordan? There's like sixty pills there!"

"You said to buy three grams. This is what three grams looks like." My bad.

"I thought three grams equaled three doses," I admit. "Way off on that, eh? I should probably reread my *Big Book of Keeping Your Kid off the Horse.* I feel like I may have missed an important part. The metric system is hard, right? The pills look a lot like Razzles, though, don't they? Remember? First it's a candy, then it's a gum?"

"Clearly, you're the one who is high, Carricoe. They're smaller and aren't bumpy. These much more closely resemble SweeTarts."

"Oh. Em. Eff. Gee." We notice Blake standing over us, gazing down into Jack's boot. "You two need to bring your bestie Molly to an after party at our place, like, right now."

I whisper to Jack, "Mission accomplished."

She replies, "Who's Molly?"

• • • •

"Anything?" I whisper to Jack. A few minutes ago, she excused herself to use the bathroom off of Ingrid's room, where she was supposed to search Ingrid's computer.

"Password protected."

"Damn it."

"All y'all bitches need to get turnt!" Hallee shrieks, waving a bottle of tequila. I feel like she's not going to be at her sharpest behind the reception desk tomorrow. "Body shots!" She cranks the music and flips on a strobe light. My goodness, I hope none of the clubgoers who joined us here are epileptic. Seizure city. Crowds of guests begin to hop around in an approximation of dance. Wow, I'd hate to live downstairs.

As Hallee waves the bottle and points at us, I feel my first pang of panic. "I can't do a body shot! The alcohol's going to pool in my C-section scar. They'll realize we're not Patsy and Edina from River North."

"Oh, to return to the land of five seconds ago, before I knew about your C-section scar," Jack says. "Please fill me in again on how your vagina's like an unfolded map. Tremendous fan of that story, too."

"Shut it. Also, you are going to have to *steal* the laptop, but mostly, shut it," I say.

"I would, but where do you propose I hide it? My dress is literally the size of an eye patch. And I can see the mole on my hip through this fabric. If I try to conceal so much as a Tootsie Roll, they're going to see it."

"Fine. Then you do body shots with Tomorrow's Leaders while I save the day. A-flipping-gain."

I make my way to the bathroom through the crowd. The roommates squeal as Jack takes her turn at bat over Hallee's navel, her face as grim as though she were facing a firing squad.

Sorry I'm not sorry.

Ingrid's room is a veritable trash heap, shoes and clothes strewn everywhere. I fight the urge to make her bed. I give the space a cursory glance to determine what she may or may not have taken with her. There's no makeup or shampoo in the bathroom, or evidence of birth control pills anywhere, so she must have packed these items. I don't see any sandals, tank tops, or sundresses in the closet, so I hold with Jack's theory that she's somewhere warm.

I take the laptop into Ingrid's bathroom and I lift the back of my dress, sliding the computer into my Spanx the long way. Because this dress is black and not completely body-skimming, the bulge isn't too noticeable, but sitting down's out of the question.

Theft complete, we have to scram before we're caught.

"Hey, bae!" Hallee calls as she positions an ashen-faced Jack on the table. "Shots, shots, shots!" As I approach Hallee, Blake smacks me on the butt.

"Ow! Your ass is like titanium, Patsy," Blake says, scrunching and unscrunching her fingers. "Why is it so hard? And flat?"

"Squats and lunges," I titter nervously.

Hallee peers at my posterior. "Hey. HEY. Are you ... Is that ... Bitch is Bogarting one of our laptops!" Jack's off the table in a flash and I'm already running when the chase ensues. Jack and I push past revelers down the apartment's long hallway. I press the DOWN button but the elevator is stopped ten floors away.

"I can't run any faster!" Jack yelps, limping behind me at half speed. "Not in these boots! Save yourself and the laptop!"

"I'm not leaving you behind because I'll never hear the end of it! Use the pills to create a diversion," I yell, yanking open the door to the emergency exit stairwell.

With one deft, Women's-World-Series-of-Softball pitch, Jack hurls the Razzles/SweeTarts/Molly at the apartment doorway and the party-goers dive for the drugs like a pack of piranhas on an unfortunate cow, effectively blocking the roommates' progress.

We make it down five flights of cement stairs and to the street just as a cab pulls up, the girls a couple of paces behind us. They must have caught the elevator. I have to dive into the car lengthwise because I can't bend at the waist. We're both screaming at the cabbie to "drive, drive" before we even have the doors shut.

"Are you ladies filming *Amazing Race*? I love *Amazing Race*! Is my favorite! Taxi make or break racers. I always want to be cabdriver on show—you ride with Mahvish, you win game." The happy man in the turban beams back at us.

Before I can say anything, Jack tells him, "Yes, and you just helped us beat the other teams. Thank you, Mahvish. You're the best."

. . . .

"You're not sleeping in the garage."

"Why not?"

"Because it's a *garage*."

"But it smells like Christmas!"

When we arrived home, we were both too keyed up to sleep, so I opened a bottle of wine while we tried to guess Ingrid's password. We had no luck with the computer, so we hatched a plan to head to Atlanta in the morning so that John-John can use his skills to help us. Jack says she has other contacts who could crack the password for us, but we decided John is the only one we can trust.

Feeling victorious, we opened a second bottle. We're currently sitting on the amazing rug Betsy gave me, as this seemed the most appropriate place to toast her.

"You're not bunking with my lawn mower when the pullout couch has thousand-count Egyptian cotton sheets on it," I reply. "So soft. Like a cloud made of marshmallow fluff."

"But I loooove your garage," Jack says dreamily, lying back on the rug. "I hate these boots, but I want to marry your garage." The moment we arrived home, Jack donned underwear and now the daisy cutout is filled with the striped pattern of her sensible high-hipped panties.

"And I love my chicken cutlets," I say, hugging my chest. "But we're not getting married. We're in a committed domestic partnership. We're very progressive."

"There's a slight possibility I may be drunk," Jack says. "Very slight. Yet still possible."

"Me, too."

Jack hums something to herself and I can feel my eyelids grow heavy. I swear this has been the longest day of my life. Did Ken just leave for Miami yesterday? Were we at the funeral this very afternoon? Reflecting on the past two days makes me even more exhausted than I already am, far too tired to even climb the stairs, let alone change out of this dress.

I tell Jack, "You go sleep on the couch. I'm going to sleep right here on this rug. For Betsy." Jack is already horizontal, so I lie down as well, feeling the not-unpleasant scratch of the wool beneath me. As I lie here and look up, I wonder . . . should I paint my ceiling a contrasting color?

"For Sars," she echoes, more to herself than to me.

"Hey, Jack?"

"What?"

"Should I paint the ceiling in here?"

"With frescoes? Like the Sistine Chapel?"

I was thinking "a lighter shade of iridescent dove gray" but her way sounds much better, ultimately more pin-able. "Yes."

"Absolutely."

"Cool." My body feels very heavy against the rug. "Hey, Jack?"

"What?"

"We're kind of a good team."

She takes so long to respond I believe she's already asleep, until she replies, "We are. And I don't hate you right now."

I reach over and pat her on the face. "I don't hate you, either."

She pats me back, saying, "Whoa." Her arms drop back to her side.

"Right?" I ask.

The house is quiet, save for the occasional clink of the ice maker and the soft whir of the air conditioner.

"Good night, Kitty Cat Carricoe."

"Good night, Jack NotBouvier Jordan."

Her breathing slows, as does mine. I pull the edge of the rug over to use as a blanket, drifting off into the most well-earned sleep.

"Hey, Kitty?"

"Yeah?"

"Did you say we have lice?"

CHAPTER EIGHTEEN

Jack

....

En route to Atlanta
Thursday

"I'm hobbled."

I flex my foot, desperate to soothe the cavalcade of pain from toe to heel. Why am I in such agony? My extremities are accustomed to discomfort. I've humped a fifty-pound rucksack over a twenty-five-mile tactical road march in the scorching desert sun. I've run the BMW Berlin marathon, twice. I've had bones shaved when *hallux rigidus* set in after mountaineering the Wrangell range. But nothing could have prepared me for how my poor dogs barked in those hooker boots last night.

"You're not hobbled. Millions of women wear heels every day. Trust me, you'll rally."

"You're speaking to me again?" I glance over at Kitty in the driver's seat. Much like me, she's all pale skin and dark circles this morning.

She keeps her eyes fixed on the highway while maintaining a strict fifty-six miles per hour, a pair of huge plastic sunglasses balanced on the tip of her nose, even though it's not bright out. "Only long enough to tell you you're not hobbled."

A truck honks at us and then passes on the right, despite this stretch of road having a sixty-five-MPH speed limit. "When you do start speaking to me, can you explain the breakfast cereal bit?" I ask. I massage my foot to no avail—it's still throbbing.

"Breakfast cereal is Special K," she replies, offering the trucker a friendly wave. "Those are both slang terms for ketamine."

"Ketamine—the NMDA receptor antagonist, which is a Schedule III controlled substance?" I ask.

She pushes the big plastic glasses up on her head to hold back her hair. "Yep, it's a club drug, similar to ecstasy and Molly, which is supposed to be the purest form of MDMA. Pure, my aunt Fanny! The newest batches of Molly have been coming out of labs in China. I say, if we can't trust the Chinese not to poison our pets with tainted dog chow, there's no way they're selling a pure form not cut with anything. That's why these substances are such a clear and present danger. I hate that we were on the wrong side of the War on Drugs last night, but I didn't see any other way."

How does Captain Carpool know about club drugs when I don't?

"And you learned all of this . . . how?"

She glances over at me. "Because I have a fifteen-year-old to protect not only from the world but also from himself and his fifteen-year-old impulses. I have to be perpetually one step ahead of him. A lot of parents—the decent ones, not Brooke Birchbaum, *ahem*—keep track of what their kids are doing by reading their texts. Kids caught on, so they started texting in code, especially when it came to illegal substances."

"Like the Enigma machine famously used by the Nazis to generate cyphers via electro-mechanical rotors?"

"Sure. Exactly like that."

"Your glasses are off; I can see you rolling your eyes at me."

"Excellent. I wasn't trying to hide the fact. Anyway, I made it my job to stay abreast of the lingo because I am *not* about to be a forty-year-old grandmother or have my kid hooked on anything other than Phonics. Before you even say it, no, I give zero craps about his Fourth Amendment rights when I'm trying to keep him safe. He doesn't have a right to privacy when he's fifteen. And P.S., still not speaking to you, so please stop speaking to me. Unless you spot a Starbucks. In which case, grunt."

I was about to compliment her on her parenting skills, but now I shall keep my kudos to myself. Still, I'm very impressed by her level of commitment to her children, even if this is the reason she's currently freezing me out.

At least I *understand* her silent treatment this time around.

I gaze out the window as the miles rush by. We're on a desolate part of I-65, somewhere in northern Indiana, on our way down to Atlanta where John-John will help us hack into Ingrid's computer. We tried booking a flight, but the airlines are still in a state of chaos after the massive storms yesterday—my God, was that just yesterday?—and we'll arrive quicker by driving.

We ride for another twenty minutes of silence. We'd been listening to the nineties station on Sirius until a David Gray song came on. In the spirit of making benign conversation, I mentioned how this song had been used at GITMO as part of the advanced interrogation program to solicit information from prisoners. That's when she snapped off the radio.

I say, "To confirm, you're mad about the hair, right?"

It has to be the hair this morning, because we were chummy by the end of the night, drunk on victory, and to a lesser extent, chardonnay. Overall, our interaction was, dare I say, pleasant. Perhaps all we ever needed was a common cause. She even turned on the charm first thing this morning when Bobby brought me a few changes of clothing, sending him back to Teddy's with a Tupperware full of squash-laden scones. So the hair has to be her sticking point.

Kitty glowers at me, her face pasty under two rage-based circles of pink on her cheeks. "Ding, ding, ding."

"I was trying to get us on the road as expediently as possible," I say. Silence.

"It's an effective solution," I say. "The US Army wouldn't have used it if it weren't."

Angry silence.

"I'd never suggest anything I wouldn't do myself," I say.

Punishing silence.

"Wouldn't have been an issue if you'd accepted that Birchbaum person's offer to send the Hair I Go Again technician," I say.

"Don't try to justify your actions, okay? Do not pin this on me. How do you not realize YOU CAN'T SHAVE AN EIGHT-YEAR-OLD'S HEAD?" she shouts in reply.

"She was game," I reason. "She recognized we were trying to get on the road as soon as possible and she wanted to do her part."

Kitty presses down harder on the gas pedal, grimacing the whole time. We jump from fifty-six to seventy-six miles per hour in what feels like a millisecond. (Perhaps the quote should be *'Cadillac, there is no substitute.'*)

Kitty seethes. "First, no one shaves heads anymore for lice. Doesn't happen. That's so flipping outdated. As for 'do her part'? There's no *do her part.* She's eight, okay? *Eight.*"

"I beg to differ. I was doing my part when I was eight. My mother always insisted we do our part to be quiet when she had one of her 'headaches,' do our part grocery shopping, do our part in cleaning the house, planting the flowers . . . I don't know if I ever told you—she and my father met in law school. She left before third year to get married, so mostly we had to do our part in amusing ourselves when she went back to school to complete her degree and then worked to pass the bar."

Kitty pulls an odd face and I don't know how to interpret her expression.

"How did her putting pressure on you to 'do your part' work out?" she asks.

I reflect on the unrelenting stress. "Not well. We'd try our frantic best to complete our tasks to her specifications, perpetually disappointing her, only to be 'rewarded' with her stony silence. Then she'd grab the damn cat and retreat to her office for hours. She'd never explode at us, only quietly implode. I clearly remember two things—one, that she never yelled at us and, two, that I wished she would have. Probably would have been easier. Anger dissipates. Indifference can go on indefinitely."

"That had to be hard."

"It was." To this day, I despise silence as a form of punishment. I'd much prefer to deal with someone's ire.

In a softer tone, Kitty explains, "Here's the thing—at eight, the prefrontal cortex is barely developed. Children are by nature irrational and impulsive. So if you, a person she likes and trusts, tell Kassie she should allow you to shave her head as a delousing solution, she's likely to submit. Kassie's less mature than many of the girls in her class, so she still wants to please everyone. You and I had the hour to spare. That was time enough for the lice shampoo to work and for me to strip and wash everything. Buzzing off her hair wasn't ever the best long-term solution, particularly since she didn't even have nits. Would we have saved the hour it took me to comb through her hair? Yes. But then she'd be the only bald girl starting third grade at Lakeside. That's why I slapped the clippers out of your mitts and called you a 'flipping ninny.'"

Even though she's speaking rationally to me, she's still clearly upset. At this point we're traveling almost ninety-four miles per hour.

"I am very sorry, Kitty. Truly. I overstepped my bounds and I apologize. Kassie's a great kid and I regret that my actions could have potentially caused alienation. I remember how singled out I felt in Saint Louis as the only girl in class without a two-parent family. The teachers used to huddle, talking about me in hushed tones. I hated being the object of pity. I wouldn't wish that level of discomfort on anyone, particularly a little girl as sweet as Kassie."

She's quiet but I can tell she's processing my words.

I suggest, "This is where you say, 'I forgive you, Jack. Your heart was in the right place.'"

Kitty eases off the gas and we drop back down to the fifties. "I've known you for twenty years and this is the most I've heard you speak about your mother."

"Not my favorite topic," I reply. "My mother was . . . a chasm of icy contempt. Our whole family bore the mark of her dissatisfaction. We walked on eggshells. I always think about the line from *Anna Karenina*, 'Happy families are all alike; every unhappy family is unhappy in its own way.' Callous as it sounds, we were better off after she was gone. I feel like my childhood began when we moved to Evanston. I prefer not to remember a lot of what came before."

Kitty lightly touches my shoulder with her right hand. "I forgive you, Jack. Your heart was in the right place. I'm sorry I overreacted and the next time you make me mad—which, let's be honest, is probably just around the corner—I'll tell you why."

I actually believe her apology.

We pass a few miles of cornfields before I speak. "Your children—your Littles?—are very lucky to have a mom who's so invested, so involved. My brothers and I would have done anything to garner that kind of attention. Kassie, Kord, and Konnor are going to grow up healthy and strong, mentally and physically. Able to face problems, rather than run from them."

"There are no guarantees in life," Kitty says. "The best I can do is start them off with a solid foundation; the rest is up to them."

"If Ken's half the father you are a mother, then you have nothing to worry about."

She looks over at me. "Are we veering dangerously toward a Hallmark moment?" Kitty asks.

"I'm afraid so. We'd best discuss Malaysia," I reply and we share a genuine laugh.

"So . . . Malaysia is really spectacular, huh?" Kitty asks.

"God, yes. Singapore's spotlessly clean, and modern to the point of feeling space-aged. The city is a blend of Eastern and Western culture and architecture, so it's fascinating. Then, if you travel far enough north, you'll hit the rain forest, which feels prehistoric with the leaf canopy and wildlife like orangutans and tigers. And the foliage? Not to be believed. Imagine Kassie's drawings come to life. The flora's like something out of *Charlie and the Chocolate Factory*. Last time I visited, I saw a type of rafflesia, better known as the corpse flower. Reminded me of the flowers on your dorm comforter, except this one can grow up to three feet in diameter and smells like rotting flesh."

"Why does it stink?"

"To attract bugs for pollination. This was not my favorite part of Malaysia. Still, what a spectacular country. Definitely in my top ten."

"I'd love to see it." Kitty sighs and then adds, "Someday."

"Look at us, engaging in conversation," I observe.

"And wearing underwear."

"Tremendous fan of that."

We both go quiet, but now it's a comfortable silence.

After a few more miles, I say, "Regardless of what we find out about Trip, our finally making peace will have a profound impact on Sars."

Kitty raises an eyebrow. "You mean Betsy."

I grin. "That's more like it."

"Hey, while we're not fighting, can I ask you something personal?" Kitty says.

I shrug. "Depends."

"What's the deal with *Top Gun*?"

I turn entirely in my seat to face her. "*That?* That's what you want to know? Not, *'Jack, why didn't you ever get married?'* or *'Jack, what are your greatest triumphs or regrets?'* Not even, *'Jack, what about you and Petraeus?'*"

She shrugs. "Eh, those questions tell me what you've done, not who you are. I'm curious because as Bobby was leaving earlier, he said to remind you that the plaque for the alternates is down in the ladies' room? I assume that's another *Top Gun* quote. I don't personally understand the reference, but he wasn't saying it for my benefit. Obviously, this thirty-year-old film is important to you; I want to know why."

"How long do you have?" I ask.

Kitty glances at the GPS. "Seven hours."

I pause to collect my thoughts. How do I explain without exposing too much of myself? Or is it truly time to let down my guard?

Ultimately, I choose the second option.

"We lost my mother in the spring of 1986. That's no secret. My father didn't know what to do with himself, let alone four shell-shocked kids. We were just . . . zombies. All of us, just going through the motions at school, at practices, in our home. How do you process something like that?"

"I really am sorry."

"I appreciate hearing that, Kitty. So, *Top Gun*. We were all numb at the time. Hollow. No highs, no lows. Then, one day we saw the trailer for the film and we all forgot to grieve for a minute. When you suffer a tremendous loss, even when the situation wasn't ideal in the first place, you mourn. But for the one minute and thirty seconds of the trailer, we were just a bunch of American kids who wanted to see a cool movie.

"When Dad realized we were excited about something—anything—he jumped on it. He took us to see the movie on opening day and it was transformative. One of his law school buddies did entertainment law, and he somehow managed to secure an early VHS copy of the film, too. Getting lost in that movie for two hours gave us back something we'd been missing—joy. *Top Gun* became a touchstone for us. A common love. The ritual of watching became far more important than the movie's content. Our broken family began to slowly knit itself back together, stronger than before, and the movie was the impetus."

Kitty's listening, really listening, as I speak. "None of us knew how to articulate our thoughts back then. Therapy wasn't a *thing* yet. *Top Gun* gave us a way to feel the gamut of emotions within a safe space. Maybe we couldn't cry over our mother, but it was just fine to pop in the VHS and tear up for Goose. *Top Gun* has always been the language of love for my brothers and me. Our family isn't terribly demonstrative, so when Bobby quotes 'it's time to buzz a tower,' I know what he really means. That's why I lost my mind when you ripped my poster, starting the whole chain of events that—well, you were there. No need to rehash."

"I truly had no idea," Kitty said. "Maybe if we'd had this conversation twenty years ago, we'd be in a different place."

"Perhaps," I agree. "But we're here now. That's enough."

"I feel like I should watch the movie sometime."

I am incredulous. "Hold the fu—*flip* on. You've never seen *Top Gun*? How's that possible? It's such an important part of American pop culture with the music and the styles and the stars—how have you avoided it for almost thirty years?"

Kitty shrugged. "I don't know. I guess I preferred Meg Ryan movies?"

"But she's in it!" I exclaim.

"Really?"

"Yes. Pull off at the next exit. There's a Walmart. We have a DVD to buy."

. . . .

While Kitty's watching the movie, I've been piloting the Escalade. I'm deeply, profoundly in love. I haven't felt this deeply drawn to a vehicle since I sat behind the stick of my first Cessna.

As the credits roll, I ask, "Thoughts?"

"I liked it a lot, especially understanding what it means to you. Still, I have questions," Kitty replies. "Many questions. For example, how come Goose didn't get to take off his shirt during the volleyball game? And why was everyone so sweaty the whole time? They were mostly in San Diego—isn't San Diego famously temperate? Is it wrong that I found Tom Skerritt to be the hot one?"

Kitty's a font of surprises. "That's what you got out of it? You don't feel the need, the need for speed? You're not concerned your ego's writing checks your body can't cash? You don't want to climb into an F-14 and go screaming across the sky, chasing MiGs?"

"No, thank you," Kitty replies. "I'm good here. I guess I was most surprised by how homoerotic the whole thing was."

"What?" I practically swerve off the road, which causes the Driver Awareness System to pulse my seat bolster. I quickly right our path.

"Oh, yeah." Kitty nods. "Like, how many shower scenes can you pack into two hours? Also, all underpants, all the time? And my goodness, the suggestive dialogue? 'Iceman's on my tail, he's coming hard.' 'Damn it, I want some butts!' Homo. Erotic. Nothing wrong with that, just pointing it out."

"You have quite the overactive imagination."

"Disagree." Kitty whips out her smartphone. "I'm going to Google 'Top Gun' and 'gay.' And . . . fifty-three million results. I'm obvi not the first to have noticed."

"Can I use your phone? I need to make a call."

She points at the dash. "Bluetooth enabled. You dial through the console. Here, I'll do it for you—what's the number?"

I give her the digits and wait as the phone rings. "Ted Jordan speaking."

"Teddy, it's me. Quick question—was *Top Gun* homoerotic?"

He bursts out laughing. "Not what I expected to hear from you, Jack-o."

"Well, Kitty and I are having an argument—"

"Discussion," she interrupts. "We're having a civilized discussion. P.S. we're on speakerphone. P.P.S. We're friends now."

"Glad to hear it," Teddy says. "So, you're both calling to confirm that *Top Gun* was homoerotic?"

I say, "Or deny. Feel free to deny."

"Let me put it to you like this," Teddy says. "Val Kilmer was my first crush. That answer your question?"

I feel all the breath leave me. "I . . . don't even know who I am anymore. This alters my whole worldview."

Teddy says, "Kiddo, this doesn't mean *Top Gun* wasn't the best thing to happen to the Jordan family. Just means we each took something different away from it. Nothing's changed. You're fine."

"I'm driving, so I have to go," I reply.

"See you later, Teddy," Kitty says.

"Don't kill each other, you two," he says by way of good-bye.

I shoot Kitty a look. "No promises," I reply.

• • • •

"Uncle, okay? I finally see it," I say after our second and third viewings. "No need to rub it in."

"We can both agree that it's a terrific movie that stands the test of time. I'll leave the DVD in the car so the boys can watch," Kitty says. "See? Now we're bonding. Everyone wins!"

"Just in time. John-John's house is right around the corner."

We pull into his driveway and I have a new appreciation for the property surrounding his house. Excellent tree-to-grass-to-home ratio. Proportionate. Leaving our bags in the car, we grab the laptop and hustle inside. We realize the clock's ticking and now that the drive's over, we have a mystery to solve, preferably before the story breaks on Sunday.

After greeting John's wife and kids, we settle into the dining room to watch John do his magic. He's always bragging about his mad hacking skills, so I'm interested to watch him perform.

"How long will it take you to get in?" I ask.

"Can't say for sure," he replies. "I'm using John the Ripper, which is a password cracker. The amount of time's dictated by the length and strength of her password. If it's heavy on alphanumerics, could be a while, so get comfortable." I hover over John's shoulder while Kitty pokes around, admiring the decor.

"I'm in love with your toile," she says, examining the curtains printed with pastoral scenes.

"I don't know what that means," John replies.

"Girl stuff," I say.

Naturally, she and John's wife, Heather, got on like a house on fire. I'm sure they'd be the best of friends if they lived closer, likely trading recipes and child rearing secrets. But I have a new respect for how hard Kitty works for her family, which is why I suggested John finally buy his wife the jetted tub. I suspect she's earned it.

"Cute pic of your kids at the Millennium Park bean," she says, holding a photo of the whole brood.

"Thanks. I can't believe they stood still long enough for us to snap the shot," John replies. Because he's helping us, I don't mention exactly how much light his rapidly balding head reflects from the chandelier.

She gestures toward a picture of a different family.

"Cousins?" she asks. "Lots of family resemblance."

"No," I reply. "*Not* family."

Before Kitty can question why I'm suddenly curt, John says, "I'm in."

Who knew John wasn't bullshitting about his actual capabilities? Color me impressed. "Already?"

"People, this is why you don't use PASSWORD1234 as your password," John replies.

"You're kidding. Did we just waste ten hours in the car?" I ask.

"I wouldn't say waste," Kitty replies. "Our drive was worth it."

I can't disagree.

John establishes Ingrid's e-mail password almost as quickly, and Kitty and I begin our search for clues.

Unfortunately, there's little to see, save for marketing e-mails from places called Gilt and Net-a-Porter.

"There's nothing," I say, cradling my face in my hands. "All of that effort for nothing."

"Oh, please, you're not even trying," Kitty says. She sits down next to me and pulls the computer over to her. "You've never kept tabs on a fifteen-year-old boy, have you? Three words: browser search history."

The Safari cache is a veritable gold mine. We uncover everything from an Expedia.com search for hotels in Miami to information about chartering flights to the Cayman Islands to scuba gear reviews. We have a dozen hot new leads, one of which will surely lead us to Trip.

This laptop is the smoking gun. I'm sure of it.

Kitty and I are in the preliminary stages of planning our next step—driving to Miami—when John returns from the kitchen. "I told you I'd do something for you if you did something for me. Time to pay up."

He steps into the butler's pantry and opens the swinging door. He makes a motion for someone to join us, saying, "She's done. Come on in."

I instantly recognize the sound of high heels clicking on the travertine and my body tenses. Now I'm furious with myself. Why did I think I could trust John? How have I learned nothing from forty years of his self-serving douchebaggery?

"Hello, Jacqueline."

Suddenly, I'm not distracted by the pain in my feet or the daunting task of finding Trip. Instead, I am entirely focused on this moment.

I stand up to face her head-on.

"Hello, Mother."

CHAPTER NINETEEN

Kitty

....

Atlanta to Miami
Thursday

"I beg your pardon. Did you say *'mother'*?"

But no one answers, or even looks in my direction.

Jack did not just say this elegant, ageless, polished, Escada-clad woman was her mother, right? Not possible. Except . . . they do resemble each other. Same heavy hair, same cheekbones, same almond-shaped eyes, although hers are two different colors. Same quiet confidence. They're even standing the same way, with perfect posture and squared shoulders.

But Jack's mother is dead. Jack's said it a million times. Hasn't she? Is this lady a ghost?

"Why are you here?" Jack says, practically spitting out every word.

"I live in Atlanta now," her mother (?) replies.

What is happening? Why does Jack seem ready to strangle someone? (And why am I so relieved that it's not me she wants to strangle?)

"Well, isn't that nice for all of you? Family first," Jack replies. Her voice is downright acidic.

"It's not like that," John pleads. "They just moved here."

"They," Jack hisses. "You're a traitor, John-John."

"You don't understand, Jack. It's different when you have kids," he says. "They have a right to know all their grandparents."

"What'd she promise you this time, John? Another new car? An even bigger house? How much does it cost to sell out your real family? What's your asking price?"

With an icy calm, the woman replies, "Jacqueline, I'll not have you take that tone."

Jack gets right up in her face. "Really? What are you going to do about it? Run away?"

"I'm not the one who runs, my dear. You practically left skid marks, you couldn't get away from us in Chicago fast enough."

"*Bullshit.*" Jack's balling her fists as though she's the aggressor, but I sense there's an imbalance of power here, not favoring Jack. I feel an almost psychic tug of her desperately wanting someone on her team, so I stand at her side, placing a hand on her back. She does not pull away from me.

"We've been over this again and again," the woman replies, the very picture of calm repose. Everything about her is impeccable, from the tips of her red-soled, patent leather stilettos to her immaculately groomed Anna Wintour–style bob. "Frankly, I'm tired of your histrionics. You and I have needed to hash this out for a very long time. We're both here, so we'll speak now."

"No, we fucking won't!"

"Language, my dear."

Jack tells me, "Grab the laptop. We're leaving. Now."

"Why? What am I missing?" I ask, collecting the MacBook and stuffing it in my purse.

Eyes locked with the woman, Jack says, "I can't be in a room with her, not after what she did to us."

"C'mon, Jack. At least hear her out," John implores.

The elegant woman clucks her tongue. "That was almost thirty years ago. Grow up, Jacqueline. Discuss your issues like an adult."

"How about this? Kitty's a detached third party. We were sworn enemies until yesterday, so she's bound to be impartial. Let's each tell her our side and she can decide who's at fault here."

I'm still touching Jack's back and I can feel her tremble.

Jack takes a couple of ragged breaths and starts to explain. "This is my mother, Lucille Allen. No, wait, the Honorable *Judge* Lucille Allen. Honorable, my ass."

"No need to be juvenile, my dear."

"The Honorable Judge Allen was my mother up until 1986 when she decided she no longer wanted the job. She'd passed the bar that spring and was eager to practice law, like she'd originally intended thirteen years earlier. But, instead of, say, trying to strike a work-life balance, or seeking counseling, talking with our minister, filing for divorce, or even having a fucking *conversation* with my dad, she left. Went out for milk and never came back. Literally."

My mind is reeling. "She didn't die? She's alive? She's alive and well and right here in kind of a fantastic power suit? Sorry, that part doesn't matter. To confirm, she walked away but she *is* of the living."

I've never seen Jack so upset—given our past, that's really saying something.

Jack says, "She's dead to everyone but John, apparently. See, that's not nearly the best part. Oh, no. For two weeks, we thought she'd been abducted. No one just disappears without a trace, without a note, right? The police were involved. There was a search. They used cadaver dogs. We made posters. *Posters.*"

The idea of a young Jack and her brothers huddled around the kitchen table, using oak tag and colored pencils to make Missing posters cracks my heart clean in two. Crafts are meant to be happy, damn it!

Her mother purses her lips. "You're being overly dramatic."

"Am I, *Mother*? God, I'm sorry. I'd hate to be overly dramatic describing what it's like to spend two weeks of your childhood worrying every minute that your mother's either dead in a ditch or chained up in some sicko's basement."

Lucille's gigantic diamond catches the light of the chandelier when she flicks her wrist, covering a wall with refracted prisms. "I wasn't dead; I was at a friend's cabin. Terrible misunderstanding. I needed time to regroup and I didn't have access to the news. I had no idea there was such a to-do. Your father is overly dramatic, too. That's where you get it from," Lucille sniffs.

John's standing off to the side, clearly conflicted. Heather steps in for a second with a big plate of cookies, notes what's unfolding, and immediately exits. I feel like I shouldn't be here, either, but I dare not leave.

Jack is ramrod straight as she speaks. "You know what finally tipped us off? The cat. *The fucking cat.* We didn't even realize Tom Kitten was missing at first. He had a cat door and came and went as he pleased. With everyone in and out, we assumed he'd been staying away. But about two weeks into her disappearance, we realized his bed was missing. So when she left, *she took the cat with her.* Not us. Just the cat. And her terrible, indulgent parents supported her decisions. They also knew where she was the whole time; they just didn't tell us. They were more concerned with keeping their spoiled little girl happy than they were about their grandchildren's well-being. Unforgivable."

"Mimi and Poppy made it up to you with the trust," her mother replies, completely unaffected by Jack's diatribe.

"Of course, yes, *the trust* tucked me into bed at night and *the trust* held my hand when I had a bad dream. Tell *the trust* thanks for teaching me how to use a tampon, will you?"

John winces.

"There's no need to be crude, Jacqueline."

I feel queasy hearing these details. I can't imagine what poor Jack's been going through all these years. No wonder she was so slow to warm up to other women. No wonder she was so livid when we had our falling-out. No wonder she's always been bonded to Betsy, clinging to that which was solid and sane and sweet.

"You have to understand how it was for me," her mother says. "I was suffocating in that house. The noise, the chaos, the awful dogs. The *smell.* Everyone perpetually saying, *'I want this, I need that.'* What about what I wanted and needed? I tried to make you my ally, Jacqueline, tried to raise you right, but you wanted none of it, refusing to wear dresses, fussing when I tried to braid your hair. You just wanted to be one of the boys."

Lucille takes a cigarette out of her chic calfskin clutch and lights it with a silver lighter. John discreetly sets a crystal ashtray next to her, like a well-trained waiter. They've done this dance before. She takes a quick drag and continues. "I was twenty-four when Teddy was born, swept up in the romance of it all with your father. Nice man. Not ambitious enough. You see, I was the only child of wealthy parents. I was accustomed to people taking care of me, not vice versa. I wasn't used to how *needy* children were."

She takes another puff. "I didn't comprehend what it took to be a mother. And there we were at the beginning of the feminist movement, and the same shackles I'd been rallying against suddenly bound me. I marched for the Equal Rights Amendment, you know. So if you enjoy the freedom to be a woman in a man's world, Jacqueline, you have me to thank. Your brother has forgiven me. It's time you and the rest of the boys do as well."

A tear streams down Jack's cheek, yet she doesn't even notice it. She says, "I could understand our family being too much. We're a lot to take. And I've always blamed myself for not being 'girly' enough for you."

Lucille exhales a thin stream of smoke, showing no reaction to what Jack's saying. Whether that's a function of being cold or having too much (excellent) plastic surgery, I can't be sure.

Jack continues. "I could even sympathize a bit with your abandoning us to live your dream. I understand the need to break free and the satisfaction of devoting your life to your profession. I do. I've been there. What I can't get past, what I can't forgive, what will keep me angry to the grave, is that after throwing us away for your career, you started an entirely new family. Hell will freeze over before I allow you back into my life."

"You have another family?" I say to Lucille, dumbfounded.

"Yes, I do. Two beautiful daughters, Caroline and Rose." She gestures toward the photo I'd admired earlier with her cigarette and ash falls on the linen tablecloth. They're both younger, more feminine versions of Jack. "When the girls were old enough, I felt it was important that they know the rest of their family, so I got in contact."

"Was this in 1999? September or so?" I ask.

"Let's see, Caroline was around twelve and Rose was ten. Yes, September of 1999 sounds about right," she says.

"How could you possibly know that?" Jack asks me. She's since fallen into a chair at the table, emotionally spent, fight completely knocked out of her, leaving Lucille standing in a more dominant position. Doesn't matter that Jack's almost forty; in this instance, and in her mother's eyes, she's perpetually a child.

To Jack, I say, "I'll explain in the car. Short story is, I owe you an apology and a debt of gratitude. But not important now." Then I do the math. "You have a daughter who was twelve in 1999? Caroline?"

Jack's mother smiles. "That's correct. She's started her medical residency at Emory. We're very proud. That's why her father and I retired to Atlanta."

"So you left in 1986 and she was born in 1987?" I ask.

"Do you have a point, my dear?"

"Where'd you go when you left Saint Louis? Were you alone or were you with someone? Like the owner of that cabin?"

She picks a nonexistent piece of lint off her beautifully tailored jacket. Aubergine, I think that's what the color is called. Somewhere between a purple and a black. So chic. "I hardly find these inquiries relevant."

"Please tell me you didn't leave one family to start another. Say that's not true." I can feel my pulse throbbing in my ears as I speak.

"Kitty, take it easy," John says. "Not your circus, not your monkeys."

Jack's mother meets my gaze. "The great irony is that no one blinks an eye when a man does the same. Pity. For as far as women have come, the sisterhood still has more ground to cover. My dear, what I did was leave to claim my destiny. That I began another family so quickly was a fortuitous happenstance. Second time around, I had a husband who supported my career. I had the baby and I was back at my desk in less than a month. I had a nanny and a housekeeper. Never touched a diaper myself. Eventually, we hired a cook, too. I found that motherhood was so much more rewarding with someone else attending to the heavy lifting."

The speed and ferocity of my backhand takes us all by surprise.

• • • •

"I can't believe you hit my mother." Jack's face is illuminated by the glow of the dashboard. She'd prefer to drive, but I prefer to confirm she's calm before handing over the wheel.

I reply, "I know. You keep saying that. And I keep saying I can't believe you *have* a mother for me to hit."

"'Mother' is not a title she's earned." She sounds more hurt than bitter.

"Lucille's lucky I have tennis elbow or I'd have knocked her through a wall," I reply.

"Pfft, the Ice Queen feels nothing. She's probably just mad that you messed up her helmet." Lucille's first reaction was to fix her mussed hair, smoothing her professionally honeyed bangs before bemoaning my own parentage. Jack had to hold me back before I went in for a second round.

"I feel terrible, even though she deserved it. How many times have I talked to my Littles about violence being on the Never Never list? To use their words and not their fists? What is it about Jordan women that turns me into Mike Tyson? I feel like such a hypocrite. Still, given the chance, I'd do it again. I wish I had all night to swat the smug off her face. What's wrong with me? Maybe I should add kickboxing to my workouts?"

Jack asks, "She makes others irrational, right? Giving her a wide berth all these years felt like my only option."

"Um, trust? Afghanistan isn't far enough from that horrible woman. Personally, I'd have been exploring the space program," I confirm. We pass an exit for Macon, Georgia. "Hey, are you fine with us pressing on or do you need me to take you somewhere to decompress?"

"How far is West Palm from here?"

Originally, we were planning to spend the night at John-John's house, but Jack figured that we were now about as welcome in Atlanta as Sherman. She made herself laugh, which is why I didn't ask for an explanation. (I'll Google it later.) So we're headed south, following Ingrid's browser history clues.

"We have about seven hours to go," I say, executing a small stretch in my seat.

"If you're exhausted, I can drive. Or, we can stop at a motel."

"I'm too full of adrenaline to sleep. Plus, Kelly's expecting us. I said we wouldn't be there until close to dawn, so she gave me the code to the door. We'll rest, shower up. Then Miami's about a hour and a half away. Sound like a plan?"

"Yes." Jack opens one of the Diet Cokes I packed, and without my needing to ask, hands me an open can as well. "Is her door code still 666?"

I glance over at her. "Are you really in a position to throw shade on anyone else's family right now?"

She clamps her eyes closed. "Shit, Kitty, I'm sorry. Old habits."

"Teasing you, Jack. Like friends do. Get used to it. And yes, Kelly is still Kelly. Not as anti-Christ-y as before, though. She's mellowed. Unfortunately for her, both her girls are teenagers now and they're exactly like she used to be."

"Sweet, sweet justice."

"Yeah, that's what my folks say, too."

Jack sips her soda, then scrubs at her eyes. "Sorry you had to witness all of that. Now you know everything, or close to it."

"Please, I know the crappy, hurtful stuff. Tell me about the fun stuff! Did you really shower with that famous general?"

"Never even met the man."

I take a drink. "Boring! No offense. What else? I want gossip."

"I was almost engaged once."

I give her a playful small shove. This is what I'm talking about! "Get out of here! When? What happened?"

"Over a decade ago, but we were off and on for a long time before that. We split for a lot of good reasons—the timing was off, we were both married to our jobs, I was halfway around the world."

"Did you have a big Betsy-style breakup?"

Jack laughs. "Jesus, no. For such a sober, serious woman, I never understood the histrionics. Did you? Remember senior year when she keyed Jeff Windsor's car? Or when she egged Peter Archer's apartment?"

I say, "I didn't realize that was Peter. I thought she lost it over Steve Reynolds."

Jack pulls off her ponytail holder before refastening it a little more loosely. "Eh, I can't remember. Youthful indiscretions, right? My breakup was amicable, though. No eggs, no damage to his car's finish or gas tank. We kept in touch for a long time, until we didn't."

"Again, boring. No offense. Ever wonder what might have been?" Kitty asks.

"Constantly. That's why I'm considering coming home for good."

I choke on my soda. "You're kidding! Isn't your whole identity wrapped up in being this big foreign correspondent, no offense?".

Jack reaches for her right foot and begins to rub the arch. "None taken. It is. It was. But I can't live this lifestyle forever. I can stand the heat, the cold, the danger, the deplorable living conditions, the crushing sadness of what I've witnessed. I just can't take the loneliness anymore. My job isolates me. While I've had relationships here and there—"

"We are talking about men, right?"

Frowning, Jack glances up from her foot. "I'm starting to take offense."

"Why?" I ask. "An hour ago, I didn't know your mother was alive. Sue me for verifying the facts."

"Yes, Kitty. Men. Being back home, seeing Teddy and Terry, my dad and Gloria, everyone else my age coupled up, I realize I'm finally ready for more. Take your life, for example. You're *surrounded* by love. Even Nana Baba's crazy about you. She only tells you what to do because she's not one to express her true emotions. Trust me, the Jordans are expert on this maneuver."

"What? Baba? I thought she just got off on being critical."

"Not from where I sit. Thought you were a cautionary tale, Kitty, the poster child for everything I was trying to avoid. But now I've seen you in your element and I realize I want something like that. A smaller house and a bigger yard, no offense, but otherwise, your life seems ideal."

If Jack's being so honest, there's no reason I can't be more forthright.

"'Seems ideal' is the operative term. So much of what I do now is for show that sometimes I forget what's real and what's a staged photo op. You want to talk about crushing loneliness? Try being stuck at home with three kids under eight years old, in the snow, without having a single adult conversation all day. You love them with your whole soul, but it's so much giving with so little receiving. And when you do see another adult, the conversation isn't ever about you—it's about potty training or growth percentiles or immersion language class. You stop being 'Kitty' and start being 'Kord's mommy.'"

"What my mother said—did you identify with any of that?" Jack asks, now massaging the opposite foot.

"Yes and no. Every stay-at-home parent feels overwhelmed from time to time. You just have to find a way to not lose yourself. For me, I became involved in the Parent Teacher Organization and I started my blog. I felt like I had good ideas and I wanted to share them to make the road easier for other moms. You figure out how to make it work; you don't just leave and take a massive do-over like Lucille. That's despicable."

"I knew Sars had to like you for some reason. Only took me twenty years to find out why."

I admit, "Eh, don't be so quick with your praise, especially on the Web site. I started off with such good intentions, and it became a real source of pride . . . but it morphed into vanity. In the past year or so, I've been so concerned with presenting an impeccable life that I now live a life I can't afford. Ask me about the four hundred dollars' worth of flowers I buy each month, just to keep up appearances. I feel like the financial stress has made me phony and so envious of what everyone has that I don't."

"Money trouble—that why you keep insisting I pay for everything?"

I redden in the darkened front seat. "Guilty as charged. Worse? I've focused so much on presenting myself as the perfect mom that I kind of forgot to be a good wife. I put everything into my children and my home. Sure, the kids are thriving, but not my marriage. I need to have a long talk with Ken when he gets back from Miami. I have so much to apologize for and I want us to have a fresh start."

"It's never too late for a course correction."

"I hope you're right. What's funny is your brother is the one who helped me figure this all out. My God, was it just yesterday?"

"Bobby's a great listener."

"Definitely. He's insightful, maybe more than you realize. At least I understand how I've gone off track and I've come up with a plan to right it all. Wish I didn't have to wait a week for Ken to come home. I want to start my do-over now, you know?"

"Wait, did you say Ken's in Miami?"

I nod. "Dental conference at the Delano Hotel."

Jack reaches for Ingrid's computer. "Hold on, let me check something." She pulls up the browser history. "Serendipity! Kitty, we have a new plan. We'll drive straight through because the Delano's one of the hotels we need to investigate, along with the Wintercourt Miami. We can book a room there—yes, on me—and you can surprise him tomorrow. Who knows? Maybe we'll find Trip quickly and you'll have a little second honeymoon together. Sound good?"

"So good," I confirm. "But is this just because you want to avoid spending time with Kelly?"

"No."

"No?"

"Maybe a little. I've had enough drama for one day."

"Fair enough," I agree.

"There's just one thing," Jack says.

"What's that?"

Jack looks pointedly at the steering wheel. "I'll need to drive."

CHAPTER TWENTY

Jack

....

Miami, Florida
Friday

"I want to believe it was that easy, but I can't," Kitty says.

"What if it can have been that easy?" I reply.

"To find Ingrid here before you even left this hotel to ask around at the Wintercourt? It's unbelievable."

We arrived at the Delano around five thirty this morning and slept like the dead for the next six hours. The plan was to split up—Kitty would discreetly inquire here as to Ingrid's whereabouts and I was taking the Wintercourt. Kitty claimed the first shower, so I was only just now ready to head out, which is no longer necessary.

Kitty says, "Seems a little too convenient. There I am with Ingrid's picture on my phone, and I ask the doorman, 'Have you seen this woman?' and he's all, 'Am I on *Dateline*?' because she's standing ten feet away getting out of a limo with a bunch of bags. The doorman was the first guy I even asked! Then I had to hide behind a palm tree because I didn't want her to see me. We've met a few times and I'm sure she'd recognize me."

"Thank God she didn't," I say. "She's headed out to the pool?"

"Yes, according to whomever she was loud-talking to on the phone. I wanted to tell her, 'Inside voice, honey!' Even Kassie knows how to adjust her volume in public spaces. I want to have a word with every one of these Millennials' parents. No flipping manners. BTW, I took a bunch of twenties out of your wallet so I was able to bribe the driver who picked her up. He said she was coming from Bal Harbour."

I ask, "Should I be familiar with Bal Harbour?"

"Only if you care about the best shopping in Miami."

"So, no."

"Here's what I don't get, Jack. You said she must be out of the country because of the error messages, but she's *here.*"

"That is puzzling. I guess the explanation doesn't matter—she's here and now I can question her." Kitty has a hand on her hips and she's shaking her head. "Now what?"

"Did you learn nothing from our caper at the Monaco?"

Her meaning's immediately clear. Only now do I notice that she's carrying a bag from the hotel's boutique. This? Right here? Is why I never did covert investigations. "Not again."

"Yes. It's all you, babe. I can't go—she knows me. I already bought the accessories you'll need, too. Charged them to the room. I have sunscreen, celebrity magazines, a couple of cool bangles, awesome sunglasses—they're Chanel, dibs when you're done with them—and a bikini. And P.S. I bought you two razors, because, damn."

· · · ·

Kitty suggested that I download the tracking app she uses to GPS her kids' locations and then hide my phone in Ingrid's bag. However, if Ingrid does leave the country, I'm not sure the software would work. We couldn't determine a clear answer from our Google search, and John hung up on me when I called to ask him. So I'm going old school, with the goal to befriend Ingrid. I've traveled enough to understand the quick camaraderie inherent between two strangers who are both far from home. But simply embracing the geography game here won't be enough.

And because I'm running this op alone, I can't rely on simply spewing text-message language while Kitty does the heavy lifting. Back when we were together, Sean used to crack up whenever I'd do my Kitty impersonation for him, even long after either of us had any contact with her. Funny is funny, regardless of the context. The minute I take the chair next to Ingrid, clad in her roommate's gingham bikini, I begin to channel my inner-Kitty, circa 1995, so she's with me in spirit.

Flipping through my *Us* magazine, I say aloud, more to myself than anyone else, "Ohmigod, I love Kimye so much." Thanks to Kitty's crash course through the bathroom door while I groomed, I'm armed with the latest in pop culture.

I've piqued Ingrid's attention, but I pretend not to notice. I liken this to the time Sean and I fished for red salmon in the Alaskan Russian River the summer before he left for med school at UCLA. Because red salmon are fairly passive, we used the flossing method (since fallen out of favor in the fishing community), which entails casting out the hook and then yanking it back as the salmon swims by. They don't bite so much as they are inadvertently snagged by quickly reeling in the hook.

I flip a few more pages. "Welcome to Stalkertown, Taylor Swift. Population, You."

Ingrid's definitely paying attention now.

"Oh, Khloé, honey, no. Could you be any more try-hard? P.S. your mom is tragic."

Ingrid closes her own magazine and angles herself to enable conversation with me. I ignore meeting her gaze. (Too try-hard.)

A waiter comes by and I hold out my menu, bracelets clinking merrily as I point. "Okay, I want something delish, but not, like, too carb-y, you know? What do I want then? Am I more raspberry mojito or spicy mango margarita? Or should I just get both, because hello, vacay!"

"You should totally get both!" Ingrid exclaims, unable to contain herself.

"Would you drink whichever one I don't like?" I ask her.

"Totes."

To the waiter, I say, "We'll have both, thanks!" I turn toward her. "I never know what to get when I'm at the pool bar. Bottle service is so much easier, amirite?"

"The best!"

Is she buying my act? I rather suspect she is. I only have so much inane conversation/slang terms in my arsenal, so I need to move along the process. Next step? The geographical bond.

"I was just in Chicago visiting the bros and we went to the *sickest* club! It's this place called the Monaco—"

"I'm from Chicago and I love the Monaco! We're there every Wednesday night for DJ Illuminati!"

"Hashtag no way! I relocated to London a few years ago, but I'm thinking of moving back to Chi-town just for the Monaco. London is, like, enough with the shitty pubs and warm beer already, right? Da fuq?"

(I'm sorry, London. I don't mean it. Sean was right and you're my favorite of all European cities.)

"Word." Her phone beeps with a text message. She looks at the screen, scowls, and taps out a hasty response.

"You cool?" I ask.

"Yeah. I just keep getting obnoxious texts from randoms, so I've been replying '504: AT&T Error Message, Subscriber Not Found.'"

One mystery neatly solved and I must admit, her response is kind of brilliant. I say, "Why not turn off your phone if the ratchets can't take a hint?"

"I'm waiting to hear from my boyfriend. Meeting him in the Caymans tomorrow and I need the deets. He's sailing in from Belize."

Yes! The pieces are coming together now! I hadn't even considered where Trip's boat *The Lone Shark* might have been. If he's off to live incognito, doing so on a boat provides quick egress and no permanent address, especially if he disguised the boat and changed the name and the hull identification numbers. Really, anything can be camouflaged, given enough cash. Hell, thanks to a flashy swimsuit, sunglasses, and diligent shaving (shameful), I've been disguised for less than five hundred dollars.

Ingrid continues, completely unaware that I'm turning cartwheels inside. "He was supposed to be there yesterday but there was this big storm and he was delayed."

Ding, ding, ding! More verification! But how best to express my great joy and this tremendous victory for Sars and all those investors poised to seek justice as soon as Simon's story hits the news cycle? "Awesomesauce!"

"Right?"

"What kind of sailboat does he have? My friend has a thirty-three-foot Watkins Seawolf on Belmont Harbor," I say, describing the boat Bobby lived on one summer in Maine, about twelve years ago.

"Um . . . his is a l'il bigger than that."

Yes . . . by approximately one hundred and thirty-four feet. How was no one suspicious when Trip's takeaway from watching *The Wolf of Wall Street* was not that he should conduct his business with integrity, but that he should add thirty feet to the back of his yacht to accommodate a helicopter landing pad?

Our drinks arrive and I take the margarita while she opts for the mojito. "Proost," I say, raising my glass in salute.

Before she can reply, her text alarm beeps again. She reads the screen and lets out a small squeal. Has to be from Trip—girls don't squeal over notes from other girls.

I need to read that text.

While she beams at her screen, I say, "Whoa. So much hotter in person! I would hit that so flipping hard."

Ingrid looks up. "Who?"

"Leo. He just walked by."

"*DiCaprio?*"

"Affirmative. I mean, *totes*. He was headed toward the spa. Major Speedo action."

Ingrid bolts up from her chair, the idea of a famous millionaire in the hand greater than the billionaire she already has in the bush. I snatch her phone and quickly transcribe the information. She's flying into Grand Cayman first thing tomorrow morning and meeting him at the International Bank of the Caymans at nine a.m. Then they'll take a private plane to Little Cayman at nine forty-five and the boat will pick them up on Sunday after a resupply run. I have to read the text a few times, due to Trip's inability to incorporate punctuation.

I replace Ingrid's phone but a moment before she returns. "I didn't see him."

"Ugh, TCBY, right?"

"What about yogurt now?"

Shit. "I mean, STBY." Before she has a chance to become suspicious, I say, "Listen. Gotta motor. Bikini wax appointment. Catch you on the flippity-flop."

What I mean is, catch you *and* your scoundrel boyfriend on the flippity-flop.

. . . .

"This is my unhappy face," Kitty says, lips pressed tight, brows knit.

She's been upset ever since we tore out of the Delano in order to catch a three-thirty flight to the Grand Caymans without her yet having found Ken. I'd spotted someone who looked like him at the pool, but that guy was rubbing oil all over some woman, so I was clearly mistaken.

"I'm sorry, Kitty. Truly. But this was the only way we were going to get here ahead of Ingrid. And since you refuse to fly with me, we had no other choice," I reply.

Little Cayman is just that—little, populated by only a few hundred permanent residents. Nonstop flights from Miami to Little Cayman don't exist. The island isn't a direct entry point to the country; both visitors and residents must ingress from one of the larger Cayman Islands. So, we're staying on Grand Cayman tonight and puddle-jumping to the little island in the morning to stake out where Ingrid and Trip plan to stay.

I'd suggested we rent a plane and I could take us to Little Cayman myself. I've kept my license current by logging hours each time I'm back in the States. However, Kitty wasn't on board with this plan. At all.

"Your aggressive driving scares me enough. There's no way I'm leaving the ground with you. No flipping way."

"Your loss," I reply, because if anyone *should* feel the need for speed, it's her.

"I'll live."

"I hope you don't mind my pointing it out, but you seem out of sorts.

What's going on?" I ask. Our collective experience has been so positive that I don't understand the sudden mood change.

"I just can't believe the first time I'm using my passport is with *you*. No offense. I've been dying for a trip to the Caymans since Kord was in kindergarten. With my husband. I don't want to eat fruit naked on a private beach with *you*."

"Not on my personal Top Ten list, either," I reply. "On the bright side—now you'll have been here and when you and Ken come back, you'll be a pro."

"Little. Flipping. Comfort."

"You're not enjoying a moment of this? Because we can go back to our rooms." We're sitting outdoors at the Ritz-Carlton (the only last-minute reservation I could snag), sipping frozen piña coladas on the terrace of Bar Jack, a spot chosen not only for the name, but also because it boasts the best view on all of Grand Cayman. The sun's a small melon ball on the horizon, while the rest of the sky has exploded in shades of fuchsia streaked with tangerine and gold. The daytime aquamarine-colored sea is now lilac in the reflected twilight.

"I might want to stay a few more minutes," she admits.

Our dinners arrive and we dive in, having had little time to consume anything that wasn't Diet Coke over the past few days. So fresh. There's a cessation of conversation as we polish off two orders of crispy crab fritters, piquant with lime aioli, and coconut shrimp, topped with tangy mango salsa. Then I tuck into the Mahi tacos and Kitty practically inhales her lobster roll and double order of sweet potato fries.

When the waiter clears Kitty's empty plate, she tells him, "That was terrible. I want to send it back."

"Hey," I say. "You made a joke. You must be rallying."

Kitty's smile fades. "Gallows humor. You realize we have to call Betsy. How's that going to go? 'We have good news and bad news. The good news is your husband isn't dead. The bad news is, neither is his girlfriend.'"

"'P.S. he's stolen a boatload of money,'" I add. I'm really starting to sound like Kitty, aren't I? "I'll call her when we go back to our rooms."

Kitty says, "You don't have to do that. She and I are closer—I'll take care of it."

"Yes, but we're much older friends, so it's on me."

"I feel like it should be me," Kitty says, a little louder this time.

"And I feel like it should not be you," I say, raising my own volume as well. "Wait. Stop. We're breaking this pattern once and for all. We'll do it together. At least our being on speaking terms will soften the blow."

"Shall we shake on it?" Instead of offering her hand, she shimmies in her seat and I laugh out loud.

"I completely forgot about that," I say. Literally shaking on it was our first of many running jokes once upon a time. "I wish we hadn't wasted all those years."

Kitty nods. "Me, too. But you wouldn't talk to me and everything spiraled from there."

"No, *you* wouldn't talk to me," I said.

"Wrong. I only stopped talking to you after you stopped talking to me that day in the food court," she replies.

"Is it possible we were both in the wrong?" I say.

"Never," she replies with a wink.

"Did you just wink at me, Kitty Carricoe?"

"I admit to nothing."

"Then Kelly trained you well." We both sit quietly for a minute. "Now what? Shall we settle up and go call her?"

"Definitely. I want to check in with the kids before it's too late, too."

I sign for the bill before we adjourn to my room. Side by side, I punch the number into Skype. When Sars answers on her end, Kitty grabs my hand in a show of support.

I say, "Hey, Sars. We need to talk."

• • • •

We have to decompress after we brief Sars, and catch up with our respective families, so we meet on the beach an hour later. She tells me Kassie and the boys say hello and we have a quick laugh about how this was not the moonlight Cayman stroll Kitty had been dreaming about for so long. But the night's too warm and clear to not make do.

As for Betsy? "That was *not* the reaction I expected," Kitty says. "I thought Breakup Betsy would come out, full of fury and ready to crack some skulls together."

The waves gently ebb and flow as we walk. "My expectation was for a mix of sorrow and relief. She was almost . . . detached? Is that how you'd describe it?"

"She *has* to be in shock. That's the only explanation for why she was so robotic. Are you surprised she wants to be here when we confront him?"

"A little. Likely, she's gathering her resources now, either placing calls to the SEC or bringing in private security to accompany her."

"Makes sense. What time are we meeting her plane at the Little Cayman airfield again?"

"Nine thirty. Ingrid and Trip are landing at ten fifteen, so that gives us enough time to stage ourselves where they're staying."

"Are you going to be able to sleep tonight?"

"Not a wink," I admit. "But imagine how poor Sars feels."

"Betrayal sucks."

We walk north, the ocean to our left. We can see the lights on the incoming boats—I wonder if one of them is Trip's.

Kitty kicks up little puffs of sand as she walks. Then she says, "So . . . in the spirit of full disclosure, I should tell you something. Do you remember the summer of 1995?"

"I'm not senile—of course I remember. After freshman year. I had an internship at the *Trib*. What a terrible summer—all those people died in the heat because they lived in bad neighborhoods and were afraid to open their windows. I tagged along with a couple of the reporters covering the aftermath. Awful."

Kitty stops. "Can you find the buzzkill aspect on any topic?"

"My entire career points to 'yes,'" I reply.

"Noted. Do you remember Bobby at all that summer?"

"Again, not senile. Why do you ask, Kitty?"

"Remember all those times he said he was 'cat sitting'?"

"Yeah, and he was gone all the time that summer. I rarely saw him."

"Think about it."

Then I understand. "No!"

I can see her trying to hide her grin. "Yes. We ran into each other over Memorial Day and had a fab time together. And it went from there."

"Are we Jordans all catnip for you? Have you hooked up with my father? Try not to fall in love with me, okay?" I say none of this unkindly.

"No promises," she replies. We walk a little farther. "Are you okay with that?"

I admit, "At the time, I'd have murdered you both. In cold blood. In retrospect, I can see how you'd have been good for each other. You were so high-strung and he was so . . . high. What happened? Why'd you break up?"

"He felt like he was being too disloyal to you, so it was just a summer thing."

Oh. Poor Bobby. "Congratulations, you just broke my heart. I remember him going back to USC in a funk at the end of the summer and it finally makes sense why."

"Super, glad it's straightened out," Kitty says in a businesslike manner. "Are you finally going to tell me about Sean?"

Now it's my turn to stop. I'm not going to deny anything. "You knew? I mean, other than the morning you jumped to a massive conclusion? I never had him over after that. And we weren't guilty that day— you have to believe me. We were not innocent, per se, but not guilty by any stretch."

"Jack, I know everything that happens under my roof—you think I didn't develop those skills elsewhere first?"

"Did Sars rat me out?" I ask.

"No, probably for the same reason she didn't mention my fling with Bobby. She didn't want to drive a bigger wedge between us."

"God bless Sars."

"Amen, *Betsy.*"

She shoves me gently and I shove her back.

I say, "So how did you . . ."

"The Acqua di Parma Colonia is how I figured it out. Every other frat guy was dousing himself in Polo or Hugo Boss at the time, while Sean exclusively wore the cologne he first found in Italy. You smelled like him all the time. Thank you for not throwing it in my face back then, BTW."

"And you as well with Bobby."

"How long did you guys date?"

"Off and on until about 2003."

"Whoa! That long?"

"Yes. He came to Chicago for his residency at Northwestern and he wanted to get married. I wasn't ready, I freaked out, I went to Iraq. We tried the long distance thing. Didn't work. Game over."

"You're an idiot, Jack Jordan. No offense. He was a catch."

"Well aware. I've been beating myself up about him since Shock and Awe. He said he'd wait, and he did. Thing is, I found life covering the front line easier to manage than being at home with my thoughts, especially when my mother tried to rejoin the picture. Out in the field, I'm all about basic needs. There's no place for navel-gazing. At home, I worried all the time I might turn into her, or have to deal with her, and that I'd somehow screw up Sean's life, too, but I was safe from all of that in Iraq. So I kept finding reasons to stay."

"I wish I'd hit her harder," Kitty mumbles. "Go on."

"When it became clear I wasn't returning to live in Chicago, I ended it. I couldn't keep stringing him along. Then, a few years ago I was in a convoy and the reporter in the Land Rover ahead of me was killed. If I hadn't gone back for my canteen, I would have been the one in the lead vehicle. I'd witnessed life and death before, but never from such a vantage point. Everything I hadn't dealt with came to the surface and I thought, 'What the hell am I waiting for with Sean?' But I was too late. He was marrying someone else. She's a buyer for Saks. She *shops* for a living. Given the choice, Sean ultimately opted for a *girl*."

Kitty grabs me by my shoulders, with a force that surprises me. "How many times do I have to tell you to sign up for Facebook? If you did, you'd know his relationship status. He must be divorced now, because I just read an article about him in *Chicago Magazine*. He was voted

one of Chicago's Most Eligible Bachelors. Do you understand? He's single. Jack, he's *single*."

I am stunned into silence.

"I have to figure out everything for you, don't I?" She takes hold of
my wrist and begins to yank me down the beach.

"What are you doing?" I yelp, stumbling in the sand while I try to
keep up with her.

"We're going back to the hotel to get on the Wi-Fi so you can get
in touch with him. This instant. I'm not messing around here. Your future starts now."

"Now?" I say, overcome with equal parts trepidation and anticipation.

"Right. Flipping. Now."

CHAPTER TWENTY-ONE

Kitty

....

Little Cayman Island
Saturday

"Feel free to crown me the Queen of I Told You So," I say to Jack, who has yet to stop grinning like a complete loon.

"Did you know he was at Trip's funeral?" Jack says. "He didn't want to call attention to himself, or cause any trouble between us, so he sat in the back. But he was there, in the hope of spotting me."

"That's so romantic I could throw up in my handbag. Thank God you had on a decent dress. P.S., stop hugging me. You're embarrassing us both."

I don't actually want her to stop. I feel like I have my first *real* best friend back.

She says, "You wish," then squeezes me again for good measure. And I hug her back. "I'm seeing him the second we get home."

"Again, you're welcome. Then you'll really be glad you listened to me about the razors. Kitty Carricoe is never wrong about this sort of thing. Fact."

We hear the sound of a small plane coming in for a landing. Betsy was leaving the chartered private jet on Cayman Brac, taking a little prop plane over here because the other's too big to land on this wee runway.

Wow, is this place seriously wild and practically uninhabited. No wonder Brooke Birchbaum was able to do her laundry on the beach. I swear I just saw a goat run past us. Not kidding. The airport is basically a shed, so I'm glad we haven't had to wait here for long.

"At least stop beaming when Betsy lands. This is serious business," I say, even though all I want to do is grab a Big Gulp full of Diet Coke and sit on the sand with Jack, reveling in every detail, while I may or may not quietly congratulate myself for having been the catalyst. I love romance. I do. I wish I'd made it more of a priority over the past few years.

Betsy's agitated when she lands, understandably so. She's not her usual polished self—untucked and disheveled, tottering around on impossibly high shoes not meant for walking on a grassy runway. She has us explain everything again from the beginning. "You two are friends again? Just like that?" she asks.

"Miracle, right?" I say.

"The Lord works in mysterious ways," Betsy replies.

"Are you bringing in a team?" Jack asks. "Won't we need help getting him into custody?"

"Taken care of, no worries," Betsy replies. She gestures toward the Jeep by the "airport" entrance. "This is our ride. Sorry it's rustic, not a lot of choices on short notice here." She finds the keys under the mat and consults her map. "He's staying at an address on Point o' Sand beach on the northern tip of the island."

Jack and I look at each other and bust out laughing, as we know this is the exact pink sand–spot Brooke Birchbaum's been bragging about for so many years.

Jack points to a tree. "Let's grab some mangoes—we can eat them there afterward. Naked, naturally," and we crack up again.

"Ooh, inside jokes. Fun," Betsy says, an edge to her voice. Yet who could blame her for being upset?

"What's our strategy?" Jack asks. "How are we doing this?"

"Follow my lead," Betsy replies.

The island's less than ten miles long, so we arrive at the property in a couple of minutes, obscuring ourselves behind a big patch of Spanish cedar. I'm surprised at the simplicity of the accommodations. I expected some windswept mansion on the water, a tropical version of Steeple-chase, full of plantation shutters and banana leaf ceiling fans and butlers ferrying silver trays of iced beverages, the glasses thick with condensation. Instead, we're camped out by a spring-break-type beach shack.

"This is it?" Jack asks, also bewildered.

I'm still trying to put all the pieces of this mystery together. "Let's talk this through again. Ingrid came down with the bags to load up at the bank, right? Jack says the international regulations have changed, but surely Trip had time to convert money from his offshore account to cash-filled safety deposit boxes. So he's picking up the money here before heading out on the boat to somewhere with no extradition laws. Does that sound right? Would he take US dollars or Cayman Island dollars?" I ask. "Or maybe he's already converted the cash to the currency of where he's headed next."

"All totally plausible," Jack agrees.

Bets doesn't seem to be in the mood for chitchat, so we wait quietly. We hear Trip and Ingrid crunching down the crushed shell drive before we see them drive up in their own Jeep, then watch as they unload all the duffels. When they're both weighted down with bags, Bets gives the signal. "Now."

We leap out of the car like we're a bunch of Navy SEALS, which is a lot easier for those of us in sensible shoes and capri pants. We all run up to the couple and surround them. This? This is so much more exciting than anything the PTO has to offer!

"Hello, Trip," Betsy says. "You're looking well. Death agrees with you."

"Hey, Sabby!" Trip says, grinning. He's since shaved his head and grown a goatee, but with the trademark pastel sweater looped around his shoulders, he's undeniably recognizable. "What are you doing here?"

"We could ask you that as well," Jack replies, obviously confused by his answer. Shouldn't he be panicked? Shouldn't Trip be aghast that his fake death's been uncovered? Jack and I trade glances, both of us silently shrugging.

"No way! The Miami margarita girl is here!" Ingrid adds, waving at Jack. "Small world!"

"You had to be stupid," Betsy says to Trip, pacing unsteadily on her high heels. Uh-oh. Batcrap Breakup Betsy's about to make an appearance. Jack and I gravitate toward each other.

"You couldn't just stick with the plan," Betsy says. "You had to free-style and ruin everything. I had it all set up. It was bulletproof. Do you know how many people I had to pay off for that 'plane crash'? And having the whole Gulfstream disassembled! *Millions*. The operation cost millions. But, no. You couldn't just be happy on your own, waiting for me to join you after a reasonable interim. You needed the immediate company of a woman fifteen years your junior. A bimbo. And she's still probably your better in terms of emotional maturity."

"Who's the bimbo here?" Ingrid asks, looking around. "Is it me?"

Breakup Betsy's out in full force. Someone is getting something thrown at his head, and soon. P.S. Don't get too attached to your car's unslashed tires. "How long did you wait to get in touch with her? Two days? You had to be a fucking cliché, didn't you?"

"Betsy, what's going on?" I ask. None of this is unfolding like I'd envisioned. Jack seems equally flummoxed.

"What's going on? Oh, I'll tell you what's going on. Golden Boy here started making bad investments about five minutes after I was ousted from CFG. His sexist old man didn't believe that I'd earned my seat at the table, despite his not even being a board member. So, at Daddy's behest, Trip bounced me. Asked me to 'please understand.' After that, Trip began to drink the media's Kool-Aid that *I'd* set in motion from Day One and started to believe he'd built CFG on his own, just like he 'earned' his MBA on the back of my efforts."

"Bobby nailed it," Jack says quietly. "Whoa."

Betsy's not paying attention to either of us, her entire focus on Trip and Ingrid. "I'm telling you, Peter Pan here invested in some stupid shit. Want to know how much he wasted on a company that created online gyms? Four hundred and twenty million dollars. For a gym. Online. And not for a company whose apps allow customers to download workout guides to use in the privacy of their living rooms. Or software that tracks your effort and holds clients accountable for exercising. No. The gym offered virtual exercise. With an avatar."

"But you could make the little guys do one-handed push-ups and they'd get all sweaty!" Trip argues. "It was hilarious!"

To Jack I say, "I always suspected Betsy was the brains of the operation."

Betsy continues. "And that's just a drop in the bucket of the bullshit you invested in; you were ruining the company *I* built, while cheating on me every chance you got." She turns to us. "Two years ago, when this mouth-breathing moron realized what a mess he'd made, he came to me for help. He was in deep and it was only a matter of time before the SEC climbed up his ass. I wasn't going to let that happen. Because even though he didn't *steal* billions he was going to be destroyed for pissing them away. So I figured out how to buy time and temporarily prop up earnings by courting new investors at my charity events, using their funds to provide returns to earlier investors. I built a house of cards. I perpetrated *fraud*, yes, for my *husband*. Our lives on US soil would be over, but we could maintain our lifestyle abroad. All this idiot had to do was *keep it in his pants* for once."

"He hit on me, you know, Betsy. Frequently. He sent me an e-mail right before the crash saying things were about to change and he wanted me by his side," I tell her, trying to validate her point.

Trip seems offended. "No way, Jose! I flirted with you because Sabby told me to. No offense, but I don't wanna hook up with someone's mom. Ruins you *down there*. Sab said Ken was cheating on you and I should give you attention to make you feel better about yourself. But I never e-mailed you. That part's messed up."

I'm suddenly, profoundly, consumed with rage.

"You're such a liar, Trip," I shriek. "Ken is not cheating on me. Stop trying to deflect here and own up to your actions."

Betsy snorts. "Honey, he is *absolutely* cheating on you. I caught your precious Ken one day about three years ago. I stopped by after hours because of a loose filling and walked right in on them."

I feel like I can't take a breath, no matter how hard I try to inhale. I'm light-headed and I fear I'm about to pass out.

No.

NO.

This cannot be true.

But what if it is? Damn it, I knew Brandi was bad news. I knew it! Is Ken a cliché, too, going through his own midlife crisis? Although, how would Betsy have caught him with Brandi? She hasn't been with the practice that long. Were they an item before she was hired? I can't—

"How do I put this delicately, Kitty? Someone was caught *with his hand in the Cookie jar*," Betsy says with a laugh that seems awfully unkind.

Cookie? Oh, God, oh, God, that's so much worse. Brandi makes sense. But the Harley-riding nana? Does not compute.

"If that's true," I sputter, trying desperately not to scream or cry, "then why didn't you tell me? You're my best friend; you're supposed to have my back."

"Like you had my back when you bailed on moving to New York?" Betsy snaps.

"It was part of the plan, wasn't it, Sars?" Jack says. "Kitty, do you follow? Trip didn't e-mail you. Sars did."

At this point, my knees go out and I collapse on the pink sand. "I don't understand any of this."

Jack squats down next to me. "Plausible deniability. She likely cast a wide net, contacting every woman in his orbit with news that 'things were about to change.' She was putting it out there that he was about to bolt, thus making him look like the guilty party. That was her extra insurance policy."

"The ever so clever Jack Jordan strikes again," Betsy hisses. "But if you're so smart, how come I got into Stanford and you didn't?"

"You could have gone to Stanford without me. No one forced you to attend Whitney," Jack says, rising to face her. "W3 is bullshit, too, isn't it, Sars? Did you ever build any wells?"

Betsy shrugs. "A couple, in the beginning. But then this nimrod had to fuck everything up and I needed a way to funnel cash to countries with friendly governments willing to, let's say, *extend courtesies* to potential new residents."

"Everything has been a lie with you, hasn't it?" I say, kicking myself for not having trusted my first impression of her back in college. "Each action has been a means to an end. You didn't want Jack and me ever making up because you couldn't have us comparing notes. You needed us to go back to our lives and not ask any questions. So you kept telling lies to keep us away or otherwise occupied. I would have leaned on you heavily if you'd told me about Ken. And Jack would have been back to the States years ago if you didn't spin a yarn about some fake Saks-buyer fiancé."

"That was a lie?" Jack asks.

"Our finding Trip alive ruined your plans to collect the insurance money before taking off before the SEC caught up with you. You spent everything to get ready to flee and you needed that money. Steeplechase is mortgaged to the hilt, isn't it? Trust? I know what it looks like when someone's in over their head financially."

"So smart. You're both so fucking smart," Betsy spits.

"Flipping," I say automatically, the second before I realize she's holding a rather large handgun.

Urge to puke rising.

Jack is oddly calm. "You don't have to do this, Betsy. Just take what's in the bags and go. We won't stop you."

With her gun trained on Trip, Betsy inspects the bag's contents, pulling out flippers and masks and oxygen tanks. "Where's the cash?"

"What cash, Sabby?" Trip asks.

"The cash you were picking up from your secret offshore safety de-posit box," Betsy says.

"I have one of those?" he asks.

"Yes! Why else would you have your whore meet you at the bank this morning?" Betsy yells.

"Because it's next to the dive shop and there's free parking in the bank lot. You said I was supposed to be on a budget until we got to Bru-nei," he replies. "Plus, Ingrid says the scuba diving here is amazeballs. Lotta shipwrecks and stuff."

The flash and subsequent crack of the gun is so sudden that we as-sume there's been a misfire. When we see Trip writhing on the ground, the extent to which Betsy means business becomes evident. He's alive, but if he's to stay that way, we have to stop the blood flow. Jack rips off her Jungle Jane safari shirt, leaving her in a tank top. She tosses the blouse to Ingrid. "Elevate his head and apply pressure to the wound, now!"

With the calm countenance of a serial killer, Betsy says, "You will not ruin everything for me *again*."

"When did you start to hate us, Sars? If you're going to shoot us, you at least owe us an explanation," Jack says, trying to mirror Betsy's eerie calm. "What did I do?"

"You had to be the best at everything you tried. 'Ooh, looky-here, Jack Jordan got the highest grade on the essay again.'"

"But I was words, you were math—that's what we always said," Jack says.

"The IMF thought my old essay about a single world currency was brilliant. They didn't give a fuck if every single word was spelled right. Let me ask you something—do you know how hard it is for a woman to gain traction in such a male-centric business? No, you don't, because you were basically a boy! Never even occurred to you that you couldn't achieve something because of your gender. Everything has always been so easy for you. 'Look at me, I'm so pretty I don't have to wear makeup. I don't even need a head of hair to be stunning. All the boys in the neighborhood fight to have me on their team.' I had to work ten times as hard as you ever did and I never got half your credit."

"You can resent me, but Kitty hasn't done anything wrong," Jack says.

"She stole Teddy from me!" Betsy shouts, pointing at Kitty with her free hand.

"Sars, he was gay," Jack reasons, trying to talk her down.

Clearly, Betsy's not well and probably hasn't been in a long time, at the very least since she lost her folks. She did start to withdraw after that. I feel like a terrible friend for not having noticed her break from reality. And yet she's the one waving a gun at us, so I'm the injured party here. More so Trip, but still.

"She made him that way!" she howls, pointing at me.

"Now that's just offensive on all counts," I say. "Science has shown that homosexuality—"

"Shut up, shut up, shut up!" Betsy begins to sob. "I have always been a second thought to everyone and I'm sick of it! None of you ever put me first! Even my parents took in every damn stray kid in the neighborhood instead of focusing on me. With him, it was, *'Boohoo, I need your help, Sabby, I fucked up the company.'* As for you two? *'Oh, Betsy, I have to have a baby and a whole new life without you. You'll be fine in New York alone.'* Or, *'I'm off to a war zone, Sars, because how much I love my perfect boyfriend scares me!'* What about *me*? Why don't any of you ever consider what I need?"

Betsy is going more and more off the rails, waving her gun wildly as she gestures at each of us. "When you two met, you were instant best friends. You were going to shut me out. I was irrelevant. When I saw the opportunity to push you apart, I took it. So heart-warming how you both wanted to talk to the other one after your fight, to find a place of forgiveness and understanding, but *I wasn't having it.*"

Ingrid's still across from us, on the ground attending to Trip. He's conscious, but barely.

Jack says, "So you lied all these years in order to perpetually pit us against each other. What I don't understand is why not use *all* your ammunition? Why didn't you tell me about Bobby and Kitty? Or tell her about Sean and me?"

Flecks of spittle fly out of Betsy's mouth as she rages. "To keep you needing me! Secrets are power! But now you're the best of friends with your road trips and your inside jokes and I'm going to be left behind *again*. Everyone has to stop taking what's mine, starting with my fucking name. I am *Sarabeth Octavia*, God damn it, and I am done here. On your knees, Jordan; as my oldest friend, you're first."

We are not dying on this beach right here, right now, at the hands of a woman who's come unhinged. I am going home to my children. That's nonnegotiable. The cheating *dentist* I married is not about to raise my family in my house. We have to take Betsy down before anyone else gets hurt.

"I'm not kneeling. You can look me in the eyes here. Kitty, run! The keys are in the Jeep. Go get help for Trip. I can take Sars," Jack says. "Save yourself!"

"Aw, Jack Jordan, ever the hero, putting her new bestie's life above her own," Betsy singsongs.

I never stood up after my knees buckled. When Betsy advances in front of me in order to go point blank with Jack, Jack and I lock eyes. I pray that she understands what I'm about to say, since it comes from the integral moment during *Top Gun* when Tom Cruise flies upside-down over the Russian MiG.

"Inverted!"

I grab the heels on Betsy's shoes and yank them toward me with all my might. She loses her balance and begins to topple forward. In the split second that she starts to fall, Jack leaps up and out to the side. Were Jack to have not understood I was about to turn Betsy upside-down, she'd have naturally gotten low instead of going high, and the bullet would be lodged in her liver, not in the banyan tree behind her.

I hop on Betsy's legs to hold her down and Jack pounces on her back. The three of us struggle to regain possession of the gun, which is a few inches away from any of our grasps.

"Jack, grab the gun. I can't reach!" I cry. She and I are both strong, but Betsy's powered by The Crazy and she's putting up one hell of a fight. Betsy is a bucking bull beneath us, writhing all over the sand, and I can barely keep my hold on her thrashing legs.

"It's too far!" Jack replies.

Betsy's right limb comes free from my grip and she knocks me back by kicking me in the shoulder. I think I hear something snap and I can grasp her with only my right hand, as fireworks of pain erupt from my neck down to my wrist. Betsy wrests an arm free and throws a handful of sand in Jack's face, blinding her.

"I can't see!" Jack shouts.

Even though we're both trying to hold her, Betsy begins to rise up beneath us, like Godzilla coming out of the ocean, her insanity-fueled adrenaline allowing her to bat us off of her like so many hapless Japanese villagers. Betsy lunges for and finally reaches the gun's grip and that's when I know it's over. "Jack, I'm so sorry!" I cry.

"You last thoughts are of that bitch?" Betsy says. "Oh, I'm going to enjoy this."

I hear her cock the gun and I squeeze my eyes shut, not wanting to witness what comes next.

A metallic clang rings out, followed by a heavy thud, and then the whole universe is silent for a solid five seconds.

I open my eyes to see Jack scrambling to brush the sand out of her eyes. Other than what will surely be scratched retinas, she appears to be fine and whole. I spot check myself, but I feel no pain or discomfort outside of the collarbone or the myriad scrapes and bruises.

Ingrid, covered in Trip's blood, is standing over Betsy's prone body. She's holding an oxygen canister, with a petulant look on her face.

"That basic bitch ruined my tropical vacay."

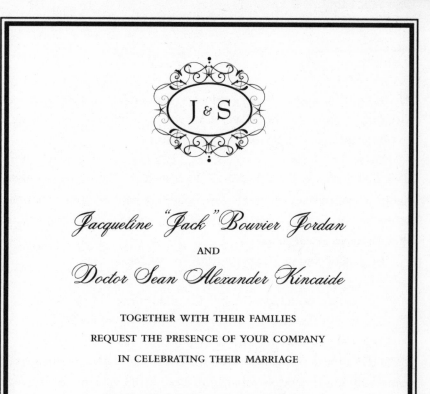

CHAPTER TWENTY-TWO

Jacqueline "Jack" Bouvier Jordan

AND

Doctor Sean Alexander Kincaide

TOGETHER WITH THEIR FAMILIES
REQUEST THE PRESENCE OF YOUR COMPANY
IN CELEBRATING THEIR MARRIAGE

SATURDAY, THE TWENTY-FIFTH OF JUNE
TWO THOUSAND AND SIXTEEN
AT SIX O'CLOCK IN THE EVENING

AT THE HOME OF KATHERINE KORD CARRICOE
NINETEEN MOCKINGBIRD LANE
IN WEST NORTH SHORE, ILLINOIS

WITH THE RECEPTION TO IMMEDIATELY FOLLOW.

Jack

West North Shore, Illinois
One Year Later

"Hydrangeas *and* peonies *and* gardenias. Yes. That's what we're having," Kitty says, tapping at her iPad. "Can you imagine a better pairing of texture, size, and scent? No, no, you cannot."

"Don't forget the white tree roses," Terry adds. "We'll have twenty of them. That's ten on each side of the aisle. Love! Now, are we under-planting the tree roses with blooms, housed in painted birch containers, or are we opting for a more simplified look, wrapped in burlap and tied off with moss-green raffia?"

"Burlap, of course. Always burlap," Kitty decides.

Terry claps with glee. "Perfection, we love it!"

"By '*we*' you both mean '*Jack*,'" I remind them.

"Right, right, of course," Kitty says, with a flip of her hand.

"Did you just wave me off?" I ask, incredulous.

"I did no such thing. But if you wanted to check on how the boys are doing building the gazebo, that's just fine," Kitty replies. "Kassie made some lemonade and you're welcome to bring it out to them. Scurry along! I'm sure they're thirsty."

"I've been dismissed. You just dismissed me from planning my own wedding," I say.

"Oh, honey," Terry replies. "This wedding stopped being yours the second you told us, 'I don't care, as long as you're all there.' That's what's called a forfeit."

"Everything has to be on point; I'm using the shots in my portfolio since this is my first wedding," Kitty says. "And you're going to flipping love it!"

Kitty launched An Affordable Affair while still in her shoulder sling, less than two weeks after we returned home from the Caymans.

Her event planning business has completely caught fire in the past year, given her ability to blend the beautiful with the economical. I'm so glad she's channeled her post-divorce energy into something positive. Ken wanted to save the marriage but Kitty couldn't get past his betrayal. They sold the big North Shore house at a loss and now Ken's stuck in a small condo in Rogers Park. Alimony's a bitch. (And so is Kitty when she's wronged. Trust me, been there.) Cookie dumped him, too. Apparently he was a lot less attractive with six thousand fewer square feet of real estate under his belt.

Kitty's new Cape Cod is far smaller than the old place, but she's content living more simply in the rural portion of West North Shore on three acres, five miles removed from the pressure of North Shore proper. The boys were able to stay in their schools, but Kassie had to transfer to Calvin Coolidge Elementary. When Kitty explained to Kassie she was switching schools, Kassie cried with relief, delighted to finally be away from Avery Birchbaum.

I guess it's never too early to have an enemy.

The backyard here is lush and green, surrounded by woods, with a barn and small paddock, room enough if Kitty were to want to buy a pony for Kassie. Nana Baba lives in a cute little cabin next to the barn. Baba completely sided with Kitty during the divorce, appalled at her son's behavior. She sold her Chicago home for ten times what she originally paid forty-five years ago and she helped Kitty buy this place. Baba's here for the kids anytime that Kitty's off-site at an event and not working in her home office.

Kitty says she's not ready to date, but I have my suspicions. Bobby seems to be her first and only choice whenever she needs someone to manage the liquor portion of her events. He expected me to believe he was really "tearing down the catwalk" for five hours last week after the Sweet Sixteen mocktail party they worked.

That's a negative, Ghost Rider.

I carry the lemonade outside, where Konnor, Kord, Teddy, and Bobby are finishing applying cedar shake shingles to the roof of our wedding gazebo in the early summer sun. They drain the pitcher in a minute flat. Sean helped frame out the gazebo, but he's currently on a volunteer mission in the Dominican Republic. He'll be back in plenty of time for the ceremony two weeks from now.

We're honeymooning in London, of course.

John-John will also be here for the wedding, along with my half sisters, Rose and Caroline. After seeing my life flash before my eyes in the Caymans, I figured it was time to get to know them; none of the business with our mother has ever been their fault.

Those two young women give "girls" a very good name.

I'm not ready to reach out to the Honorable Judge yet. Maybe I will eventually, maybe I won't. Too soon to tell. But having my sisters in my life has been a blessing. They're even standing up with me at the wedding, along with Ashley, who insists on doing my hair, Sean's sister, and, of course, Kitty. I thought she and Terry were going to throw down over who'd be my maid of honor. Sean saved the day, asking Terry to be his best man.

P.S. I am *not* having a bachelorette party.

Part of me still wishes Sars was her old self, and that she could be here, too. Despite having become a terrible adult, she was there for me as a kid and I won't ever forget that. I visit her at the psychiatric hospital sometimes, taking her flowers from Kitty's garden. She pretends not to know me, but I'm cynical enough to believe that her psychotic break will last exactly as long as Trip's trial.

As for Trip? He recovered from his gunshot wound and is currently under house arrest at Steeplechase, thanks to his family's connections and maneuvering.

I don't have high hopes that justice will be served.

But at least I can tell the whole story and let the public draw their own conclusions. That's what I'm working on now—an exposé of the whole mess, told from my perspective. *The Lone Shark: Profiles in American Greed* comes out next year. I hope to—and honestly, need to—finish the manuscript in the next six months.

I'm sitting in the shade of the porch, watching the guys work. I'd help, but I'm hesitant to climb any ladders right now. Not prudent. Kassie opens the screen door, and tells me, "Auntie Jack, Mommy wants you to come inside and model your dress for Uncle Terry."

In the past year, I've learned that family isn't only who you're related to; it's also who you choose.

And I'm so very sorry that Sars opted out.

I step back inside, following Kassie down the hall to Kitty's office.
She and Terry are in there already, each clucking over the way they'd
embellish the dress, if I weren't so stubborn.

I insisted on something plain, without ribbons or bows or tulle, so
I'm walking down the aisle in a simple knee-length gown, sleeveless
and fitted on top, with a swirly skirt. Kitty says it's an A-line, scoop-
necked, satin something or other. Don't care. I'd happily marry Sean in
flip-flops.

The first wife was one of Sars's lies. Sean never married. He insists
I was worth waiting for.

I slip out of my shorts and T-shirt and slide the dress over my head.
The two mother hens gather behind me to work the zipper and buttons.

"You? Need to lay off the mini-pies, girl," Terry says, huffing as he
tries to force the zipper all the way up my back. "We're going to have to
have this taken out! Oh, Jack. What are we going to do with you? No
one gains weight before her wedding. No one."

I glance over at Kitty, who is ramrod straight, mouth agape, pointing at my midsection, and staring directly into my soul.

I truly can't hide anything from her, can I? I'm not out of my first
month; I haven't even told Sean the good news yet.

I reply, "No, it can happen. Happened to a friend of mine. My *best*
friend, actually."

Kitty squeezes my hand, leans in close, and says, "Welcome to the
dark side; we have cookies. And P.S., they're made with squash."

ACKNOWLEDGMENTS

First, thank YOU for (I hope!) liking this book enough to want to continue reading what I've written even now that the story's over. I won't go all Ferris Bueller here and tell you to hit the bricks after the credits roll. Instead, I offer my appreciation for your continued support. You're the best. Fact.

I wasn't terribly familiar with embedded journalism when I started this project, but learned so much by researching books and articles by reporters such as Ann Jones, Kirsten Scharnberg, David Ignatius, and Patrick Cockburn. I didn't realize exactly how in harm's way these journalists could be until I visited the Imperial War Museum and saw the wreckage of the Reuters Land Rover hit in the Gaza rocket attack. Let me be really clear here—I'm not worthy to be listed on the same page as them. But I hope I've done them a small bit of justice with Jack's character. All mistakes are my own.

I'm so thankful for the support I've received from the whole New American Library family—Kara Welsh, Claire Zion, Tracy Bernstein, Craig Burke, Jessica Butler, and each department that helps propel the author's work forward, from copyediting to production to sales to art. You all are my "takes a village." Thank you. Mean it.

Fletch and I would like to offer our collective thanks to Trident's Scott Miller. You are perpetually the ocean of calm that supports this ship of fools. (FYI, the adult tricycle has since been donated.)

As always, big love to my girls Stacey, Tracey, Gina, Joanna, and Laurie for putting up with all the canceled lunch dates and general flakiness when I'm on deadline. And much respect and admiration to the amazing community of female authors out there for always rallying around one another. Knowing that writers are readers makes my heart smile; you're class acts, every one of you.

I kind of want to thank Jack and Kitty here, even though they didn't actually do anything and, also, they're not real. (But I wish they were.)

Finally, for Fletch, who really ran the show this year while I completed two books. Thanks for being right there to pick up the slack. You are my hero! (And, yes, fine, your beard deserves its own Facebook page.)